Rescued by the Ranger

Also by Dixie Lee Brown

The Trust No One Series
All or Nothing
When I Find You
If You Only Knew
Whatever It Takes
Tempt the Night

Rescued by the Ranger

DIXIE LEE BROWN

AVONIMPULSE
An Imprint of HarperCollinsPublishers

Excerpt from *Right Wrong Guy* copyright © 2015 by Lia Riley.
Excerpt from *Desire Me More* copyright © 2015 by Tiffany Clare.
Excerpt from *Make Me* copyright © 2015 by Tessa Bailey.

EPub Edition SEPTEMBER 2015 ISBN: 9780062328403

Print Edition ISBN: 9780062328427

AM 10 9 8 7 6 5 4 3 2 1

*This book is dedicated to the three ladies
who helped me make it shine.*

*To Karissa, who dropped everything when I asked,
stayed up all night reading my manuscript, and
wrote copious notes and suggestions as she went—
thank you for your help, your friendship, and for
allowing me to adopt you as part of my family.*

*To amazing author and friend Sharon Struth,
who has an extraordinary voice, and whose books
I read just to see how it's supposed to be done—
I was honored to have you critique the opening chapters
of this book. Your input was honest, insightful, and spot
on. Thank you for giving so generously of your time.*

*And finally, to my editor, Chelsey, who I'm
pretty sure poured her heart and soul into
the editing of this manuscript—
thank you for all your hard work, your understanding,
and your encouragement. Thanks also for always
being just an e-mail or a phone call away.*

*I feel fortunate to have worked with you.
You've made it fun.*

Chapter One

A FAINT WHINE from the shotgun seat jerked Garrett's attention back to the narrow road hugging the side of a steep mountain in the middle-of-fucking-nowhere, Idaho. Gravel crunched beneath the tires as he came close to the drop-off on his right, and he immediately guided the Jeep closer to the white line down the middle of the chipped and broken asphalt. Clearly, either he was lost, or naming this strip of pavement a state highway was someone's idea of a joke. Whatever the case, this wouldn't be the best place to lose his focus. It was a damn-good thing Cowboy was watching out for him, as usual.

Garrett scratched beneath the chin of the German shepherd in the seat beside him, and the dog gave another worried whimper. With no words at his disposal, Cowboy still managed to convey his opinion about the last-minute road trip they'd embarked on late last night, and at this point, Garrett was tempted to agree with him.

"Relax, boy." Garrett cocked his head toward the navigation system resting on the dash. "Matilda thinks we're almost there, and she hasn't gotten us lost in a long time."

That earned him another whine and a hopeful thump of the dog's tail. Cowboy's tongue lolled from the side of his open mouth as he stuck his head out of the window and resumed his panting.

Maybe Garrett should have listened to his little brother Luke. Cowboy might have been better off staying with his father at the senator's residence in Sacramento. But Garrett had balked when Luke brought it up. The dog belonged with him. Constant companions for the past two years—watching each other's backs, eating together, sleeping together, flushing out Sunni militants together—Cowboy was the closest thing to a guardian angel Garrett would ever see.

When they'd both been injured in a firefight outside the Iraqi city of Fallujah, Cowboy had not only led them out of the ambush, but also stood guard over him and the other surviving member of their unit until help had arrived in the early hours of the morning. At the field hospital, Garrett had insisted the dog receive the best treatment available and, a couple of weeks later, had pulled out all the stops to secure the necessary approval to bring him home.

He knew what it was like to have someone you love suddenly and permanently disappear. And it wasn't happening to Cowboy. Not if Garrett could help it. He hadn't left the dog behind in Iraq, and he wasn't going to leave him now. Unless he was able to pass the stringent physical requirements that would allow him to rejoin his Ranger unit. As hard as he'd worked toward making that a reality, the odds were against him. If by some miracle he did, his half sister, Shay, would keep Cowboy, but even thinking about leaving him made Garrett's gut ache. So, for right now, they were staying together. Besides, he just might need some moral support if he was going to see this mission through to the end.

"Sorry, bud. Needed you with me on this one." He rested his hand on the dog's shoulder just above the ragged scar where a bullet had torn through muscle and tissue. Cowboy had recovered surprisingly well, but the wound had ended the career of the best military dog Garrett had ever been teamed with.

Cowboy's big, brown, soulful eyes studied his for a moment before a barely audible *woof* broke the silence.

Garrett chuckled and patted the dog's furry side. "Good boy. That's right—use your indoor voice. You'll need to be on your best behavior while we're here. Shouldn't be long, though. I can't imagine there'd be anything to keep us here beyond the end of the day."

Why *had* he come anyway?

Aunt Peg's letter. His temper flared remembering the confrontation between him and his father after Garrett had stumbled upon the year-old letter in his dad's desk drawer.

"Looking for something, son?" There'd been wariness in his father's voice.

Garrett had dragged his gaze from the envelope in his hand to study the senator. "I misplaced Shay's telephone number. I thought I might find it in here." The call to his sister momentarily forgotten, he'd held the letter up so his father could see.

The senator had looked away, his expression shuttering over. "I meant to give that to you, but both you and Luke were out of the country when it arrived and, frankly, it's not something you should worry about. You need to concentrate on getting well," his father had said, but the way his gaze bounced around the room instead of meeting Garrett's told a different story.

"Dad, I've been in the States for six months. Two months at the VA hospital and four months recuperating right here in this house. Luke's been here a week. What were you waiting for?" Garrett had held the letter out in front of him. " 'Garrett and Luke Harding.' " He'd read the first line of the address out loud and then jerked the letter away as his father made a grab. "Peg Williams. That's Aunt Peg, isn't it? Did it cross your mind at all that Luke and I might be interested in what our mother's sister had to say?"

"Your mother passed away a year ago. Peg invited you to the reading of the will. Hell, your mother didn't have time for you while she was alive. Why *would* you be interested now? Hate me for it if you want—I took it upon myself to keep the letter from you. I didn't think it was important twenty-nine years after she walked out on you boys." Anger had hardened his father's expression.

Garrett had sucked in a breath as the words pelted him, reopening a wound he'd thought long closed. After all, they hadn't heard from the woman their father had said was a drug addict in nearly thirty years. Now she'd apparently left them something in her will—as though she'd have anything they'd want. Wasn't that just the icing on the cake?

Garrett had straightened his six-foot-one frame until the muscles surrounding the six-month-old wound in his back protested sharply. "You had no right to make that call."

"I had every right. I wasn't going to let that woman hurt you again."

Steel-gray eyes, so like his own, had stared back at Garrett. "Are you sure that's the reason, Dad? Or could it have had anything to do with keeping the *senator's* ex-wife off the front page of the newspaper?" Silence had stretched for at least thirty seconds, during which Garrett had had ample time to regret his words.

His father, ever the diplomat, had smiled faintly. "Let's table this discussion until cooler heads prevail, shall we? You have your letter, and I have a meeting I'm going to be late for." He'd grabbed several folders from his desk and hastened from the room.

Guilt had descended upon Garrett as soon as he was alone. He had no idea why the deception and his father's explanation had gotten him so hot. He'd agreed with nearly all of what the senator had said. Hadn't he been bitter and angry with his mother most of his life? Still, the questions he'd carried with him for a long time screamed to be answered, and a road trip seemed to be just what he needed.

He'd hoped to convince his brother to tag along since the letter was addressed to him too, but Luke, home on leave from the navy, opted to stay in Sacramento. With a wink, he gave a halfhearted promise to join Garrett if pretty girls or manual labor was involved. Though disappointed, Garrett had understood. Luke had been only three years old when their mother left and had avoided most of the bitterness, the loss, and the sense of worthlessness that had ensnared Garrett at the age of five.

So, he and Cowboy had jumped in his Jeep and typed Grizzly Gulch, Idaho, into Matilda's electronic brain. The GPS had been named after his high school principal, Ms. Matilda Banks, because the snarky impatience in its computerized voice was a dead ringer for the woman who'd refused to give up on him even after he'd gotten himself kicked out of school. She still checked up on him now and then just to make sure he was staying out of trouble and on the right path. Garrett had enjoyed the idea of setting the electronic Matilda on his dash and letting her tell him where to go.

He'd driven seventeen hours, stopping only to sleep beside the road, fuel up, and grab a bite to eat. Now, as the only vehicle on a road looking like something from the apocalypse, Garrett was beginning to have second thoughts. He swerved to miss a pothole. Matilda said they were right on target so their destination had to be close, but this narrow mountain road had him wondering if he'd taken a wrong turn somewhere. Maybe these winding backwoods trails had thrown Matilda for a loop.

Around the next sharp corner, the road straightened for about five hundred yards. On the left, a graveled parking lot surrounded a substantial log structure, its metal roof reflecting the light of the sun. One vehicle, a dilapidated pickup, waited out in front, engine running. A sign hanging from the eves over swinging double doors said COUGAR RIDGE WATERING HOLE.

He braked and pulled off the road as two men in the old rusted Ford pickup backed away from the building, turned, and started in his direction. They slowed to a crawl, both glaring with obvious malice as they drove by, then hit the gas and spun tires on gravel until they reached the two-lane ribbon of asphalt. Garrett would have laughed if he hadn't been so damned tired. Cowboy added his sentiments with a his-ass-is-mine growl.

"Yeah, I wish, boy, but unless we start hearing banjos, we don't want any trouble." Garrett pulled into the spot the old Ford had vacated. "Stay in the Jeep, bud. I need some coffee, and I'll find out if this is the best way to get to Aunt Peg's lodge…in case Matilda doesn't know what the hell she's talking about." GPSs weren't infallible. Just a couple of months ago there'd been a story on the news. A family had become stranded on a snow-packed, impassable road after their navigation system sent them on the shortest, most direct route to their destination, rather than the most well-used, safest road. The father had gone for help and ended up freezing to death.

The dog's whine turned into a grumble as Garrett stepped out of the Jeep and strode toward the swinging doors. The sun felt good on his back and thigh, which were still stiff and aching from two bullet wounds, courtesy of his last tour. After seventeen hours of sitting and sleeping in a vehicle, his muscles were all tied up in knots.

He was going to wish he hadn't skipped out on his P/T appointment yesterday. Stretching his upper body, he climbed the short set of steps to the open deck that ran the length of the building.

The second he pushed one of the swinging doors open and stepped onto the rough plank floor, the skin at the back of his neck began to crawl. He stopped as every muscle in his body tensed, and he slowly removed his dark glasses to give his eyes a chance to adjust to the dim interior. At first glance, the place appeared empty. His gaze leisurely swept the tables to his left, searched the length of the bar—made from a monstrous piece of old-growth pine—and stopped when he zeroed in on a man, a punk really, and a woman sitting at a table to the right of the burnished log. Apart from them, the Cougar Ridge Watering Hole was deserted.

He kept one eye on the couple as he stepped purposefully toward the bar. His gut had twisted into a massive knot, a sure sign something wasn't right.

The male was a good-sized kid, no more than nineteen or twenty. Long, dirty hair slapped against his collar as his gaze followed Garrett farther into the room. The woman's shoulder-length red hair framed an attractive face, and bangs, in slight disarray, slanted across her forehead. She sat ramrod straight in her chair, and a glimpse of amazing green eyes grabbed Garrett's attention when she glanced his way before turning her watchful gaze back to her companion.

The kid gripped one of the woman's hands, pinning her to the table in an awkward position. They were so clearly not just a boy and girl holding hands. Garrett would lay odds that the pretty redhead couldn't bear the man's touch.

So, what was their story? A lover's spat? He doubted that. A domestic dispute? Something more sinister? Goddammit. Why did he have to walk into the middle of it?

"Bartender around?" Garrett leaned one elbow against the bar and glanced over his shoulder.

"Yes." The woman was quick to reply and would have jumped to her feet if the jerk beside her hadn't twisted her arm, forcing her to remain in her chair. A grimace of pain flickered momentarily across her features.

"No," the guy growled. "There's no one here but me and Rachel, so *you* might wanna be goin'."

A wave of anger hit Garrett hard as he watched the red-haired woman school her expression into patient nonchalance, yet she couldn't hide the fury that burned in those green eyes. Garrett, taking his cue from her, forced a smile and shifted his weight to one of the barstools. "Huh! They just left the place unlocked?" He stared directly at the kid. "Seems reckless. Any slimy piece of riffraff could wander in and sit himself down." A faint smile crossed quickly over Rachel's face, but apparently the idiot beside her was too stupid to take offense. Garrett would have to try harder.

The kid leaned back in his chair, and a black scowl twisted his features. "I won't be tellin' ya again to clear out. A fella stickin' his nose in around these parts is askin' for a beatin'…or worse."

Garrett's gaze shifted to Rachel as she slowly lifted her eyes to his. She studied him curiously for a second before the slimeball squeezed her hand cruelly and she bit her lip, muffling a small sound. The tautness of her body and the determined set of her jaw telegraphed her intention ahead of her movement, and Garrett started toward them seconds before she jumped to her feet, sending her chair flying backward. Rachel fisted her right hand and flung a haymaker at the punk's nose. Obviously quicker than he looked, the kid saw it coming and easily caught her wrist, yanking her arm behind her back. With one foot, he pulled the closest chair into position and forced her to sit, then turned to face Garrett with a make-my-day smirk on his face. Clearly enjoying himself now, he twisted Rachel's arm higher, bending her over the table, and a cry escaped her this time. "As I was sayin', it's time for you to go."

Garrett held his ground. The woman's eyes still flashed with fire, but fear seemed noticeably absent, if the instinct to knock the kid on his ass was any indication. Maybe they *were* a couple and this was their idea of Saturday-afternoon foreplay. Damn. He hated getting involved in family matters, but he'd never been able to abide violence against women.

A deep breath later, he'd committed himself to what was likely to follow. "Thanks for the warning, but I think I'll hang around for a while. Unless you want to let this pretty little bartender here sell me a drink."

The guy took a step toward the edge of the table, still grasping Rachel's wrist. "Hey! You hard of hearin' or somethin'? You've got two seconds to git back on the road or I'm gonna kick your ass."

Garrett laughed, then let his forced humor fade as he squared his stance. "You can try if you want."

The guy roared like a wounded rhinoceros, released the woman's wrist, and lurched around the table toward Garrett. Rachel didn't waste a second. She darted away from the table, vaulted over the top of the bar, and dropped out of sight on the other side.

Garrett braced for the lunatic's clumsy attack, but with three strides still separating them, he heard the distinctive sound of a Winchester lever-action rifle. The charging bull in front of him obviously recognized the sound as well.

He skidded to a stop and threw his hands in the air. "Now, Rachel, baby. You don't wanna do that."

"I sure as hell do, you sorry excuse for a single-celled amoeba. I told you if you ever laid a hand on me, I'd kill you, and I meant it." Rachel's voice was silky smooth and hard-edged.

She stood with elbows braced against the far side of the bar, drawing down on the kid with the rifle she gripped like a modern-day Annie Oakley, and Garrett didn't doubt her threat for a minute. Clearly, however, the dimwitted kid didn't have the sense to take her seriously. Shit. It chapped his ass to have to take this worthless scum's side. "Uh…Rachel is it? Maybe we should let the police handle this."

A disbelieving laugh burst from her. "The *police* are worse than Riley here."

With her attention solely on the young Riley, Garrett sidled up to the bar, shoved the barrel of the rifle up, and pulled it from her hands. "Trust me. He's right about this. You don't want to do that."

Riley picked that moment to laugh.

"Damn it. Shut up, kid, if you know what's good for you." Garrett's patience was at its breaking point.

Rachel inhaled sharply, and Garrett's attention jerked back to her. She stared at the door.

"Drop the rifle, Mister." The new voice was deep and raspy, and it was followed by the sound of footsteps moving closer.

Garrett slowly turned to see the two men from the old Ford pickup standing one on each side of the swinging panels. Both carried sawed-off shotguns. They reminded him of Darryl and Darryl, two no-doubt inbred brothers from an old sitcom he'd watched once. These two weren't quite as funny, though.

Riley hooted, strode toward Garrett, and confiscated the Winchester. "What the hell are you boys doin' back here? I told you to go pick up the supplies."

"We saw this yahoo park and go inside. Thought there could be some trouble." Darryl #1 smirked as though that's what he'd been hoping for.

Riley gave him a playful shove. "Oh, and you didn't think I could handle it by myself?"

"Naw, Riley. Just didn't want you havin' all the fun."

Darryl #2 chewed on a toothpick as he studied Rachel, then swept his gaze to Garrett. "Thought we was just supposed to git the girl. What we gonna do with him now?" The older of the two jabbed his shotgun toward Garrett.

"What d'ya think?" Riley smirked.

What the hell was going on here? This wasn't some awkward kid trying to coerce a kiss out of a reluctant girlfriend. Not even close. Both parties seemed willing to kill over whatever the stakes were in this little game, and Garrett was sadly out of the loop. He met Rachel's gaze and cocked an eyebrow in question.

"I'd say I told you so, but the satisfaction would be short-lived. Bet you wished you'd stayed on the interstate now." She lowered her eyelids, and it appeared she was studying something below the level of the bar, then she slowly opened them again until she was looking into his once more. There was a message in her green depths—if he could only figure out what it was.

His imagination might be working overtime, but it sure did look as though the young lady had just given him a signal. Was there something under that bar that she was hoping to get her hands on? Something that could help them out of a tight spot? If that was the case, by God, this time he'd let her use it. He wished to hell he hadn't left *his* handgun in the glove box of the Jeep.

"Git him out of here. Take his rig. I'll bring the girl, and we'll meet up at the mine." Riley started toward Rachel, but she stayed where she was, spouting a stream of colorful adjectives sure to piss him off even further. Damned if she wasn't a handful once she got good and mad.

Darryl and Darryl advanced on Garrett, and he lifted his hands, palms toward them, raising his voice to be heard over the commotion behind him. "Easy, Cowboy."

A streak of black and tan running in under the swinging doors went unnoticed until the dog charged and leaped, hurtling ninety-five pounds of muscle and fury toward Darryl #1. The man turned to face the threat at the last minute, and Cowboy hit him squarely in the chest. The back of Darryl #1's head walloped the floor, and he didn't get up.

Darryl #2 backed away as Cowboy stalked him with a menacing snarl, wrinkling his muzzle. Before the man could get his wits about him and think to use his shotgun for something besides a shield, Garrett stepped between them and let go with an uppercut that dropped the man in a crumpled heap. There was no movement when Garrett nudged him with the toe of his boot. Tapping his leg, he called the dog to his side. "Take no prisoners." He spoke softly, and Cowboy dropped to his haunches and stood guard over the fallen enemy.

Garrett swung around to locate Riley, but Rachel already had that situation under control. She gripped a .38 special in her hand. "Jesus. How many more guns do you *have* back there?"

"I suppose you want this one, too?" She barely moved the weapon as her gaze flicked over Garrett dismissively.

"Not at all. It appears you've got this handled. I'm not too proud to admit when I've been wrong." He waited, giving her time to think things through. After about thirty seconds of silence and nervous vibes inside the dimly lit establishment, he figured she'd had enough. "Are you going to kill him?"

"Aw, Rach. I was just havin' some fun. I wasn't gonna hurt ya." Riley backed away as he whined.

"What *were* you going to do, you moron? Leave us at the bottom of Addison's Mine? I wonder what your mama would think of you now." Rachel raked one hand through her hair, brushing it back from her face. Frustration and uncertainty were clear in the deep furrow between her brows.

A twinge of protectiveness rocked Garrett when her chin trembled for the first time since he'd walked in the door. She was a fighter—no doubt about that—but something was going on here that clearly had her off balance.

"Who said anything about Addison's? We was just out drinkin' and havin' a good time. Problem is you've always thought you was too good for me and the boys. But then I met an old friend of yours, and he told me you know how to party real good." Riley leaned his hands on the bar and grinned lecherously.

"Who? Who's been talking about me? Did someone put you up to coming in here today and causing trouble?" Damned if Rachel's voice wasn't shaking more now than when they'd had a gun on her.

Riley smirked. "If I told you, it would spoil the surprise. No can do, Rach."

"Okay, that's enough." Garrett was surprised by the intensity of his anger. Seeing Rachel scared for the first time since he'd walked through the door hadn't helped. "Either shoot him or give me the gun." He held out his hand.

Rachel darted a glance at him, a wisp of a smile floating over her face. She apparently considered her options before placing the revolver in his outstretched hand. Humor flashed in her eyes and lifted the corners of her mouth ever so slightly. When she spoke, though, she was still nervous and edgy. "I wasn't kidding when I said the cops are useless…so…maybe *you* could shoot him."

Garrett held his breath and searched her face. She looked serious enough except for a sparkle in her eyes that disappeared a heartbeat later when she lowered her lashes. She'd proved she wouldn't use her weapons as anything beyond a warning, so this suggestion had to be a con intended to drive her point home to the not-so-bright Riley. Obviously, she didn't want Garrett to shoot him either, no matter what kind of vermin he was. Okay, he'd play her little game…to a point.

He turned until Rachel was the only one who could see his face and gave her a wink. Then he braced his arms against the log bar and dropped his head toward his chest. A heavy breath escaped. Behind him, Cowboy whined, no doubt sensing his subterfuge. Garrett flashed a hand signal for the dog to stand down so he wouldn't interfere.

He nodded. "Okay, I can do that, if you're sure that's what you want."

"I think it's the only way," she replied.

"Now, wait just a doggone minute." Riley sputtered and started shuffling backward. He tripped over one of his buddies and almost fell. His buddy came to, scrambled to his feet, and stumbled for the door, keeping a wary eye on Cowboy.

"If you don't shoot him, he'll just come back next time I'm here alone." Rachel cast an accusing glance at Riley.

"Are you bat-shit crazy, bitch? I'm never settin' foot in this place again." He turned and raced for the exit, hitting the swinging doors with such force they slammed shut on him halfway through, and he had to shove them apart again. Once Riley was outside, Garrett heard the pickup roar to life and its tires squeal away from the Watering Hole before silence finally settled over the bar.

It took Rachel a moment to regain her former confidence, but when she smiled, she revealed a dimple in each rosy cheek and no small amount of amusement. "That was fun. We make a good team."

Garrett chuckled as he handed her the revolver and had to tear his gaze from her exuberant expression. "If that's your idea of fun, I'd hate to have to entertain you for any length of time."

She laughed easily, her delight contagious, and suddenly all Garrett could think about was finding an excuse to stay a little longer and get to know her. The women he usually met were nothing like this girl. She was all sunshine and clean mountain air, and something about her intrigued him.

Darryl #2 was still out cold when Garrett bent to check for a pulse and then hauled him over his shoulder and dumped him outside in the parking lot. The old Ford truck was nowhere to be seen. Riley and his friend hadn't waited around for their comrade.

When he stepped back inside, Rachel was rearranging the chairs that had been disturbed by the three miscreants. Garrett watched her move gracefully around the floor—as if it wasn't the first fight she'd ever cleaned up after. She wore a white button-up shirt made of some kind of gauzy fabric, knotted at her hips. The first three buttons were undone, revealing a lacy camisole and the fullness of her breasts. A short denim skirt hugged her hips and then flared out to midthigh—and damn fine thighs they were, too. Equally nice calves disappeared into red cowboy boots. Simmering heat began to grow in his abdomen.

Rachel finished her chore and sashayed behind the bar. "That drink is on the house if you still want it."

He hadn't realized earlier that a band of darker green outlined the pale of her eyes. Strikingly attractive, they pulled his gaze away from the red tresses that fell, curly and untamed, to cover her shoulders.

"Actually, I think I've got a ways to go yet. I was hoping for some coffee…and directions."

"I'll put on a fresh pot. Won't take a minute. What's your dog's name?" She turned her back to start the coffee, giving Garrett ample opportunity to scrutinize her nicely rounded backside, and his manhood, having been on an enforced hiatus, twitched in appreciation.

"Uh…Cowboy." The dog padded up alongside him and waited attentively to see why Garrett had called his name. "We served together in Iraq. When it was my turn to go home, I brought him with me. He's got my back."

"He's gorgeous, and obviously devoted to you."

"So what was that about? Riley and the other two— what did they want from you?" Garrett stared at her back until she flipped on the coffeemaker and turned to face him.

Her smile was gone. "Riley wanted me to go for a ride with him, and when I refused—well, you saw the aftermath. I don't know what he was thinking, but from the things he said, I'm afraid it could have something to do with"—Rachel crossed her arms and averted her eyes—"you know. I'm sure I'm not the only one with skeletons in my closet."

"You think that's why he mentioned an old friend of yours and spoiling his surprise?"

Rachel gave a nod of her head, but didn't look up.

"The best way to keep someone from spilling your deep, dark secrets is to be the first to share them. The worst that can happen is people finding out, right? So if you're the one who gives it away at a time of your choosing, *he*, whoever he is, has nothing." Garrett leaned in on his forearms, hoping she would look at him.

Her green eyes darted to his and she wagged her head side to side. "That's *not* the worst that could happen—not by a long shot. And you're not suggesting I confide in you, are you?"

Garrett shrugged. "No…but since you brought it up…I am a stranger. I have no preconceived ideas about you. Chances are pretty good you'll never see me again after today. If you don't have anyone else you can talk to, I'll listen and maybe I can help."

Rachel was silent long enough that Garrett thought she might actually be considering his offer, but then she laughed and waved her hand in the air, dismissing the idea. "Nice try, but I don't think so." Laughter eased the worry lines on her forehead and brought out her dimples. Garrett would probably have reached out and caressed her flawless cheek if she hadn't turned her back to him.

The coffee was almost done, its aroma calling to him. Rachel pulled a foam cup from below the counter and set it next to the gurgling coffeemaker. "You said you needed directions. Where are you headed?"

"Well, I think I'm close but I'd feel better if someone besides Matilda—uh…that's what I call my navigation system—if someone else confirmed that. I'm looking for the Cougar Ridge Hunting Lodge and Resort. Heard of it?"

Her back stiffened instantly, and after she poured the coffee into the cup, she slammed the glass decanter down on the burner. With shaking fingers, she fumbled with the lid until it locked in place. Then she pivoted to meet his gaze. There was no longer anything neighborly or even remotely friendly in her green eyes. Was it his destination that had triggered her response?

She pushed the coffee toward him. "I thought you looked familiar. Which one are you?" The controlled anger in her voice accused him of something, but he couldn't for the life of him figure out what. A shame too, because not two minutes ago the thought had crossed his mind to ask her to dinner.

At a loss to know what he'd done and not understanding the question, he continued to study her face.

"You're one of Amanda's boys, aren't you?"

At the mention of his mother, his jaw clenched, and every muscle readied in preparation to bolt. He shoved his hands in his pockets and forced himself to stand still. "Garrett Harding—at your service." The words escaped without emotion, and Cowboy whined. Obviously, he didn't understand the turn in the conversation either.

Garrett searched Rachel's eyes again. They were filled with defiance and something bordering on disgust. He had no clue why she was suddenly treating him like something she'd scraped off the bottom of her shoe, but he was pretty sure it had something to do with his mother. He could totally understand if Rachel's ill will was directed at the woman who gave birth to him, but it was foolhardy to blame him for his mother's actions. Rachel couldn't know that he'd been five years old the last time he'd seen Amanda, however, and since he was only passing through, he should just let her think whatever she wanted.

"Does that mean you don't know where the resort is?" He slid his hand around the coffee cup and turned to go.

"You've been on Peg's land for the past thirty minutes. This bar is part of the resort. There's a bed-and-breakfast and a restaurant, too. The resort is about a mile farther up the mountain." Disdain permeated every word.

If there was one thing Garrett had learned, it was that you couldn't change someone's mind if they weren't receptive. Rachel clearly wasn't into listening, and it irked him for some reason. That and a mysterious ache in his core drew him up short, not willing to quit on the conversation just yet. There was something going on here that defied his understanding, but he couldn't shake the feeling that Rachel was in serious trouble. If she was right about the secret from her past catching up to her, then Riley was probably the least of her worries. But Riley was the trouble Garrett had seen, and there was nothing stopping him from returning to the bar once Garrett and Cowboy left. That was unacceptable.

He turned slowly. "You shouldn't be here alone. I've got a hunch those local boys will be looking for a chance to get even. I could give you a lift somewhere, or I could stick around until the rest of the evening shift arrives. I'll be quiet. You won't even know I'm here."

The glare she fixed him with was flat-out hostile. She braced her arms on the bar and leaned toward him as though to impart a whispered confidence. Her lips parted in a half smile, and her voice, as sweet as honey, turned the knife in his chest. "The dog can stay...but no Harding will ever be welcome here."

Chapter Two

THE INFAMOUS GARRETT Harding displayed a split second of surprise before he turned and stomped his big army boots to the door. One hand on the swinging panel, he stopped and stared into the parking lot, then his head dropped toward his chest, and he huffed an irritated breath. He scrubbed a hand across the back of his neck, and a barely audible growl carried across the room.

Rachel Maguire might have mistaken it for the dog if Garrett hadn't whipped around, looked straight at her, and motioned for her to come and look. "They're back."

Every nerve in her body vibrated—and not in a good way—at being commanded by this man who'd broken Amanda's heart. His biological mother, yet he'd ignored every one of her letters, turned his back on her, and let her die without the one thing she'd desired more than anything—to see him one more time. Lower than pond scum—that's what he was. He'd had a multitude of chances to drop in when his mother was still alive. What was he doing here now?

Had Peg contacted him? She was ever the devoted sister…but this was going too far. Damn it. It was too soon. Amanda's sudden death had hit Peg hard. It'd only been three months since she'd gotten out of the hospital, having managed to crawl back from the black hole of depression that had sought to claim her. No way would Rachel let her get to that point again.

Rachel's chin jutted forward, and she crossed her arms. Garrett's heated gaze was a physical force, nearly knocking her off balance. When he started back toward her, his steps determined and angry, it was only stubborn pride that kept her where she was.

Garrett halted two feet in front of her, his lips pressed into a thin line, his steel-gray eyes narrowing dangerously. Clearly he'd surpassed the limits of his patience. Perhaps, under the circumstances, she'd been a bit uncooperative. Still, if he presumed to lay a hand on her, he wouldn't walk away without a scratch. Her life at Cougar Ridge had taught her many things, not the least of which was how to defend herself should that skill ever be required.

A few seconds into their stare-down, his gaze fell to her lips and lingered there as he rested his hands on his hips. Indecision, among other harsher emotions, registered on his face, but the angry inferno in his eyes slowly dissipated. His voice was gravelly as he started to speak, so he cleared his throat and tried again.

"Riley and the other two clowns are parked across the lot. I'm going to discourage them from hanging around. I want you to wait inside." He started to swing around.

Rachel caught his elbow. "Discourage them how? I was only joking when I talked about shooting them. I thought you knew that. They're just kids—barely twenty. You can't hurt them, Garrett."

He scowled. "Yeah, well, they're old enough to be packing weapons and issuing threats. I don't plan on hurting them...unless there's no other way."

"There has to be. Let me handle this. I've known Riley Metcalf and his brothers, Arnold and Matt, for half their lives. I was there when their mother passed away. Those young men are my neighbors. They're not going to hurt me. "

Riley's mother had died when the boys were still in high school. Rachel, Amanda, and Peg had brought meals to the family and helped wherever they could while Mrs. Metcalf was sick. Amanda had tried to keep the boys in school, too, but Arnold dropped out and the other two soon followed. After that they'd gone wild and seemed to always be in trouble. Still, they'd treated Rachel with respect...until now. She'd assured Garrett they meant her no harm, but truthfully, there'd been a glaring difference in Riley's visit today.

Garrett snorted his disbelief, and his hands found rest on his hips again as he glanced toward the door. Finally, he swept his gaze slowly back to hers. "What in the hell do you think they had in mind earlier? From where I was standing, it looked pretty damn serious. I'm not leaving you. Believe me, I'd like to, but I can't. So, you've got two choices. Call someone—boyfriend, brother, friend—someone who can stay with you and then see you safely home. I'll hang around until they get here. Or you can lock the place up right now. I didn't see any other vehicles out there so I'm assuming someone dropped you off. Call 'em. If they can come right away…fine. If not, let me give you a ride home. Please."

Rachel stifled a giggle. He'd almost choked on that *please*. Apparently the big man wasn't well versed in the niceties of society. Still, he seemed genuinely concerned with her safety. She hadn't expected kindness or concern from Garrett Harding, but why else would he be putting himself in harm's way to protect her?

He'd encroached on her space, and his size alone was intimidating. It wasn't that he was so tall, although he was at least six feet—maybe a little more—but his shoulders, arms, and thighs were thick with muscle. Every ridge and plane of his chest and abs was outlined on the black T-shirt he wore tucked into snug-fitting blue jeans. A set of dog tags hung to midchest and called attention to his well-formed pecs.

His dark brown hair was cut short, and the cowlick in back suggested he may have slept on it recently. It was obvious he hadn't shaved in a day or so. She hated to admit it, but the overall package was off-the-charts hot.

Nothing wrong with enjoying the view, but no way would she let her guard down simply because he looked damn good in a T-shirt—not *this* man. It didn't matter that Garrett Harding was strong, muscled, and wore dog tags. It made no difference that he'd served his country, returning with a slight limp that he tried hard to hide, or that he was a sucker for dogs. He'd helped her, a complete stranger, out of a jam, and now he refused to leave her with the threat of danger. None of that was important. She wouldn't allow herself to be taken in by him—not by Amanda's heartless and unforgiving son.

Skirting around him, she hurried to the door, peering over the top of one of the panels. That stupid rusted-out pickup sat at the edge of the lot right where he'd said it was, and that probably wasn't good. What did Riley want with her? At first, she'd thought he'd just meant to scare her, but when he'd grabbed her and made it clear she was leaving with him whether she wanted to or not, she'd immediately recognized that this was something outside of Riley's expertise. He was obviously taking orders from someone. But who?

Was it possible that Jeremy had found her after all this time? She'd become complacent. She was supposed to be hiding from her stalker here in the backwoods of Idaho, but she'd gotten comfortable in her new life. Living out in the open, where anyone might see her—recognize her. She hadn't taken Jeremy seriously ten years ago either, and the consequences had been disastrous.

Rachel bit her lip as a tremor started between her shoulder blades and radiated outward. Jeremy's phone calls had started again about five years ago. When he called, often she wouldn't hear anything on the other end—other times just heavy breathing. If he spoke, his voice was always muffled, and he'd ask about whom her friends were and if she was dating. Her answer was always the same—she had a couple of girlfriends and no, she never dated. Forcing herself to talk to her stalker, trying not to anger him, would cause her to break out in cold sweat and usually always culminated in her heaving the contents of her stomach. When each call was over, she'd throw her old phone away and buy another, yet somehow he'd always get her new number and call again. Maybe she was being naive, but in a way, his calls had made her feel safer. Common sense said if he could find her phone number, discovering her address couldn't be that much harder. But as long as he wasn't leaving her notes or flowers in the privacy of her dwelling, or calling and complimenting her on how she looked today, she clung fast to the belief that, for now at least, he didn't know where she was. Fully aware that circumstances could change in a heartbeat, she'd remained ready to leave on a moment's notice.

The *click, click* of the dog's toenails drew her attention as he sidled up beside her and leaned his head against her thigh. His eyes were big and curious, and Rachel couldn't help smiling as she reached to scratch under his collar. He was a big dog, and with him close by, she felt protected. Her sense of security had absolutely nothing to do with the testosterone-laden hulk whose gaze she could feel boring into her back even now.

Making up her mind, she swung around and started toward the bar. "There *is* no boyfriend or brother. I was only here to pick up something for Peg. It's too early in the season—the bar isn't even open yet. I walked down from the resort. That's where I live." She stopped in front of him. "If the offer is still good, you can give me a lift home…but then you have to go. I won't have you upsetting Peg."

"Peg is *my* aunt. I'm not here to upset her. I just want answers." For a heartbeat, anger simmered just below his dark look, and she was sure he would open up and let her have it, but his facial features slowly relaxed until he almost smiled. "What else do you have to do? Can I help with anything?"

"I need to grab some papers from behind the bar, pour out the coffee, grab my purse, and lock up on the way out." Rachel performed the first three chores as she spoke.

Garrett tapped his hand against his leg and the dog loped toward the door ahead of him. A quiet command brought him to a halt just inside the bar, swinging his head around to see what the holdup was. Garrett ran his fingers through Cowboy's fur as they both waited at the door. Rachel stood still and watched them, feeling guilty for the warm glow that started in her stomach at the obvious affection the two shared. Was it possible for a bad man to care about an animal the way Garrett clearly cared for Cowboy? Rachel didn't believe so, but he was putting on a pretty good act.

Just as Garrett glanced back for her, she busied herself searching through her purse. Then, with keys in one hand, she slid the strap of her purse over her head and hurried toward the waiting pair.

"Are they still there?"

"Evidently, they've got all the time in the world." When Garrett glanced down at her, she suddenly realized how close they were.

He took a step toward the door, laying one hand on top of the swinging panels. "Any idea how far these fools will go to get what they want? It's none of my business, but it might give us some insight as to how they'll react once they see us leaving."

"If there's trouble anywhere around, Riley's usually right in the middle of it." She peered over the doors beside him. "Matt would follow him off a cliff, but Arnold usually has a mind of his own, though apparently not today. No, I don't know how far they're willing to go. This is the first time anything like this has happened."

"If that's true, why are you so well armed behind the counter?"

"Everyone around here carries. Some hunt, some come here running from something and wouldn't be caught dead without a weapon, and some are involved in bootlegging or white supremacy. They're all my neighbors, and sooner or later they all end up in my bar. I'd be crazy not to be well armed—crazier still not to be able to handle myself if the situation were to arise."

He searched her eyes for a little too long before he finally faced the door again. "Cowboy and I will get the Jeep. If your friends think I'm leaving, they might wait, hoping they'll catch you alone again. As soon as I'm outside, you lock up just like you always do. By then I'll have the Jeep running and your door open. My ride's not that fast, but I think we can outrun that rusted piece of shit they're driving." Warmth stole into his voice as he ended on a chuckle.

Rachel forgot herself for a moment, returning his grin as merriment bubbled over her defensive shields. As soon as she remembered whom it was standing beside her, her good humor vanished, leaving her cold and bitter. "Let's not prolong this. I'm sure you have someplace you're supposed to be."

She glanced away, but not before one of his brows shot up toward his hairline and an irritated scowl blackened his features. He mumbled something as he shoved the wooden door back on its hinges, but she couldn't tell if he was commanding Cowboy or grumbling at her. She almost hoped it was the latter because annoyed and angry was a lot easier to deal with than kind and protective.

As soon as Garrett and Cowboy stepped off the porch, she followed them, pulling the secondary doors into position and locking them. She turned to find the Jeep purring softly directly in front of her, the passenger door open about two steps from the porch. As much as she wanted to, she couldn't keep herself from glancing across the parking lot. The instant she did, the engine of Riley's truck rumbled to life.

Rachel jogged down the steps and scrambled into the Jeep. Calm and unhurried, Garrett ignored her as he checked the rearview mirrors, but Cowboy barked impatiently, wagging his tail from side to side.

"Hand me my gun from the glove box and buckle up. Here they come." Garrett peeled out before she got her door completely closed.

A quick glimpse over her shoulder confirmed his announcement. The pickup was closing the distance between them. She faced the front and gripped the edge of the seat while her world spun dangerously for a few seconds. The young men in the truck behind them were her neighbors—members of the community where she'd lived for most of her adult life. If she handed Garrett his gun, what would he do? Did she care? Lord only knew what they'd have done to her if she hadn't gotten free— if Garrett hadn't stopped by. Funny how the suspicion that Riley and his brothers might be working for Jeremy changed the direction of her moral compass.

She jerked the glove compartment open and felt around the dark interior until her fingers bumped hard steel. A Colt .45 semiautomatic. Garrett apparently had excellent taste in weaponry. She smoothed her hand along the gun barrel until she saw him watching her curiously, then shoved the weapon toward him. His big hand wrapped around it, and he slid it between his thigh and the seat.

Another quick glance from the rear window told her Garrett was beginning to leave the old Ford pickup behind. Fumbling with the seat belt, she became more self-conscious with each unsuccessful attempt to close the buckle. After a few mumbled expletives on her part, he reached over and easily seated the metal latch inside the clasp.

An electrified jolt hit her as his knuckles brushed her hip. Her gaze darted to his, and the anticipation in his darkened eyes said she hadn't just imagined it. Evading the intensity of his perusal, she eased away from his lingering touch. *So* not happening. It'd be a cold day in hell before anything heated up with the likes of him.

"Sorry," Garrett rasped as he returned his hand to the steering wheel. "Just trying to help."

"No problem." Rachel forced herself to act as though his touch hadn't reached into her bone marrow and turned her to mush. What was wrong with her? She despised Garrett Harding for callously remaining silent in spite of every letter, every invitation, every birthday card Amanda had sent him over the past twenty-some years. Rachel had been there for the last ten, and she'd seen firsthand the heartbreak he'd inflicted on his mother. The other one—Garrett's brother Luke—had hurt his mother too, but he'd been little more than a toddler when Amanda left. He probably didn't remember her or understand why she'd gone. But Garrett would have, and yet he'd withheld the most precious gift he could have given her—his forgiveness—and now it was too late.

Okay. She banished that spark of desire, or hormones, or whatever it was. Loathing swelled within her again for the man in the driver's seat.

Garrett was covering ground rapidly—albeit in the wrong direction, but before she could point out that they should be traveling uphill, he slammed on the brakes and skidded around. Stomping on the gas pedal, he straightened the wheel, and now they were barreling straight toward Riley's pickup. Rachel gasped and shrunk down in her seat.

"Chill, Cowboy." Immediately, the dog dropped to the floor, his head lying partway between the seats. Garrett glanced at Rachel. "Get down lower."

She freed the latch on her seat belt and slid onto the floor, squished uncomfortably between the seat and the dash. Garrett was obviously expecting Riley's crew to have more weapons than the ones they'd left in the bar—and he was probably right.

"What about you?" She searched his face, trying to convince herself that her concern wasn't for him, but rather for herself if anything should happen to him.

"Why, *Rach*, if I didn't know better, I'd think you cared." A thin smile mocked her.

Okay, she'd deserved that, but if he was waiting for her to apologize, he'd have a very long wait.

Irritated, she rose up until she could see out the window. The old Ford pickup was so close, her knuckles whitened on the edges of the seat in anticipation of the crumpling of steel around her as the two vehicles met. At the last minute, Riley swerved, the truck spinning 360 degrees and balancing on two wheels for a second before slamming down to all four.

The Jeep raced past them, and she heard the whirr of their starter as they tried to get the pickup going again. Garrett grabbed another gear and accelerated up the mountain road. Rachel pulled herself onto her seat again, studying him from beneath lowered lashes. So, Garrett Harding knew how to play chicken and win, and he'd never even broken a sweat. Why couldn't she help admiring that?

Rachel glanced behind them periodically as they rolled along the narrow chip-sealed road. Garrett kept one eye on the rearview mirror too, but it was Cowboy who alerted them with a rumbling growl seconds before the old Ford rounded a corner and came into view behind them.

"They're gaining on us." She whipped around and stared straight ahead, then leaned forward and pointed. "Take a left up ahead where the sign is…and lay on the horn."

A quizzical glance was directed her way. "The *horn*?"

"Just do it," she snapped.

Despite his grumbling, he fishtailed onto the gravel road beside the rustic billboard with its arrow pointing toward the Cougar Ridge Hunting Lodge and Resort. Accelerating as much as the winding trail allowed, he slammed the palm of his hand on the center of the steering wheel, and the blaring bark of the horn drowned out everything else.

The Jeep slid around a corner, gravel flying in its wake, and Rachel welcomed the sight of home up ahead, surrounded by green, forested landscape. The road dipped through a meadow filled with spring wildflowers, crossed a small bridge over a narrow but deep creek, and then swung into a long cul-de-sac and parking area in front of the idyllic log buildings of the resort.

As soon as they crossed the bridge, Rachel turned to peer out the back. A smile formed when a huge, dark-haired man walked calmly to the center of the bridge and stood with arms crossed, staring at Riley, who had stopped his pickup and clambered out. Relieved, Rachel laid her hand on Garrett's arm.

He let up on the horn as his gaze sought the rearview mirror. "What the hell…Who is that?" He slammed on the brakes.

Rachel would have jumped out, but he caught her arm. "Friend of yours?"

"It's Jonathan. He works for Peg." It was none of Garrett's business, but Jonathan was also her best friend. It had been his idea to have a signal she could use if she was ever in trouble. With all the new people moving into the area—strange people—he hadn't liked her going out alone or working in the bar late at night. Too damn dangerous, he'd said. Of course, Jonathan had secrets of his own and was probably more paranoid than he needed to be. Rachel had simply refused to put up with a 24/7 bodyguard, so he'd had to settle…right after he'd taught her basic self-defense and shooting skills.

The signal had worked exactly as planned. Jonathan had blocked the road after she'd passed and stood ready to deal with the trouble for her. No doubt he'd give her hell later for accepting a ride from Garrett Harding.

She opened the door and jumped out. Turning toward Garrett, she started to tell him to wait in the Jeep, but all she saw was his back and Cowboy's furry rear end as they exited the other side. She scurried to the rear of the vehicle and was barely able to keep up with his huge, angry strides as he stomped toward the confrontation at the bridge.

Riley paced angrily in front of his pickup. He didn't appear to be armed, but the two waiting in the truck probably were.

Jonathan wore his Sig openly in a shoulder holster, the weapon left over from a law enforcement career he seldom mentioned. That, coupled with a seriously dark and dangerous demeanor, pretty much guaranteed that the Rileys of the world didn't mess with him.

"You *boys* have business here?" Jonathan stood in the middle of the bridge, his legs spread slightly and his arms folded across his impressive chest.

Riley blanched for a second, then jutted out his chin. "We was just makin' sure Rachel got home okay. Pretty little thing like her shouldn't be takin' rides from no stranger."

Rachel stepped alongside Jonathan and opened her mouth to retort.

"You're right," Jonathan growled, glancing sideways at her. "But, as you can see, she's fine. Rest assured I'll have a talk with her. Thanks for seeing her safely home, Riley, but I'll take it from here." Jonathan's tone dismissed him.

"He's a liar," Rachel said. She stood close to Jonathan and spoke quietly while she explained what had happened, the rushing of the water below ensuring their conversation was private. "He came into the bar looking for trouble. He was trying to force me to go somewhere with him. If Garrett hadn't walked in, there's no telling what he might have done." Rachel seethed at the idea of those jerks getting away with harassing her.

Jonathan didn't say a word—just stared at Riley, a warning in his eyes that was no doubt enough to convince most men they didn't want to argue. His silence was unnerving her.

Riley continued to huff and pace on his side of the bridge, but finally returned to the truck and crawled inside. He backed up until he found a place to turn around and threw gravel getting out of there.

Garrett stepped closer with Cowboy right beside him. "Appreciate your help. I'm Garrett Harding." He stuck out his hand.

Jonathan eyed him speculatively. "I know who you are." He turned away and fixed his gaze on Rachel. "You okay?" He waited only long enough for her to nod. "We'll talk about this later." Jonathan strode toward the house.

"*Jesus!* Is everybody around here as friendly as you two?" A dark scowl left splotches of red on Garrett's face.

Even though Jonathan had been majorly rude, Garrett had no room to talk. "Yes, we are. Lucky for you, you're leaving now. Thanks for the ride." She turned her back and hurried toward the resort.

"Sorry to disappoint you, but I'm not leaving yet."

She swung around and stared, her heart sinking.

"I've driven a long way to speak with Peg, and I'm not leaving until I do."

Her fists clenched as she retraced her steps until she stood a couple of feet from him. "That wasn't what we agreed on."

A scornful smile barely showed itself as he jabbed his index finger toward her. "I didn't agree to anything except giving you a ride home…and I don't take orders from pissed-off, spoiled brats. If you think I'm going to swallow your rude-ass remarks much longer without coming back with some of my own, you've been queen of fucking nowhere too damn long."

"Garrett?"

Rachel gasped as she whipped around toward the voice. Peg stood at the end of the cul-de-sac with a sheaf of papers in one hand and her reading glasses in the other, staring at Garrett. Her shoulder-length silver hair shimmered in the afternoon sunlight, and her chin trembled.

"See what you've done?" Rachel hissed.

Garrett stepped from behind her. "Yes, ma'am. That's me."

Rachel held her breath as Peg started forward, her gaze locked on her nephew. Tears welled in her eyes, and a wistful smile captured her lips. She didn't stop in front of him, but kept going until her thin arms slid around him, the top of her head reaching the middle of his chest.

"I knew someday you'd come." A tear rolled down her cheek.

It was a full five seconds before the man put his arms around her and hugged her back. When he did, he held her awkwardly, like a man holding a baby for the first time. It was just as Rachel suspected—Garrett Harding didn't have a caring, nurturing bone in his body. He would end up hurting Peg exactly as he'd hurt Amanda. What was Peg thinking, welcoming him? Even Cowboy sat nearby, dusting the ground with his tail. Was Rachel the only one who could see that Garrett was heartless?

He cleared his throat. "I need some answers."

Peg stepped back and wiped her tears. "Of course you do. Let's go up to the house and we'll talk. You can pull your Jeep in front of the garage. We'll meet you inside." She linked arms with Rachel and started to turn toward the resort before she paused. "If the dog is well-mannered, you can bring him in, too."

Rachel scoffed. "Give me the *dog* any day."

"Cowboy won't be a problem, ma'am." He signaled, and Cowboy followed him to the Jeep, jumping into the passenger side. Garrett shoved the door closed behind him and turned a scathing glance toward Rachel. "Would it kill you to be civil?"

"Let's shelve the *ma'am*, if you don't mind. You used to call me Aunt Peg, but if you're not comfortable with that yet, you can just call me Peg."

"Peg it is, then." Garrett climbed behind the wheel, started the engine and drove toward the resort.

Peg seemed to ignore the slap in the face she'd just gotten, but Rachel seethed under the weight of it. "I'm sorry, Peg. I didn't want to bring him here. We should have Jonathan send him on his way."

An incredulous frown carved a trough between Peg's brows. "Rachel, I'm surprised at you. Garrett is family. You know how long and hard Amanda tried to reconnect with him. Would she want us to send him away now?"

Rachel felt the heat of a flush creep into her cheeks. "No, but he didn't get here in time to see Amanda, did he? Have you forgotten how many times we had to bring her back from the depths of despair when he ignored yet another letter?" It was true Amanda hadn't been her blood relative. But she'd unselfishly filled the gaping hole in Rachel's life left by a mother too busy man-hunting to care about her. Rachel couldn't have loved Amanda any more if she'd been born into her family.

Sadness swept over Peg's expression. "Remember, there are two sides to every story. No, I'll never forget my sister's heartache, but today she'd be happy. Can't you just see that big smile on her face?" Peg drew Rachel close for a hug as fresh tears rimmed her eyes. "We're going to treat him like Amanda's son, whether she's here or not. Can you do that for her, dear?"

Rachel blinked hard to keep her own tears from falling. It was so unfair that Amanda couldn't have seen this day. Rachel *could* imagine the smile on her face and the joy in her eyes, but to forgive Garrett Harding would mean letting go of some deep-seated bitterness. It might be easier to stay away from him, and he'd probably appreciate that just as much.

The expectant look on Peg's face said she was still waiting for an answer. Rachel forced her trembling lips to cooperate. "I'll try, Peg. Or maybe I should go stay with Sally for a few days until he leaves." Her friend Sally Duncan lived in Huntington, about twenty miles away. She'd been the first person Rachel met when she first moved here, and they'd become close.

"You're old enough to make your own decisions, but I'd hate to see you run away with your bitterness intact. Stay. Face it. Do it for Amanda." Peg ran her fingers down Rachel's face. "She loved you so much. But she loved him, too. She'd want the two of you to be friends."

Garrett and Cowboy were waiting outside as they approached the front door, and Rachel panicked, despising her tears and red-rimmed eyes. She'd already been reduced to needing this man's help once today. She wasn't about to let him see her fall apart now.

Peg must have sensed her tension. "Dory will be starting dinner. Why don't you go help her?"

Peg's cool hand on Rachel's arm grounded her, and she managed to pull herself together. She pecked a kiss on Peg's cheek, straightened her spine, and walked past Garrett without a glance. She felt his gaze on her back long after she was out of sight.

Chapter Three

THAT WAS ONE fiery redhead, and damned if Garrett wouldn't mind getting to know her better under different circumstances. Unfortunately, she was majorly pissed off, and her anger appeared to be directed solely at him. What the hell was that about? She'd given no explanation for her antagonism except for the hostility with which she'd mentioned his mother. After Peg answered his questions, he'd be out of here, and it wasn't likely he would ever know what had her panties in a twist, but that didn't stop him from speculating.

A smile eased his rancor as he remembered Rachel earlier in the bar. She was tougher than she looked, displaying no fear while facing Riley down. Yet she hadn't been *all* gunpowder and bravado. Garrett had enjoyed the soft, feminine, humorous side of her, which had peeked free for a moment after they'd run the lowlifes out the door. He felt sure he could appreciate *that* side of Rachel…if he was ever allowed to see it again.

For all he knew, she may have handled worse situations than this, but his instinct told him she was underestimating the danger that Riley represented. Garrett's plan had been to drop in, get his answers, and get the hell out. No reminiscing. No time spent renewing old acquaintances. He'd come to exorcise the memory of his mother—not to wallow in what might have been. Now, however, when he contemplated his eminent departure, a twinge of regret chipped away at his resolve. Someone should get to the bottom of Riley's motives. Would it hurt to stay another day or two?

With Cowboy by his side, he followed Peg inside the lodge, traversed a large, impressively appointed lobby, passed a smoothly lacquered pine registration desk, and entered a small room that clearly contained the financial workings of the resort.

Peg's office was small, but organized and nicely furnished. Shelves lined the wall behind her desk and were filled with journals, reservation books, and accounting ledgers in chronological order. Like the lobby, the office was rustic and comfortable.

She motioned him to a straight-backed chair facing a medium-sized white cedar desk, and Cowboy plopped down on the floor beside him. Peg sat in a brown leather office chair, took a large, flat envelope from the center drawer of her desk, and placed it in front of her. Removing her reading glasses, she smiled sadly.

"I'm *so* happy you've come, Garrett. We have a lot to talk about."

Garrett frowned as resentment twisted his gut, and anger seeped into his words. "Less than you think. I'm only here to find out about Amanda Harding. I want to know what kind of mother walks out on her family. What was so much more important that she couldn't take care of her own kids? After it was all said and done, did she find what she was looking for? Was she happy? Did she ever think about Luke and me? Tell me that, and I'll be on my way." He stopped, choked by the lump of sadness that had formed in his throat.

Emotions flitted across Peg's face faster than he could recognize them. He'd expected sorrow, but the anger that burned in her eyes the longer he talked surprised him. The room grew quiet as she studied him, then rose from her chair and strode to the window, her back to him. Unmoving, she stood there in silence for so long he felt as if he was alone in the room.

Suddenly, she turned and unshed tears glistened in her eyes. "What did Senator Harding tell you?"

"This isn't about my father."

"It is, Garrett—more than you know."

Garrett clamped down on the temper rising to the surface. He would answer her question, but then, by God, she would answer his. "He said she was sick—some kind of a drug addiction—and it was too dangerous for her to care for me and Luke. He wanted her to get treatment, but she wasn't interested. She skipped out in the middle of the night, and we never saw her again."

Peg dropped into her chair, expelling a tired breath. "Part of that is true. Amanda became addicted to pain medication after a skiing accident at Vail. There were symptoms that made it hard—yes, even dangerous—for her to take care of you and Luke. She was causing problems for your father, too. He was running for governor then—the Democratic Party's shining hope in California."

Garrett leaned back in his chair, crossing his legs. He didn't like where this conversation was headed.

"Douglas convinced Amanda that she had somehow put you boys in danger. She was horrified and agreed to do whatever he said as long as you'd be safe. Rather than get her help, he insisted it was too risky for her to be around the two of you. So he agreed to cover the cost of her detox and give her a small settlement if she'd quietly divorce him. The only thing she cared about was your safety." Peg's chair squeaked as she leaned back. "She was addicted to pain meds, and she wasn't thinking straight. She didn't understand that she'd be losing custody of you forever." Peg's gaze never left his face.

"It took her two years to shake the drugs completely. As soon as she was well, she contacted your father and asked to see you. He was governor by then, and he said no—that if she tried, he'd have her arrested." Peg laughed scornfully. "Ever the diplomat, he agreed that she could write as long as the letters were mailed to him. He said that if you or Luke ever expressed an interest in seeing her, he'd make the arrangements. Until then, he thought it best not to disturb your lives again."

Garrett gritted his teeth. What was she saying? That his father had known where his mother was the whole time? Hell no—that couldn't possibly be true. His father had done the best he could. It was hard the first couple of years, but eventually, he'd remarried, and his new wife, Meredith, had fit snugly into the empty hole left by Amanda—everywhere but in Garrett's life. He'd wanted nothing to do with her. His father, insisting Garrett give the woman a chance, had only widened the gap.

Dad had always been distant, leaving the nurturing to Meredith. Of course, for the sake of his political career, it had always been important that his family give the appearance of a storybook existence. Perhaps that was the real reason behind the senator's dismay when Garrett, at seventeen, borrowed a police cruiser and ran for the state line with lights flashing and sirens wailing. Yeah, that had probably stolen a few years from the senator's life. Not to mention having the potential to derail his aspirations—the ones that might eventually land him in the White House.

Garrett had been on his way to the bottom in a nonstop hurry. His teenage years saw him hanging with the wrong crowd and making poor choices. His father had been forced to watch helplessly while Garrett edged closer and closer to a rebellious blunder he couldn't bounce back from. Ultimately, he'd gone too far and gotten in trouble with the law. His father hadn't missed a beat calling in favors so that Garrett could become the army's problem.

Except that had turned out to be the best thing he could have done. Rather than it being the lesser of two evils that Garrett had expected, the military had given him a place to verify his worth. Basic training had been a godsend, but when he'd completed the rigorous eight-week Ranger training and put the elite unit's tab on his sleeve, he thought he'd finally rid himself of all the old memories…right up until yesterday when he'd found the letter from Peg in his father's desk drawer.

His relationship with the senator had been strained for some time, but surely, during the darkness of Garrett's teen years, his father would have told him if he'd known where Amanda was. Their confrontation after Garrett found the letter had ended with his father walking out. Still unanswered was the question of why he'd never mentioned the letter, dated nearly a year ago.

Garrett scrubbed a hand over his face. "Did she write?" The words came out more forcefully than he'd intended.

Peg nodded once, then looked at her hands on top of the envelope. "Once a month like clockwork. And then we'd wait…and check the mailbox…to see if, this time, you might respond. It was agonizing for her, but she insisted on sticking to the verbal agreement she'd made with Douglas. After her initial call to him, she never picked up the phone again. I tried to convince her to go to California and see you. I told her I'd go with her. But she'd have none of it—not even after you left home. Douglas wanted her to communicate through letters sent to him…and it would have taken an act of God to divert her from that. I suspected he was purposely keeping you and Luke from her, either by filling your heads with lies or intercepting the letters. She refused to believe any deception on his part. I think it was the guilt she carried. Whatever happened back then to make her leave was so devastating, she never got over it."

"She didn't tell you what happened?"

"She would never talk about it. I didn't push, even though I could see it tearing her up inside."

Garrett jumped up and paced across the small room, anger at his father vying for supremacy over irritation with himself. He'd had no intention of allowing Peg to make him *feel* something deep down inside. He didn't want to suffer empathy for the woman who'd deserted him, yet it was far too easy to see his father as the villain in all of this. He'd admitted to hiding one letter. Could he have hidden hundreds?

He stopped in front of his aunt. "We never saw *one* letter." He slammed his fist into the desk, and Peg flinched. "Are you going to sit there and tell me she wrote twelve letters a year for twenty-nine years?"

"I knew Douglas was to blame. I should have tried harder to convince Amanda. I could have gone to Sacramento myself." Peg dissolved into tears, burying her face in her hands as quiet sobs racked her body. Her grief was a physical force, and he sensed the anguish buried deep within. Even as a child, he'd recognized the bond between his mother and this woman. What reason could she possibly have to lie to him now that Amanda was dead?

To believe her would change everything he knew. His tenuous rapport with his father and his stepmother, the love and acceptance of two half brothers and a half sister, and possibly even the bond between him and Luke. What would his brother have to say? He'd been too young to fully understand what had happened back then, but the telltale signs of a life spent overcompensating were recognizable to Garrett because he knew them so well. Would this new information destroy Luke's ability to pretend his life was picture-perfect?

Garrett wouldn't take a chance where his brother was concerned. The first order of business would be finding out just what role the senator had played in their mother's disappearing act. Had his father hidden the letters—and the whereabouts of his mother—out of concern for his sons…or his political career? One way or another, Garrett would discover the truth.

His brain was on overload, and his gut ached with his need to exact justice somehow. But at the moment, it wasn't *his* perceived injustices he was worried about. Nor Luke's. Garrett would always worry about his little brother, but Luke was strong and capable, and when the time was right, he'd deal with the fallout from this revelation with his usual good humor and determination.

With a jolt, Garrett's gaze fell on Peg. His aunt had apparently stood up for his mother when no one else would. Even now, after Amanda was gone, Peg carried the burden. If what she had told him was true, he wouldn't rest until he found a way to make this whole damn thing right…for his mother and Aunt Peg.

He stepped closer and laid his hands gently on her shoulders, trying to convey with a touch what he couldn't possibly put into words. After a moment, he returned to his chair and sat, bracing his elbows on the desk, giving her as much time as she needed. Finally she dried her eyes.

He studied her and tried one more time to detect any duplicity within her. Her eyes, though glistening with moisture, were as clear and honest as the last rays of the Idaho sunshine outside her window. He shook his head as he drummed his fingers on the desk. "You need to know that I'd have come if *one* of her letters had reached me. I don't know what happened to them…but I intend to find out. If the senator is responsible, he'll be held accountable."

A fleeting smile told him what he already knew—it was too late to change what had happened. "But you must have received the letter telling you of Amanda's death and the will, right?"

He laughed mockingly. "I found it accidentally in my father's desk drawer."

Garrett leaned back in his chair. If not for that one improbable find, it would be hard to believe his father had hidden or destroyed hundreds of notes and letters in order to perpetuate the lie about their mother. Garrett had lost respect for his father during his troubled teen years. Though they'd healed the hairline fracture in their relationship in recent years, nothing could regenerate the bond that had been destroyed. As hard as he tried, Garrett couldn't dredge up an iota of loyalty for the man. He should be innocent until proven guilty, but deep down where the pain of his mother's desertion throbbed to life, Garrett put the puzzle pieces together and handed down a guilty verdict.

Still, he needed to know for sure. Needed proof. Should he call his father first? Or his PI buddy who was going to love digging in the senator's sandbox?

"There's something else." Peg opened the envelope and pulled out some papers. "You'll want to read the will."

Garrett accepted the document she handed him, though it made the hair on the back of his neck stand up. He turned the pages slowly, reading every word, digesting their meaning. When he was finished, he let it fall into his lap as he looked up and met her steady gaze.

"She left everything she owned to Luke and me."

Peg slowly bobbed her head.

"Who else knows about this?" Was this bombshell the reason Rachel and Jonathan had been less than hospitable?

"No one but the two of us and Amanda's attorney. That's the way she wanted it, with her half of the resort run by me until one or both of you stepped up to claim your inheritance."

"I'LL HAVE TO contact Luke, but as far as I'm concerned, this place is yours. I'm not going to take any part of it away from you." Garrett handed her back the will. Everything was happening too fast. He needed time to think.

"It's what Amanda wanted. It's what she worked for every day of her life. At least stay a few days before you make up your mind. Maybe you'll find something here worth staying for." Peg took the document and returned it with the envelope to her desk drawer.

Garrett took a deep breath and blew it out slowly. A new contentment left him feeling lighter. The silver-haired lady across the desk seemed to hold no bitterness toward him—no greed for Amanda's half of the resort.

This apparently selfless woman only wanted to honor the memory of her sister by welcoming him like a long-lost son. The barriers around Garrett's heart wobbled a bit. Calm nipped at the edges of his frayed nerves as he considered the idea of spending a day or two here on this remote mountain. It just might do him some good. "Yeah. Maybe that'd be okay...Aunt Peg." The name came out naturally, as though almost three decades hadn't separated them.

A pleased smile slowly spread across her face, and she nodded. "All right then. I'll get you set up in a room and have your bags brought in. Dinner will be ready at six o'clock. Make yourself at home."

Garrett rose. "One more thing—how did my mother die?"

"Heart attack. Her drug use weakened her heart. It happened so fast. She didn't suffer."

Garrett took her hand in his, aware how hard it had been to answer him. "Thanks for telling me...and for the warm welcome. You didn't have to be nearly as gracious under the circumstances, but it means a lot." Sensing her need to be alone, he gave her a warm hug and strode from the office with Cowboy at his heels.

A surprising tranquility had settled over him. As if he had the key to the mystery—the answer to the questions that burned inside him. He had to keep reminding himself that there were two sides to every story—that his father deserved to be heard. But with every passing moment, Garrett became more certain of the validity of Peg's story. He would wait for adequate proof before confronting his father, but it was almost as though Garrett had known all along.

He dreaded calling Luke and considered putting it off for a couple of days, but his little brother would worry if Garrett didn't at least let him know he'd arrived safely. Still, how was he going to explain the whole sordid mess over the phone?

Garrett stepped outside onto the deck that ran the length of the building and stopped at the top of the steps, leaning his hip against the rail. Cowboy continued down the steps to find a spot in the shade. The creek bubbled along its winding path not too far away. Timbered slopes rolled down toward the meadow, alive with bachelor buttons, black-eyed Susan, and about a hundred other varieties of wildflowers. The tops of other mountains filled the skyline as the sun slowly marched toward obscurity.

His mother *had* written to him and Luke. If Aunt Peg could be believed, Amanda had wanted to be a part of their lives. Hell, he hadn't even gotten his PI friend started on the investigation to confirm Aunt Peg's story, and already he was free of the debilitating weight he'd been carrying around since he was about twelve years old. Was it because he wanted to believe it so badly? Or because he'd suspected there was something off in his father's handling of the whole event?

Quick footsteps drew his attention over his shoulder.

Rachel, dressed now in tight-fitting jeans rolled up to show slender ankles, a blue calico button-up shirt, and red canvas shoes, barreled out onto the deck, her head down, oblivious to his proximity. She was parallel with him, one foot poised to take the first step off the deck, when he cleared his throat to warn her of his presence. Her head whipped toward him, her eyes widened, and her saucy lips puckered into a perfect O.

As quickly as she made eye contact with him, her head turned back toward the steps. She was clearly off balance, and her gaze darted frantically toward the railing. Only problem was, *he* stood between her and the railing, and she would obviously rather tumble down the steps than chance touching him in her bid to regain her footing.

At the last second, Garrett snagged her waist with one arm and swung her away from the edge, up against his chest.

With a small squeak, the entire length of her body collided with his. Her blush was crimson and instantaneous, priceless considering her earlier bold behavior. Soft, full breasts crushed against his chest, even as she tried to push herself away. Her thighs brushed his, and her enticingly toned stomach leaned against a part of him that awoke with a fully formed agenda of its own.

Her wavy red hair came to just beneath his chin, and the sweet scent of jasmine warred with his practicality as it swirled around him. He set her down a safe distance from the steps. Without thinking, he dipped his head to breathe in her honeyed aroma.

She expelled a furious gasp and jammed her palms against his chest. "*What* do you think you're doing? Let go of me, you Neanderthal!"

What the hell *was* he doing? Garrett raised his head to face the heated anger smoldering in her gorgeous green eyes. He couldn't seem to stop smiling like a fool. Nor could he help wanting to hold on to her for a little while longer.

Wanted to—but he let her go anyway, trying not to take offense as she backed a half dozen steps away. "I don't bite, you know. I was only trying to keep you from breaking that pretty little neck of yours. You have nothing to fear from me."

Rachel pulled herself up straight. "I'm *not* afraid of you." The way her eyes focused somewhere on his chest seemed to say otherwise.

"Okay. Look, obviously we got off on the wrong foot. Maybe we could start over again. I'm thinking of sticking around for a couple of weeks." He quirked an eyebrow, waiting to see how she would take that news.

"*A couple of weeks?*"

He chuckled, having gotten the expected response. "There you go again…making me feel welcome."

"You're not a guest." Her tone clearly implied that this was possibly the worst news she could have received.

Garrett didn't fully understand why he was yanking her chain since he'd planned to stay only a day or two, but he wasn't ready to let her off the hook yet.

"Aunt Peg asked me to stick around for a while. I'm considering." He turned back to the gorgeous landscape beyond the deck, leaning his weight against the railing. He could almost hear the explosion building within her.

"*Aunt* Peg? Well, it didn't take you long to figure out who to cozy up to, did it? But why? For that matter, why are you here at all? Peg doesn't owe you anything.

Showing up here, after Amanda is gone, only causes more sorrow. Don't you get it? *Amanda* wanted to reconcile with you and your brother. You missed out. Now go back to wherever you came from. Peg is the only one who wants you here, and trust me, you're not doing her any favors by hanging around." The words rushed out as though she'd been holding them in for a long time. Her chest heaved with her effort to catch her breath, and tears rushed to her eyes but didn't fall.

Garrett caught her in a sideways glance. "If I thought I was causing Aunt Peg to suffer, I'd leave in a heartbeat. I think you're the only one who doesn't want me here. You can't forgive me for what you see as my callous mistreatment of Amanda Harding."

"Her name was Amanda *Williams*. She stopped using her married name a long time ago. Can't imagine why she wouldn't want to be associated with the Harding family." Scorn burned hot in her eyes as she stared him down.

Maybe he should tell her he'd never received one of the letters his mother supposedly wrote in all those years. It was highly unlikely that she'd believe him, though. He was just another man passing through her town— one who'd managed to get on her bad side without even trying. On the other hand, that she'd obviously loved Amanda when he couldn't, automatically granted her access to a soft spot in his heart.

Suddenly, he wanted to get to know this woman more than anything in the world. He wanted her to understand how badly it had affected him to lose his mother. And he wanted her to know how fast he would have camped on their doorstep if he'd received even one of Amanda's letters.

Clearly, the only way Rachel would change her mind about what kind of a man he was, would be if she spent some time with him…got to know him. He was on the verge of pleading his case when he caught the contempt that furrowed her brow and curled her lip. It was obvious that she despised him. If he told her the sky was blue right now, she probably wouldn't believe him. But…maybe there was something he could do to increase his odds.

Rachel backed another couple of steps and started to turn.

"Tell you what. I'll make you a deal." Garrett watched her casually, schooling his expression to play down his sudden and significant need for her to hear him out.

She stopped, her gaze searching his distrustfully. "What kind of a deal?"

"It's Saturday. You give me the next two days—show me around this place that was Amanda's home. If you still hate my guts by Tuesday morning, I'll leave."

Melodious laughter fell from her lips. "That's all I'd have to do?"

"One more little thing. You have to be *nice* to me." Garrett nearly laughed at the look of abject horror that crossed her face.

An unladylike snort escaped and she slammed her hands on her hips. "How nice?"

"Well, hell, don't you know how to be pleasant? Lay off the snarky comments. Be polite. Pretend you like me. We'll spend a couple enjoyable days getting to know each other while you show off what Amanda and Peg built on this mountain."

Rachel crossed her arms in front of her. "How do I know you'll really leave?"

"Scout's honor."

"Right. Like you were ever a Scout." She narrowed her eyes. "Just one thing wrong with that plan. I work for a living. I can't let my other chores slide to babysit some city boy."

Garrett's ego cringed at that description. Was that really how she saw him? "Now, see? That was a perfect example of *not* being nice." He scowled until she looked away. "Anyway, I'm sure if I asked Aunt Peg, she'd arrange for someone to take over your duties so that you could help me out for two days."

Rachel chortled. "Peg doesn't show preferential treatment to anyone, so if you can get her to agree…you're on. But if not…you leave today." She turned toward the door again. "I wouldn't bother unpacking if I were you."

He chuckled. "See you at dinner, Rachel, and don't get too cocky. The game hasn't even started yet."

She disappeared inside without another word. Garrett shook his head and blew out his breath. *What in the hell just happened?* He could no longer deny the attraction he felt for her, but this was the act of a crazy, desperate man. Yep—that seemed to describe him right down to his boots, all right. Still, a small spark of resolve swelled within him at the thought of the challenge ahead. He had to admit that he'd likely be going down in flames unless he came up with a plan to reinvent himself in her eyes.

That wasn't going to be easy because Rachel held her bitterness with both hands, and she was determined to see him out of here in two days…or sooner. That meant he had very little time. He'd have to move fast.

First thing on the agenda was to search out Aunt Peg and find out how she felt about rescheduling the help so that Garrett could spend two days with the lovely, though sharp-tongued, Rachel. While he was at it, he'd better ask Peg to keep the details of his mother's will quiet for the time being. If his best guess was right, Rachel would waste no time in putting this mountain behind her if she learned he might actually be her boss.

Chapter Four

RACHEL STOPPED JUST inside the door to let herself fall apart. How would she ever get through the next few days? Peg had practically begged her to treat Garrett Harding like the honored guest he would have been if his mother was still alive. Now, he'd offered her an easy way out if she'd show him around and *be nice* to him for two days. It sounded simple enough, but it had taken a surprising amount of effort to stand her ground and agree to Garrett's proposition.

Her breathing started to slow as she leaned against the wall. There was no chance Peg would concede to trade her shift out, but it would have been worth it to get Garrett out of their lives in two days. She wouldn't even consider whether she could have been *nice* to the egomaniac for that long, because it was probably a challenge that was doomed from the beginning.

Why did she have to literally bump into him anyway? The resort was big enough that she should be able to stay out of his way. Sure, he'd saved her from a nasty tumble, but then he'd held her too close...for too long...and she hadn't stopped him quickly enough. The heat of a tell-tale blush crept up her neck and into her face. Damn it! She hated him. So why had his arms around her been so comfortable and made her feel so safe? She drew a ragged breath and leaned her head against the door. He was going to drive her crazy if he stayed for more than two days.

Rachel pushed away from the wall and made a bee-line for the stairs and her room on the second floor. She had a few minutes before she needed to join Dory in the kitchen to help with dinner. That would be enough time to change and wash away Garrett's musky scent so she wouldn't have to relive her embarrassing moment every time she breathed.

Five minutes later, clean and clothed in khaki slacks, a salmon-colored T-shirt, and wedge-soled sandals, she closed her bedroom door and skipped down the stairs. It smelled as if Dory's famous pot roast was on the menu tonight. As she passed Peg's office, she caught a glimpse of her talking to Garrett. Rachel couldn't help wishing Peg would put the outsider in his place firmly enough that he'd take his bag and his dog and go home.

Well, actually, he could leave Cowboy. The dog at least was well-mannered and didn't talk all the time. That put a smile on her face as she entered the kitchen.

"There you are." Dory's consistently cheery voice came from halfway inside the oven where she was test-ing the temperature of the meat. "There's a new guest in the house tonight. With you, Peg, Jonathan, and Mr. and Mrs. Taylor, that makes six. When you set the table, be sure to put the new hunk next to you."

"He's not a guest," Rachel mumbled. But was Garrett a hunk? He was attractive, she'd give him that, but as soon as she'd discovered who he was, he ceased to be anything but the detestable man who'd made Amanda cry once a month like clockwork and probably other times in between that no one had known about. Rachel had learned that outward appearance usually meant zilch. What was inside made the man, and as far as she could tell, Garrett didn't have it in that department. "Why would I want him to sit by me?" She returned Dory's impish grin with a scowl. The other woman's sparkling blue eyes and dimpled cheeks soon had Rachel choking on a laugh.

Dory chuckled loudly. "That just proves it right there, girl. When was the last time you made hot monkey love with the likes of Mr. McDreamy out there?" Her gaze skewered Rachel, demanding an answer.

Dory Sullivan was about as cute as they came. Two years older than Rachel, with a petite figure that could stop traffic, she had no trouble getting dates. She also had no qualms about dispensing advice to those less fortunate, a position Rachel had found herself in more times than she cared to count.

"We've talked about this, Dory. Still not interested." Rachel sidestepped the question, but couldn't escape the shiver that feathered along her spine. So she didn't trust men easily. What was so wrong with that? There'd been a time, many years ago, when she'd given her heart, soul, and body to the man of her dreams. Those dreams had somehow turned into a living nightmare. She was happier and safer on her own, despite what Dory thought.

Dory straightened, and her blonde head wagged back and forth. "You're not getting any younger you know, Rach."

They both laughed. "Yeah, well, the last time I checked, twenty-eight was still too young for assisted living." Rachel grabbed an apron from the hangers beside the refrigerator and tied it around her as she stepped forward.

"It all depends on who's doing the assisting, in my opinion." Dory's grin widened.

Rachel rolled her eyes and grimaced. "Would you stop, please? Tell me what you want me to do."

"Set the table. And then stir the gravy while I whip up my famous broccoli salad." Dory handed Rachel a wooden stirring spoon as she passed her on the way to the refrigerator. With one hand on the door handle, she stopped and looked over her shoulder. "Are you still getting those calls?"

Rachel stiffened even as she pasted a phony smile on her face. If only she hadn't confided in Dory last week after her friend had witnessed her answer three calls in a row with either heavy breathing or silence on the line. Thank goodness she'd sworn her to secrecy so Rachel didn't have to worry about Peg finding out. "No. Must have just been kids playing pranks." She grabbed plates and silverware and headed toward the dining room, hoping Dory would buy her lie.

After making quick work of the table settings, she folded simple place cards and put one at each seat. It would be foolish to deny her friend's suggestion completely when it was within her power to ensure that Garrett sat as far away from her as possible. Upon returning to the kitchen, Dory was occupied with last-minute preparations, and Rachel was relieved to tend to the gravy without any further questions.

A few minutes later, she and Dory carried the food dishes into the dining room table as Peg, Jonathan, and the guests started filing in. Dory went back to the kitchen, while Rachel turned toward her seat.

Peg sat at the head of the table with the Taylors, a couple from Colorado, on her left, but Jonathan sat on her right...where Rachel's place card should have been. A quick glance revealed the worst-case scenario. Her name was on the placard next to Jonathan...and Garrett was already seated on her right. *Dory.* Oh, how her friend was going to pay for this.

As she circled the table to take her place, she caught a smug grin from Jonathan, which shot *him* to the top of her most likely culprits list. She should have known he wouldn't want to make small talk with Garrett any more than she did. Still, it was unforgiveable, and she narrowed her eyes, hoping he'd understand that she *would* get even.

Just as she reached her seat, Garrett jumped up, pulled her chair out, and smiled as he waited for her to sit. She slid onto the seat and allowed him to push her in while her stomach did a little flip-flop, which she assured herself was only hunger.

Mr. Taylor, Alan, paused in the conversation he'd been having with Peg to watch curiously as Garrett seated her. Realizing that everyone had now fallen silent, Rachel felt the smoldering heat of embarrassment. If only a hole would open in the floor, she would gladly disappear through it. Alan exchanged a glance with his wife, then studied Rachel for a moment before he grinned.

"You're making the rest of us look bad, son." A good ten years Garrett's senior and considerably smaller in stature, Alan's low, raspy voice vibrated with humor as he extended his hand toward Garrett. "Alan Taylor, and this is my wife, Linda."

Garrett shook hands and introduced himself. "I've been in the military for the last fourteen years. Women are rare. Pretty ones are even harder to come by. You learn to make an impression any way you can."

Everyone but Rachel laughed—even the traitor, Jonathan. Was that what Garrett was trying to do—make an impression? Well, he'd have to pull out the big guns to impress her.

"I understand completely. And it's nice to see that chivalry is still alive and well." Alan winked at Rachel. "In spite of what they'll tell you, women like their men to make them feel special. Sure…today's woman can fend for herself just fine, but that doesn't mean she'd object to being set up on that pedestal now and then. Right, honey?" Alan turned to his wife, the slant of his lips forming a crooked smile.

Linda's gaze swept to her husband, and Rachel was surprised at the vacant stare that made her seem miles away. Then, as though Linda suddenly realized where she was, she laughed softly, wrapped her hand around Alan's forearm, and looked around the table. "That's what I love about Alan. He's always coming up with new ways to show me I'm the only woman in his life." She leaned toward him and gave him a quick peck on the lips.

Alan smiled proudly, but Rachel was struck by how quickly Linda detached emotionally from the conversation, apparently resuming whatever internal thoughts had occupied her before her husband pulled her into the discussion. Was there trouble up on that pedestal? Rachel sincerely hoped not. They'd seemed so happy together whenever they'd come to stay at the lodge. Rachel hadn't analyzed their marriage before... and it would be best if she didn't start now.

Rachel usually enjoyed these dinners with travelers from across the country, learning where they were from and where they'd been. The Taylors were almost always the first to arrive each spring. This was the sixth year in a row they'd been guests of the lodge for the early bear hunts. For all intents and purposes, they were practically family. They'd grown to know the area and many of the local people.

Hanging on their guests' every word was normally the high spot of each day for Rachel, but today's dinner seemed to drag on forever. All too aware of Garrett's imposing form beside her, she found it nearly impossible to concentrate on the conversation. Instead, her attention focused on her food, which she shuffled around her plate. On the other hand, Garrett was apparently completely comfortable, joining in the discussion as though he'd sat around this same table all his life, much to Rachel's annoyance.

Alan Taylor leaned his elbows on the table, his rapt attention evident in the bobbing of his head and the consideration in his penetrating gaze. Linda looked from speaker to speaker, her shoulder-length red hair flipping against one side of her collar and then the other. Their words all blurred together for Rachel—until Alan mentioned that he'd grown up in Texas and still had family there.

She jumped as though electricity had zapped her nerve endings, then went rigid, her arms braced on the edge of the table, hoping it hadn't been as noticeable as she feared. Her skin tingled beneath Garrett's curious stare, and she could feel Alan's gaze on her as well. That answered the question. Even Peg eyed her with concern etched in the lines around her mouth. Rachel made a conscious effort to relax, which failed big-time. Sad when the mere mention of Texas, her home when her stalker began threatening her, could send her into full-fledged panic.

As though he knew the reason for her tension, Garrett turned the subject away from Texas. The Taylors had a winter residence in Garrett's home state of California, so the discussion moved to the housing problems, the economy, and politics. With an uneasy glance toward Peg, Garrett admitted that his father was a US senator from the Golden State.

"You don't say. Well, hell, I didn't vote for him," Alan said.

Everyone chuckled except Garrett. Rachel studied him from beneath her lashes, immediately picking up on his discomfort and animosity. Was this a chink in his armor? Something she could use to hasten his departure? In the next breath, a tiny sprout of sympathy unsettled her as red splotches appeared on his face.

Anger? Was there trouble in paradise? Or was Garrett embarrassed by something about his old man?

When Amanda had mentioned that her ex-husband was now a US senator and worth a lot of money, Rachel hadn't given it much thought. Now, however, she could imagine growing up in that household, where the only parental figure had spent most of his time in Washington, DC, and when he'd been home, was probably more concerned about his image than his sons.

Oh no. If she wasn't careful, she'd be feeling sorry for Garrett next. The Taylors finally excused themselves, and Rachel immediately began gathering empty dishes, unable to wait another minute to make her escape.

"Rachel, I'd like you to show Garrett around our mountain while he's here." Peg's words wrapped around Rachel's thoughts, and for a moment she forgot to breathe.

"What? What about the Watering Hole? We're opening in two weeks. I have to take inventory and order supplies." She glanced at Garrett, and to his credit, he seemed as curious about the answer to her question as she was.

"There's plenty of time for all that. And Jonathan said he'd check for needed repairs, so that will take quite a bit off your plate, dear. Garrett isn't sure how long he'll be staying yet, but I know Amanda would want him to see as much of the mountain and countryside as possible. I'd give him the grand tour myself, but I just can't get away right now." The sadness in Peg's eyes implored her.

Rachel bit back the refusal poised on the tip of her tongue, because Peg's wistful smile told the real story. She was asking for Amanda…for her son's visit to be all that Amanda would have made it if she'd been there. No matter how unfair life became, no matter how angry Rachel was, it didn't matter. There or not, these were Amanda's two days. And since when wouldn't she cut off her right arm for either Peg or Amanda?

Rachel had agreed to Garrett's deal thinking Peg would refuse his request. She should have known Peg would likely grant him anything within reason. She'd walked right into that one and now she was stuck, but she didn't have to like it.

Rachel breathed deeply and straightened, tamping down her desire to storm out of the room. She smiled, probably a wobbly, pathetic stretching of her lips. "Of course, Peg. I'll be happy to show Mr. Harding around." She turned toward Garrett, wishing looks really could kill. "What time would you like to start?"

One corner of his lip twitched slightly, and his eyes shone with amusement…at her expense. "That's really *nice* of you, Rachel. Is oh-eight-hundred too early?"

"Not at all. I'll have time to get my run in before we start." Rachel lifted the pile of dishes she'd accumulated and started to push her chair out.

Garrett was instantly behind her, moving her chair away from the table. As she brushed by him he laid a hand lightly on her arm, and that same pulse of energy that had leaped between them earlier in the Jeep hit her full force again. "You run? I'd like to get a few miles in myself. Would you mind if I joined you? Especially after what happened at the bar today. It might not hurt for you to have some company."

Oh no! Rachel closed her eyes and waited for it.

"What happened at the bar today?"

She turned to face Peg's questioning gaze. Jonathan scowled blackly in Garrett's direction and leaned back in his chair, looking as though he'd like to disappear right along with her. She and Jonathan had an unspoken agreement—they didn't worry Peg unnecessarily. Too bad Rachel hadn't taken into consideration the likelihood that Garrett would mention the events of the day.

"It was nothing, Peg. Riley and his brothers had a little too much to drink and were out having fun." Rachel forced a smile.

Peg nodded, and the whole darn thing would have gone away if Rachel could only have found a way to shut Garrett up. She whirled on him as soon as he started to speak.

"Wait a minute. It was a hell of a lot more than that. Those hoodlums were intent on taking Rachel somewhere without her consent. Where I come from, that's called kidnapping. And they were *having fun* with two sawed-off shotguns." His gaze swept from Peg, to Jonathan, to Rachel.

When his eyes turned to her, his *oh-shit* moment was obvious, but it was too late.

Peg left her seat and strode toward her. "Are you all right, dear?"

"Of course. I'm fine, and there's nothing to worry about. Jonathan had a talk with them, and I'm sure they won't do anything like that again." Rachel glared at Jonathan, hoping he'd back her up, but he remained silent.

"Jonathan knew about this, too, and neither of you thought to tell me? Well, thank goodness for Garrett." She smiled fondly at him. "Riley's bunch has gotten out of hand. Something needs to be done about them. I think it's time to have a talk with the sheriff. For now, Rachel, I don't want you outside the lodge alone until the sheriff has had a chance to check into this." Peg waited for Rachel's dutiful nod before she dropped her napkin on the table and started for the door. "Jonathan, may I have a word, please?"

Jonathan groaned and glowered at Rachel as he stood and pushed his chair back. "You're going to be the death of me, girl."

"It wasn't my fault. It was…"

"*He* didn't know we were keeping that information from Peg, did he? I'm afraid this one's on you, Rachel." Jonathan nodded briefly at Garrett and followed Peg's path from the room.

Okay, so maybe she was at fault, and if she ever got Riley in her sights again, she was going to shoot the worthless vermin, but why was Jonathan suddenly siding with her least favorite person?

Garrett stepped in front of her, raising his hands as though in supplication. "I'm sorry, but even if I'd known,

I still would have told her. Someone needs to take this seriously."

Rachel let out the breath she'd been holding, and with her next inhale, she choked on a bitter laugh. "Jonathan's right. It's not your fault—it's mine. I should have told Peg myself. And if I get my wish for a total do-over for today, everything will go back to normal in the morning." She tried a smile as her gaze met his, but had a feeling it turned out completely cheesy.

Regret clouded his eyes for an instant as he studied her. "I apologize for my part. Obviously, I'm the last person you wanted to have show up here. I'm hoping to change your mind about that, but if not, I want you to know that I'll keep my word and be out of here come Tuesday."

Rachel had the perfect retort, but for some reason, she couldn't force the words out. Maybe his apology was too genuine, or perhaps the sadness that had fallen over him in an instant had stolen her derision. The longer she stared into his eyes, the less she wanted to own the hatred she'd held on to for so long.

Garrett's steel-gray eyes darkened as his gaze swept over her face and lingered on her lips. Self-consciously, Rachel turned to take the stack of dishes to the kitchen, but was stopped when his hand gripped her elbow. The strength and warmth of his gentle grasp made her breath hitch as she met his eyes again. No humor waited there now…no sadness…only longing.

Unexpectedly, a shiver engulfed her, and an ache of something long forgotten flared to life deep inside. For endless seconds, she couldn't look away from his eyes, until the rattling of the dishes she held between them broke the spell. Rachel pulled from his touch, but it was another second before she broke eye contact, feeling strangely weak and shaky. Afraid her voice would give her away, she let the silence stretch for a moment. No one moved. "Six thirty in the morning…if you still want to run. Don't be late," Rachel said, then turned and hurried from the room.

Chapter Five

THE ALARM WENT off on the bedside table, and he slammed his hand down on the button to cut the annoying sound. Cowboy rose from his bedroll on the floor and stuck his nose in Garrett's face.

"At least one of us slept, huh, boy?" It wasn't Garrett. Between his mother's unanswered letters, his father's probable deception, and Rachel's enigmatic pull on emotions that hadn't been heard from in a while, he'd tossed and turned most of the night.

He'd been crazy to make that ridiculous deal with her. On a scale of one to ten, Garrett's chances of getting Rachel to change her mind about him sat pretty close to zero. Right now, he'd settle for her merely tolerating him. From divulging the information to Peg that Rachel had intended to keep to herself, to mistakenly concluding she would abide his touch, he'd managed to lessen his odds considerably in the space of only a few hours. He should probably leave now and save himself the humiliation.

But he wouldn't, even though his original plan had been to get in and out of here the same day with answers to his questions about his mother and with no emotional commitment to Aunt Peg. So why did he care what Rachel thought of him?

Fact was, he'd drawn his first totally peaceful breath in as long as he could remember after walking out of Peg's office yesterday. It was a feeling he wouldn't mind holding on to for a while. Plus he hadn't quite gotten out without a scratch in the emotional commitment department. Irrational though it might be, he felt he owed Peg something. He didn't need Rachel's permission to stay, but it would make things easier on both of them if she didn't hate his guts.

She'd obviously been close to Amanda, and the idea of seeing his mother through her eyes intrigued Garrett, but he'd be lying to himself if he didn't admit that he was drawn to her, too. Rachel was an attractive, intelligent, sexy woman, and her charms weren't lost on him. Usually she was bristling with put-downs and smart-ass remarks, but he'd gotten to see the softer, vulnerable side of her twice now, and he wanted to get to know that woman better. A chuckle escaped, sounding more like a grunt, at the foolish idea he might actually break through the barriers she had. That would probably take an act of God *and* Congress.

Cowboy's tail wagged slowly as Garrett swung his feet to the floor and rubbed his hands over his face. It

RESCUED BY THE RANGER 77

was 0600 hours. He had time to throw on some running clothes, make a couple of phone calls, and still meet Rachel before she took off without him.

He patted the dog, then grunted with the effort to stand. The damaged muscles in his back had stiffened on the long trip, and a night of restless sleep hadn't helped. He'd need to get back on a regular exercise routine to keep his muscles warm and pliant. Turning on the table lamp and glancing at the clock again, he shuffled into the bathroom. A few minutes later, he slipped into a pair of old sweats and a charcoal gray army T-shirt. After donning socks and running shoes, he pulled his cell phone from the pocket of the jeans he'd worn yesterday.

He moved to the window as he dialed a number. The call was answered on the first ring. "Hey, Luke. Still up at the crack of dawn, I see."

"Garrett. It's damn time you called. I was about to come looking. Did you find Aunt Peg? Tell me about our inheritance." His brother's familiar voice, filled with humor, drifted over the distance, making Garrett homesick.

With them both in different branches of the military, a sadistic machine that didn't seem to care whether their leaves coincided, they'd had to snatch bits of time when they could in various ports of call. Regardless, no matter how long it'd been since he looked his brother in the eye, Garrett would always put his faith in the strength of their shared bond. "It's a long story, Luke. I've got a lot to tell you…and I'd rather not do it over the phone."

"Good. When will you be home?" Luke punctuated his question with a yawn.

Garrett hesitated only a second. At some point during his sleepless night, Garrett had toyed with the idea of asking Luke to come to the lodge, but he hadn't made a decision until the words came off his tongue. "I need you to come to Idaho. I found Aunt Peg, and I think you should hear what she has to say about our mother." He waited through the silence on the other end.

"Sure. I can probably get out there in a few days." Luke's tone made it clear he was certain Garrett had lost his mind.

Garrett grinned. If Luke thought he was crazy now, wait until he told him the rest. "Actually, I need you out here tomorrow."

"What the hell's the rush, man?"

Garrett considered avoiding the truth of his agreement with Rachel...but he'd never lied to Luke before, and this wasn't the right time to start. Maybe coming clean with the whole embarrassing truth would pique his brother's curiosity. "There's a kick-ass gorgeous redhead here that I'm trying to impress."

Luke was quiet for a moment before his deep laughter dispelled the awkward moment. "In the first place, you were supposed to call me if there were any pretty girls around. And second, that doesn't explain why you need me *tomorrow*."

"The problem is the young lady detests me. So, I asked her to give me two days to change her mind. If I can't manage it, I'll be back in my Jeep, on my way home, day after tomorrow."

"What's the problem? I've never known you to lack confidence or shirk a challenge." The warmth in Luke's teasing voice put a smile on Garrett's face.

"I've managed to screw up a couple things already— bad enough to make me think I might actually be out of here by Tuesday." Garrett grimaced at confessing his clumsiness to his brother.

"Wait a minute. Are you saying you'd really leave there because of this…agreement?"

"You haven't met Rachel yet. I'm fairly certain she'd have me hung from the nearest tree if I reneged."

Luke hooted. "All right. I want to meet this girl who has you trembling in your boots. I'll be there tomorrow. What's the closest airport?"

"Lewiston, I think. I'll text you directions from there. You'll have to rent a car." Garrett stopped and breathed a sigh of relief. "Thanks, little brother. I appreciate this."

"Wouldn't miss it for the world, bro." Luke disconnected the call.

Garrett squeezed the phone tightly. For just a second, all of the familiar abandonment issues rushed to the forefront of his mind. He loved his half brothers and his half sister, but Luke was his only real family and the closest connection he had to his mother. Every once in a while when they'd say good-bye or part company, the loneliness, still hanging over him from his mother's desertion, jabbed its claws into him again. This time, however, anger followed close behind, which he easily transferred over to his father. He glanced at the clock again before dialing another number.

This time it rang at least ten times before a sleepy voice mumbled into the phone. "Do you know what the fucking time is, man?"

"Whatever it is there, it's an hour later where I am. Times a-wasting, Jase."

Poor Jase merely groaned.

Garrett wiped the grin off his face so his friend wouldn't hear the amusement in his voice. "You don't have to talk, Jase. Just listen. I assume you still have your private investigator's license?"

Jase's growl sounded as though it was in the affirmative.

"I've got a job for you. I think you'll enjoy this one."

"Why's that?" Movements sounded through the phone and, when Jase spoke again, he seemed more awake and almost alert. "Are we digging into the fucking president's liberal fundraising campaign?"

Garrett smiled. "Even better."

Jase scoffed. "What could be better than that? You're not jerking my chain, are you?"

"I want you to investigate my father."

Stunned silence was Jase's only response. As one of Garrett's oldest friends, Jase Richards had spent a good deal of time under the senator's roof while they were growing up. He probably knew the man as well as Garrett did.

It wasn't often he'd left Jase speechless. "I need you to find someone who remembers what happened between my mother and father before she left. And there's a bonus in it for you if you dig until you find something in the neighborhood of three hundred letters addressed to Luke and me." Garrett's jaw tightened as he said the words.

"What's going on? Do you think there was more to your mother leaving than what your father let you believe? What kind of evidence do you have to back up what you're insinuating about the senator?"

"All hearsay. I ran into someone with a different version of what went down. That's why I need you. Will you scrounge up the truth for me?" Garrett glanced at his watch again and scratched Cowboy's ears, trying not to show his impatience.

Finally, Jase exhaled a long breath. "For you, Garrett, I'll do what I can."

"I knew I could count on you. Call me, day or night, if you need anything." Cowboy pressed against his leg, his way of saying he was ready to go.

"Will do, buddy. Listen, how's it been going? Are you taking care of yourself, you know…like you're supposed to? I get the feeling you're not in Sacramento. Where are you?"

Garrett frowned. Clearly, Jase was worried about him because of his injury. That's what his friends did now, and Garrett was tired of being treated like an invalid. The truth was his wound had probably healed as much as it would. The only thing left to do was tone and push his body to reach the peak physical condition he'd maintained before his injury…and then learn to be happy with the best that he could do. In reality, that was the easy part. Dealing with the guilt he woke up with every day because he'd survived when ten good men had died— much more difficult.

"I'm okay, Jase. Thanks for asking." As much as it grated on him, Garrett wouldn't hold it against his friends for being concerned about him. "I gotta go. Call me, okay?"

"I'll keep you posted." Jase was gone.

Garrett shoved his phone in his pocket, retrieved his sweatshirt from the back of a chair beside the bed, and donned it on the way to the door. Cowboy loped along beside him, obviously excited to be on the go.

Not another soul was stirring in the hallway outside his room, the stairwell, or the lobby downstairs. It was so quiet, Garrett began to wonder if Rachel had given him the wrong time to meet, but the moment he stepped out onto the front porch, he saw her.

Her posture was rigid, her body language beyond tense as she stood in the shadows at the end of the covered porch to his right. She appeared to be staring into the trees and shrubbery at the side of the lodge, her back to him, giving no indication that she knew he was anywhere around.

Garrett tapped his leg, signaling for Cowboy to be quiet, and swallowed the greeting that was poised on his tongue as Rachel slunk backward a step into the deepest shadows. Garrett stood still, listening, trying to see into the darkness of the tree line beyond the lodge. Nothing moved. It was as still as a cemetery—yet the skin on the back of his neck prickled with apprehension. Something was wrong.

He closed the door without a sound and moved silently toward her. A foot or so behind her, he stopped and reached to tap her on the shoulder. As though she'd received a blow, Rachel whipped around, balled one hand into a fist, and threw a clumsy punch toward his jaw. Cowboy growled his warning.

Garrett caught her wrist just before she connected, but she inhaled sharply, her mouth came open, and he was sure the scream she intended to let loose would wake everyone inside the house and succeed in scaring away whoever or whatever she'd been watching.

Garrett pressed his hand over her mouth and pushed her back against the wall. He watched her eyes go from wide and startled to narrow and distrustful, and the realization of just how much she despised him caused a strange ache in his chest. "I'm going to let you go, okay?"

She nodded.

Garrett still pressed her against the lodge, but removed his hand from her mouth and rested it on her shoulder. "What's out there? What did you see?"

Her eyes flickered beyond the railing again. "I thought I heard something—someone moving through the bushes—but I didn't see anyone."

"I'll go check it out. Stay here." He stepped away from her and immediately felt the loss of her warmth along his body.

"I'll go with you." She stared at him with that same challenge in her expression that he was starting to find appealing in a strange way.

Suddenly, Cowboy's frenzied barking jerked Garrett's attention toward the woods. The dog paced the width of the porch, his gaze locked on something in the shadow of the trees. A hurried movement caught Garrett's eye, accompanied by the sound of running footsteps.

"Stay here," he growled over his shoulder as he vaulted the top rail. Cowboy hit the ground right behind him, and they both followed the sounds of the intruder's flight through the trees toward the creek. He didn't have a significant lead, yet Garrett caught only glimpses of the man's silhouette between the large pine trees.

He pushed himself to overtake the stranger, but each jarring step on the uneven, unfamiliar ground sent a sharp pain shooting through his thigh, straight to the weakened muscles of his back. The stranger could easily have outdistanced him, but appeared to purposely stay within fifty feet or so. Taunting him, as though the man knew Garrett's limitations and had nothing to fear. As he disappeared into the shadows again, frustration and anger burned in Garrett, and he slowed to a walk, then stopped, bracing one arm against a tree to take some of the pressure off his bad leg.

Cowboy, trained to stay with him, circled anxiously, waiting for the command to take the enemy down. Garrett raised his arm, ready to issue the words, but something about the situation made him hesitate.

An instant later, an unfamiliar voice cut across the darkness. "Don't make me shoot him."

Garrett's gaze darted ahead to the creek, not forty feet away, where the man was just stepping out from behind a tree. For a split second he was framed by the feeble light of the horizon. It was long enough for Garrett to get an impression of their intruder and to spot the shoulder holster the man wore over his black turtleneck, his hand resting on the gun handle.

"Chill, Cowboy."

The instant the dog dropped to his haunches, the man saluted Garrett, turned, splashed through the creek, and disappeared into the forest on the other side.

What the hell had just happened? Garrett didn't regret his split-second decision that probably saved the life of his dog. The stranger had apparently known exactly what Garrett had intended to do, and Garrett had no doubts that he had been prepared to kill Cowboy and anyone else who stood in his way. The question was...why?

That one look also blew Garrett's theory out of the water. It wasn't Riley who'd stood outside the lodge under cover of darkness, waiting, and it wasn't Darryl or Darryl, either. This man had all the appearance of a trained professional. But what was he after? If he'd wanted either Rachel or Garrett dead, he could have accomplished that easily.

He turned at soft footsteps to find Rachel behind him. She touched his arm tentatively, and the worry in her eyes when she looked into his pleasantly surprised him.

"Are you all right?" She drew her cool fingers over his forehead. "You're bleeding."

A swipe of his own hand across his brow confirmed that she was right. He must have run into a low-hanging branch and drew blood without realizing. "It's nothing. Just a scratch."

"Why do big tough men always say that? You could get an infection from that as easily as I could." Rachel turned on a huff and started back toward the lodge. "Come on, Cowboy. We're taking this stubborn, pigheaded friend of yours back to the house to put something on his cut. Although, his head is almost certainly so hard, it couldn't possibly have hurt him."

Cowboy *woofed* and wagged his tail, and Rachel glanced back at the dog with a smile that warmed Garrett's heart, even if it was his reputation being impugned for their enjoyment. As soon as her gaze swept to him, her amusement disappeared, but only a portion of her former wariness returned. He was making progress.

"Do you know who that was?" Garrett fell in beside her, his arm brushing hers as they walked.

Rachel looked sideways at him. "It wasn't Riley, was it?"

"Whoever that was, he's way more dangerous than Riley." They climbed the steps to the porch.

Rachel stopped and turned toward him. "Do you think he'll be back?"

"It depends on whether he got what he came for. If he was after something inside the lodge, seeing you on the porch might have put a crimp in his plans temporarily. Or…maybe it was *you* he was waiting for." Garrett searched her eyes and picked up on her fear seconds before her expression shuttered over.

She looked down, focusing somewhere near the center of his chest. "Why would someone be waiting for me?"

"I was hoping you could tell *me*. Maybe this *does* have something to do with Riley and his boys. Maybe they hired some professional help after you outsmarted them." He stepped closer, waiting for her to look at him again. "If there's something you'd like to tell me, I'm a good listener."

Her scornful laugh was clearly forced. "Of course not. That man could've just as easily been looking for you. You're the only newcomer on the block." Her adamant denial, followed quickly by pointing fingers at him, cast doubt on her truthfulness even before her gaze shifted away from him. She stepped toward the door.

Garrett reached for her hand and stopped her. He'd lay odds that Rachel knew more than she was letting on, but for now, he had to pick his battles. "There's one more thing we need to discuss before we go in there."

Her brow furrowed as she searched his face.

What he was about to say would no doubt put an end to the mostly amicable conversation they'd been having, and he was surprised by how much he regretted that. But there was no doubt they'd graduated from a standoff with Riley and his two buffoons, to what Garrett's instincts told him was a totally dangerous and deadly adversary.

He drew a deep breath. "We're not keeping this from Peg. She has a right to know."

Rachel's worried expression pulled at him, and the warrior in him wanted to rise up and protect her, starting with pulling her against him and calming her fears. With no small effort, he made himself stand still.

Finally, she nodded. "You're right, but that doesn't mean I have to like it. Can we get you cleaned up before we tell her? She'll get the point without seeing you dripping blood."

"That's a bit of an exaggeration." He pushed the door open for Rachel, still holding her hand, and waited for

Cowboy to squeeze through ahead of him. "Where are we going to do this...medical procedure...where she won't see?"

Rachel thought for a moment, then frowned. "I have a first aid kit in my room."

She was so obviously uncomfortable with that idea that he couldn't help taking pity on her. "The place was deserted when I came down a few minutes ago. Is Peg even up? Maybe we don't need to sneak around."

"She's an early riser. She'll be down any minute."

"Your room it is then." Garrett threw her a grin he hoped would put her at ease.

Rachel sighed. "You'll be in and out of there in sixty seconds, so don't get any ideas."

"What? I'm perfectly capable of tending this little scratch by myself. You're the one who's worried about it getting infected. I'm beginning to think *you're* the one with ideas." Garrett started up the stairs with her in tow before she had a chance to blast him.

Upon reaching the second-floor landing, she jerked her hand from his grasp, and the fire that flashed in her eyes clearly said he'd pissed her off again. "Oh, I've got ideas all right, but you've somehow brainwashed Jonathan, and I'm afraid he wouldn't help me hide the body."

Garrett threw his head back and laughed as Rachel stomped down the hallway to the right, pushed the door to her room open, and motioned hurriedly for him to get inside. She closed the door softly behind Cowboy.

Garrett was still trying to hide his smile when she tossed some clothes from an armchair near the bed and told him to sit, then disappeared beyond the open door of the bathroom. Garrett stepped toward the chair, taking note of the unmade bed, her nightclothes strewn across the sheets. At least three pairs of shoes and a pair of boots littered the space. Ms. Maguire apparently wasn't Susie homemaker.

He slouched in the chair, shoving his legs out in front and crossing them at the ankles, just as Rachel reappeared with the first aid kit and a wash towel. She'd pulled her red hair into a ponytail, and a worried frown drew her brows together. Instinctively, he knew her concern was for something other than any ideas he might come up with. She was clearly worrying about Peg—something she seemed to do frequently.

"Am I missing something, Rachel? Aunt Peg seems like a strong woman. Why are you so worried about telling her?"

Garrett watched Rachel as she set the first aid kit on the edge of the bed and moved to stand beside the chair. The wash towel in her hand was warm, and she was surprisingly gentle as she cleaned the wound. He closed his eyes and savored the feel of her so close. It was a few seconds before he realized her hands were shaking, and some deep need to connect with her had him reaching to pin her wrists before she could move away. He raised an eyebrow as he gazed into eyes filled with sadness.

Rachel stared back, turning sideways to sit one hip on the arm of his chair. Her lips parted and she bit her bottom lip, then sighed, a breath Garrett felt all the way to his groin. Her eyes misted over as she tore her gaze from his.

"Peg *is* strong, and I'm going to make sure nothing changes that. Amanda's death was so sudden. Understandably, Peg took it hard. No one realized how hard. About a month after the funeral, she just gave up. She closed everyone out, stopped getting dressed in the morning, wasn't interested in the lodge. Eventually, she wouldn't come out of her room. Jonathan and I had to get her help at a...hospital. I hated seeing her in that place, but she had to get better." Rachel's gaze seemed to beg him to understand.

"You did what you had to do, Rachel. Thank God you and Jonathan were here." Guilt slammed into Garrett as the realization followed that *he* should have been there. Not knowing didn't seem an adequate excuse at the moment.

Her lips trembled, making her smile appear weak, but it was a smile nonetheless. "She's only been back three months. I'm scared to death she'll relapse. That's why I didn't want you here reminding her of Amanda. And why I didn't want her to find out about Riley. Telling her about someone sneaking around outside the lodge can't be a good idea, either." Rachel's eyes took on the shine of impending tears as she pulled her wrists free and stepped to the bedside to rifle through the first aid kit.

Garrett studied her with a new respect. Apparently Rachel took her responsibilities here at the lodge seriously—and then some. "Thank you for telling me. I still believe she's stronger than you think, but I'll do my best to not upset her. We'll alert Jonathan about the intruder, along with any other employees on staff. My brother Luke is arriving tomorrow. He'll be able to stick around for a few days…you know…in case I have to leave Tuesday morning."

As she turned toward him with a Band-Aid and some hydrogen peroxide, Garrett winked at her, intent on putting that smile back on her face.

The corners of her mouth barely lifted. "What makes you think it'll be any easier having Luke here than you?"

"Luke's a lot better-looking." That earned him more of a smile.

"I doubt that." Rachel, apparently realizing what she'd admitted, blushed an attractive crimson color and wouldn't meet his gaze as she perched on the arm of the chair, preparing to swab his scratch with peroxide.

"Ms. Maguire, are you flirting with me?" Garrett chuckled as she tried to hide a sheepish grin.

"Don't be ridiculous. I don't even like you." She set the bottle of peroxide on the floor and concentrated on ripping open the Band-Aid's wrapper. With one smooth swipe she pressed the bandage in place on his forehead. "You're right. It *was* just a scratch." Rachel laughed and slid off the arm of the chair, moved to the bed, and began to close up the first aid kit.

Encouraged by the way she'd shared her concerns with him and her warm smile that didn't seem to hold any of the reservations he'd seen there before, he leaned back, unwilling for their brief interlude to end. "And yet you took far longer than sixty seconds to patch me up. I think you're starting to appreciate my charm." He gave her a wink when she glanced over her shoulder, a disbelieving smirk pulling at her lips.

Rachel turned slowly, regarding him thoughtfully as though she had a weighty decision to make. The green in her eyes captured him, and his gaze traveled slowly to her slightly parted lips and lingered there while he entertained the prospect of kissing her. Foolhardy at best. It was way too soon. She'd only just reached a point where she could look at him without contempt flooding her expression. One wrong move on his part would send them back to the starting line. Kissing her thoroughly was definitely something he intended to do…but timing was everything. He cleared his throat and forced his attention from her lips.

A rosy pink tinged her cheeks. "I'm not saying I like you or anything, but…I wonder if we should postpone our *deal* until we figure out what's going on. For Peg's sake, of course. Would you be willing to stay a while longer?"

Relief flooded Garrett. He'd been trying to figure out how to broach that very subject. But his gut told him it wasn't Peg who was in danger. He'd wager it was the sexy spitfire standing next to his chair, that she knew it, and was withholding information. Whatever demons chased her, they must be formidable to convince Rachel to let him stay in exchange for his help.

He could live with that. Additional time was what he needed to get to know his aunt all over again, and to break through Rachel's barriers. He would never tell her, of course, but he hadn't planned on leaving with a gunman running around the mountain anyway.

Still, if yesterday and today were any indication, he was sure to have a problem keeping his libido in line. If he stayed, he already knew he would want to talk with her, and touch her, and protect her, and…Shit yeah…that could definitely be a problem.

"You got it. I'll stay as long as you need me." He might be sorry, but he'd take his chances.

Chapter Six

RACHEL WATCHED THE green vegetation blur past Garrett's Jeep. The mountain that had been her home for ten years seemed foreign and merciless today. As though sensing her preoccupation, Garrett's dog pushed between the seats and pressed against her thigh. The small offering made her smile, and she looped her arm over Cowboy's back, burying her face in his fur long enough to take what comfort he volunteered.

She hadn't felt sorry for herself in over a decade. There was no sense starting now.

Texas had been a lifetime ago. She'd left it all behind her, including the drawl. Still, she'd lived in fear that, eventually, a man intent on finishing what he'd started would succeed in tracking her down. And now she was afraid he had. As if the threatening calls that had become routine weren't enough...now he shows up on her doorstep? Was it Jeremy? She didn't want to believe it, but who else could it be? By not informing Garrett, Peg, and Jonathan of the possibility, was she endangering them all?

"Hey. Are you all right?" Garrett laid his hand on her arm.

Rachel raised her head and looked over Cowboy's back. "Fine. Just…overwhelmed I think."

Why did he have to look so good in his snug-fitting jeans and light blue shirt, the sleeves rolled up and three buttons left undone, showing a smattering of curly chest hair? Kindness and understanding shone in the warmth of his eyes. Damn it! Why couldn't he have been selfish and hateful, the way she'd pictured him? Why did he have to be dark, handsome, and built like a friggin' tank? How was she supposed to despise him if he wasn't…despicable?

He stroked her arm once, then placed his hand back on the steering wheel. "I'm still not convinced we shouldn't have warned the guests about our uninvited visitor, but I think Aunt Peg handled the news okay, don't you?"

"Jonathan will keep an eye out for trouble. Peg didn't want to frighten the Taylors needlessly. But then…I didn't notice you telling her that the intruder was armed…or that he threatened to shoot your dog. So considering she didn't have all the information, Peg handled it amazingly well. I just wish she hadn't insisted we go to town and inform the sheriff."

"It can't hurt. What do you have against the man, anyway?" His tone wasn't disbelieving, only curious. Figures he'd ignore her dig about withholding the juicy bits from Peg, though.

"He uses his office to bully and steal…and hurt good people. He's the biggest crook in Grizzly Gulch." That was the reason she would never consider confiding the secrets of her past to Sheriff Connors. She didn't trust him.

A heated scowl darkened Garrett's steel gray eyes. "Did he hurt you?"

"No." She forced herself to meet his gaze, knowing she'd answered too quickly. She had to give him something to wipe that I'll-kill-him grimace off his face. "A friend of mine. She lives in Huntington now, with her eight-year-old daughter."

Garrett's fingers tightened on the steering wheel until his knuckles whitened. "Why don't you wait in the Jeep with Cowboy while I talk to him?"

"I don't back down, Garrett. Especially not from scum like that." She smiled faintly and faced the passenger-side window again. It felt nice to have someone offer to stand up for her. She could get used to that if she let herself.

The cab of the Jeep was quiet for a couple of minutes before Garrett squirmed in his seat and stretched his left leg out as far as he could. One hand massaged his upper thigh.

"Does it hurt?"

"Naw. Not anymore. Just cramps up on me now and then. A good massage usually takes care of it, but I skipped my P/T appointment today."

Rachel frowned, wishing there was something she could do to help, all the while kicking herself for caring. "Were you shot?" The words seemed to come of their own accord.

He searched her face. "You sure you want to hear this?"

She lowered her lashes in case he might recognize the uncertainty in her eyes. "I wouldn't have asked if I didn't."

He turned his attention to the side mirror, then faced the front. A muscle on the rim of his jaw flexed with tension, and his expression hardened. "My unit was twelve strong, thirteen counting Cowboy. Rangers all of us, the best soldiers I ever served with." Rachel could hear the emotion in his voice, and he stopped to clear his throat. His grip on the steering wheel tightened again. "The colonel sent us into Fallujah at nightfall to bring out an American doctor that a particularly nasty militant group was holding for ransom. Fallujah was a hot spot. All kinds of shit going down there."

Rachel's stomach tightened with dread. Maybe she *didn't* want to hear this.

"When we reached the compound where they were holding the hostage, we split up. Six stayed outside to guard the exits. Six of us and Cowboy went inside the bunker. Our information was good. We knew where they were keeping the doc. We took out four enemy targets along the way, and then everything went to shit.

"They'd left the fucking door to the man's cell unlocked. Hell, we knew he was dead before we even saw his mutilated body. They *let* us get that far because they had no intention of letting us get out. The insurgents opened fire…and ten good men died that night. Sergeant Cole was wounded bad and unconscious. I was hit once in the back and once in the upper thigh. Cowboy got it in the shoulder. We'd have never made it out of there if it hadn't been for him. I carried Sarge, and Cowboy did what he was trained to do—tracked the enemy, luring them out into the open where I could get a shot.

"When we got out and I saw we were the only ones left, we dragged ourselves into an alley and waited for help to arrive." Garrett hit the steering wheel, anger twisting his face into a mask. "I should have known it was an ambush. *It was just too fucking easy.*"

Rachel reached out to comfort him, her hand resting on the hard muscles of his arm as they lay tense beneath his shirt. "You couldn't have known it was a trap."

A tortured smile lifted one corner of his mouth. "I was commanding officer. It was my *job* to know." His voice was hoarse, and it was obvious how close he was to losing it, but he quickly pressed his lips together and looked away.

Tears tingled along the backs of her eyelids, and Rachel fisted her hand, jabbing her fingernails ruthlessly into her palm in an effort to distract herself. What happened to him should never happen to anyone. But it did—and her soul ached for him in spite of the fact she should be glad he'd suffered. Not even she was that callous. But sympathy wasn't what he needed, and he wouldn't expect it from her.

"Did the sergeant survive?"

It was a few seconds before he replied. "Cole lost his left leg, but his wife met him on the tarmac at Fort Benning, Georgia, and, last I heard, she still hadn't left his side."

"You sound surprised. Is it hard for you to believe that kind of devotion exists?"

A myriad of emotions tumbled across his face. Finally, he turned an obviously forced smile on her. "Not at all. Not anymore. I only mentioned it because it was the one good thing to come out of that night."

"What about you…and Cowboy? You both survived. You even seem fairly well adjusted." Rachel tried hard to stay detached, but damn—apparently she was a sucker for hot military men who were willing to give everything if called upon to do so.

"Sure. Cowboy was a hero. He deserved the ceremony, the medal, every honor he received. But he'd have been just as lost as Sergeant Cole out there in civilian-land by himself." Garrett's grin flickered mischievously. "Instead of an attentive female to keep him company, all he got was me."

Rachel choked back a laugh as she scratched Cowboy's muzzle. "*He's* not feeling sorry for himself."

Garrett gave a short laugh. "Ouch! Meaning, of course, that I am?"

"Well, Cinderella…if the shoe fits." She released the words and then waited, ready to deal with whatever his reaction would be.

A kaleidoscope of emotions tumbled across a face too surprised to mask any of them. Anger changed abruptly to guilt, then annoyance, then a spark of amusement appeared. And Garrett started to laugh, a low chuckle at first, building gradually into a full belly laugh that caused his eyes to sparkle with warmth.

His laugh was contagious, and Rachel couldn't help smiling.

When he'd regained control, he pinned her with a glare. "You think you're a real hard-ass, don't you?"

The smile slipped from her face as she averted her eyes. She'd come a long, long way from the sweet, naïve eighteen-year-old she'd been. She'd never thought of herself as a hard-ass, but if she was, it was because Jeremy had been such a good teacher.

With little notice, they rounded a curve and entered the tiny town of Grizzly Gulch. Garrett let off the gas and slowed down.

"The sheriff's office is the brick building in the middle of the next block." Did Garrett see the same thing she'd seen ten years ago when she came to town? Grizzly Gulch hadn't changed all that much. It still had rowdy-looking bars on almost every block, a one-pump service station, a feed store that shared a building with the grocery, a K–eight elementary school, and a dilapidated old church that saw more town meetings than worship services. Even the population sign at the edge of town still touted 137 residents.

Basically, it was a small town where strangers stood out like a fully clothed person on a nude beach…and where no one would ever think to look for her.

Garrett pulled to the curb across from the sheriff's office. The brick building also housed the mayor's workplace, the tiny post office, and City Hall. Members of the community were out in force today, so there'd be no shortage of gawkers to wonder who Garrett was and plenty of gossipers to overhear their report of an intruder and transfer the buzz to the well-oiled grapevine. The certainty that she was making a fool's mistake lay heavily on her chest. What if the stranger outside the lodge wasn't Jeremy…and what if reporting the incident led to her picture in the local newspaper—which was then picked up by the AP because of the beautiful scenery or a general lack of interesting news anywhere? It wasn't likely, but she'd heard of catastrophic events set in motion by less…a mistake…a quirk of fate. However improbable, the result she feared was Jeremy spotting her picture and knowing where to find her. Ten years ago, someone had died because she'd refused to believe evil like that would ever touch her life. She'd been wrong, and now she had a whole new circle of friends to protect. She loved them, and she didn't want to leave, but to keep them safe, she'd do anything.

"Are you all right?" Garrett's hand covered hers where she still hugged the dog.

"I'm good." She plastered on a smile.

"Ready?"

She was so *not* ready, but she opened her door anyway.

"Chill, Cowboy." Garrett stepped out on the other side.

Rachel drew a deep breath as they crossed the street together. Somewhat emboldened by Garrett's substantial size beside her, walking so close his arm brushed hers every few steps, she almost worked up the courage for what they were about to do.

That lasted until Riley and his two grinning buffoons filed out the door she and Garrett were headed for. A groan escaped her, and Garrett stepped closer, his hand going to the small of her back, encouraging her to keep moving.

Riley grinned when he saw her and stopped just outside the door. "Hey, Rach. I wanna apologize for my behavior yesterday. Me and the boys had too much to drink. It won't happen again. We been friends a long time. I'm hopin' you won't hold it against me." His words would have sounded good if not for his usual sarcasm in the delivery. He held his hand out as though to shake on it, but Rachel ignored his overture.

With a scornful grin on his face, Garrett stepped to within inches of Riley, looking down on him slightly. "You've got a lot to learn, kid. Some things can't be apologized away. Bringing guns into a lady's bar and threatening to kidnap her are just a couple of them. You're lucky to still be in one piece. If you ever see a gun in her hand again, I wouldn't stand around wondering if she was going to pull the trigger if I were you."

Riley glanced at his brothers and then smirked. "Yeah? Well, I wasn't talkin' to you, Mister. Rachel can speak for herself. She don't need no stranger to stand up for her." He made the word *stranger* sound like a four-letter word.

Rachel had listened to about all she could stand. She stomped forward, pulled her arm back, and threw her fist into Riley's nose with all her strength. Blood flew before he grabbed his wounded snout, muffling his screams and the harsh expletives that flowed like water. Matt backed quickly away from the reach of her fist while Arnold ducked his head and refused to look her in the eye.

Garrett's piercing gaze flew to hers, clearly surprised, but something else shone from his eyes as well—something like pride—and warmed her heart, making it hard not to smile.

She turned her attention back to Riley and pounded her finger into his chest. "Two mules and a coal train wouldn't make that apology worth the ink to write it down. I don't ever want to see you back in the bar—any of you." She extended her warning to include his brothers.

Riley straightened, letting the blood run down his face. "Be careful, Rach. You don't want me as an enemy." His voice now contained a heavy lisp.

For a moment, she got the impression he knew something about her that no one should know, and a chill made her shudder.

Garrett must have sensed her apprehension because he stepped closer. "You haven't left her any choice. You may have been a friend once, but not after yesterday. I don't know what you think you're doing, but I *will* find out."

Riley's expression turned cold. "This is between me and Rachel. You should probably stay out of it…if you know what's good for you."

Garrett's smile didn't reach his eyes. "Well, that's the best part, Riley. You see…any enemy of Rachel's is an enemy of mine. And I take it personally when you attack her, physically or emotionally. Now, if *you* know what's good for *you*, you'll get out of our way so we can go about our business."

His eyes were almost black as he faced off against Riley, daring him to make the first move. She saw it in

Riley's expression the instant he got the message—Garrett wouldn't back down. Riley stepped aside, trouncing on Matt's foot. Matt jumped and let out a yowl.

As Rachel brushed past Riley, he stroked one finger up her arm. She jerked away from his touch and her gaze darted to his.

He leaned toward her, keeping his voice low. "Been gettin' any mysterious phone calls, Rach?"

She nearly stopped breathing from the effort to show no reaction. How did Riley know about the phone calls? Dory was the only other person who knew, and she'd sworn not to tell—and even if she *had*, it wouldn't be to the likes of the Metcalf brothers. Dory had her standards after all. It had to be *Jeremy*. Her first instinct had been right—it had been Jeremy outside the lodge, watching her. He'd found her. Terror flowed freely, leaving her trembling in its wake. She couldn't stay here and wait for him to hurt her or one of her friends. Not this time.

As soon as they were inside, out of sight, Rachel let her breath out and pulled away from Garrett. She leaned against the wall, clasping her handbag to her stomach as she gasped for air, her mind going at mach nine. Moving on would be so hard, but what better time than when Garrett Harding had showed up out of the blue wanting a whole new relationship with Peg? It was perfect...if she could convince him to stay on a more permanent basis. How was that for irony?

He propped himself beside her. "Are you going to tell me what he said that has you so upset?"

Rachel forced her breathing back to normal, stood straight, and glanced at him. "Nothing. Just more of his drivel. Thanks for what you said, Garrett. It meant a lot, especially after the way I've treated you."

He nodded. "I meant it, but I don't believe you're telling me the truth about Riley, so we're going to continue this conversation later." He gripped her hand. "Let's visit with the sheriff so we can get out of this town."

She allowed him to pull her toward the sheriff's office down the hall, as anxious to be out of there as he was.

Garrett glanced over his shoulder. "By the way, *two mules and a coal train*?"

She laughed as his sexy smile grabbed her attention. "I've had ten years to pick up some local color. You should be thankful I'm selective in what I'll repeat."

"Sure. I get that. I guess I've picked up some color in the army too, only mine's a lot more predictable than yours, and I try not to repeat it." He winked and squeezed her hand.

She was off balance. That had to be it. It was the only excuse she could think of. Here she was talking, smiling, actually enjoying the company of the man who only yesterday she hated with a passion. Who knew he would turn out to be a hard man to hate? At present, she couldn't even drum up a decent scathing remark. Part of her felt like a traitor to herself and Amanda, but another part realized her lack of animosity would make it easier to convince him to stay so that she could make her escape with a little less guilt.

Garrett pulled her down the hallway and straight through the open doorway of the sheriff's office. Millie, the receptionist behind the counter, smiled at Rachel, then stared appreciatively at Garrett. Sheriff Mike Connors turned and scowled at them. Rachel tensed, and Garrett, no doubt hoping to avoid another bloodletting, stepped toward Mike, shoving her behind him.

"Sheriff, my name's Garrett Harding. Rachel and I are here at the request of my aunt, Peg Williams, to report an intruder out at the lodge."

An instant of surprise turned to skepticism before the sheriff's gaze slid away from Garrett and swept full-length over her, while she forced herself to stare right back. Eventually, he gave up on intimidating her and acknowledged Garrett's presence. "I heard Peg's nephew was in town. Well, Mr. Harding, you saved me a trip. I got a complaint about a dog belonging to you, and I was just on my way out to see you." The sheriff's voice held a high-pitched, nasally quality that grated on Rachel's nerves.

She gasped and glanced at Garrett. The muscle flexing in his cheek said it all. Nobody messed with Cowboy. It had to be Riley complaining about the dog after Cowboy had defended Garrett in the bar yesterday. Hard to tell what lies he'd told. Rachel seethed with anger.

"It was Riley, wasn't it? Mike, you're not seriously going to take Riley's word for anything without hearing both sides of the story, are you?" Her hand slid around Garrett's arm, hoping to calm him.

All of five-eight and thick around the middle, Mike must have recognized the rage brewing in the bigger man's expression and backed away a few steps. "Of course not. That's why I was coming to see this dangerous animal for myself."

A growl emanated from Garrett's throat as though he was warring with himself. Apparently, he lost because he stepped in close to the sheriff. "Dangerous? You don't know what dangerous is, Sheriff. That *animal* is a highly decorated war veteran who saved hundreds of US military personnel by flushing out insurgents and finding unexploded bombs. He's trained to take the point on missions that would make your balls wither and fall off, and he never once hesitated to rip the throats out of the al-Qaeda scum that threatened his unit."

The farther forward Garrett pushed, the farther away Mike leaned, and it was all Rachel could do to tamp down a giggle.

But Garrett wasn't finished yet. "In case honor, loyalty, and gratitude don't mean anything to you, Sheriff, and you have any lingering thoughts about touching my dog, you should probably know that I can have several high-ranking army officers, news teams from CNN and Fox, and a US senator here in a matter of hours with one phone call. They'll be very interested in how you handle complaints against war heroes like that *animal* you're referring to. I can almost guarantee they'll turn your little town into the biggest media circus you've ever seen if there's any hint of impropriety."

Millie watched with a slight smile while Garrett berated her boss. Mike's face was about as red as it could get, and he held his hands in front of him as though to ward off a physical attack.

"Calm down, Mr. Harding. I was led to believe your dog was running loose and endangering the residents on the mountain. I understand now that I've been…misinformed. As long as you can assure me the dog is under your control at all times, that'll be the end of it."

Garrett still viewed the sheriff distrustfully, but he backed off a step. "He's under my control," he growled.

Mike threw his hands in the air. "Fine, then. What did you folks need from me?"

Rachel bit her lip, trying not to smile, as she waited for Garrett to continue.

"I think we're done here." Garrett took her arm and turned her toward the door as her mouth dropped open. Something in his eyes warned her not to argue.

As they left the building, with the sheriff grumbling behind them, and strode toward Garrett's Jeep, Rachel kept glancing at him, no longer able to keep her smile under control.

When they were a few feet from the vehicle, Garrett swung toward her. "What?"

Her smile widened. "Overprotective much?"

Chapter Seven

GARRETT OPENED THE Jeep's door for Rachel and closed it after she tossed her handbag in ahead of her and pulled herself into the passenger seat. Cowboy rose from where he lay in the back to shove his head between the seats and watch Garrett as he crossed to the other side of the vehicle. The intelligence in Cowboy's eyes never failed to impress Garrett, and this moment, with the dog's tail wagging leisurely, was no exception.

Hell yes. Rachel had nailed it. Cowboy was worth two or three of that backwoods sheriff, and Garrett would be damned if any unappreciative civilian would ever touch him.

He slid behind the wheel, but just as he was about to turn the key in the ignition, he stopped, his gaze fixed on the dashboard. "Okay. You're right. I'm a little overprotective where Cowboy's concerned…but I'm not going to apologize for that. He's saved my life more times than I can remember. The least I can do is—"

Movement in the corner of his eye caught his attention just before she touched him, and his gaze traveled from where her slender fingers stroked the contours of his bicep to her rose-colored cheeks and her soft, pink mouth, closed on a wisp of smugness.

She smiled when his gaze reached hers, transforming her pretty face to hauntingly beautiful, and he lost himself for a moment in the depths of her green eyes. For a heartbeat, he forgot to breathe.

"You don't need to explain. The bond between the two of you is obvious. I have nothing but respect for the way you defended him back there." Rachel self-consciously removed her hand from his arm.

"Yeah? You mean I actually earned a couple points by standing up for this mangy dog?" He winked and started the engine. If he'd only known it was that easy.

Rachel laughed. "Don't get your hopes up. You lost a few for not talking to the sheriff about our intruder like Peg asked."

"Oh yeah—that. I don't think he was really interested in anything we had to say. Actually, he convinced me to come over to your way of thinking. The less the sheriff knows about our business, the more comfortable I am. We'll handle the intruder on our own." Garrett looked in his side mirror and pulled away from the curb.

"Didn't I tell you he was a crook?" Rachel latched her seat belt, clicking it home on the first try.

"And I should have listened to you." He studied her for a moment before his attention swept back to the road. What was it about her that was so damned appealing? Long, slim legs stretched from beneath a short brown skirt, worn with a sleeveless white shirt that gathered just under her breasts and draped across her flat stomach. The picture she presented stirred something deep within him. But, it was more than just her physical appearance, although she didn't lack for anything in that department. The contrast between her almost angelic face and the sharp bite of her words when she was riled presented an enigma that tantalized him.

"Oh no. Don't give me that BS story. I'm not going to suddenly start thinking you're this okay guy just because you flatter me and tell me what you think I want to hear. I don't care whether you agree with me or not or how good you are to that dog. Nothing will change the way I feel about how you treated Amanda." She actually mustered a tiny bit of an accusing scowl as she stared at him.

Garrett didn't buy it. He no doubt had a ways to go yet, but he was getting to her. She was starting to let down her guard now and then—to show the real Rachel beneath the barriers.

He focused straight ahead as they left Grizzly Gulch behind. "You're so full of shit, I'm surprised your eyes are still green." A slow grin formed as he felt her gaze burning into the side of his face.

"Seriously? You think I'm not being honest with you? I'm not going to forget the nine years' worth of anguish

I witnessed Amanda go through simply because of one honorable act."

Ouch! Then again, maybe he was wrong about making headway with her. Perhaps his best course of action would be letting her hold on to her anger for the past he couldn't change and focus on his more immediate concern. "You're not even being honest with yourself. You're hiding something. Not just from me, but Aunt Peg and Jonathan, too. That stranger lurking outside the lodge this morning shook you up. My guess is you're afraid he was waiting for you. Someone who's probably been keeping tabs on you for a while and would know what time you'd be leaving for your run. He didn't have any way of knowing I'd be there though, or Cowboy, and it ticks you off that I probably saved your ass. Am I close, Rach?"

She remained silent for several seconds as she turned to look out the window, then sighed deeply. "It doesn't matter what you think. Whether you're right or wrong, it doesn't change anything." Her voice was low and heavy with sadness.

"That's where you're wrong. Something *has* changed. Whether you ever decide you can forgive me or not, you were there for my mother, and I owe you for that." He bit back the rest of his words before they could escape. Truth was he didn't know how she'd react to his admission, and he was more than a little afraid she'd turn away from him entirely. That was the last thing he wanted, but there were also a couple of good reasons to continue, not the least of which was to let her know she could trust him to tell her the truth. If she also got that he wasn't just a drive-by, that would be a bonus. What the hell—he was going for it.

"While we're at it, here's some honesty for you. I realize that you might always think I'm a snake and that's your right…but I'm attracted to you. I haven't stopped thinking about kissing you since I first saw you at the bar. Even before you learned who I was, I knew I wanted to see you again." He stopped and glanced sideways, hoping for some clue as to her reaction. She still looked out the window as though she hadn't heard him.

"You probably think I'm a stalker now." Garrett laughed nervously. "I'm not. I promise. You can trust me with whatever your secret is. While I'm here, I just want to help. Let me help you, Rach."

He looked her way in time to see her stiffen, and then she remained silent for so long he started to worry that he'd been right and his honesty had been the final straw.

A couple of minutes passed before she sighed and seemed to relax again. She glanced at him. "What do you want to do today?" By the spark of determination alight in the pretty eyes she turned toward him, he might as well accept that she was finished with his topic of conversation.

He didn't blame her for changing the subject. Her business-as-usual question told him she didn't plan to back away from the tenuous truce they'd cultivated, and that though she'd tried to hide it, he'd gotten his point across. It wasn't the breakthrough he'd hoped for, but it could have been worse, and he'd take it. "Why don't you surprise me."

"Would you like to see where Peg and Amanda lived when they first came here?"

Excitement tinged her voice, and he grinned at her. "Perfect."

She pointed to a dirt road up ahead. "Take a right."

RACHEL WAS QUIET for the rest of the ride, unless she was telling him where to go. The gravel road they ended up on fifteen minutes later was fairly smooth and well maintained. It led to a parking area beside a quaint log cabin that perched not thirty feet from the banks of a river. The water near the bank was shallow and meandered slowly, but the farther out he looked, the faster the water rushed by. Garrett parked and killed the engine, staring at the picturesque scene in front of him for a few minutes before he sensed Rachel watching him.

"Sorry." He reached for the door latch. "This is where they lived?"

"Uh-huh. Until they built the lodge." She jumped from the Jeep and was already waiting for him beside his door as he let Cowboy out.

"It's really something. Who lives here now?"

Rachel's expression filled with pride. "It's closed up all winter, and we open it in the spring after the last frost. I was just here last week, getting it cleaned and stocked with a few staples. It's ready to go for the season. Once in a while, Peg rents it out to a select few if the lodge fills up, but most of the time it's empty. When Amanda was alive, she used it as a studio for her painting. Her work is still inside."

"She painted?" So much he didn't know about his mother—so unfair. Anger at his father began to brew again, and he very carefully stuffed it away for a later date. "May I see?"

"Of course." She withdrew a ring of keys from her small handbag, sorted through them quickly, as if it wasn't her first time, until she found the one she was looking for, and held the ring out to him. "I'm going to stay out here. Take your time."

He accepted the keys, and she immediately walked toward an aged boat dock that protruded a few feet into the river. A small aluminum fishing boat with an old Evinrude outboard was moored there. Garrett gave Cowboy a signal to stay with her, and the dog silently trailed along behind. Rachel kicked her shoes off, padded to the end of the dock, sat, and hung her legs over the side just as a flock of wild geese skimmed the water and landed downriver.

The sky was a brilliant blue, and the sun warmed the otherwise cool mountain air. Garrett was tempted to forget the house and go sit beside her, but one look at the key and he knew he had to see what was waiting there. He turned away from Rachel and Cowboy, striding toward the cabin. A well-worn deck lined the front and held two oversized wooden rocking chairs under a covered porch. Three windows stared blankly back at him.

The key she'd chosen turned easily in the lock, and he pushed the door open, then hesitated. Stepping across the threshold took more fortitude than he would have imagined.

The main room was furnished meticulously in an early western motif, much as the lodge had been. A tiny kitchen nook took up one corner toward the back, and a wooden spiral staircase curled its way upward to a loft, which appeared to answer the question of sleeping arrangements. A large stone fireplace was centered along the wall to his left, and a gnarled branch, sanded and lacquered until it shone, formed the mantel. Garrett stared at the pictures lining the shelf.

He pushed the keys in his pocket and stepped closer. The first one was an image of his mother with Peg in the boat right outside. The beautiful sunny day had been eclipsed by the smile on her face. It eased some of his burden to see that she'd known happiness, but all the more he felt cheated and betrayed.

Next to that picture were several of him and Luke as toddlers, playing in a large grass-covered yard. There was also one of Rachel, younger than she was now, standing in the snow against a backdrop of trees. A knit scarf partially covered her hair and coiled around her neck, and a mysterious smile curved her lips. Her obvious sweetness tugged at his heart. He laughed quietly, realizing how ticked off she'd be if she knew he'd thought of her that way.

The next frames practically rocked him back on his heels. Because of who their father was, it had apparently been newsworthy when Garrett joined the army and again when he'd earned his Ranger tab. Same for Luke when he entered the navy. Someone—no doubt his mother—had cut those pictures from a newspaper, framed them, and set them in a place of honor on her mantel. For a few breaths, Garrett was afraid his heart would burst with pride…with sorrow…with longing for a different ending to their story. He turned away as his eyes misted and his vision blurred.

Seconds later, he was able to focus on a painting that hung on the opposite wall—an autumn mountain scene with a small herd of elk in the foreground, drinking from a clear stream. Even before he approached close enough to read the artist's name, he knew it was hers. There were two other paintings in the main room that bore her signature as well—Amanda Williams.

He found the rest when he climbed the staircase. Leaning against the walls on both sides of the full-sized bed were dozens of his mother's paintings. They were in various states of completion. Garrett couldn't help wondering which one she'd been working on in the days before her death.

Okay. He was getting too sentimental. Enough for one day. Learning about Amanda's life was the main objective. There was nothing he could change about her death or the fact she'd been ripped from his life when he was too young to stop it. He could have done something later, when he was grown…if he'd known. Again, he refused to allow anger to gain the upper hand.

He jogged down the stairs and headed for the door. Just inside, next to the exit, was a narrow wooden box containing board games, bats and baseballs, Frisbees, and other supplies. Rachel had said they sometimes rented it out now. These games were probably meant to occupy guests after they'd had their fill of hiking and boating. Garrett stopped and snagged a football, turning the grainy leather over in his hands.

Stepping outside, he squinted toward the dock where he'd seen Rachel last. She was still there, leaning back on her arms, letting the sun bathe her face. Her bare legs beneath her short skirt swung alternately as she dangled her feet just above the water. Looking carefree and oblivious to his presence, she presented a truly enticing picture. He'd definitely like to slide his hands through her thick and silky-looking hair, maybe grabbing a fistful so he could guide her lips to his. Imagining how soft she would feel next to him led to the beginnings of an arousal. He smiled ruefully as he shoved his daydreaming aside.

Garrett descended the porch steps and stopped, gripping the football with both hands. "Hey, Rach."

She turned her head with a curious expression.

"Go long." He laughed as he spiraled the ball toward her.

Rachel came to her feet in one lithe movement, her eyes on the ball. Garrett had planned for it to sail over her head, but at the last second, she jumped into the air and caught it like a pro. Her triumphant laughter carried to him, and he whooped and applauded as she landed on the dock…almost. One bare foot only got partial purchase on the wooden planks, and the angle of her landing knocked her off balance. She threw her arms out to catch herself, but it was too late. The *oh-shit* look on her face was priceless as she toppled over the side. Cowboy barked, ran to the edge, and looked back and forth between them.

How deep could the water be? Was the current danger-ously swift? Did she even know how to swim? All things he should have considered before he threw the ball. Gar-rett raced to the dock and reached the end just as Rachel made a one-handed grab for the wooden structure.

"You okay?" He knelt on the edge of the planks, pushed Cowboy out of the way, and grasped her wrist.

Coughing and sputtering, she brushed her sopping-wet hair out of her face and focused on him. "C-cold."

He barely suppressed a grin, so relieved was he that she was all right. "Give me your other hand and I'll help you out."

She thrashed about in the water until she was close enough for him to grip her other wrist. Then he lifted and pulled her toward him, hauling her far enough out of the water that he could enfold her and roll. He ended up on his back with her on top of him, and he was nearly as wet as she was.

As soon as he stopped moving, she pushed herself off his chest far enough to meet his gaze. He braced himself for the tongue-lashing he figured he had coming, but he wasn't prepared for the amusement that sparked in her eyes, or the spontaneous laughter that fell from her blu-ish-colored lips. The dog pushed his nose into her face, clearly confused by her reaction too, and gave her a big lick.

Garrett laughed then too, until he realized her white cotton shirt was gauze thin and transparent, revealing a tiny scrap of lace, masquerading as a bra, which did nothing to hide her all-too-apparent charms. Worse yet, his body was reacting to her being so close and so damn desirable and, any second, she was sure to notice.

Rolling her off him, he lunged to his feet and drew her up beside him. "Your teeth are chattering. Let's get you inside and out of those wet clothes." He started walking with her hand in his.

Rachel planted her feet and wouldn't move.

Garrett stopped as soon as he felt her unyielding weight and already had an idea what the problem was before he turned to face her. Her impish smile combined with her uncontrollable shaking from the cold made him want to pull her into his arms and employ whatever methods necessary to warm her up. Probably not a good idea under the circumstances. "I didn't mean that quite the way it came out." Although, it didn't sound half-bad. He forced himself to keep looking at her face and not allow his field of vision to drift farther down. Otherwise she would see through any other assurances he might give her. "Amanda taught me the basics of being a gentleman, and I wouldn't think of disappointing her, if that's what you're worried about."

She smiled at that and gave in to the tug of his hand, leaning slightly away from him to scoop up her purse from the dock where she'd been sitting. "Thankfully, my phone was in my bag and didn't go in the drink with me, so it's all good."

"That's what I like. A girl who looks for the silver lining. Now all we have to do is find you something to wear while your clothes are drying. I think I saw a dryer in there somewhere." They climbed the steps, crossed the deck, and he opened the door for her. "Go on in the bathroom and I'll go upstairs and see if I can find a robe or something."

After she disappeared, Cowboy plopped down in front of the closed bathroom door and made no move to follow Garrett to the spiral staircase. Garrett made a face at him. "Traitor."

He dashed up the steps and swept his gaze around the room. The small chest of drawers was empty, as was the closet. For a moment, he considered offering Rachel *his* shirt. She wasn't likely to be pleased with that solution, not to mention that seeing her in his clothes wouldn't particularly *enhance* his gentlemanly behavior. After swinging around twice, his gaze dropped to the bed. The comforter would have to do. He grabbed it, rolling it into a ball, and headed downstairs.

Garrett nudged Cowboy out of the way and knocked on the bathroom door. When Rachel opened it a crack, he held up the comforter. "Sorry. It's all I could find."

"It'll work." She opened the door a little wider so he could shove the comforter through and then pushed it closed.

He stuffed his hands in his pockets and glanced again at the mantel. Then he headed for the door and straight for the dock. The football was probably long gone, having landed in the water the same time Rachel did, but he scoured the bank downstream anyway and was surprised to see the ball caught in an eddy where a patch of tall grass grew close by. After grabbing one of the oars from the boat, he jogged the hundred yards or so and was able to drag the ball to shore without getting more than his feet wet.

By the time he returned to the cabin, Rachel sat on a love seat in the main room, wrapped from head to toe in the cream-colored comforter. Her cell phone lay on the coffee table beside her. Gorgeous green eyes followed his movements even as twin spheres of red emblazoned her cheeks. Just knowing she had nothing on beneath the comforter set his blood pulsing through his body.

He tossed the football back in the box and strode to the kitchen nook. Quickly rifling through the cupboards, he took stock of what was available. "How about something warm? Instant coffee or hot chocolate?"

"Hmm…hot chocolate sounds good. I don't suppose there are any little marshmallows left?"

Garrett checked the cupboards again. "Afraid you're out of luck." He found a teapot, filled it halfway with water, and set it to boil on the gas stove. After spooning hot chocolate mix into two cups, he turned, leaning against the counter, and studied the back of her head as she sat, unmoving, on the love seat.

What was her secret? She was hiding from someone—he was sure of it. But who…and why? The man outside the lodge was obviously a professional. Had someone put out a contract on Rachel? Or was the law looking for the redheaded beauty who exuded innocence as easily as her next breath?

The teapot started to whistle, and he swung around to turn off the burner, pour water in each cup, and stir. He couldn't explain his need to know what was clearly so personal to her, except that it was tied to the intense protectiveness she'd unleashed in him. Still, he couldn't help her unless he knew where the danger was coming from, so he'd make it his business to find out.

Garrett set her cup on a coaster beside her cell phone and stepped to the other end of the love seat. "Okay if I sit here?"

"Sure. Thanks for the hot chocolate. This almost makes a dunk in the river worthwhile." She threaded one arm free of the comforter to reach for her cup and took a sip.

He set his mug down and gave her an apologetic smile. "Obviously I didn't mean for you to land in the river."

Her laughter was sweet, and his stomach tightened in response. "This isn't the first time I've taken an unexpected dip in that exact spot, and it probably won't be the last." She turned sideways and pulled her legs up underneath her. "Jonathan always tells me I'm a klutz."

"Not this time. This one's on me. I shouldn't have thrown that ball. I don't really know why I did, except…I was so overwhelmed with everything of my mother's in here…I guess I just wasn't thinking." He turned sideways and threw his arm along the back of the love seat, his fingers within a couple of inches of where her hair splayed on the suede fabric. The urge to reach out and touch the wet strands contended with his common sense.

"She was a great artist. Some of her paintings are still in galleries all over Idaho, Montana, and Colorado." Rachel fell abruptly silent, and bitterness again clouded her eyes.

Clearly, she'd tried to put her feelings aside in light of their new arrangement. Asking him to stay indefinitely, until the stranger casing the lodge could be dealt with, obviously hadn't been as easy as she'd made it look.

He had to tell her the truth, even if she refused to believe him. The desire to have her look at him with anything other than disdain made him reckless and impatient. He needed her to believe in him—to know that he was inherently a good person. Otherwise, she'd never open up to him and allow him to help her, and suddenly, that was of the utmost importance. Telling her why he never came to see Amanda while she was still alive was the first step, and this was as good a time as any. Garrett took a deep breath. "Aunt Peg said my mother wrote to Luke and me regularly."

Her gaze locked on his. "You *know* she did." Her icy tone accused him.

He pressed on. "Two days ago, by accident, I found Aunt Peg's letter telling me of Amanda's passing. Up until that day, neither Luke nor I saw any letters, cards, or notes from Amanda or Peg."

Suspicion flared in the green of her eyes, and she unfolded her legs as though to leave.

Garrett put his hand on her arm and leaned closer. "Think about it, Rachel. Two days ago, I saw the only letter I've ever seen. I loaded up Cowboy and drove straight through to get here. If I'd gotten even *one* of Amanda's letters, do you think anything could have kept me away? I waited for her to come back my whole life. I'd have moved heaven and earth to see her again."

Indecision wavered on her pretty face as she searched his eyes. "What are you saying? Someone hid the letters from you?" She snorted in disbelief.

"One or two letters might have gotten lost. Over three hundred? Probably not. I have my suspicions. That's why I hired a private investigator to find the answers."

A soft gasp escaped as fire slowly smoldered in her eyes. "*Your father!* That hateful man. I'm right, aren't I? It has to be him. He's the one who insisted the letters be mailed to him."

A flutter of anger awakened in him as though in agreement with her words, but he tamped it down, refusing to give it a voice. He wouldn't waste time being furious with the man until he knew for sure. Nor would he accuse him. "If I find out it was him, I'll deal with it. Right now, my only concern is that *you* believe me. You were here with her when I didn't know where she was. You helped put that smile on her face in that picture on the mantel. I know it's a lot to ask…but please believe me, Rachel. I don't know why, but it's important to me."

Confusion skittered across her face. "I…I don't know. I'd like to believe you, but you have to admit it's a lot to swallow. I need some time." Her eyes softened with an emotion that seemed to ask him to understand.

He smiled briefly. "Well, at least you didn't call me a liar to my face. I wish you could believe me now, but sooner or later I'll get the proof I need, and then there won't be any doubt."

She turned toward him, her face inches from his. "I've blamed you and Luke for hurting Amanda for years. That proof of yours will have to be pretty damn convincing to make me change my mind now." The challenge that shone from her eyes was different from her usual defiance— hopeful, playful almost. A wisp of a smile appeared and disappeared in the same heartbeat, and then her gaze wandered slowly to his lips and stayed right there.

The only sound in the room, besides Cowboy's slow and steady breathing from his spot near the door, was Garrett's own breaths, the rhythm becoming harder to maintain with each passing second. Rachel was so beautiful and so lusciously, innocently sexy he had to remind himself that she didn't know him. If he moved too fast, he'd scare her off and ruin everything...although he was at a loss to identify exactly what *everything* was. She smelled of citrus and sunshine, and clean mountain air. Her scent wound around him and pulled him closer.

And then he lost what little sense he had left. His right hand slid behind her neck, the sudden contact making her eyes widen. He smiled and lightly stroked her cheek, nudging her hair away from her face. His gaze fell to her full mouth, lips trembling somewhat.

Blinded by his need to possess those lips, he pulled her toward him and leaned in slowly to meet her. Tenderly, he covered her mouth, moving lazily, sipping her sweetness again and again before backing off slightly to focus on her closed eyes.

She must have finally sensed him watching. Her eyes opened languidly, and she looked up at him. She blinked and worry darkened the nearly transparent green. "What's wrong?"

"Not a thing," he whispered before taking her lips again.

Rachel released her grip on the comforter to fist her hand in the collar of his shirt and tug him closer, and her lips parted beneath his.

Enticed by her subtle invitation, Garrett slid his tongue along the opening, and then pushed through to sample her sweet flavors. She met each thrust of his tongue with a stroke of her own that sorely tempted him, and the heat level between them rose by several degrees.

Hyperaware that she was naked beneath the comforter she no longer clutched with both hands, his body responded all too quickly with a rock-hard erection that ached for release. The prize he was after, however, wasn't an impromptu roll in the hay. He wanted Rachel to trust him. He raised his head and tipped her chin so he could have his fill of the most sensuous eyes he'd ever seen. They were hazy with lust and curious now. She watched him, perfectly still except for the tip of her tongue, which ran slowly over her bottom lip. *Shit!* Why couldn't he have both?

Ever so slowly, he leaned in and covered her lips again, nipping at the one she'd just licked, and then grinding his mouth over hers. Damn, she tasted like honey, and she was so soft. He found an opening in the comforter and slid his fingers inside to rest against her stomach. He didn't miss her instant of tension as he began to stroke her bare skin, but then she wrapped her arms around his neck and the comforter slipped off her shoulders.

Garrett smiled and lightly kissed her eyes and the tip of her nose before finding her lips again and losing himself in them. Rachel settled into his arms as if she belonged there, and he pulled her closer.

A raucous country tune blared from somewhere, and it was a couple of seconds before Garrett realized it was coming from Rachel's cell phone, and that she was pushing away from him to reach for the device on the table beside her.

Rachel glanced at the screen, turned off the ringer, and tossed the device back on the table. Without looking at him, she pulled the edges of the comforter together and crossed her arms. The sudden tension that emanated from her filled the log cabin with an air of anxiety.

Was it the intimacy they'd shared that had her in such a state, or the phone call? Garrett decided to go with the latter. "Aren't you going to answer that?"

A forced smile appeared briefly. "Unknown number. Probably a telemarketer." She stood awkwardly, trying to hold the comforter in place. "My clothes should be dry by now. We should get going." She turned her back and left him sitting there.

Well, that lie had come easily enough, but he'd seen the guilt written all over her face. Garrett watched as she disappeared into the bathroom. Cowboy rose from his place near the door and dropped down in front of the love seat. Garrett patted him absently. It hadn't been an unknown number. He'd barely gotten a glimpse before the screen had gone dark, but he'd been trained to focus on details, so the number was forever ingrained in his memory.

If it wasn't the call that had upset Rachel, why would she lie about it? Perhaps he should dial the number and see who answered—or have his friend Jase find out who the number belonged to. Or maybe he should mind his own business—but hadn't he already decided to make Rachel's problem his business?

The same country tune broke the silence again, and Garrett reached automatically for her cell phone. The number was the same that had appeared only minutes ago. For an instant, he debated taking the phone to Rachel, but that would only end in the same result: She'd ignore the call. For agonizing seconds, he held the phone, staring at it, before he remembered his decision. Right or wrong, he couldn't help Rachel unless he knew what she was afraid of.

He stabbed the answer button. "Yeah." A vacuum of silence echoed eerily on the other end before Garrett detected a sound that indicated someone was there. "Hello. Who is this?"

"How about if I ask y'all the same thing. Did Rachel put you up to answering her phone?" The man's muffled voice dripped with scorn, delivered with a deep southern drawl.

"I'm a friend. Name's Garrett. Rachel isn't here right now, but I can tell her you called if you want to leave your name." He really wanted that name to give to Jase. It was likely the only way he'd find out why this guy had been able to turn Rachel's world upside down just now. And all of Garrett's instincts were on high alert. Something wasn't right here.

"I'm Jeremy. Rachel's my girl. So, as you might imagine, I'm more interested in who *you* are and why you're with her. Wait. Let me guess. Are you thinking you'll get her into your bed, *Garrett*? Uh-uh…it'll never happen. She knows better. I'd find you and kill you." His words were matter-of-fact.

Garrett bit back his angry reply as rage tore through him, leaving flecks of red in his field of vision. *Stalker*—had to be. Was this who Rachel was hiding from? The lunatic sounded deranged, yet just lucid enough to be dangerous. Jase would be able to find out who he was, and they'd put a stop to his harassing Rachel.

"What's the matter, Garrett? She didn't tell you about me, did she?" Jeremy grunted a laugh.

Garrett's jaw clenched so tightly it ached. "Why don't you tell me, Jeremy? Where did you two meet?"

"Garrett?"

He swung around at the desperation in Rachel's cry. She stood just behind him, dressed again in her skirt and sleeveless top, one hand on her stomach as though she was nauseous, with confusion and fear in her eyes.

"Uh-oh! You're fucking busted!" Jeremy's foul words echoed Garrett's own thoughts and were punctuated by contemptuous laughter just before the call abruptly ended.

Garrett lowered the phone and searched for the right explanation to erase the betrayal in Rachel's expression. None came.

She stepped toward him and jerked the phone from his grasp. "What did you do?" More accusation than question, it hung in the silence long after she'd turned and hurried from the cabin, leaving Garrett caught between guilt and good intentions.

Chapter Eight

RACHEL HIT THE ground beyond the steps at a full-out run, desperate to put distance between her and Garrett. She'd peered out from the bathroom, curious about whom he was talking to, but his back had been turned, and she'd seen the phone pressed to his ear—her phone. Still oblivious, she'd walked toward him. He evidently didn't hear her approach, but she'd heard him use Jeremy's name, and it had stopped her in her tracks.

Had Garrett picked up her phone and dialed the last number? *Who did that?* Her instant anger had given way to horror as the realization of what Jeremy might have said to him settled over her.

Garrett had finally turned when she'd forced his name from her dry throat. She'd ripped the phone from his hand, ignoring the shock and puzzlement in his gaze, and then, unable to face him, she'd run. That *was* what she did best, after all.

Having no idea where she was going, except away from Garrett's prying and questions, she ran past the Jeep, following the dirt road they'd driven in on. Sixty seconds later, she heard soft footfalls echoing her own and, from the corner of her eye, saw Cowboy running beside her.

Damn dog. "No. Go back, Cowboy." That's *all* she needed. Garrett would never leave her in peace if his dog insisted on following her. Behind them, the Jeep's engine fired to life and its tires crunched on the gravel.

Rachel stopped and grabbed Cowboy's collar, turned him around, and gave him a totally ineffectual shove back toward Garrett. Instead, the dog sat, leaning against her legs, and watched the approaching vehicle.

As soon as the Jeep came to a halt a few feet away and Garrett hopped out, Rachel started walking backward away from him. "Call your dog. He won't pay any attention to me when I tell him to go away."

Man and dog both trailed her now. "That's because I told him to stay with you. He'd die before he left your side." Garrett kept moving closer. "We need to talk, Rachel."

She shook her head. "Well, you're not exactly on my most-trusted list at the moment, and I don't care what you need. I can't deal with this right now, so that's not going to happen. Just go away."

Garrett glanced around the lonely forest pointedly. "I'm not leaving you—not here. Not after what happened yesterday and this morning. Let me take you home, and you can have some time, but we *are* going to talk about what happened back there."

Rachel snorted. "Maybe where you come from it's okay to snoop in other people's business, but we tend to frown on it around here. So, what you think is going to happen and what's really going to happen…are two very different things." She whirled around and started jogging again.

Garrett said something in a low voice that she didn't catch, and then Cowboy was suddenly right in front of her. She stumbled in her effort to avoid him, rolling with the fall the way Jonathan had taught her. Unhurt except for her pride, she sat up, casting a scowl at the dog, who appeared to be waiting for her to get to her feet and resume their game. Garrett stood over her, one hand extended to help her up, which she ignored with her best *drop dead* expression.

"You're right. I shouldn't have answered your phone, but I did. And now that I know there's a lunatic on the other end, I'm not walking away. I'll find out who he is with or without your help, but it makes more sense for us to work together on this. For what it's worth, I think we'd make a pretty good team. How long has this guy been harassing you? Don't you think it's time you confided in a friend?"

Rachel swept the hair out of her face with a dusty hand, too close to tears, and desperate not to let him see her fall apart. He made it sound so easy. Talk about it…work together…find Jeremy. If only it were that simple, but Garrett didn't know how dangerous Jeremy really was.

She couldn't be sure Jeremy actually knew where she was. If her hunch was wrong and the stranger at the lodge wasn't Jeremy, he could still be working for her stalker—looking for her. Either way, she wouldn't take the chance. Now more than ever, she had to put this place behind her. Leaving was the only way to guarantee he wouldn't come near the people she loved.

Garrett had inserted himself right in the middle of it. She had to warn him, yet if she did, he'd likely try to stop her from running. After she was safely gone, she'd find a way to send him a message. If he left—went back to California—this might all blow over. Her plan to somehow convince him to stay on for Peg's sake had just gone up in smoke, but she couldn't worry about that now. Her first priority was finding a new place to hide—a new life. A tear rimmed over her eyelashes and rolled down her face. Brushing it away with a dirt-covered finger, she focused on Garrett.

He still stood with an outstretched hand, one brow raised in question, a smile of assurance, and eyes filled with sincerity. His obvious belief in her and his promise to help made her feel even worse...if that was possible.

She reached for his hand and let him pull her up. "Okay. You promised me some time, but after that I'll tell you everything you need to know about Jeremy." Stepping around him, she tried to remove her hand from his, but he held on and turned with her toward the Jeep.

He smiled slightly. "That's great. You made the right decision. You won't be sorry, Rachel." He opened her door. "Can we talk later? After dinner tonight?"

"Peg asked me to do some letters confirming reservations tonight. She prefers everything the old-fashioned way. Hand typed and personalized. No electronic reservation system or group e-mails for us. It might be a late night. How about in the morning? I'll come to your room. That way no one will interrupt us." Guilt hit her hard, and she forced a smile. She hated lying to him, knowing that she would be long gone in the morning when he expected her. Still, the comical way his brow hitched upward when she mentioned his room tugged strangely at her heart.

"Sure. That works." Garrett circled the front of the Jeep.

As soon as he opened his door, Cowboy jumped in and, if it was possible for a dog to look shamefaced, this one did. Rachel laughed and scratched his scruff. "It's okay, boy. I know it wasn't *your* fault."

The dog pushed past her for the backseat while Garrett climbed in. He dug a white towel from the console between them and turned toward her. "I'm sorry, too, and I don't want you to forget what a good day we've had." He took her hand and pulled her toward him, gently wiping the dirt from fingers to elbows before kissing her lips tenderly. When he was done, he winked and handed her the towel. "You can probably do a better job than I did."

This time, Rachel's smile was real. How did he do that? Make her forget who he was—who she was? Cause her to believe that she could have a normal life for more than just a little while? She'd been lucky. Ten years in one place was more than she could have hoped for. It was bittersweet though. With time to foster genuine relationships, now it would be that much harder to let them go.

But Garrett? He'd dropped into her life yesterday. Before that he'd been only a fixation—one that she'd despised. She shouldn't have any regrets about saying good-bye to him. Yet, in some unexplainable way, she did, which was all the more reason she had to leave. She couldn't be responsible for what would happen to him if she didn't.

"Hey." He gently stroked her hand where it twisted around the towel in her lap. "Relax. Why don't you give me the rest of my tour?"

Rachel's gaze swept to the mountain road and the dense forest outside the windows. A smile pulled at her lips, and she filled her lungs with the clean pine-scented air, grateful beyond words for something else to concentrate on.

EVEN WITH HER talking nonstop, visiting every scenic vantage point and describing every historical reference along the way, the trip back to the lodge had ended too soon.

Garrett, with Cowboy bringing up the rear, walked her to her room. When they stopped at the door, he turned her toward him. "I had a great time. Thank you for a wonderful day." His gaze was so intense it sent a shiver up her spine.

"My pleasure. I had fun." Rachel amazed herself with her confession.

Garrett's brow hitched upward. "Yeah? So, tell me, if we were still working on our original two-day deal, would you be sending me home?"

"Hell yes." She had to hide a smile as she met his eyes.

"What?" Garrett laughed. "I don't believe you." He stepped into her, pushing her against the door.

She held her breath as his gaze burned into hers. He leaned toward her in painful slow motion until the breath of his lips warmed hers. When he finally covered her mouth, it wasn't with the same gentleness as earlier in the day. Heat radiated between them as the need in his kiss became obvious, and she responded to his demand to open her lips.

He slowly and thoroughly plundered her mouth, tasting, exploring, his tongue tangling with hers. Rachel's legs grew shaky as though they'd melt right out from under her, and she grasped his shoulders to hold herself up. His hands dropped to her hips and pulled her against him, and his erection pressed into her, long and hard. Her eyes flew open and searched his.

Immediately, he released her and stepped back. His eyes were almost black, and a sheepish grin lifted one corner of his mouth. "Guess it's no secret what you do to me."

Rachel struggled with a need that clearly matched his, but rather than give in to the foolish idea of pulling him inside her room, she stepped around him and reached for her doorknob. "Whatever this attraction is between us, Garrett, nothing can come of it."

"Why not? Because of Amanda? I thought we'd made some progress on that today." Garrett reached for her hand and held it close to his chest.

She trembled with the effort not to lean into him. "We're at the same train station, Garrett, but you're getting on and I'm just seeing you off. Ships passing and all that. There's nowhere for us to go with this. It doesn't matter if you leave in two days or two weeks, the point is you're not staying. Your life is elsewhere. I suppose you're used to having a girl in each port, but I'm not that girl. I'm also not prepared to have my heart broken." As lame as that no doubt sounded, she couldn't tell him the real reason. In less than twelve hours, she'd be gone, and it wouldn't do either of them any good to stir the embers of a fire that was about to be smothered.

"Do you distrust all men this much, or is it just me?" He shook his head, a shadow of sadness passing momentarily over his expression. "Frankly, it's insulting for you to think casual, meaningless sex is my MO. If it was, you'd know that already. And I've had my heart broken too, so trust me when I say I don't want that to happen to you." His thumb stroked across her knuckles.

It was clear he was talking about his mother. Rachel had always thought of what happened to Amanda as her losing her family because of events that were out of her control. It was obvious Garrett viewed it as his mother abandoning him. Maybe a little of both was true, but she wanted to slap herself for reminding him yet again. Rachel rested her forehead against her fingertips for a second before meeting his gaze. "You're right. That was out of line, and I'm sorry. But there's no time for this to go anywhere."

"Because you think I'm leaving right away?"

Rachel dropped her gaze. "Well, aren't you?" *Careful. Don't give yourself away.*

"You asked me to stay until we figured out who the intruder at the lodge was, and I agreed. I also plan to hang around until we identify and put a stop to your stalker. Even then there's nothing back home waiting for me. My military career is all but over. Signing the discharge papers will be the next step. Maybe this place that my mother helped to build is where I belong for a while. Maybe I want to get to know *you* better." He closed the small gap between them.

Garrett leaned toward her as though to kiss her, his breath caressing her ear, but then his hand covered hers on the knob, turned it, and pushed her door open. "I'm not going to rush you, though. We'll go as slow as you want." He winked and a crooked grin made her insides do a flip. "Hell, it's only been twenty-four hours and already you've gone from hating me to tolerating me."

Rachel laughed in spite of herself. "Yeah...not because you haven't tried to piss me off."

A smile tipped one corner of his mouth even as anger brewed deep in his eyes. "I said I was sorry about answering your phone...but I'm not. We're going to get this sick son of a bitch, Rach. He won't bother you again."

Rachel forced herself to smile. Garrett really believed he could make that happen. Maybe he could, but she wasn't willing to take the chance. It was Garrett who would ultimately suffer if he was wrong.

She stepped across the threshold. "I have to change and go help Dory with dinner."

"And I have to find Peg and explain why we didn't tell the sheriff about our intruder. How angry do you think she'll be with me?"

A slight smile escaped though she'd tried to be serious. "I wouldn't worry. I think you're her favorite."

Garrett grinned, an endearing blush coloring his cheeks. "Good to know. I've never been anyone's favorite before."

The image of him as a little boy, growing up without a mother in what Rachel could only assume was a cold and unfriendly environment, wrenched at her heart. She struggled to keep all of the emotions invoked by her musing from parading across her face.

His gaze locked on hers and dropped to her lips for a heart-stopping moment. "Save me a seat at dinner, will you?" He turned to go before she could answer.

Rachel closed the door and leaned against it as his footsteps faded. How had she let him get to her? He was so disarmingly sexy, his lips like a drug she couldn't do without. *No excuse.* She couldn't afford to get close to anyone, least of all Garrett Harding.

She stripped off her dusty clothes and stood under the shower only long enough to rinse herself off. After dressing in a clean denim skirt and burgundy knit top, she headed down to the kitchen.

Dory was making her own recipe of French chicken tonight, and she recruited Rachel to chop potatoes, onions, and green peppers. When everything was ready, they carried the two main dishes, along with a veggie salad and fresh, homemade rolls to the dining room table.

The Taylors had made reservations to stay through the early bear hunt, which started next week, and they were chatting animatedly with Peg and Garrett. Same as last night, the only seat left open was between him and Jonathan, but she stepped around the table without hesitation. Funny how her opinions had changed literally overnight.

She searched Garrett's face as he stood to pull out her chair. "Did you tell her?" Her voice was low and meant only for him.

He nodded indiscernibly and leaned closer to her ear. "You were right. I *must* be the favorite. They're a little upset with you, though." He chuckled as he pushed her chair in and took his seat.

Rachel wanted to laugh in the worst way—to shake off the pall of gloom and anxiousness that dogged her steps and really enjoy herself. It had been a while since she'd felt that free, probably not since Amanda died. It was Garrett who'd given her something to smile about—something to look forward to…if she were staying. As quickly as the realization came, an ache settled in her chest. He was forbidden. His smile, his touch, his kiss…as dangerous as they were enticing.

She knew what she had to do. Her plan was set. In a few hours it wouldn't matter one way or another. If she could just get through this dinner. Choke down this food. Forget that Jonathan would be hurt by her sudden disappearance. That Peg would no doubt blame herself.

And Garrett? The man with the easy laugh, scruffy good looks, and hard, muscled body that begged to be touched—what would *he* do? She'd wanted him to stay and help Peg, but under the circumstances, he would be much safer if he hightailed it back to California and counted himself lucky that there hadn't been anything here to hold him.

Rachel forced herself to join in the conversation that Alan and Linda were having with Garrett. Not that she knew much about cattle ranching and raising hay, but that's what she loved about these dinners—learning about other people's lives beyond Cougar Ridge. Now that she was moving on, maybe some of the information she'd gleaned over the years would come in handy.

"Say, I heard there was some excitement around here this morning. Someone trying to break in or something?" Alan grinned, obviously pleased with the gossip and its effect on the group around the table.

Peg choked on a bite of food and raised her napkin to her mouth, darting a glance toward Jonathan. She couldn't have looked guiltier if she'd tried. Jonathan, usually calm, cool, and professional, pushed his plate back and offered a dark scowl that no doubt would have silenced anyone who didn't already know what a soft-hearted tough guy he was.

Rachel swallowed a lump in her throat and concentrated on Alan Taylor's curious expression instead of the dread that the memory evoked. "Nothing so dire, I assure you. Probably just one of the area residents cutting through the property on their way back to town."

"But I heard he ran. Why would he run unless he was up to no good?" Alan's brow furrowed in confusion and, possibly, regret that there wasn't more excitement to the story.

Garrett leaned forward, resting on his elbows, his arm brushing against hers. "I understand there's quite a lot of poaching in these mountains. Our visitor probably *did* have something to hide, but I doubt the lodge was the target of his misconduct."

Rachel glanced at him and, as their eyes met, something subtle passed between them. Earlier, he'd told her he thought they'd make a good team. She hadn't realized their first collaboration would involve lying to a guest.

"I hadn't thought of that. You're probably right." Disappointment was obvious in Alan's expression for the space of a heartbeat, and then his familiar teasing grin appeared. He turned to his wife. "That'll teach us to listen to gossip at the diner, honey."

"You heard someone talking about our trespasser in town today?" Garrett studied Alan, obviously paying closer attention.

She sensed Jonathan bristling on her other side, too. With good reason. No one but the three of them and Peg knew about the incident. She and Garrett had left town without filing a police report today. The only other person who could know was the intruder himself. An involuntary shiver cascaded through her.

Garrett leaned back and dropped his arm beneath the tabletop, finding her hand where it rested in her lap. He squeezed it lightly, and the warmth of his touch grounded her.

"Yes. We were having lunch. I stepped up to the counter for some mustard and overheard a couple of guys talking. They looked like locals, but I'd never seen them before. Had you, honey?" Alan draped his arm around Linda's shoulders.

"I didn't really get a good look at them, dear." Linda smiled apologetically.

"No reason to worry. I'm sure Garrett and Rachel are correct in their assessment." Peg patted Linda's hand reassuringly. "I'll impose upon Jonathan and Garrett to have a look around before they turn in tonight. We've never had any trouble here, but we do have an alarm system that we could set after everyone goes to bed if that would make you feel safer."

"No, no. We're perfectly comfortable with the way things have been. You've always taken good care of us." Alan raised his glass in a toast to Peg.

Rachel's heart pounded with a new worry. What if Jonathan and Garrett stood watch tonight? What if she couldn't slip away unseen? She was still fretting over the possibility when the Taylors said goodnight and took their unfinished wine with them to their room.

Peg barely waited for their guests to hit the stairs. "Garrett, in light of this new information, are you sure it wouldn't be wise to file a report with the sheriff?"

"The sheriff and I didn't exactly get off on the right foot, Aunt Peg. I don't think he's going to care about anything I have to say. Maybe you or Jonathan could speak with him the next time you're in town?"

A smile slowly worked across Peg's features. "So much like your mother."

Garrett's visage brightened. "Really? How so?"

"Amanda was forever forming first impressions about new people from which she'd decide whether they could be trusted or not."

Garrett laughed softly. "Yeah? How'd that work for her?"

"She was never wrong," Peg said.

"That's a good thing, right?" Garrett cocked an eyebrow.

Peg nodded and pushed her chair back. "That's a very good thing."

Rachel shoved her chair out and stood as soon as Peg and Jonathan headed for the door. "I'm going to help Dory with the dishes and then go to the office."

Garrett stood and placed a hand on her arm. "Are you sure I can't help? I'm a mean typist."

Dread lay heavy in her stomach. "Thanks, but no need. It'll actually go faster on my own."

"Have it your way. I'll have a look around outside before I turn in tonight."

"Maybe it's not necessary. It could really have been one of the locals." She searched his face hopefully.

Garrett stepped toward her and cupped her jaw, one thumb tracing her lower lip. "It wasn't. We both know that. Anyway, it won't hurt to have a look around. Would a goodnight kiss be out of the question?"

"Suddenly you're asking?" Rachel raised her eyebrows, then tensed with anticipation as the warmth of his breath on the side of her face turned her legs to rubber.

A soft brush of his lips on hers and a quick kiss on her cheek was all she got, but it was enough to start her heart beating erratically. When he straightened in front of her again, he grinned as though he knew he was leaving her wanting more.

"My room, in the morning. Don't forget, or I'll come looking for you." He winked and strode away.

Rachel's heartbeat reverberated in her ears. He could look for her all he wanted. He wouldn't find her. That thought initiated a pain in her chest and made it hard to breathe. She shook her head. It wasn't important. She had dishes to do and a phone call to make. Then she would go to the office long enough to finish the letters she'd promised to send out welcoming the guests who'd made reservations for the season. It wouldn't take as long as she'd led Garrett to believe.

Then she would pack…a few belongings. Not much would fit in one bag, but she didn't have a lot. It had always been in the back of her mind that she'd have to run again so she hadn't accumulated material things. The nearly eight thousand dollars she'd saved was more critical.

She went through the motions, doing her chores, saying goodnight to Dory and Jonathan before she climbed the stairs to her room. Pretending that it wasn't the last time she'd ever see her friends was the hardest thing she'd ever done, but there was no other way to make it through this. Once alone, the first thing she did was call Sally. Her friend was the only person who knew the whole story about Jeremy, and there'd never been a doubt in Rachel's mind that Sally would help her disappear, no questions asked, and keep her whereabouts quiet. She was that kind of friend. Rachel was going to miss her like crazy.

"Rachel? I'm so glad you called, but it's kind of late. Is everything all right?" Sally's bubbly greeting slowly faded to worry.

Rachel glanced at her bedside clock, wishing she could reassure Sally, but her friend knew her too well. Rachel would normally never call her after 10:00 p.m., knowing that Sally's daughter, Jen, would likely be sleeping. "I need your help, Sally, and you can't tell anyone."

Heavy silence stretched into seconds. Finally Sally sighed. "What do you need, Rach?"

"It's time for me to move on. I need you to pick me up by the lodge sign on the highway. If anyone comes looking for me after I'm gone you have to tell them you haven't seen me in weeks. Can I stay at your house tonight?"

"Of course, but where are you going?"

"I can't tell you, hon. You'll be safer if you don't know." The silence again, but Rachel pushed on. "Can you be here by midnight?"

"Sure. I'll arrange for Jen to stay with one of her friends," Sally said.

"That's a good idea. I can't thank you enough."

"You don't have to. You know that. I'll be there at midnight."

Rachel held on to the phone long after her friend was gone, wishing things could be different. As the silence settled around her, the immensity of what she was doing crashed over her, leaving her breathless and vacant except for a lump as hard as stone in her chest.

Leaving without saying good-bye to Peg would be devastating…for both of them. She tried to keep herself busy, not willing to give in to self-pity. There'd no doubt be plenty of time for such pursuits later.

Forcing her sadness to the back of her mind, she jerked her satchel off the top shelf of the closet and opened it on the bed. Just one pair of shoes and a few clothes followed by her favorite picture of her with Peg, Amanda, and Jonathan two summers ago on the dock at the cabin nearly filled the bag. Lastly, she took a shoebox from the very back of one of her drawers. Inside was the .38 special she'd bought before leaving Texas along with a handful of extra shells. She'd been so embarrassed when Jonathan had found the gun helping her move in. Somehow he'd known that she hadn't had a clue about guns, and he'd shamed her into learning how to use one. As she loaded the cylinder, pocketed the remaining ammunition, and laid the weapon on the top of her clothes, she was immensely glad he had.

Finally, she retrieved a sheet of stationery from her desk drawer and sat stiffly, penning the hardest words she'd ever had to write. She meant it to be for all of them, but upon rereading, it sounded as though she was talking to Garrett. Damn him for getting inside her head and messing with her preconceived ideas. She'd have been better off if she'd continued to hate him. Now, she would miss him and always wonder what might have been.

But nothing could ever have come from her association with Garrett. As long as Jeremy was alive, the danger was very real that Garrett would end up dead if she let herself get too close. And it would be her fault because...*hadn't she been warned?*

She glanced at her watch again. A deep breath came hard as the minutes ticked by. If she hesitated now, she'd never leave. She slipped into a dark-colored jacket, slung her bag over her shoulder, tiptoed down the stairs, and slipped out of the lodge.

A full moon illuminated her path as she followed the gravel road across the bridge, through the meadow, and down the drive. She'd never been afraid walking in these woods, but tonight the shadows swayed with an eerie presence, and the hairs prickled along the back of her neck as she glanced over her shoulder at every sound. Her hand rested on the .38 special at the top of her bag, and she kept walking.

Ten minutes later as she neared the highway, she heard a car's engine. It was nearly midnight, and the narrow mountain roads didn't see much traffic after dark, but she stepped into the shadow of the trees anyway. It would be best if no one saw her leave. She couldn't take a chance that someone would mention to Peg or Jonathan that they'd seen her—not until she was far away.

As soon as she recognized the old gray Ford Explorer, Rachel stepped back onto the roadway, into the light from the oncoming vehicle.

The Explorer came to a stop and the front passenger door opened. Rachel strode forward, deposited her bag on the floorboard, and slid into the front seat opposite a petite brunette who studied her rearview mirror before glancing over.

Rachel leaned toward her, giving her the briefest of hugs. "Thanks for coming, Sally."

The woman behind the wheel looked Rachel over, misgivings apparent in her expression. "You call...I come, but are you sure about this, sweetie?"

Rachel shook her head. "I don't have a choice, Sal. I think Jeremy may know where I am. If I don't leave, a man I only met yesterday will end up dead, and I'm not going to let it happen this time."

Chapter Nine

FRUSTRATION PROPELLED GARRETT down the stairs, the lavender-colored envelope and sheet of paper half-crumpled in his fist. *Damn stubborn woman!* Rachel owed him an explanation—one he needed if he was going to figure out why that Jeremy character scared the shit out of her. She'd agreed to come to his room this morning. When she didn't show by 8:00 a.m., he'd gone looking for her and found the note in her room. *Her good-bye note!* Why couldn't she see that she was safer here than out there…alone?

An irritated grumble escaped in spite of his efforts to rein in his simmering temper.

As Garrett's feet hit the landing halfway between the lobby desk and the front door, he glanced around. "Jonathan?" Where was everybody? Faint voices drifted in from the dining area, and he scrunched the lavender paper tighter as he started that way.

Without warning, the lodge door swung open. A tall, broad-shouldered hulk of a man with dark brown hair, cut military short, stepped across the threshold. His ready smile crinkled his boy-next-door face and revealed matching dimples that he'd been teased about unmercifully all of his life. Garrett skidded to a stop.

"Luke!" He never could set eyes on his younger brother's happy-go-lucky mug without giving up a grin of his own, no matter how black his mood.

"Hey, bro. Don't look so surprised. You told me to haul ass." Luke cocked his head. "Here I am."

Garrett closed the distance between them and grasped Luke's outstretched hand, then pulled him in for a hug. Damn, it was good to see him.

Releasing him, Garrett stepped back. "You're just in time. I'm going to need your help." He ignored the quizzical expression he received in return and resumed his march toward the dining area as Luke fell in beside him.

They no doubt seemed a formidable pair, filling the doorway, because Jonathan and Aunt Peg both rose and stared at them. The Taylors weren't in attendance yet, which Garrett was thankful for. The fewer people present the better when he demanded Aunt Peg tell him what the hell was going on. Before he could say anything, though, she emitted a small gasp, and her hand flew to her throat.

"Luke?" She glanced at Garrett. "This *is* Luke, isn't it?" Her gaze flitted back to his brother as her shoulders slumped, and she grabbed for the edge of the table, her eyes rolling back in her head. Garrett leaped forward,

Luke close behind him, but it was Jonathan who caught her before she hit the floor.

With a black scowl drawing his brows into one, he scooped her into his arms, carried her out the door and up the stairs to her room, leaving Garrett and Luke nothing to do but follow. Jonathan laid her gently on the handmade quilt that covered her bed and rounded on Luke with contempt in his eyes.

"Well, you Harding boys are living up to your fucking reputation today, aren't you? First him," he said, jerking a thumb toward Garrett, "now you. Have you *ever* given a thought to another human being in your fucking life? Spoiled…thoughtless rich kids…it's all about *you*, isn't it?"

Luke threw up his hands and backed away from the fury that radiated from Jonathan as he moved ever closer, but Garrett knew his little brother would only back so far before his training and his natural inclination to defend himself kicked in. Garrett had seen people try to bully Luke before, fooled by his easygoing nature and those damn dimples. That meant Garrett had about ten seconds to restore order before all hell broke loose. Remembering the paper in his hand, he held it up and stepped in front of Luke.

"Jonathan, I understand how much you care about Aunt Peg, but you're overreacting. You need to get a grip. Neither of us knew she would respond by fainting, least of all Luke. Let's make sure she's okay, and then we need to find Rachel." Garrett extended the lavender paper toward him and saw him flinch for the first time, as though coming back from somewhere far away.

His gaze pierced Garrett's and dropped slowly to the paper before any cognizance appeared in his eyes. "What do you mean—find Rachel?"

Rustling from the bed behind him seemed to indicate that Aunt Peg was regaining consciousness, and Luke skirted around both of them to reach her side. She'd pushed up on her elbow, so Luke pressed her back down gently and knelt beside the bed.

"You must be the Aunt Peg my big brother said he'd found. I don't remember you, but I'm pleased to finally meet you." Luke took her hand between his.

Jonathan whirled around, watched the two for a heart-beat, then started toward them. Garrett grabbed his arm, hoping that this confrontation wouldn't come to blows right here in Aunt Peg's room. Jonathan stopped, but if the glint of warning he turned on Garrett was any indication, no danger would ever get close enough to touch her if he had anything to say on the matter.

Couldn't hold that against the man. Didn't Garrett feel the same sense of responsibility toward Rachel? "Aunt Peg, I dropped in out of the blue on you day before yesterday, and then Luke blasted in today with no warning. Jonathan was right—I showed no consideration for you, and I'm sorry." Garrett included Jonathan in his apology and received a curt nod in return.

"I'm sorry too, Aunt Peg." Luke added his charismatic smile to the moment as he brought her fingers to his lips.

Aunt Peg leaned toward him, sliding her fingers free so she could hold his face in her hands as she studied him, a soft smile relaxing her face. "Your mother always said you were a charmer."

Garrett again pushed the paper toward Jonathan. "Rachel's gone. I found this note in her room."

"What?" Another gasp from Aunt Peg and a frown from Jonathan made Garrett wish he'd taken this outside the room. On the other hand, she might know something that could help him find Rachel.

Shit! Was he overstepping his bounds? Without conscious thought, he'd taken on the task of finding her. He'd met her only two days ago. If she wanted to move on…who was he to say she was making a mistake? Yet he couldn't rid himself of the niggling sensation that she hadn't run solely because of that asshole Jeremy, but rather because Garrett had answered her phone and spoken to the bastard. That's what had put the dread in Rachel's eyes—almost as if she was afraid of *him*.

That was unacceptable. Hell yes, he'd find her and convince her that she *could* trust him, and he'd use everybody in this room, and then some, to help him do just that.

"Okay, Aunt Peg. You can sit up, but let's take this one step at a time. We don't want you fainting on us again." Luke stood as she swung her feet to the floor.

She focused on Garrett. "How do you know Rachel left?"

"We were supposed to meet this morning. When she didn't come, I went to her room. I found this note addressed to all of us." He motioned to the note clutched in Jonathan's hand.

"What does the note say?" Her strained whisper told Garrett she'd just asked a question she didn't really want the answer to.

Damn, he wished he didn't have to be the one to break her heart. He stepped to Luke's side, took Aunt Peg's hand in his, and helped her up on unsteady legs. "She said the years she spent here were the happiest of her life. That she considers you all her family. She'd hoped her past would never catch up with her here, but after yesterday, she thinks it might have. If that's the case, to stay would place you all in danger, and she won't allow that to happen."

Jonathan cleared his throat before he started to read aloud. *"I'll miss you all like crazy. Please don't try to find me. I can't come back."* He lowered the hand that held the note and let it fall to the floor.

Tears shimmered in Aunt Peg's eyes as she looked up at Garrett. "What happened yesterday?"

The steadfastness in the woman's expression told him she wasn't going to let him off the hook, so he dived in. "Well, there was the trespasser yesterday morning. She didn't seem that bothered by the incident. But…Riley and his two brothers met us out in front of the sheriff's office, and Riley said something to her that I didn't catch. Whatever it was, it hit home. I could tell she wasn't quite the same after that. Then on the way home, she offered to show me the cabin where you and my mother lived when you first came here." Garrett allowed himself to relive the moment when he kissed her, the feel of her lips on his, and her body trembling under his touch…until her phone rang.

"She got a call that she didn't answer, but it put that same scared look in her eyes." Garrett shrugged. "So, when Rachel was in the bathroom, and the phone rang again with the same number on the screen...I answered it. It was some guy named Jeremy. He's evidently been stalking her for God knows how long, and he's not above issuing threats of violence. Rachel clearly has reason to believe he'll make good on those threats. She had a melt-down when she saw what I'd done."

Aunt Peg's wistful smile instantly made him feel guilty. "Well, you *did* invade her privacy, dear. But why wouldn't she confide in us?" She glanced at Jonathan, then turned to face him. "Did you know anything about this?"

He straightened and shrugged his massive shoulders. "She told me that someone was looking for her, and that if he ever showed up here she'd have to find a new place to hide. I pressed her for details, but she wouldn't budge on that. Said I'd be in danger if I stuck my nose in. So I taught her how to use that old revolver she always carried and made up some warning signals that she could use if she was ever in trouble, and that seemed to make her feel safer...up to now."

"Do either of you know where she might go?" Garrett looked back and forth between them.

Jonathan shook his head. "Not for the long term, but I don't think Rachel would leave the area without saying good-bye to Sally Duncan and her daughter, Jen. It's any-one's guess how long she'll be there, but I'm betting she'll make a stop in Huntington—twenty miles to the north."

Garrett nudged Luke's arm. "I'm taking off as soon as I get my dog from my room."

"I'm going with you," Luke said.

Jonathan started from the room. "Somebody has to show you city boys how to find the place."

Garrett sought Aunt Peg's chocolate-brown eyes and found the corners of her mouth turned up in a weak smile. With a huff, she pulled her hand from his grasp. "If it's me you're worried about—don't. I've been taking care of myself for a while now. Dory is here, as well as two groundskeepers and a river guide. I think even the Taylors will be here most of the day. Besides, I've got my old Winchester behind the counter." She wagged her finger at him and Luke. "You just find Rachel and bring her home."

Five minutes later, Garrett, with Cowboy by his side, met Luke and Jonathan in the parking area. After some discussion, they decided to take Luke's rental, a nearly new Chevy Tahoe, which would afford them more room than Garrett's Jeep. Jonathan rode shotgun with Luke since he supposedly knew a shortcut, and Garrett and Cowboy spread out in the backseat.

The sun shone brightly, the brilliant blue of the sky tempered by thin wispy clouds. The temperature was already in the seventies with the sunrise only a couple of hours old. The pristine air rolled through the open window Cowboy's head was stuck through, whipping Garrett's short hair onto his forehead.

The Tahoe lurched to the left suddenly, and Cowboy slammed into Garrett's chest before he caught his balance. Garrett glanced through the windshield at the road up ahead. Actually, *road* was a fairly optimistic term for the one-lane, overgrown trail they followed, chiseled from the side of a cliff. Luke apparently had the pedal to the floor as they barreled along with a river on their right.

As his head turned to take in the river, Garrett could see Luke was enjoying himself. Pushing the envelope was what his little brother did best. He thrived on it—just as Garrett had before he was wounded.

He was glad to see that Luke and Jonathan were talking. Between the engine and the airflow, he couldn't hear what they were saying, but they both seemed relaxed and amiable. That was good. It would've hurt Aunt Peg if there was bad blood between them.

Damn, he hoped Jonathan was right about Rachel going to see her friend, and that she was still there. If they missed her, he'd likely never see her again. Something clenched in his chest as the possibility took root. *What the hell?* His concern for the shapely redhead seemed inflated considering he'd known her not quite two days and most of that time they'd spent sniping at each other. Nonetheless, there it was. She'd gotten under his skin, and now he itched for want of her.

This was a good place. He'd felt more at home here than he had anywhere for a very long time. He could start over here—maybe start a family. That thought immediately brought Rachel back to the forefront. Why he cared was anyone's guess. So far she'd kicked him out of her bar, told him she despised him and wanted him out of Peg's life, and then lied to him. She'd never intended to explain who and what Jeremy was to her. Her delaying tactic was just that—until she could get out of town and never have to face him again.

Garrett wasn't going to let her out of his sight again until she told him what the hell was going on, even if it meant staying with her 24/7. Except that scenario brought up images of a totally different kind, and the tightening in his groin warned him to think of a safer topic—such as finding her.

A few minutes later, the vehicle slowed, and Garrett reached to steady Cowboy before he lost his footing again. When he glanced out the front, they were on a paved street surrounded by small, older, well-kept houses. Garrett sat forward in time to hear Jonathan instruct Luke to make a right turn. Another right, then a left, and Luke pulled the Tahoe to the curb beside a yellow two-story home with a big front lawn and a stereotypical white picket fence.

Jonathan pointed to an older, run-down, concrete-block house across the street. "That's Sally's place."

No fence. That was good. No trees, either. Not so good. Nothing to hide their approach and keep Rachel from dashing for the back door as soon as she caught sight of them. "Cowboy and I will take the back. Give me two or three minutes. Then knock on the front door."

Luke raised one brow. "You think she'll run?"

"Hell yeah." Garrett and Jonathan answered at the same time.

Garrett released the dog from the right side and slid out behind him. After closing the door silently, he tapped his leg and Cowboy fell in beside him. They moved as one away from the rear of the car until Garrett judged that they'd no longer be seen by anyone who happened to glance from Sally's windows. He ducked between two homes and came out near an alley one house-length away from Sally's back door. Crouching low, more from habit than any illusion that he could remain unseen, he raced across the open grass. Cowboy kept stride with him as they ran, circling and sitting when Garrett reached his goal and pressed his back up against the side of the house. Cautiously, he peered around the corner at the back steps leading to a small covered porch and a door.

It was quiet inside the house. Was anyone even home? They'd know in a minute, because Luke and Jonathan were walking across the street, heading for the front door. A few seconds later, the knock echoed through the entire house, and abruptly Garrett heard muffled voices followed by running footsteps.

Seconds later, the back door flew open, and Cowboy came to his feet, growling low in his throat. Garrett signaled him to stand down and the dog sat on his haunches, his ears and hackles saying he was still ready to go. Garrett looked around the side again. Clearly ready to bolt, Rachel stood on the porch carrying a small satchel, her pretty red hair an attractive mess, obviously listening to voices that he couldn't hear. He pulled back as she looked both ways, vaulted the handrail closest to him, and hit the ground running directly for the corner of the house where he hid.

Cowboy whined at the sound of her hurried approach. Pressed tight to the wall, Garrett waited. As she burst from cover, looking over her right shoulder and away from him, he stepped toward her. Catching her around the middle, he swung her off her feet and up against his body, holding her tightly with both arms. "It's me, Rach. Take it easy. I just want to talk."

She stopped struggling, so he loosened his hold as he set her back on her feet. Mistake number one. She dug her fingernails into his forearm, scratching until she drew blood. As soon as he leaned over her shoulder to grab her hand, she whacked his jaw with the back of her head, hard enough to send him stumbling back a step. He shook his head to clear the stars in time to see her swing that black bag.

"Wait a minute, Rachel!" Garrett tried to duck, but her shorter height gave her the advantage. She caught him across the side of the head, and there was apparently something heavy and damn hard in her bag. He staggered, lost his balance, and went down.

She looked surprised for a second before determination steeled her expression. "I told you not to look for me. What didn't you understand about that?" Shifting her bag onto her shoulder, she turned, and started running down the alley.

"Well, shit." Garrett glanced at Cowboy and damned it if didn't look as if he was laughing. "Okay, already. You were right. Saddle up, Cowboy."

The dog took off, his long strides closing the distance to Rachel's retreating back easily. Garrett stood, brushing the dirt off and taking a moment to stretch the ache from the wound in his back. Then he jogged after the girl and the dog. He'd seriously underestimated Rachel today.

Cowboy had his instructions to stop her, but keeping her there would require a whole different set of commands—ones that Garrett would never utter where Rachel was concerned.

Ahead of him, the dog ran circles around her, making the circle smaller each time. When she finally stopped, keeping a wary eye on the animal, Cowboy dropped to a walk, his tail wagging as he angled toward her. Though she didn't move, her body, tense and ready, said she was on high alert. Garrett picked up his pace to reach them.

Rachel looked over her shoulder, obviously noted the diminishing distance between them, and grabbed for her satchel. The next thing he knew, the damn hard object she'd hit him with—a small revolver—was in her hand and she was pointing it at Cowboy.

"You need to stay where you are, Garrett, and call your dog or…I'll shoot him."

"Cowboy, chill." The dog dropped to the ground, watching Garrett carefully. "This is what it's come to then? You want to get away from me so bad you're willing to shoot my dog?"

She shook her head dejectedly. "That's not what I want, but I will if I have to."

"I don't believe you, Rach. That dog's just following orders. My orders. Shoot me if you want to hurt somebody." Garrett moved a few steps closer.

Rachel laughed scornfully. "Did you miss the part where I tried to leave without anybody getting hurt?"

"No. I get that you're worried about Peg, Jonathan, and the rest of the people at the lodge, but damn it, Rachel, they love you. They want to understand. They want to help if they can, because that's what people do when they love someone. They don't sneak off in the night, leaving their *family* to wonder what happened."

"I can't—" She lowered the weapon until her hand hung at her side. Her eyes closed for a second, then she sat abruptly amid the grass that bordered the alley.

Garrett walked up to her and knelt down. Prying the gun from her fingers, he placed it back in her bag and zipped it up. "Yes, you can. I'll help you." He tilted her chin up so he could see the sheen of her expressive green eyes. "Give me a chance, Rachel. What have you got to lose?"

She jerked her chin from his fingers and averted her eyes. "It's never been about me."

"You promised me an explanation, remember? If you can convince me and your friends in there that the best course of action is for you to leave, I'll help you disappear. Deal?"

She threw her hands in the air and scowled. "Do I have a choice?"

He stood and caught sight of Cowboy, waiting patiently. Rachel would never have hurt him. She was simply at the end of her rope. She did, however, deserve a lesson.

Stepping aside, he motioned for the dog. "Cowboy, kill."

Cowboy leaped toward Rachel, wiggling and wagging like a pup, while he covered her face with doggy saliva.

She squeaked in protest and tried to protect her face with her hands, to no avail. Finally, she gave up and laughed, throwing her arms around Cowboy, and hugged him close. Grudging humor mixed with uncertainty in her eyes, as she tilted her head and looked up at him. "I owe you big-time for this."

He scooped up her bag and reached out a hand to help her. "Good. Stick around and there'll be plenty of time to get even."

She accepted his hand and rose gracefully to her feet. "Kill, huh? Does he really have a command for that?"

"I'm afraid so."

She raised an eyebrow. "What is it?"

Garrett moved his hand to the small of her back and turned toward the house. The warmth of her body so close to his sent a surge of desire through him. Barely resisting the urge to pull her against his side and wrap his arm around her trim waist, he had to think hard for a moment to remember her question. When he did, a grin pulled at the corners of his mouth. "That's classified, sweetheart."

Chapter Ten

JONATHAN HAD GREETED her with distrust. Sally looked as though she'd like to crawl in a hole somewhere and pretend this wasn't happening in her safe little home in Huntington. Who could blame her? Thank God Jen had spent the night with one of her friends.

Luke Harding was charming to a fault, and Rachel liked him right away, but it was obvious that he'd vote with his big brother if it came to that. True to his promise, Garrett stayed protectively by her side, encouraging her with a look, a touch, or one of his silly winks. Rachel, Luke, and Jonathan took seats around the kitchen table while Sally made fresh coffee, poured five cups, and handed them out. Garrett pulled up a chair next to Rachel's, and everyone else became quiet, apparently waiting for him to start the show.

He smiled reassuringly. "Who is this Jeremy?"

Great! The worst possible question first. "I don't know. It could be anyone." Shaking her head, she looked around the room at the skeptical stares leveled at her. "I swear. To my knowledge, I never met the man. Anyway, it's not like he'd have walked up to me and introduced himself as my stalker." She dropped her gaze to her hands resting in her lap. Let them think she was crazy if they wanted. It was nothing she hadn't already wondered about herself.

Garrett touched her leg, drawing her attention back to him. "But you're sure he's after you?"

"Yes…I mean no, not exactly. I mean…"

He grasped her hand and squeezed. "Why don't you tell us how this started?"

It'd been so long ago, yet the images were as crisp and clear as if it had happened yesterday. A shudder rolled along her spine, and Garrett stroked her hand with his thumb. She sucked in a deep breath. "It was ten years ago this August. I was living in Plainview, a small town in northern Texas, and working in a nightclub, trying to save enough money to put myself through school. One of the regulars asked me out. His name was Chance."

Chance was everything she'd been looking for in a guy. Nice, from a good family, easy on the eyes. The clincher was that he planned to leave that Podunk town someday. Rachel fell for the *idea* of him before they even had their first date.

"A day or two later, I received flowers, except they weren't from Chance. The card was signed *Jeremy*, and his message was clear. Don't go out with Chance again or something bad would happen."

Luke leaned toward her from the other side of the table. "You didn't know anyone by that name?"

"No. I thought it was somebody's idea of a stupid joke. I ignored it. The next week, I got more flowers and another card with the exact same warning. I told Chance, and he laughed. Said one of his friends was probably trying to be funny." Rachel knew she was talking too fast but couldn't seem to slow herself down.

"Then Chance's cat was stabbed through with a butcher knife…inside his apartment. We went to the police and told them everything. They investigated the flower deliveries but it was a dead end. Unless we could find out who Jeremy was, they couldn't help us." She stopped to catch her breath, and Sally set a glass of water in front of her. Rachel took a sip, then placed it back on the table.

"What happened next?" Garrett's calm voice nudged her.

"I wanted to call it off."

"Stop seeing Chance?"

She met Garrett's eyes. "You sound just like him. He scoffed at the idea, too. Said no one was going to break us up by harassing us." A choking sob escaped, and Rachel dropped her gaze to the table. "I let him convince me. The next night when I got home from work, there was a new flower arrangement…inside my house…and the card said *I warned you*." Rachel hated how vulnerable the recounting of this story made her feel. Hated not knowing what the others in the room were thinking.

Consciously stiffening her spine, she continued in a monotone voice, distancing herself from the actual events. "I called Chance, but there was no answer. So I drove to his house and let myself in." She paused to draw a shaky breath. "He was there...in the bedroom. He was tied to the bed and bludgeoned to death. The killer had carved the words NO NO RACHEL on his chest." She tapped her fingers on the table as though to put a period after the climax to her story.

"Is that why you left?" Garrett's words were angry.

A scornful laugh worked free. "Isn't that enough reason?"

"That's not what I meant, Rachel. Did this guy continue to harass you in Texas? Did you leave right after Chance died? I need the whole story, sweetheart."

She studied his face for a second. That was the second time he'd called her *sweetheart*. Was it simply a reaction to the stress they were both under, or did it mean more? She couldn't decide if she wanted it to, but there were all the reasons in Texas why it was a really bad idea.

"I stayed until after Chance's funeral. I got two more bouquets. The note with the first one said: *Sorry I had to hurt you.* The second one was longer. It said: *I suppose you had to attend the funeral, so I'll forgive you this time. Now we can get back to normal.* I packed a bag and left that night.

"I went to Las Vegas and tried to lose myself in the crowds, but I hated the glitz, so I kept moving around until one day I ended up here. Got this great job with nice folks. For years it was everything I could have wanted. Then, about five years ago, Jeremy started calling. Every time he called, I got rid of my old phone and bought a new, disposable one. That seemed to work for a few months...and then he'd call again."

Jonathan grumbled under his breath and all eyes turned toward him. "That's why you've been switching phone numbers faster than a fisherman cuts bait? I should have known."

"Over the last three or four years, the calls have become more frequent. Changing numbers hasn't helped. Maybe I should have gone to the cops, but they couldn't help me in Texas, and I figured the fewer people who knew the better. I kept thinking if he really knew where I was, he wouldn't call—he'd just show up. So I stayed, thinking I was safe here. But now I'm not so sure. If he could get my phone numbers so easily, how hard could it be for him to learn my address? Don't you see? He knows where I am, and not only am I not safe here anymore, but I've endangered all of you."

She turned toward Garrett. "Especially you. If I don't answer the phone, he always leaves a message. He asks if I'm seeing someone and then laughs before he hangs up. Do you understand what you've done by answering my phone yesterday?" If she could only make him grasp how much danger he was in, surely he'd let her go.

"I think I do. I woke the sleeping bear. With any luck, we'll draw him out into the open and put a stop to this for good. He won't be able to sneak up on us easily at the lodge, especially now that we know he exists." His gaze swept first to Luke, then to Jonathan, who both nodded in determined agreement.

Rachel slapped the table. "*No!* You don't get to make this decision." She wrenched her hand from his. "I stuck my head in the sand ten years ago, and it cost the life of a good man. I'm not taking this problem back to the lodge and putting all of you and Peg in danger. I'm sorry you've come all this way for nothing, but it's time for you to go home now." She rose, pushing her chair out with her calves.

A faint groan came from Sally, and Rachel looked up to meet her friend's gaze. The apprehension on her face immediately made Rachel sorry she'd picked Sally's house as her dropping-off point. Sally had known enough fear and pain in her own life. She didn't need to share Rachel's. She mouthed the words *I'm sorry*, but Sally only shook her head, got to her feet, and took her coffee cup to the sink.

Jonathan scowled, and his voice was harsh with obvious frustration. "We told Peg we'd bring you back, and that's what we're going to do. She doesn't deserve this, Rachel. She and Amanda took you in off the street and treated you like a daughter. And this is how you repay her? By leaving a fucking see-you-never note?" He shrugged his broad shoulders and stepped toward the kitchen windows, staring out at the alley while waves of anger rolled off him.

When he turned back a few seconds later, he was more composed. "Use your head, girl. You're safer back at the lodge where we can keep an eye on you. No one will get close that we don't see coming first. Besides, if what you say is true, it's Garrett who should be watching his back." He glanced at Cowboy lying a few feet away. "But between him, that dog, and Uncle Sam, he seems like a man who can take care of himself."

Rachel sensed Luke's eyes on her and she raised hers to meet his. He obviously had something on his mind. Maybe he could talk some sense into his brother.

A smile raised one corner of his lips. "You don't know me so you probably don't give a damn what I think, but for what it's worth, here's my two cents. Jonathan's right. Seems to me this Jeremy wants you scared enough to run. He'd like for you to leave your friends behind and set out alone. Do you know why that is?" He didn't give her a chance to hazard a guess. "Stalkers get off on their victim's fear, and he doesn't want you to think about anything but him. These last few years, you've surrounded yourself with friends who've been watching your back. I'm guessing he doesn't like that. I'm surprised he hasn't tried to flush you out before now so he could have you all to himself. You'd be foolish to believe that just because he killed your friend he doesn't also have some unpleasant plans for you."

Sally inhaled sharply, and Rachel glanced at her again, leaning against the kitchen counter, in time to see her hand fly to her mouth and tears well in her eyes. She was shaking uncontrollably, and her unsteady legs appeared as though they'd give out any second. Rachel started for her friend, but Luke jumped to his feet and reached Sally first, helping her to the closest chair.

Rachel circled the table and dropped her arm around Sally's shoulders. "I'm so sorry. I shouldn't have come here."

"Yes, you *should* have!" Sally's assertion was immediate and forceful. "Haven't you been listening? You can't go off alone and let that crazy psychopath have what he wants. Go back home, Rachel, please. You'll be safe." Her tear-filled gaze held a plea that was hard to resist.

But Rachel had to stand firm, because it wasn't only about her. "Please try to understand. I can't go back to the lodge." She raised her eyes to Luke. "If what you say is true, maybe he'll follow me and leave all of you alone. I *have* to believe he will because losing another friend…like that…I couldn't take that again."

She straightened her spine and looked first at Jonathan, then Sally and Luke, purposely avoiding Garrett's eyes, afraid to see the disappointment in them. "I'm going. You can either wish me well…or be pissed off. Your choice." She stepped around the table and grabbed the strap of her bag that was sitting by the back door.

A sob escaped Sally, nearly breaking Rachel's resolve. Luke kicked back in his chair, crossing one leg over the other, and shook his head. Let them think what they'd like. She wasn't wrong about this. Hadn't she kept herself and everybody she'd left behind safe for the past ten years?

Jonathan gripped her arm and turned her roughly. "Enough, Rachel. You're coming back with me, and I'm not above locking you in your room to make sure you stay there."

She pressed her lips together to keep from smiling. Jonathan was gruff and liked to bluster on occasion, but he was one of the kindest souls she'd ever met. It was why she loved him so much. He'd been her big brother and best friend for a long time now. His fear for her shone clearly in his dark chocolate-colored eyes. She raised a hand to touch his stubble-covered jaw.

"Wait a minute."

The words were uttered quietly, but everyone turned to look at Garrett.

"She's right."

"You can't be serious." Jonathan fisted his hands and stared incredulously.

"If this asshole is as obsessed as we believe he is and he didn't see Rachel leave in the middle of the night, he'll walk through hell to find her again. If we tell everyone who'll listen that she's gone and isn't coming back, he'll have no choice but to look elsewhere. Aunt Peg will be in the clear, which is what we all want. And we'll buy ourselves some time to find out who he is." Garrett looked back and forth between Luke and Jonathan as though they were the only ones he was worried about convincing.

Rachel stared at Garrett, unable to believe what she was hearing. He'd driven all the way to Huntington to stop her from leaving and now it appeared he was throwing her to the wolves. Unexpectedly, she was getting what she'd wanted, but her relief was mixed with confusion as conflicting emotions collided. She swallowed hard, trying to dislodge the gigantic lump in her throat. If she didn't leave now, she might never find the courage to walk out that door. With no strength left for good-byes, she strode to the door and turned the knob.

Suddenly, Garrett was behind her, closing the door and turning her to face him. An odd light shone from his eyes. "I didn't tell you the best part."

Rachel stared, curious what he could say that would possibly make any difference. She wasn't going to like his announcement. His apologetic expression gave him away. Still, his strong hands on her shoulders and his barely there smile held her motionless, waiting.

"I'm going with you." One of his shoulders lifted in the hint of a shrug.

Rachel blinked and then blinked again. *Did he say .*
. .? She took a step back and slammed his chest with the palms of her hands. "Are you crazy? Did you listen to a single thing I said?"

Garrett hardly flinched from her blow, but at least that cockeyed grin was erased from his face. "I didn't hear anything that convinced me to let you go alone. If *you* go…I go. That's the deal. Take it or leave it."

A furious breath whooshed from Rachel. "You miserable…arrogant…controlling simpleton! There's just one thing wrong with your little plan. I'm an adult. I don't need your permission to walk out that door, and I don't *want* you to come with me!" Tension sparked in the air. A second later, it took a gargantuan effort to ignore the glint of amusement flickering in his eyes. Anger settled over her with its red haze obscuring her good judgment. She curled her right hand into a fist, drew back, and let it fly toward his chiseled jaw.

Garrett ducked back and caught her fist an inch short of its mark to accompanying laughter from the other men in the room. Emotions tumbled across his handsome face. Surprise and amusement, and then his eyes darkened in warning as he grabbed both of her arms and shoved her against the door, dwarfing her with his hard, muscled body pressed against hers. Jonathan and Luke went silent.

Garrett smiled through cold, thin lips. "You heard the deal. I'm not going to repeat myself. Now, if you can't behave yourself, I'm going to hunt up a pair of handcuffs just for you, sweetheart."

"You wouldn't dare." She pushed against him without budging him an inch.

"Don't bet on that." His voice was hard, but he stepped back and gave her some room. "Luke, sorry to run off as soon as you arrive. I hope you'll hang here for a few days and get to know Aunt Peg. Ask her about our mother."

"Just so happens I've got some free time. I was hoping to spend it with my big brother, but I'll catch you later." Luke strode forward and shook Garrett's hand.

"Sally, I think you and your daughter would be safer at the lodge for a few days…just in case Jeremy knows about your friendship with Rachel and comes looking for information." Garrett flashed a quick smile.

She nodded, stealing a look at Rachel, then focused on Garrett. "Will you take good care of her?"

"I promise, nothing will happen to her." Garrett nodded at Sally.

Rachel huffed. Of course, he'd think he was bulletproof enough to pull that off, but it wasn't her he should be worrying about.

"We'll need a car. Is there a rental place in town?" Garrett's arm brushed lightly across the front of her as he swiveled, and Rachel's breathless reaction made her press back against the door as far as she could.

"Jonathan, can you give us a ride to the lodge?" Sally grabbed her purse from the counter. She looked through it and came out with a set of keys that she handed to Garrett. "Take my Explorer. It's old, but it runs like a champ."

He grinned. "Looks like we're set." He turned back to Rachel and she averted her eyes. The amusement in his voice said he couldn't care less if she was still mad. "We'll check in now and then. For obvious reasons, we'll keep our destination a secret. I'll be calling a buddy of mine, Jase Richards. You remember him, right, Luke?"

"Jase used to be a Ranger too, didn't he?" Luke returned to his chair.

"He's a private dick now. I've got him working on something else at the moment, but I'll have him put this on the front burner. We'll find this SOB." Garrett started to reach for Rachel, but her glare must have changed his mind.

The house fell silent—so silent Rachel could hear her own breaths. Apparently, no one was feeling justified enough to speak to her directly. Not even Cowboy would look at her, having eyes only for his master. Had she behaved so egregiously, endeavoring to keep her adopted family safe from the maniac who dogged her steps? If they couldn't forgive her for her actions, so be it. She'd done what she thought best.

As for Garrett—she didn't know what to think. Earlier, he'd promised to help her through this, and apparently that was a promise she could take to the bank. Oh, but his bossy, domineering ways drove her crazy. In spite of that, she was attracted to his strength and chivalry, and yes, he was a hunk. She bit her lip to keep from smiling. No sense in trying to understand her feelings, but she had to admit it. Garrett was a good guy. He was determined to stand beside her, ignoring the danger to himself. That was worth something, and she should give him a break. While she was at it, she might as well admit to herself that he was growing on her. She liked him, damn it. And because she did, she wasn't in a position to ignore the very real threat Jeremy presented to him. So, she'd swallow her pride, keep her hands to herself, and go with him until she was far away from here. Then she'd leave *him* behind as well. He had to sleep sometime.

Chapter Eleven

GARRETT GLANCED AT the woman in the seat beside him, staring out the passenger window. She'd turned her back to him as much as possible, one leg folded beneath her and arms crossed over her chest as though she was cold. If only that were the case, but he knew better. Rachel had completely shut down as soon as they left Sally's place thirty minutes ago, but beneath that quiet, stoic exterior, he suspected a flame burned, preparing to erupt into a wildfire at any moment. So far, she'd ignored his attempts to draw her into conversation, and the tension inside the vehicle was at about DEFCON 2. Even Cowboy gave a low whimper every few minutes, wagging his tail and doing a little happy dance with his front legs every time Garrett looked his way. Rachel ignored him, too.

"Are you hungry, Rach?" It wasn't in his nature to give up, especially since he'd be sleeping with one eye open from now on if he couldn't make peace with her.

"No. Thank you."

Garrett managed to hide his grin. He'd gotten actual words—polite words if you didn't count the churlishness with which they were delivered. It was a start. "Luke put some water in the back. Thirsty?"

"I'm fine. Thanks." She glanced over her shoulder, but her eyes didn't quite meet his.

"Before I forget, you should turn off your cell phone. We'll check it later for messages."

Rachel hesitated briefly before leaning forward enough to pull the phone from her back pocket. She cradled it in both hands then finally hit the off button, and the screen went black. Even then, she continued to stare at the blackness, and when trembling seized her shoulders, it was a few seconds before Garrett realized she was having a meltdown.

He had to clamp his hands around the steering wheel to keep from reaching for her. It was purely instinct that told him she'd react badly to any comfort he might offer. As hard as it would be, he had to wait for Rachel to turn to him.

At the next wide spot in the road, he pulled over, let Cowboy scramble out behind him, and gave Rachel her privacy. As the dog investigated the brush, Garrett dialed Jase's number and got his voice mail. "Something's come up. I need you to put the investigation on hold for now. I've got a more urgent matter that needs your magic touch. Call me as soon as you can. Thanks, Jase." He ended the call and stared at the phone, debating whether to call his little brother. He couldn't tell Luke that they were headed northeast toward Coeur d'Alene. Tonight, after they found a place to stay, he'd call to make sure Aunt Peg was adjusting to the changes.

Cowboy was still smelling and claiming the new territory. He never wandered out of Garrett's general vicinity. It'd been ingrained in the dog to always be within sight of his handler. It was barely midmorning, and traffic was scarce on the narrow but well-maintained state highway they traveled. Still, not a good idea to stay out in the open too long.

He skirted the front of the Explorer, glancing through the windshield. Rachel leaned back in the seat, her eyes closed. He propped himself against the side of the vehicle just beyond her door. Crossing his legs and jamming his fingers in the front pockets of his jeans, he waited.

After about five minutes, she cranked the window down a few inches. "What are you waiting for?"

He smirked. Her impatience was showing. "Nothing. Just enjoying the sunshine."

An indelicate snort reached his ears before she closed the window. He didn't move. Just waited some more.

Two minutes passed before she opened her door and stepped out. Cowboy bounded up to say hello, and she knelt down and gave him a good scratch. He was in heaven. Shit. Garrett would have been, too.

She finally straightened, closed her door, and leaned beside him. "Where are we going?"

"Coeur d'Alene or maybe Sandpoint." Garrett itched to free his hands from his pockets and pull her against him—to wrap his arms around her and keep her safe.

He'd never had any woman bring out this need to protect before.

"Why?" Her voice was breathy as she glanced toward the ground.

"It's far enough from the lodge that if Jeremy's going to follow us, he'll have to forget about the folks back there and move on. And there are more people. He may get careless if he thinks he's just another face in the crowd." Garrett sneaked a glance at her, but her thick red hair covered the side of her face, and he had no idea how she was reacting.

As though in response, she pushed away from the side of the Explorer, resting her hands on her hips, and looked straight ahead. With no warning, she swiveled and stepped into him, the top of her head coming to just below his chin. The smell of jasmine filled his senses and wreaked havoc with his self-control. Surprise kept him from putting his arms around her until she'd snuggled tightly against him from thigh to chest, her hands fisted in the fabric of his shirt at his waist.

When he finally gave in and hugged her to him, she fit just right to his body as if she'd been made especially for him. She felt right in his arms. The intensity of his posses-siveness shocked him, and he instinctively loosened his hold on her. Turning to him for comfort was definitely a step in the right direction, but her emotions were all over the board right now and it probably wouldn't take much to make her turn away again.

"I'm sorry. I don't know what came over me. I just needed to feel the warmth of another human being." She didn't move away, but tilted her chin so she looked in his eyes.

"Don't apologize. I'm happy to provide that warmth anytime you feel the need." Her lips were so close to his, it would be a true test of his resolve to resist them, especially having already tasted their honeyed sweetness.

Rachel smiled wistfully and looked down again. "I hope I didn't hurt you back there…you know…when I knocked you down."

Garrett chuckled ruefully. "Only my pride."

She locked gazes with him again, a sparkle of amusement in her eyes. "You kind of deserved it…sneaking up on me like that. Jonathan's been teaching me self-defense for the last five or six years, and that was the first chance I've had to practice for real. It would have worked too, if not for your dog."

He threw caution to the wind and kissed her adorable nose. "Well, there are reasons why I keep him around. He sees farther, detects odors humans can't smell, hears the slightest sound from incredible distances, runs faster, and seems to have an amazing ability to decide who's trustworthy and who isn't. I aspire to be like him when I grow up."

"I see. Will the shedding and the cold nose be part of the package?"

Garrett laughed and rubbed his nose over hers. "Only time will tell."

Threading her arms around his waist, she pulled them even closer. "Garrett, why are you doing this? If Jeremy finds us, he'll kill you."

Garrett slid his hands up her back until they landed on her shoulders, and he pushed her away slightly so he could see her face. "I hope he tries. We'll be ready for him, Rachel. We'll have each other's backs. And don't forget our secret weapon over there." He nodded toward a patch of grass beyond the graveled shoulder where Cowboy was rolling on his back.

Free and easy laughter spilled from her as they both watched the dog. She seemed reluctant to break contact, and that was okay by him, but finally he turned her toward the car and opened the door. "Time to hit the road."

She stood still for a moment as she studied his face, her gaze dropping to his mouth. Then, suddenly, she stretched up and brushed his lips with hers.

Every muscle in his body jumped to attention, and as she turned and ducked into the vehicle, he caught her arm and pulled her back. "Not fair. I wasn't ready." He dipped his head and covered her mouth with his, tasting, nipping, and scraping his teeth over her lips until she opened for him. He took her mouth, thrusting deep, the same way he longed to take her luscious body in a much more fulfilling way. But his goal was all about trust, and sex wasn't the key to earning hers. He gently kissed her twice, then reluctantly pushed her toward the open door.

Garrett called the dog as he walked stiffly to his side of the Explorer, thanks to his growing arousal. Not a cold shower in sight. Cowboy jumped in and Garrett climbed awkwardly into his seat. One look at Rachel's grin told him she hadn't missed the reason for his shuffling gait.

"Is there something you'd like to say?" His gaze dropped to her lips again.

She raised her hands in mock surrender. "I wouldn't touch that with a ten-foot pole." At which point she leaned forward and uncontrollable laughter spewed forth.

"Funny." Garrett grumbled under his breath, but in reality, he was so glad to see her laugh again after the events of the morning, he didn't mind being the cause.

He started the Explorer and reentered the roadway. They had about a four-hour drive ahead of them—farther if they decided to go to Sandpoint. The map Jonathan had given him was tucked beside his seat. If he remembered correctly, Lewiston was an hour or so up the road. Maybe he could talk her into getting a bite to eat there.

Ten minutes later, his phone rang. Jase's name and number appeared on the in-dash screen. This could no doubt spoil the inroads he and Rachel had made toward restoring peace between them.

He turned toward her. "Up to answering some questions?"

Apprehension darkened her eyes, but she nodded.

Garrett pressed the button on the steering wheel, allowing the call to be answered through the hands-free device. "Hey, Jase. Thanks for calling, buddy."

"What the hell, man? First you want me to drop everything and go chasing ancient history. Now you want to move on to something else just when I'm starting to get somewhere?" Jase sounded more excited than disturbed, which probably meant he really had found something.

Garrett ached to know what the man had uncovered, but one glance at Rachel and it could wait. "We'll get back to that. If it makes you feel any better, I need your help on a matter of life and death."

"Cool. Whose?"

"Mine, asshole. Why else would I be calling you?" Garrett grinned at the gleeful laughter coming over the speakers and the cute-as-hell smile replacing Rachel's wary expression. "Listen. This is serious and it involves a beautiful lady. Her name is Rachel Maguire, and she's sitting right beside me. So watch your language and keep a civil tongue, okay?"

Jase's voice filled the cab on a huff. "Hello, beautiful lady. Even though Garrett has impugned my reputation, rest assured that I will always be the most civil of the two of us."

Rachel smiled and amusement again crept into her eyes. "Nice to meet you, Jase. After seeing your friend Garrett in action for the last couple of days, I'm inclined to believe you."

"Hey! Am I going to have to separate the two of you already?" Garrett reached for her hand and squeezed, giving her a wink when she glanced his way. Her gorgeous smile made his breath catch.

"Okay, here's what we need. Rachel is being stalked by a man she's never met who signs his cards and notes as Jeremy. That's likely not his real name, but it *is* likely he's responsible for the death of her friend Chance, whose murder was never solved." He turned to Rachel, giving her a chance to add pertinent information, but she apparently wasn't ready to talk to Jase yet.

"And Chance's last name was…" The sound of flipping pages no doubt meant Jase was searching for a blank sheet to jot some notes.

A shadow crossed Rachel's face. "DeMaris."

"I can tell this is hard for you, beautiful lady, so we're going to get through it as quickly as possible. Okay? Where did the incident happen? And how long ago?"

Rachel inhaled slowly. "It will be ten years this August. Plainview, Texas."

"Texas, huh? You've done an excellent job of losing the drawl. Now, this guy, Jeremy, any idea where he may have come in contact with you?"

"I worked in a nightclub called Barney's. I always assumed it was someone who frequented the bar, but no one stands out in my mind. There was never a shortage of strange and sometimes unacceptable behavior exhibited by the patrons in that setting." Rachel's cheeks turned a rosy pink.

"What about the employees? Anything unusual there?"

"No, I don't think so. I didn't socialize with them outside of work, but they seemed normal." She twirled a lock of hair nervously and leaned her head against the seatback.

Cowboy whined. Garrett could relate. He reached to lay his hand on Rachel's thigh, wanting to remind her she wasn't alone. She jumped as if he'd shocked her, and she blinked a couple of times. A relieved sigh escaped her lips, and her hand covered his, twining their fingers together. Her breath came faster, but she smiled and held on as if her life depended on it.

"Stalkers are mentally disturbed for sure, but they're also smart and know how to stay below the radar. They can blend in. What about neighbors, Rachel? Did you get any weird vibes from any of them?" Jase's compassionate side came out as he asked his questions. Garrett appreciated that.

"I lived in a duplex. My next-door neighbors were a nice retired couple. I didn't really pay much attention to anyone else."

"I need the address and the name of the retired couple."

Rachel set the phone on the console and reached for her bag. She pulled out a wallet and searched until she found a small slip of paper. "Eight ninety-five South Irving Street. I was in unit A. Stan and Alice DuPont were in unit B."

"You wouldn't happen to remember the name of the homicide detective assigned to Chance's murder, would you?" Jase sounded doubtful.

"Detective Ian Michaels. He's not likely to forget my name, either. I've called him at least once a month since Chance died." Rachel glanced toward the side window, her jaw clenched.

Her eyelashes batted furiously. She was on the verge of breaking down and fighting it with everything she had. Garrett frowned. "Do you have enough to get started, Jase?"

He hesitated for only a heartbeat. "Yeah…sure, this will get me going. I'll call if I need anything more. Thank you, beautiful lady."

A smile perked up the corners of her mouth. "Of course. Thank *you*. I appreciate your help."

"And so you shall have it, milady. Garrett, I'll be in touch." He was gone.

"Sorry about him, Rach. He's kind of crazy." Actually, Garrett probably valued his friendship with Jase more the moment he put that smile on Rachel's face than any other moment since they'd met.

Rachel shifted sideways to face him. "He seems nice. Your brother seems nice, too."

"Luke is the best guy on the face of the planet. Easy-going, considerate—a truly good human being. Right up until someone pushes him too far or picks on somebody who can't defend themselves. Then someone's going to the hospital, and it won't be Luke. He just completed the Navy SEAL training program." Garrett was proud of his baby brother and aware that it probably came across in his voice.

"So both of you went into the military. That's a little odd, considering who your father is."

"No mystery in my case. I got myself in trouble when I was eighteen. Enlisting kept me out of jail, kept my name out of the paper, and made my old man happy. Seemed like the right thing at the time." He shrugged and grinned.

"I bet you were a real handful, Garrett Harding." Rachel laughed, but sobered quickly. "What was it like after your mother left?"

"It was…hell." How could he explain the emptiness to someone who hadn't been there? The sense of betrayal?

The ache in a little boy's heart every night when he lay in his bed alone? "It ripped my world apart. Every day I prayed she'd come home. My father wouldn't talk about her except to tell us she was a drug addict, and she wasn't coming home. So I made up my own stories. Unfortunately, they all ended with a mother who had no use for her own kids."

"You don't believe that anymore, do you? Amanda loved you and Luke. I saw it with my own eyes." Her uncompromising belief amazed him.

"Believe me, I'd like to see her the way you and Peg remember her, but I've got years of bitterness to trounce. I'm working on it. Just give me a little time. Okay?" They passed a green highway sign. "We're six miles out of Lewiston. Are you hungry yet? I'm starving."

She smiled and shook her head. "I guess I could eat."

AN HOUR AND a half later, they'd enjoyed easy conversation over fried eggs, ham, and flapjacks, filled the Explorer with gas, and gotten back on Highway 95, headed north. Garrett pulled over at the first wide spot to let Cowboy exercise a bit and have some food and water. The cab had been warmed by the sun when they loaded up again, and it wasn't ten minutes before Rachel was sound asleep.

She was no doubt exhausted after sneaking away from the lodge in the middle of the night, not to mention spilling her guts about Jeremy, not once, but twice. That had to take an emotional toll. He'd felt her pain as she relived Chance's murder, and yes, he *was* slightly jealous of a dead man. Go figure.

She slept peacefully now. Garrett glanced at her every few seconds just to make sure she wasn't caught in some nightmare. What was it about her that made him want to stay beside her and make sure she never had to be afraid again? Something stirred within his heart—something he'd stowed away one day when he was five. Child that he was, he hadn't known the right words then, but he'd instinctively retreated within himself, put up barriers that no one but his brother Luke could breach, and vowed that he'd never let another person get close enough to matter.

Yet there she was, sleeping in the seat beside him, and in the space of three days…she mattered.

Chapter Twelve

RACHEL JERKED UPRIGHT and reached for the door latch, fear clawing at her throat. Where was she? Her vision blurred in the bright sunlight that shone through the front windshield, and she closed her eyes again with a groan.

"Hey, you're okay." A soft, masculine voice startled her with its proximity, making her inhale sharply, and then the weight of his arm landed on her waist. "Time to wake up, sleepyhead. We're here."

She squinted and focused on him. Garrett's teasing smile hung right above her, close enough she could feel his breath on her cheek. He smelled of blended spices, the heady aroma filling her senses.

"Where's here?" She returned his smile.

"Coeur d'Alene. You slept through some pretty country, but I'm pleased to report that you don't snore." Garrett winked and leaned away from her.

The immediate loss of his warmth sent a chill skittering across her skin in spite of the sunlight that still filled the cab. "How nice of you to comment on that."

"I thought it was." Garrett laughed easily. "Let's get a hotel room for the night. Tomorrow we'll see if we can find a vacation rental, maybe on the lake. Sound all right to you?"

Rachel took a good look at the hotel outside the window. Several floors, each room with a private balcony overlooking Lake Coeur d'Alene, and the doorman dressed in his freshly pressed uniform all smacked of money. She caught her bottom lip with her teeth and chewed.

"Hey. Rach. Something wrong?" Garrett leaned toward her again, cupped her chin between thumb and forefinger, and gently turned her to look at him.

She felt her cheeks flush with heat. "I have some cash…" There was enough to last until she landed someplace and found a job…if she was careful. She'd need first and last month's rent, and probably a used car. Why was she embarrassed? Because she didn't have an unlimited supply? Or was it because she didn't want to admit how far removed she was from the lifestyle in which he'd obviously been raised? "I have to make it last as long as possible. I can't splurge on a ritzy place like this."

Dropping a kiss on her lips, he released her and sat back. "Believe it or not, I didn't drive up here and park in front of this hotel thinking I'd ask you to hand over money." He raked a hand through his hair. "It's been a long day for both of us. I'd like to take you out for a nice dinner, and make sure we get a good night's sleep on a decent mattress in a room with plenty of hot water. My treat. Let me do that, okay?"

Rachel regarded him warily, concern spawning dread in her stomach. "That sounds really nice, Garrett, but look me in the eye and tell me you're not expecting some more intimate form of payment." As soon as the words were out, she wanted to take them back.

He just stared, irritation knitting his brow tighter and tighter. His gaze drifted to her lips and then lower to her breasts before it rose again to her eyes. A scornful curl of his lips wounded her. "You don't know me at all, do you? I realize we've just met, but I'd have thought by now you'd have some idea of the kind of man I am."

His eyes never left hers, forcing her to look at him. She should apologize, but the disdain in his expression shamed her and woke her damnable pride. In the last couple of days, she'd come to know that honor, truth, and family were what made Garrett Harding tick. To him, *family* extended to everyone that he cared about. That stupid dog. Aunt Peg. And her—damn it! So, yes, she should have known better. He didn't *have* to drive cross-country with her. He could have let her go—should have. How ridiculous to suggest he'd placed himself in Jeremy's crosshairs and traveled all this distance simply to coax her into the sack.

Humiliation emptied her of pride, and she tried a tentative smile, but was pretty sure it came off more like a grimace. She drew a deep breath, prepared to issue the apology he deserved.

"Not to worry, Rachel. I enjoy sex as much as the next guy, but freely given and never owed. I don't expect anything from you. Wait here and lock the doors." Regret invaded his expression as he pushed his door open, stepped out, and closed it quietly.

Rachel stared after him until he disappeared inside the lobby. Well, now she'd done it. He was hurt and angry, and so damned controlled it scared her. Why didn't he yell at her? How was she going to make this right? Clearly, an apology wasn't going to fix things at this point.

Avoiding confrontations had never been her style, but the thought of facing him again was equally unacceptable. She'd fully intended to jump and run at the first opportunity in order to force Garrett from the danger zone surrounding her. Why not now...before he came back and pierced her with those accusing gray eyes? From here, she could easily catch a ride to Spokane or Missoula and disappear to parts unknown. Garrett would be safe from Jeremy's wrath, as would her friends back at the lodge.

Rachel glanced at the lobby entrance, then reached between the seats for her bag, having to fend off Cowboy's licks in the process. Laughing, she patted him between his ears and under his chin, staring into his big, brown, all-knowing eyes. Sadness welled up within her, and her laughter stilled.

"Don't look at me like that, you furry mutt. What do you know about sticking your foot in your mouth, anyway?"

Cowboy whined, and his tail thumped the floor.

"You know he thinks I'm a selfish, uncaring waste of his time right now, don't you? He can't even look at me without contempt. And what about Jeremy? You don't want Garrett to get hurt, do you?"

The dog gave a soft bark.

Rachel smiled. "I know you'd protect him with your life. Right? I'm glad because I want him to be safe, too." She wanted that so badly, she was willing to strike out alone, exactly as she'd done ten years ago after Chance…but this time she didn't *want* to leave. The thought very nearly put her in a panic. Aunt Peg, Sally and Jen, Jonathan, and Dory were her family. Of course she didn't want to go. Except, when she closed her eyes, it was a tall, broad-shouldered, dark-haired man with stubble on his rugged cheeks and smiling gray eyes that called to some part of her soul as though they'd always been together.

Nonsense. Yet she couldn't deny the attraction, the desire that invaded her when he was near. What would he do if she disappeared again? No doubt the egotistical man would try to find her—just as he'd done last time. For sure, he'd be even angrier than he was now.

Cowboy whined again, rising and pushing forward until his head bumped against her chest.

She hugged his neck, burying her face in his scruff. Loneliness rolled over her in waves. "Okay, maybe you're right. Maybe he deserves better than me just disappearing again. He *is* trying to help me. So, I *could* stick around and try to apologize for being a jerk." Truth was, she wasn't ready to leave Garrett. She needed to find out if the way he made her tingle with a touch of his hand was anything other than a case of nerves. Did the shiver that ran through her when he spoke in that soft baritone portend other thrills to come, or was it merely an effect of a chill in the air?

Rachel sat up straight as soon as she heard the driver's door unlock, and she tensed when he slid onto the seat. Garrett neither glanced her way nor spoke. Did she deserve that? A wispy tendril of anger hovered over her, but she tamped it down. Maybe she did. She'd give him the benefit of the doubt…for now.

He pulled the Explorer to the backside of the hotel, parked, and held out a plastic room key, again without looking at her. "Room three thirty. Go on up. I'll take Cowboy for a short walk. There's a department store down the street about two blocks. I need to pick up a few things. Is there anything you need?"

"No," she said. "Thanks."

Garrett jerked the door handle, stepped out, and called the dog. Cowboy rushed by her and jumped from the seat to the ground, only too happy to be free and with his master. The door closed behind them and neither even cast a backward look as they walked away.

Well. Rachel felt a hysterical giggle rising within her, but she cleared her throat and then bit the sides of her cheeks until it hurt too bad to laugh. She refused to give in to maniacal behavior no matter how crazy he made her. What's more, there'd be no feeling sorry for herself. She had two choices. Either she grabbed her bag, left the key on his seat, and hitched a ride as far as she could go, or she sucked it up and figured out how to fix this. Neither option seemed particularly appealing.

With her satchel slung over her shoulder, she went inside the hotel, found the elevator, and rode it to the third floor. Room three thirty was to the right, according to a sign on the wall outside the elevator. Rachel followed the arrows halfway down a long hallway and used her key card to open the door to their room.

She crossed the threshold and stopped short as the door fell shut behind her. *One bed.* What was up with that? Didn't he just get all bent out of shape because she asked if he expected payment of a sexual nature? Considering the chemistry between them, what did he think was going to happen if they shared a bed?

Taking a deep breath, Rachel forced herself to calm down. At the moment, he couldn't stand to *look* at her. There was no way he'd want her, and even if he did, his anger and pride would no doubt prevail. But what about her? That was no small amount of attraction she felt for Garrett. The memory of his kiss set her heart racing and he wasn't even in the room. How would she sleep in the same bed with him? This was shaping up to be a very long night.

The king-sized bed occupied the center of one wall, with glass doors to the right, leading to their very own balcony overlooking the lake. She dropped her bag on the foot of the bed and crossed to the doors. The view of pristine waters, surrounded by dense forest and mountains, sparkling in the late afternoon sun just beyond the balcony, was gorgeous. A leather love seat sat to the left of the bed, a table and two chairs next to that, and a gas fireplace filled the corner. The door to a bathroom opened directly across from the bed. Suddenly, a long, hot, luxurious shower was all she could think about.

Rachel stepped into the bright and spacious bathroom, running her fingers across the tiled countertops done in deep earth tones and scrubbed to a spotless finish. A huge tub sat at the far end of the room and an equally large, see-through shower stall started her wondering what it would be like to share that space with a certain tall and well-built military man—a waste of good contemplation. Whether or not that man was seriously irritated with her would be the least of her worries. It wasn't as if she had any experience at enticing men to get down and dirty, whether under running water or not. Besides, Garrett, naked in the shower, should be the last thing on her mind right now. A wave of her hand dismissed the whole silly idea.

Turning the water on, she stripped off her clothes, grabbed the hotel's sample bottles of shampoo and conditioner as well as a miniature bar of soap, and stepped into the steamy shower. She closed her eyes and braced one arm against the wall, letting the hot water pound against her bare skin, relaxing her and lessening the mysterious ache she experienced every time her thoughts turned to Garrett.

The sense of loss that had gripped her heart as she stole from the lodge last night still echoed within her. As difficult as it had been, she'd had no doubt it was the best thing for Garrett. He refused to acknowledge the danger he'd placed himself in, but *she knew*. She'd seen the results of her own denial in grisly shades of red.

So, why hadn't she slipped away again when she had the chance? Instead, here she was in a room he'd paid for, standing naked in *his* shower, wondering if he'd avoid looking at her even here. A short laugh burst from her, and she turned her back on the water to soak her long, thick hair.

Garrett was an attractive, sexy male specimen. There was absolutely no doubt about that. It'd been years since she'd responded to a man the way she had when he'd kissed her. Surely he had to know she was a lump of clay in his hands. Did she turn him on, too? It'd certainly seemed so in the heat of the moment, but now that he was angry with her, it was easy to believe her imagination had gotten away from her.

The air in the bathroom quickly went from steamy, to humid, to clammy. The glass walls of the shower were covered on the outside with a fine sheen of moisture. She'd been so eager to get under the running water that she'd forgotten to turn on a fan. Quickly, Rachel washed and rinsed her hair, turned off the water, and selected a bath towel from the plush array provided. After the last droplet of water was gone from her skin, she stepped from the enclosure, flipped on the fan switch, and glanced around.

Shoot! Her bag, with all of her clean clothes, was out there in the bedroom. Rachel stared at the door and listened. Had Garrett returned yet? It was eerily quiet. She glanced at her discarded clothes, grimy from sitting in the dirt with Cowboy this morning and wrinkled from sleeping in them. No way was she putting them on for the five seconds it would take her to grab her bag.

She wrapped the towel around her, tucking the end securely, then studied herself in the fogged-up mirror to make sure everything important was covered. With a deep breath, she opened the door and stepped into the main room. At the same moment, a sound drew her attention to the entrance.

Before she could react, the door swung open, and Garrett appeared, stopping the instant he saw her. Surprise widened his eyes as his gaze slowly traveled the length of her. Then Cowboy, entering behind him, pushed him farther into the room, and Garrett looked away, his expression shuttering over. "Nice getup." His voice was emotionless, and he brushed past her.

Rachel's instant embarrassment at being caught half-naked fell away as an irrational anger possessed her. So many ways he could have reacted...and she got ridicule? No. She didn't have to stay here and put up with that.

She retucked the edge of the towel, which had loosened with her movements, padded silently across the carpet to the bed, and grabbed her bag. His back was to her as he unpacked items of clothing from a large paper sack he carried. She watched him for a few seconds while she tried to make sense of the stabbing pain in her chest. Why were her feelings so hurt? Why couldn't she return to the emotionally safe place of hating him? She clutched her belongings against her stomach and turned toward the bathroom.

Rachel's steps slowed as she contemplated the unthinkable: getting dressed and repacking her bag, sneaking away again. Maybe he was right, and she had no idea what kind of man he was, but she *did* know that Garrett wouldn't forsake his role as protector without a fight. Still, it just seemed wrong to leave without any explanation. That he probably wouldn't listen or care didn't seem like much of an excuse.

Three feet from the bathroom door she stopped, set her bag down, and turned. Once again, she tucked the end of the towel more securely. Her heart pounded with the adrenaline rush that seized her as nervous energy made her second-guess her decision to come clean. She opened her mouth to say his name just as Cowboy sprang to his feet and gave a low woof, facing off toward the hotel door.

The words died on her tongue as Garrett swung around, his body tensed, and the muscle flexed in his jaw. His gaze feathered over her and landed on the door, his expression dark and dangerous. Quickly, he glided toward her. The same weapon he'd used outside the Watering Hole suddenly appeared in his hand.

Garrett put a finger to his lips. "Stay behind me," he whispered.

So grim and forbidding, he almost convinced her that her faceless enemy had finally come for her. Frozen in place, she forgot everything she'd ever learned about self-defense. Bleakly, Rachel nodded her compliance to his command.

With Cowboy waiting on high alert by his side, Garrett glanced toward the door just as someone rapped out a staccato rhythm on the other side. He grasped her elbow and pushed her closer to the wall behind him. Her attention focused on the door, she stumbled slightly, but easily caught herself. However, her clumsy movements had loosened the towel again, and she reached to catch it as Garrett noticed her plight and swung back to help. In spite of both of them grabbing for it, the damp length of fabric slid all the way to the floor.

Mortified, Rachel held her breath. Garrett snagged the errant cover-up and pushed it toward her, his eyes shiny and dark as they met hers for a split second before the knock came again. She straightened the towel as best she could and held it lengthways in front of her as Garrett moved to the door.

After a quick look through the peephole, he left the chain in place and pulled the knob toward him only far enough to scrutinize whoever was waiting in the hallway. Quiet conversation ensued. After a minute or so, Garrett reached for something the mystery person handed him and closed the door.

He tucked his gun in the back of his waistband and turned slowly. Clearly, he was trying to hide the amusement that danced in his eyes, without much success. He held up two postcard-sized notices. "Twenty-five percent off dinner at the restaurant downstairs. Part of the newlywed package."

"*Newlywed package?*"

He shrugged. "I figured if Jeremy was looking for you, he wouldn't expect to find you in one of the newlywed suites." His gaze kept dropping to her throat and the swell of her breasts where she clutched the towel.

"Good plan." Rachel rolled her eyes as she fumbled with the fabric, positioning it to cover more of her chest.

Wrapping some of the excess around her bare hips, she tried to hold the ends together behind her, but the towel wasn't quite wide enough. Finally, she gave up and started backing toward the bathroom.

Garrett strode forward and reached for her, his large hands catching her around the waist. Fear seized her briefly, followed quickly by searing anger. Still trying to move away from his touch, her retreat stopped abruptly when her backside came in contact with the wall. She tilted her chin and looked him in the eyes. "*What* are you doing?"

Rachel was having a hard time believing that the man she'd come to respect in just a couple of days would hurt her. Yet his proximity and her state of undress made this a whole different ball game, didn't it? Damn. She shouldn't have come out of the bathroom in a towel, but that wasn't an excuse for him to put his hands on her and back her into a corner. The last laugh would be hers, however. She wasn't helpless, thanks to Jonathan. She knew how to break a nose, crack a rib, or bust his balls if need be.

Garrett's brows shot up and an amused grin accentuated the laugh lines around his eyes. "I'm trying to help you if you'll hold still for a minute." He removed his hands from her waist, took a step back, and twirled his finger in the air. "Give me the towel and turn around."

Rachel huffed a laugh. "Not on your life."

"Will you trust me, please? I promise not to look." A smile appeared. "Well, not any more than I have to, anyway." He held out his hand, waiting to receive the towel, as he met her gaze. "Like ripping off a Band-Aid, Rachel. Quick and painless. You're not afraid of me, are you?"

No, she wasn't afraid of him, but there were some pretty powerful emotions rolling around inside her right now. Not the least of them was desire and a strong sense that she could trust Garrett. Not only here in this room with a flimsy towel between them, but out on the street where Jeremy searched for her. Should she believe the protectiveness that shone from his eyes? Or was her awakening desire messing with her head?

Making up her mind, she shoved the towel toward him and spun to face the wall.

Immediately he was directly behind her, holding the towel open against her back. "Raise your arms." His voice was slightly huskier than it had been.

She complied without hesitation, and he reached around her with the towel until the ends overlapped in front of her. Catching the corners, she pulled them together, tucked them under, and held them tightly.

When she glanced over her shoulder, Garrett was still watching her. "Thank you."

"Any time." He started to turn away, but stopped before he'd taken a step. "You know you're beautiful, don't you? You don't have one damn reason to be embarrassed." The rich warmth in his voice drew her eyes back to his.

She breathed again, feeling light-headed, as though she'd been holding her breath for a while.

Garrett's brow creased. "One more thing. I'm sorry for getting all torqued in the car earlier. You don't know me—not well anyway—and you had every right to ask what my intentions were. I apologize for being a butthead." An impish grin dispelled the remainder of his seriousness. "If you forgive me, I won't tell anyone I saw you naked."

Laughter threatened to break free, but she managed to keep a straight face. Rachel turned, studying him for a moment, examining his ruggedly chiseled face and the scruffy stubble that made him look so super sexy. She never knew who he was going to be next. The devilishly handsome army Ranger, able and willing to protect her, or the insecure little boy who teased, laughed, and sometimes missed his mother. Both versions of the man drew her, and something inside her came alive whenever he was near. If she'd ever really questioned his integrity, that issue had since been put to bed.

She tapped her index finger pensively against her lips. "I guess I could…if you'll forgive *me*, too."

He raised an eyebrow quizzically. "For . . .?"

"It's twofold, really. I have trust issues that cause me to act irrationally where new people are concerned. I'm working on them, but—"

"Nothing to forgive there. Under the best of circumstances, it's not a good idea to trust everybody you meet. Right now, I don't want you to trust anyone until you get that sixth sense that they're okay. Not even me." Garrett lifted his hand and traced her bottom lip with his thumb. "What's the second thing?"

She allowed her attention to linger on his mouth as he smiled reassuringly. Heat rushed through her and settled in her core. Suddenly, she became ultra aware that she was naked beneath her questionable covering, but she found it only slightly odd that she didn't seem to care.

Rachel stepped into him and stood on her tiptoes. "*This*," she said and melded her lips to his.

She'd meant to kiss him for only a second, but his instant and fervent response sent the idea of a time limit right out of her head. His mouth owned hers, his body pressing her firmly against the wall and holding her there while his arms formed a barrier on each side of her shoulders.

His tongue traced the seam of her mouth, and as soon as hers opened, he invaded, conquering in a way she welcomed and reveled in. Her own hunger was matched by his, and under his smoldering onslaught, her legs turned to Jell-O beneath her. She fisted her hands in the shirt at his waist and gave her desire free rein.

Garrett trailed kisses across her cheek to her ear and down the column of her throat to where the plush towel only half covered her breasts. Once he'd worked his way back to her lips, he kissed her hard and hungrily.

Her lungs demanding air, she tried to push away, but he wrapped his arms around her and drew her in tightly. "Uh-uh. Don't go. Please? Not when we've finally figured out how to get along." Soft laughter rumbled through his chest, and those molten gray eyes waited for her answer.

Her smile evidently reassured him, and he bent slightly to grip the back of her knee and raise her leg to hook around his hip, positioning her over the long, thick ridge in his jeans. Pressing her hard to the wall, he rubbed against her center. Rachel shuddered on contact, and a gasp caught in her throat. Her one leg would have been useless in keeping her upright if she hadn't been grasping his strong arms for all she was worth.

Her legs spread wide to encompass his girth, he held her in place with his powerful thighs as he rocked his hips against her. The pathetic scrap of terry cloth might as well have been nonexistent as it crept farther and farther up her hips. His lips seared her skin wherever they touched, and she ached for them to touch her everywhere. Pressure built within her, and she instinctively knew that he held the key to her release.

He raised his head, his eyes dark with lust, his lips moist and curved in a smile. "Are we good, sweetheart? I hope so, because I'm not sure I could stop at this point."

His whispered words held no threat because his eyes told the real story. Respect, truth, integrity, but most of all protectiveness. If she said *enough*, he'd honor her refusal no matter how difficult.

Her body was on fire. She didn't want him to stop. That this situation was painfully similar to a one-night stand wasn't lost on her. Something she'd promised herself she'd never do—yet here she was, close to climax against the wall of a hotel room with a man she'd known for three days. She choked back a hysterical giggle. *At least it's a fancy hotel.*

She wanted him to make love to her, to share himself so completely that the loneliness inside her would vaporize, if only for a little while. Being held in a man's arms until they fell asleep, sated and happy, was a distant memory, and the need to feel that connection to another human being burned in her heart. How long had it been? How long would it be before another man she could trust walked into her life? Many years had passed since she'd let herself get close to anyone.

Rachel smiled into his eyes and pushed against him again. After a brief hesitation, he released her and stepped back. She raised one hand to her chest and toyed with the end of the towel where it was tucked against her chest. He watched her carefully, an air of strained anticipation surrounding him. What was he expecting? Was he afraid she'd turn away from him? Surely she was easier to read than that. With one fingertip, she pulled the towel loose and let it drop to the floor.

Chapter Thirteen

GARRETT TRACKED THE movement of the towel until it hit the floor at Rachel's feet. Then he dragged his gaze slowly up her luscious frame, meeting her eyes on their way back from the same exploration. *Holy hell!* In a heated rush, the last remnants of his self-control crumbled into dust. He swept her into his arms, cradled her against his chest, and strode to the bed.

Jerking the covers back, he tossed her, none too gently, onto the sheets. She shrieked and then laughed. Garrett gave a quiet command to Cowboy, who'd followed along, probably wondering what the commotion was. The dog grudgingly found a place to lie near the door.

Garrett reached behind his back and dragged his T-shirt over his head, mostly because he was hotter than hell, giving it a toss toward the paper bags that held his new purchases. He fumbled his wallet from his back pocket and placed it on the nightstand so his condoms would be close at hand. Dropping to the edge of the bed, he made short work of his boots and socks. Then he turned, put one knee on the mattress, and stopped abruptly as a stray thought made it through the lust swirling in his brain and slapped him upside the head.

This didn't exactly fall under the category of protecting her from Jeremy.

Rachel sat in the middle of the navy-colored blanket, and the perfection of her creamy skin, bared from head to foot, went straight to his groin. Her inspection over every inch of his body clearly held desire equal to his own, but something else lurked in her hooded eyes as well, giving credence to his guilt.

Garrett crawled up the bed until he flopped on the pillows and pulled her down beside him. Her hand went to his shoulder where she gently outlined the tribal dragon tattoo that perched there, tail and wings trailing down his chest and back. She grimaced almost as though the thought of a tat caused her pain. Later, maybe he'd tell her what it meant to him—how he'd transferred his pain and anguish at loosing ten good men into a fire-breathing beast that would be with him always.

He kissed her gently and wound his fingers in her hair. "Answer one question before we go any further. Are you sure about this?" He tipped her chin up, forcing her to meet his gaze.

A tiny shrug lifted one shoulder and uncertainty changed her expression a split second before she averted her eyes.

"Okay. That answers my question. Want to talk about it?" He was relieved that she didn't pull away, stretching her arm across his chest and cuddling close instead. She breathed a sigh that tugged at his heart while he waited patiently for her to answer.

After a few seconds, she lifted her head and met his gaze. "Impulsive actions oftentimes end in regret. Most men don't want their one-night stand staring them in the face the next day, but you won't have a choice unless you decide to leave after all."

"Let's deal with the last part of that first. I'm here for the duration. Changing my mind is not an option. Got it?" He rolled on his side and reached for her arm, bringing it over his shoulder so she was hugging him around his neck.

"Now for the impulsive behavior you mentioned." He gave her a wink and got a wisp of a smile in return. "Is that what you want this to be? A one-night stand? Because I don't *do* one-night stands, sweetheart. Never have. Well, unless you count the first time when I was fifteen years old and my father's personal assistant took it upon herself to show me the ropes. Even that wouldn't have been a one-time deal if Anna hadn't bragged about it to the kitchen staff and gotten her ass fired the next day." Garrett grinned, remembering his father's anger and frustration when the story had finally made its way to him.

"Stop, Garrett." Rachel skimmed a cool hand down his roughly whiskered face. Her smooth cheeks took on a pinkish hue, and her expression registered no small amount of guilt. "Have you forgotten there's a lunatic out there ready to kill the next man I spend too much time with? This is a really bad idea." She tried to roll away from him, but Garrett anticipated her move and threw his leg over hers, pulling her snug against him.

He rested his forehead on hers. "I remember, but that has nothing to do with this. *This*…is between you and me. And I'd be mad as hell if you let something happen here today that you'll be sorry for later tonight…or tomorrow morning…or next week. I don't want to be your biggest regret, and I don't want you to be sorry you met me."

Tears flooded her eyes, and for the first time since he'd walked in her bar, she didn't try to blink them away. A big droplet cascaded over her eyelashes and rolled down her cheek. "What happened to Chance has been my first thought every morning and the last thing I see every night. I've been afraid for so long, I don't know how to separate *us* from *him*. How am I supposed to do that?"

Garrett kissed the moisture from her face, then covered her mouth with his. He smiled against her lips when her arms tightened around his neck. "Sweetheart, all of us have bad memories. I let mine define me for a long time, so I'm not the one to tell you how to escape yours. But you're going to let *me* worry about Jeremy from now on. Luke, Jonathan, and I will nail his worthless hide to the barn door. If it takes more manpower than that, I've got two brothers and a sister you haven't met yet, a dozen Ranger buddies who'd drop everything if I promised them a good skirmish, and we can always go over Sheriff Connors's head to the Idaho State Police if we have to.

Hell, I'll even ask my old man for help if it becomes necessary. All you have to do is trust me. Think you can do that?"

Her eyes sparkled with residual tears, but she nodded and kissed him back when his lips found hers again.

Garrett rolled another quarter turn until she was on her back and his weight pressed her into the mattress. He brought one knee up, spreading her legs slightly, and positioned himself in the cradle of her hips. He rocked against her, gently at first, until his engorged manhood pulsed with the need to be free of his jeans and someplace much tighter. Forcing himself to go slow, he lazily circled the peak of one breast with his thumb while with the other hand, he brushed the hair away that had fallen in front of her eyes.

A groan escaped while he fought for control and rained soft kisses on her mouth and throat. When he again searched her eyes, her luminescent smile caused his swollen shaft to harden even more. He shifted to the left side of her, unbuttoned his jeans, and lowered the fly. His arousal tented the front of his briefs as it escaped the confines of the zipper.

Rachel braced herself on her elbow and watched as he slipped to his back and shed his jeans and Calvin Kleins. She scrambled to her knees and reached for him, closing her small hand around him and squeezing, rubbing her fingers along the length of him and circling the head with her thumb while he looked on.

Shit! For a second he thought his brain might have imploded for lack of blood. When he could move again, he shoved her down on the bed and dropped alongside her. He palmed one of her breasts and lowered his mouth to the other. Instantly, her breath came faster and grew ragged. Working his thumb over her taut nipple caused her to jerk in rhythm with his fingers. His mouth closed over her other breast, sucking and nipping as he rolled his tongue to the same beat. She moaned and pulled him closer.

Garrett threw his knee over her thigh and spread her legs. One hand began a slow and exploratory journey down the front of her, and he shifted so he could capture her mouth with his. Rachel responded with every bit as much hunger as he felt. A shudder rolled through her when his hand settled on the drenched heat between her legs. So damn wet and ready for him. His shaft ached for release.

"Shit, sweetheart. I've never been this hard in my life. What are you doing to me?"

Her cute little shrug was the only answer he got, which meant it wasn't something special she did—it was that *she* did it. Garrett smiled with that knowledge, not sure why it made him feel content deep down where he hadn't known contentment in…forever.

He worked his fingers through her slippery folds, alternately rubbing and pinching her sweet spot until she was on the verge of coming. Then he pushed two fingers deep inside her, pumping hard and fast. When he pulled out and pinched her center again, she came with a cry of passion that he captured and silenced with a kiss.

Her eyes shone when she finally opened them, evidence of the tears that had gone before. Worry gripped his chest. "Tell me you're not sorry."

Her smile slowly blossomed as she looped her arms around his neck. "No. Not sorry. Not even close."

The need to make her his hit him, so powerful that it left him trembling. Hopefully, she wouldn't notice. He gave her a smug grin. "Good, because we're not done yet." He pushed himself up on his arms, extracted a condom from his wallet, and quickly rolled it on. Then he lowered himself on top of her and pressed himself to her opening.

It was too late in the game to go slow. He rocked back and shoved in to the hilt. Hot satin sheathed him and moved when he did. It was the best damn feeling he'd ever had.

Garrett found her lips and drank freely of their honeyed flavor. Rachel lifted her legs and wrapped them around his hips, giving more of herself, allowing him deeper. After taking a few seconds to absorb the sensations bombarding him, he started to move. All the way out except for the head. When Rachel started squirming and trying to affect his reentry herself, he pushed in again. Each time harder, faster, deeper, and closer to the drop-off.

Twining his fingers with hers, he rested his hands on the pillow beside her head and silently held her gaze. He kissed her, biting her lip, then massaging it with his tongue, then invading her mouth, tasting, owning, branding. As his passion built, drawing closer to the moment of climax, so did his hunger for this woman. Once would never be enough. Not by a long shot. Did she feel it, too?

Fireworks exploded in his peripheral vision as every muscle in his body went rigid. He rocked into her one last time as deep as he could go. A long, feral growl sounded from somewhere, and it must have been him. Wave after wave of spasms convulsed him, and inside Rachel, he jerked and twitched. Kissing her gently, he savored every moment he could touch her, possess her like this. Finally, he released her hands and wrapped his arms around her. Not willing to move yet, he stayed, sheathed in her warmth. Rachel slid her hands behind his head and brought his mouth to hers, kissing him soundly and then burying her face in his neck. "That was amazing." Her voice came low and muffled.

Garrett pulled back and regarded her sparkling eyes. She smiled, but worry still cast its shadow across her face.

"*Fucking* amazing!" To be exact, sex had never left him feeling so right before. It stole some of his contentment to see her still sad, even after the best damn sex ever. His half sister, Shay, would have reminded him that women needed more—they needed an emotional attachment— but anger at what Rachel had suffered and his need to fix it for her steamrolled him anyway. Jeremy had taken enough from Rachel. It was time he disappeared from her life. Garrett would be happy to help the bastard on his journey. He just needed to know who her stalker was, and he'd make sure the son of a bitch never hurt her again.

He reluctantly rolled off her. Then he hooked his arm around her waist and tugged her to spoon against his front. It felt so damn good with her beside him. Too good to be true. He'd have to be careful that he didn't do something to spoil this. Funny—he'd never cared about the *aftermath* of sex before, always heading out of Dodge before the cuddling got too intense. Was he getting in too deep…too fast? He dropped a kiss on her exposed neck, and she laughed softly in response. Maybe. But he wasn't ready to let her go yet.

Garrett stroked her hair and breathed in her clean, fresh scent. Was there anything he didn't like about this woman? Maybe her hot temper and penchant for holding a grudge—but she was also quick to forgive. To be fair, she'd had good cause to hate his guts when he arrived. Rachel leaned away from him. "Are you *smelling* me?"

He tightened his hold, pulling her back where he wanted her, and nuzzled the sensitive spot at the base of her neck. "Damn right. I love the way you smell. Is that jasmine?"

"I'm impressed. You know your perfumes. Do they teach you that in Ranger school?" The teasing in her voice came through loud and clear.

Garrett groaned close to her ear and then licked her lobe as he slid his hands lower on her abdomen and pressed her against his burgeoning hard-on. He smiled as a small hitch in her breath marked her realization that he was ready to go again. "In a way, the Rangers are responsible. A couple of years ago, my unit trained in Alaska for three weeks. At the end of it we got some R&R, and a bunch of us went into Fairbanks. The guys decided they wanted to buy their girls or wives presents—perfume. I never smelled so damn many perfumes in my entire life, but my favorite was jasmine."

Rachel drew in a soft breath. "Is that what you bought for your girl?"

Garrett laughed softly. "Are you asking if I *had* a girl-friend?" He propped himself up on one elbow and trailed his fingers along the side of her face and down her throat to splay on her breast.

She turned slightly toward him. "Of course not—did you?"

Garrett hooted, holding her arms down while he tickled her until she was out of breath from laughing. He stilled, hands clasped around her waist. "Give up?"

She snorted a laugh but it sounded more dangerous than humorous. "That'll be the day."

He rolled her onto her back and kissed her gently. Then he traced her bottom lip with his thumb. "You never give up, do you?"

The determination in her eyes instantly turned her expression serious. "No, I don't."

Garrett brushed her hair from her eyes. "Good. I like that about you, but you're not alone anymore. Let me in, sweetheart. Let me help."

Without a word, she raised her hand and lightly caressed his stubbled cheeks. Slowly, her eyes darkened to a smoldering hue of green.

Garrett lowered his mouth to hers and pulled her on top of him as he flipped to his back. He stretched for another condom, opened the package, and rolled it onto his rock-hard member with shaking fingers. Man, she did a number on him.

She clamped her lower lip between her teeth as her eyes followed his movements. Clearly lost in concentration, she jumped when he touched her sides. She dragged her heated gaze from his engorged shaft to his eyes. Her pink tongue appeared and flitted across her lip a fraction of a second before a speculative grin settled there. He answered her with one of his own. Whatever she was planning, he was pretty sure he could get on board.

She reached for him, fastening her hand around his dick. Her eyes never left his. "Take it off," she whispered low and sultry.

"The condom? Why would I do that?" He tugged her down for a hard kiss.

Pushing herself up, she raised her index finger in front of her mouth, sucked the tip between her lips, pulled it out with a slight pop, and drew a wet line over the end of the condom. "Why do you think?" Her voice was a teasing purr, and he'd apparently only *thought* he was hard before.

Aw hell! He groaned with the effort to concentrate on anything other than the promise in her eyes. "As tempting as that sounds…this is my last condom…and I kinda need to be inside you. But next time, if you'll do me the honor again, I'm all yours." He started to sweat a little at the anticipation alone.

It hadn't even occurred to him to replenish his supply before he left the base. It'd been a while since he'd needed any at all. That ambush in Fallujah had changed his perspective on many things. Not the least of which was how trivial it was, in the scheme of things, to bury himself deep in some woman he didn't even know merely for the sake of a fuck. His lack of interest had worried him at first, but the shrink his commanding officer made him see had assured him the problem would take care of itself when he was ready. Apparently the good doctor had been right. Garrett felt as if he'd been sporting a partial erection ever since he came face-to-face with Rachel.

What was so different about her? She was pretty—beautiful even—but it was more than that. She touched something deep down inside him. Maybe it was as simple as the fact she needed him, although he doubted if *she'd* see it that way. As he studied the tenderness in her eyes, he couldn't help wondering what emotions she saw on his face. He used to be a master at hiding his feelings, especially from the women who decorated his arm...and occupied his bed. Rachel, however, was chinking away at his armor. Where panic at getting too close might have bombarded him in previous years, now his need for the green-eyed redhead made him ache all the way to his toes.

Straddling him, she leaned forward until her hands were braced on the bed beside his shoulders. "Let's not waste it then." Her clear eyes held his gaze as she lowered her mouth to his.

He let her control the kiss for a few seconds before he cupped the back of her head and ground his lips over hers. Tucking her to his chest, he rolled until she was beneath him, her legs on each side of his hips, allowing him free access to exactly where he wanted to be. Leaving her mouth and ignoring her hands that tried to pull him back where he'd been, he scooted down her gorgeous body until her center was within reach of his tongue.

With the first lick, she screamed and then slapped her hand over her mouth. Muffled giggles came from beneath as she shook her head back and forth. Garrett's shaft jerked in readiness.

His tongue covered her center, circled, then nudged and teased her swollen nub. Arching off the bed, she allowed him more leverage to get deeper in her folds. She alternated between pushing against his mouth and trying to pull away from him. He locked his arms around her thighs and held her in place while his blood boiled with the need to be inside her.

Garrett guided her legs over his shoulders as he crawled upward on the bed again. When her hips aligned with his, he lowered himself into position and shoved home. *Sweet mother of all things fucking hot!* She was it for him. He opened his eyes and gazed into her exquisite face. A slight smile curved her lips as she beckoned him closer, then circled his neck with warm hands and kissed him when he complied.

She sighed, a glint of mischief in her eyes. "It was my turn to be on top."

He eased out and rocked back into her. His breath came faster. "Were we taking turns? Sorry. Next time. I promise."

She sniffed. "You do remember that's your last condom, right?" She slid her legs off his shoulders, down his sides to tangle around his hips.

Garrett covered both of her breasts with the palms of his hands, flicking her pebbled nipples with his thumbs. She trembled beneath his touch, and he couldn't hold back any longer. He started a slow rhythm, stroking in and out of her velvet softness. "I know you want me bad, sweetheart, but if you could be a little bit patient, I'm sure it's not the last condom in town."

Rachel laughed and reached toward his side, clearly searching for a ticklish spot. "Ohhhh…I'm pretty sure between the two of us, I possess the greater patience."

Garrett grinned. "I don't doubt that a bit." He pulled both of her hands up over her head and held them with one of his. His mouth covered her sweet lips even as his hips ground against hers. Internal pressure built as he plunged in and out, Rachel meeting each thrust with a force of her own. In no time at all, she tensed and shuddered beneath him, and he was pretty sure it was his name she cried out, though he muffled it with his tongue. Man, he loved making her come. If only he had one more lousy condom.

His thrusts became wildly urgent just before what felt like a volcano blew in his head, and red-hot lava flowed through his veins as he gathered Rachel tightly in his arms.

When his breathing had slowed, he showered gentle kisses on her face, then rolled to his back, tugging her with him until her head and upper torso rested on his chest. "You're going to kill me if we keep this up." The alarm in her eyes alerted him immediately to his stupid choice of words. "Shit! I'm sorry, sweetheart. I was trying to be funny."

The saddest smile he'd ever seen worked across her face, and she brushed his lips with hers. "You should probably leave the funny stuff to someone else."

Garrett dropped his forehead to hers. "Count on it."

Rachel reached for the sheet, pulled it over them, and snuggled close to him. Garrett held her tightly because to do anything else would put too much space between them. Finally, he sensed that she'd dozed off, and still he couldn't bear the thought of letting her go. He was just dropping off himself when his cell phone vibrated against the wooden top of the bedside table.

Chapter Fourteen

RACHEL JUMPED AT the sudden noise even though it wasn't very loud. Strong arms wrapped around her and kept her from bolting. *Garrett.* Still naked beside her. Memories of him making love to her, so fresh in her mind, raised her body temperature enough that she kicked her legs out from under the sheet that covered them.

"It's just my phone, sweetheart." Garrett spoke close to her ear, then stretched over her to reach the offending device. "It's Luke. I better take it."

Rachel nodded and rolled to the side of the bed. She searched for something to cover herself with, then briefly wondered why she would bother after everything that had transpired between her and Garrett. Spotting her bag on the floor, she made a beeline for it, grabbed it, and kept on going right into the bathroom. Okay, so she'd never be the kind of woman who was comfortable flaunting herself in the nude. So what?

Holding her breath, she waited for regret, shame, and self-condemnation, the harbingers of humiliation, to punch her in the gut. Surely, now that she'd satisfied her traitorous body's needs, sanity would return with a vengeance and make her sorry she was alive. She waited…and let her breath out little by little…and waited some more. The only thing she was having trouble controlling was the persistent twitch at the corners of her mouth that felt suspiciously like a smile—one that went nicely with the carefree thundering of her heart. She had no regrets. The realization made her breath catch in her throat and sent her spiraling into self-doubt. She'd just had wild and crazy sex with a virtual stranger. What did that say about her?

She sorted through her belongings for something clean to wear while keeping an eye on Garrett through the half-open door. He was sitting on the edge of the bed with his back to her and his phone to his ear. What was going on at home? Was everyone all right? Was Peg upset with the decision Rachel had made to leave? She wanted to know what Luke was calling about, but Luke was Garrett's brother. They probably had more to talk about than just her. Amanda…for example. So she'd give Garrett his privacy. Surely he would fill her in if there was something that concerned her.

She pulled the door closed all the way, turned on the shower, and stepped beneath the water, the hot drops pelting her with soothing power. Even as good as it felt, she hurried through soaping and rinsing. After all, it hadn't been two hours since she'd stood in the same spot, going through the same motions.

Finished and towel-dried, she dressed in her favorite tan skirt and a sleeveless lemon-yellow cotton top that she'd taken from her bag. She finished with a pair of comfortable sandals and a spritz of the jasmine scent that Garrett had liked. Then she brushed her long, wavy hair and used a barrette to pull the top layer behind her head and keep it off her face.

Leaving her satchel on the counter in the bathroom, she pushed the door open. Garrett had gotten up, slipped jeans on that were zipped but not buttoned, and stood on the balcony, leaning against the railing, his concentration on the phone. He must have heard the door open because he glanced up, smiled when he saw her, and beckoned.

One look at this sexy guy with nothing on but a pair of jeans sent her heart racing. What was this effect he had on her? What would happen if Jeremy found out? Rachel went weak all over as the blood apparently drained from her head to pool in her feet. *Breathe, damn it! Breathe.*

Concern instantly flooded Garrett's face. He ended the call and strode through the open balcony doorway. "Hey. Are you all right?" He reached her just as she stumbled to the closest chair and dropped down. He knelt in front of her. "Tell me what's wrong."

Rachel forced her version of a brave smile. "Nothing serious. I think I'm just hungry."

"Shit! Of course you are. It's almost dinnertime." He stood and gripped her shoulders. "You stay right here and rest. I'm going to take the fastest shower in history, throw on some clothes, and we'll go downstairs to the restaurant. Five minutes. I promise." He dropped a kiss on her forehead, grabbed the paper bags that held his new clothes, and disappeared into the bathroom.

Silence, broken only by the sounds of water spraying the tiles in the shower, settled around Rachel, along with a deep-seated dread that Jeremy would somehow find out she was falling in love with Garrett. Terror, the likes of which she'd never known before, nearly blinded her, and then suddenly the weight of Cowboy's head lay in her lap.

She hugged him and scratched his neck as he whined and licked her face. The seriousness in his intelligent brown eyes seemed to say: *What are you worried about? I've got this.*

Garrett was lucky to have Cowboy. He'd already saved Garrett's life more than once, and Rachel felt her apprehension lessen as the dog returned to his vigil, stretching out on the carpeted floor a few feet away.

True to his word, Garrett was finished and ready to walk out of the room in just under the promised time. He wouldn't leave before he promised Cowboy that there'd be a walk in it for him after dinner. The dog's tail thumped on the carpet, but that was his only indication he cared they were leaving at all.

Before Garrett opened the door, he wrapped Rachel in a hug and pulled her close. "You look good enough to kiss all over." His lips came down on hers with tenderness and a hint of his earlier passion. "Do you feel like taking a short walk before dinner?"

She studied his face for the reason behind his amusement. "Sure. I guess. Where are we going?"

"The department store a couple blocks down. I need to lay in a megasupply of condoms so I don't disappoint you the next time you can't keep your hands off of me."

Rachel huffed, but then her smile broke free. "I doubt if it's possible for you to disappoint me." She leaned into him, reveling in the hunger in his eyes.

With a very pleased smirk, he dipped his head and kissed her thoroughly, but when he pulled away, his expression seemed a little too serious. "There's news from Cougar Ridge. I'll tell you over dinner."

Rachel's breath stuttered. "Is everyone okay?"

"Other than Aunt Peg being ready to skin me alive, everybody is just fine. But don't worry...Luke will apply a little of that charm he's so good with, and she'll be back to normal in no time." He opened the door and ushered her through.

They walked the two blocks to the store hand in hand, and Garrett dragged her with him to the condom aisle. She should have been embarrassed, picking out the latest in male contraception with him, but his sense of humor and natural confidence rubbed off on her. The only one who'd blushed was the clerk behind the counter who would have apparently been happier if Garrett had stopped asking questions about sizing and just bought the damn things already. They laughed all the way back to the hotel.

The restaurant on the ground floor was busy, but Garrett employed some of the Harding brothers charm himself and the pretty blonde hostess was only too happy to show them to a secluded table. Garrett pulled out the chair against the wall and waited for Rachel to seat herself, then took the chair to her left.

By the time the waiter arrived to take their orders, Rachel had a headache from wading through the overinflated prices on the menu. No way was she paying forty bucks for something called Country Natural Beef. There wasn't a slab of meat alive worth that much.

She dropped her menu on the table and smiled at the waiter. "I'll have a house salad with ranch, please."

Garrett frowned, and she saw his argument coming. He turned to the waiter. "Let's wait on the main course if you don't mind. I think we'll start with some wine and an appetizer." He smiled at Rachel, all innocent like. "Bring us a bottle of Inglenook Cabernet Sauvignon, please. And…some calamari…and an order of the seared ahi. Does that sound all right, sweetheart?"

Rachel stared, bemused, until he nodded at the waiter and the poor man walked away. When she opened her mouth, intending to tell him how it all sounded, Garrett held up his hand.

"Do you want to know what Luke and Jase had to say? Because if you do, you're going to let me buy you a nice dinner, and you're going to order some real food with your salad." He leaned toward her. "Besides, the hotel is picking up part of it. Remember?"

"You talked to your friend Jase, too? What's going on, Garrett?" Suddenly, her observation that he was getting a little too free with his coercion didn't seem important.

He reached for her hand. "Our friend outside the lodge yesterday morning? He came back. Luke and Jonathan caught him planting listening devices in your room."

Rachel's other hand flew to her mouth. "What happened? Did they call the sheriff?"

"Apparently, Jonathan has the same opinion of Sheriff Connors as you do, so the two of them thought they could get the truth from the man themselves." Garrett went silent as the waiter returned with their wine, opened the bottle, and poured a small amount in one of the glasses that Garrett tasted and pronounced satisfactory. The waiter than poured a glass for both of them and left the bottle.

"They didn't torture him, did they?" Rachel could barely hold in her question until they were alone again. Was it possible it was Jeremy they'd caught red-handed?

"Well, as you know, my brother is a SEAL, and Lord knows what Jonathan did with his time before he moved to Idaho. But I'm going to assume the answer to your question is no since they didn't get much information. The guy wouldn't even give his name. They were just about to change their minds and call the sheriff when he insisted on talking to Jase."

The waiter returned again with their appetizers. As soon as he left, Rachel cast a disbelieving look at Garrett. "Jase? Why Jase? Jeremy doesn't know him." She had to stop to catch her breath.

"The man we saw outside the lodge is a professional. I'd bet on that. I doubt if he's your stalker, and I'd be surprised if he worked for Jeremy, either. Stalkers get off on *stalking*. Doesn't seem feasible that he'd hire someone else to do what he enjoyed most. But we can't rule it out completely." He rubbed his thumb across her knuckles, sending a tingle up her arm. "Why he asked to speak to my PI—that's something I'll have to ask Jase tomorrow. He wants to talk to me…face-to-face…before we meet with the mystery man. He refused to say why, and that's not like Jase at all. He'll be here about noon."

Garrett lifted the appetizer dishes one at a time and passed them to Rachel. She was in such turmoil over the possibility that Luke and Jonathan were holding Jeremy at the resort she forgot to turn up her nose at the tentacles on the deep-fried calamari. She had a bite anyway and washed it down with a swallow of wine.

An exasperated sigh escaped her lips, and Garrett frowned. "I'm sorry I couldn't get Jase to answer my questions, sweetheart. We'll know what's going on tomorrow, and then we'll decide if we're going back."

A question nagged at the fringes of her mind. "What happens if you decide to go back…and I decide not to?"

His expression went suddenly blank, giving her the answer she suspected. He looked away from her before he answered. "Let's not worry about it tonight. We'll have some dinner, some wine, and take Cowboy for a walk. Do you like classic cars?"

"Sure. You?" Rachel wasn't really surprised by the sudden change of topic.

"I'm obsessed—old Model Ts, muscle cars, you name it. Anyway, the clerk at the desk when I registered said there's a car show in town all week. We could check it out, if you'd like." And there it was—the little boy's grin that Rachel found so endearing.

Was it possible for her to forget about Jase and Jeremy for tonight? One look at Garrett's eager face made her hope she could. "I'd love to. As long as Cowboy can go, too. He's been stuck in that hotel room too long." She flushed with heat as she suddenly remembered why.

By the amusement in Garrett's eyes, he'd had no trouble following her train of thought. "Cowboy better damn well get used to it." He leaned across the corner of the table that separated them and kissed her ear, his breath feathering her hair and causing a shudder along her spine.

Just then the waiter returned for their order. Rachel opened her menu, then closed it and turned to Garrett. Under the table, she dropped her hand on his knee and slid it slowly upward. "You know what I like, honey. Would you mind ordering for me?"

Garrett coughed and cleared his throat. His eyes turned almost charcoal as his gaze pierced her. "Of course, sweetheart. We'll both have prime rib, medium rare, baked potatoes with the works on the side, and salads, ranch for the lady and bleu cheese for me. Can we get some water too, please? I'm suddenly really thirsty."

"Very good, sir…miss." The waiter gathered the menus and strode toward the kitchen.

Garrett's brow shot up. "Well, well. Aren't *you* full of surprises? Can't wait to see what's next."

Rachel laughed softly, absurdly embarrassed by her brash advance. She jerked her hand away, but she wasn't quite quick enough. Garrett snagged her wrist and guided her hand effortlessly to where the hard ridge lay just beneath the worn denim of his jeans. His eyes never left hers, the knowing grin he wore taunting her.

"I usually have more control, but I have to admit I like the way you get me all hot and bothered." His deep voice sent tremors clear to her toes.

The hostess led a middle-aged couple to a nearby table and still Garrett's gaze never wavered. "What now? Should we take this to our room? Or maybe we could enjoy an elevator ride. Do the nasty on the way to the top floor and back?"

Whether it was his melodramatic words or his solemn delivery, Rachel burst out laughing. And she couldn't stop.

Garrett huffed, released her hand, and threw his own in the air in a gesture of defeat. Then he started to chuckle and shake his head.

Soon, Rachel was laughing so hard tears ran down her face. Finally, ignoring the couple within earshot of them, she stood and slid onto Garrett's lap. She raked her fingers through his short hair, pulling his head down for a kiss. "You are the sexiest man I've ever met."

"Aw…and sexy makes you laugh?" His confident smile teased her.

She shrugged. "I'm laughing because I was actually considering your irreverent suggestions—so not like me. Apparently, sexy makes me want to behave with abandon."

Garrett wiggled his eyebrows above a wide grin. "I like that. You can let go of your inhibitions with me anytime.

You're safe with me." He slapped her bottom playfully, and she leaned into him, giving him an over-the-top kiss that she hoped he took as a promise of good things to come.

Garrett's cell phone vibrated, and he set her on her feet, retrieving the device from his back pocket. After taking one look at the screen, he sent the call to voice mail and turned his phone upside down on the table.

"Your wife?" Only half joking, Rachel tried to think of who else's call he would avoid so blatantly while having dinner with her.

He rolled his eyes, clearly irritated. "There is no wife."

"Girlfriend, then?" Rachel sat in her chair again.

"Don't be ridiculous." His words were almost a growl, and Rachel tried not to take them personally.

Their waiter and another staff member appeared with their salads and disappeared just as quickly. Garrett spread his napkin on his lap and started eating, obviously deep in private contemplation.

Rachel toyed with her salad greens.

After three minutes of excruciating silence, Garrett cleared his throat, causing her to glance up. He held his phone, screen facing her. The name of the person who'd just called was highlighted. She knew that name, and immediately understood why Garrett would ignore the call.

She turned sympathetic eyes on him. "Senator Harding?"

"Yeah." Garrett tossed the phone down. "I haven't answered any of his calls since I left home for the lodge. He's getting desperate."

Rachel reached for his arm. "I understand why you're upset with him. I am too, but you'll have to talk sooner or later."

Garrett scowled. "I want proof that he sent my mother away and purposely hid her efforts to contact us before I confront him. I'm afraid if he tries to deny it, I might do something stupid."

"He'll still be your father, you know, no matter what you discover." As much as Rachel despised the man for what he'd done to Amanda and his own sons, she felt compelled to search for words that would comfort Garrett. "Maybe there's an explanation—something you can live with."

"Don't defend him." He pointed an accusing finger at her, but the anger had gone out of him. "You were ready to run me off that first day even though I was trying to save your ass—all because you were sure I'd done something *you* couldn't live with." A slow smile materialized as he reached to encircle her wrist and rub her palm with his thumb. "Getting some mixed signals here, sweetheart."

Rachel cocked her head and looked him slowly up and down, then lowered her voice to a whisper. "If you are, it's because you're not reading them right. I'm glad I didn't run you off, Garrett Harding."

He winked at her as the waiter returned with their entrees.

Garrett made her feel…so many things. As if she was the most important person in the room. His smoldering gray eyes locked on hers, sliding away to follow the path of each person who encroached too closely on their table, or darting toward the door to evaluate the threat level of each newcomer who had the audacity to enter and request a table. Clearly, her safety was his priority, and his intimidating size, the muscles that rippled and flexed beneath his shirt, and the Colt .45 she suspected he carried tucked in his waistband all worked to produce her current sense of well-being.

That and possibly the wine. She pushed her empty plate away and frowned as he poured her the last of the ruby red liquid. "Wait a minute. You're still on your first glass. Are you trying to get me drunk, sailor?"

Garrett regarded her over the rim of his glass as he sipped lazily. "I should take offense at the sailor crack, but since Luke is a navy man, I'll let it go...this time. And the answer to your question is *no*. I don't want you drunk. I just want you relaxed. I imagine it's been a while since you let your guard down and tonight, while I've got your back, you can relax."

She could have sworn she felt the heat of his sincerity, and for a moment, she was afraid she'd embarrass herself by crying. Truth was she couldn't remember the last time she'd felt truly safe. That Garrett, stranger and object of her disdain three days ago, had thought to give her the gift of his protection, even for one night, was nothing short of miraculous. No wonder she harbored impossible feelings for him. Feelings she could never put into words because his stay in Idaho was only temporary. His life was elsewhere.

Nonetheless, he was hers for tonight and maybe for a few more days. Earlier, she'd paraded naked in front of him, seduced him, and let him make love to her. The secret was out—she was attracted to him, and she felt as though she'd known him all her life, not just a matter of days. Still, it was no excuse. Bottom line—she'd had sex with a man she barely knew. She'd crossed a line—done something that could never be undone—yet here she sat, contemplating how they would spend the rest of their night. In the absence of any real shame, her desire for him remained.

"Ready to go?"

Rachel glanced up at the concern in his voice. It was uncanny how he seemed to read her mind. She forced herself to lighten up and smile. "Ready when you are." She was a grown woman. She'd known what she was doing, and any consequences would be born with as much grace as possible. No way would she feel sorry for herself now. Nor was she willing to sacrifice the rest of her time with Garrett.

He motioned for the waiter, gave him a hefty tip and the two discount coupons that had been delivered to their room earlier. All the while, Rachel closed her eyes so she couldn't possibly see how much of the bill Garrett was picking up, and they left the restaurant with her arm looped through his.

As soon as they were in the elevator, Garrett hit the button for the top floor, lifted her until she wrapped her legs around him, and leaned her against the wall, all before the door ground shut. His forceful kiss seared her lips and dragged the breath from her lungs. She was practically panting when he let her up for air.

Rachel eyed the slowly closing door. "Garrett. What if someone comes in?" A second later, the door glided shut, and she breathed easier.

He slid his hands up her thighs, pushing her short skirt out of his way. "I haven't been able to get this out of my mind since the idea came up at dinner. I can be quick…when I have to."

He probably would have been, if his hand hadn't, at that instant, come in contact with the bare skin of her hips where panties should have been. Those expressive eyebrows shot upward. "Are you going commando?"

"No!" Rachel laughed. "It's a thong."

A groan broke from his chest. His hands caressed her bare buttocks and traced the edges of the fabric into intimate places. "You need to tell me about things like this. Hell, we could have had food delivered to our room." A huge grin formed as he tested the stretch of the tiny strip of fabric barely covering her crotch. He reached for his fly.

Voices outside the elevator penetrated Rachel's lust just as a beep, indicating the button had been pushed to reopen the door, was followed by clicking noises from the control panel. Slowly, the mechanism began its slow-motion journey to clear the way for whoever was waiting to enter.

Though she was confident her eyes held nothing but panic, Garrett's were sparkling with amusement as he set her on her feet, helped her tug her skirt down, and slid around behind her, using her body to hide his fairly noticeable arousal. As though on cue, a young couple stepped into the elevator at that exact moment and pushed the button for the third floor. Silence reigned in the tiny compartment as the door slowly closed once more and they lifted off with a small jerk.

The girl might have been twenty-one on a good day with the right ID, but Rachel would never have served her. Yet it appeared someone hadn't been as discriminating. She leaned heavily against the man, blowing bubbles with a large wad of gum, while she brazenly scrutinized Garrett. Rachel bit her lip to keep from laughing.

Garrett looped his arms around her middle and pulled her against him, kissing the top of her head. The girl skewered Rachel with a disgusted glare, then turned to her date and rubbed her heavily perfumed body against him. The poor guy had the good grace to at least appear embarrassed, but it was obvious she'd had too much to drink and whatever evening he'd hoped for was on a downhill slide.

It seemed like forever before the elevator slid to a halt, the door opened, and the man helped the girl stumble into the hallway. Rachel's humor disappeared with them. One more glass of wine and that could have been her. *Oh, Lord!* She and Garrett had very nearly done the deed…in an elevator…where anyone might have seen them. How dare she judge that young woman when her own behavior today had been disgraceful. Worse…because she *knew* better.

Garrett's laugh jarred her from her reverie as he stepped around her, hitting the button to close the door and send the elevator toward the top floor again. He turned and offered his hand. "Come here."

Rachel tensed and hooked her thumb toward the door. "That was our floor."

He took a deep breath, his gaze flitting over her face, the tiniest bit of concern darkening his countenance. "I know. Come here for a minute."

She shook her head slowly. "No. Garrett, did you see her? Drunk and acting like a complete slut...in public. Getting lucky was clearly a foregone conclusion for her boyfriend, but I'm pretty sure he couldn't wait to be rid of her." The words spewed from her until she finally had to stop for a breath.

Garrett's eyebrow lifted in that curious way he had, and he held his hand out to her again. "Rachel, please come here." Only two feet separated them. He could easily have reached her, yet he waited, steadfast as always.

Rachel was torn between annoyance and gratitude. In the end, it was the sexy stubble on his face that made her mind up for her. She took a step toward him.

He met her in the middle, gripping her shoulders firmly. His expression was somber and desperate at the same time. For a heartbeat, she dreaded what he was going to say. Studying his eyes, she threaded her fingers through his hair, watching each strand fall back into place. His expression softened, his jaw unclenched, and he leaned his forehead against hers.

"Are you going to tell me what's wrong?" Sadness and a hint of accusation surrounded his whispered words.

Rachel closed her eyes tightly so there'd be no chance of seeing the emotions flit across his face. Somehow he knew. Had he compared her to that girl, too? Did she come off looking just as sleazy to him? She couldn't put her finger on why it mattered—why it was suddenly so important that he respect her. She couldn't stop thinking that the girl might have been just like her at one time. Did one small indiscretion lead to what she'd become? Maybe they were more alike than Rachel wanted to believe.

"I don't want to be that—" She choked on the words.

He gave her a quick shake and her eyes popped open. "You're *not* that girl." The forcefulness of his words wouldn't allow her to look away.

Something in his strength and the trace of anger in his eyes made her stand straighter. She saw nothing but acceptance in his expression and felt the pride in his touch. Her heavy spirit began to fall away as she grabbed on to the truth of how he saw her with all of her strength. If he could believe in her that much, why shouldn't she? Self-assurance had never been lacking before.

Rachel tipped her chin so she looked directly in his eyes. "Well, just to be on the safe side, I think I'll quit drinking."

Garrett chuckled, and his concern dissolved into a crooked grin.

"And if I *ever* start to grope you in public, please just put me out of my misery."

He laughed softly and pulled her into his arms. "Don't worry. If that happens, I know just what to do."

Chapter Fifteen

GARRETT WALKED CLOSE beside Rachel on the lush green grass of the wooded acre that served as the venue for the classic car show. The lake, less than two hundred yards away, sparkled in the moonlight, adding its beauty to the surreal setting. Cowboy was on high alert beside him. The dog wasn't used to being leashed, and it always made him edgy. At least if anyone got within two feet of Rachel, Garrett would know.

Something had shifted, the tiniest fraction of an inch, between him and Rachel in that elevator earlier. As they'd returned to their room, grabbed jackets, and left again with Cowboy, a deeper trust had lingered in her eyes each time she glanced his way. He didn't fully understand, but the warmth that settled somewhere near his heart morphed into tenderness for the courageous redhead who'd grabbed his interest with little or no effort.

Now, more than ever, it was up to him to make sure nothing happened to her.

Garrett kept one eye on the crowd as they walked along a row of restored muscle cars, stopping to admire, occasionally speaking with an owner who stood ready to share information about horsepower and performance. Garrett was amazed and proud of Rachel's knowledge of the V-8 engines that powered the cars. Many times she carried the conversation herself, and he'd learn something new before they moved on.

After one particularly long interchange where even Cowboy got antsy, Garrett slung his arm around her shoulders and leaned close. "Where did you learn about cars?"

"One of my mother's many boyfriends when I was growing up was a mechanic. Unlike most of the men who hung around, he didn't mind answering my questions—until the day my mom kicked him out." She turned away, but not before he saw the pain reflected in her eyes.

"I've never heard you talk about your mother before. Why is that?" Of course, he had an idea. The *many boyfriends* reference kind of said it all. Was Rachel afraid she'd turn out like her mother? Is that why she'd had such a strong reaction to the girl in the elevator?

"We're not close. There's not much to talk about." She shrugged and tossed her head as though the small action would put a period at the end of the conversation.

Garrett chuckled and slid his arm around her waist—then stopped abruptly as he encountered the hard object against her back, hidden by the drape of her denim jacket over her hips.

He swung her around in front of him. "Are you carrying?"

"Of course. Aren't you?"

"Well…yes, but—aw hell! Never mind. I should have known you were…and that you'd keep that bit of news to yourself. Rachel, I thought we'd made a little breakthrough, but apparently not. When are you going to start trusting me?"

She pressed her palm against his chest. "I *do* trust you, Garrett. More than I ever thought possible, but that doesn't mean I'm going to be unarmed when Jeremy tries to kill you."

It always threw him when she steadfastly maintained that *he* was the one in danger—that Jeremy would go after *him* if their little ruse worked and they managed to pull him out into the open. Garrett hoped to hell she was right. He wanted a shot at the bastard in the worst way.

Over the top of Rachel's head, Garrett caught a glimpse of a familiar face. The words on his lips dissipated as he did a double take straight into the grinning mug of Jase Richards. *What in the hell?* Jase wasn't supposed to show until tomorrow.

As he stared, his friend motioned to his right where a coffee vendor occupied a temporary kiosk. Rachel looked over her shoulder, apparently noticing his shift in attention.

Irritation made him jumpy. What was going on with his friend anyway? He'd never known Jase to say one thing and do another. He must have a damn good reason. Garrett drew a deep breath to calm himself. "You remember Jase from the phone, right? How about if we go get a cup of coffee and I'll introduce you to him?"

Rachel raised one eyebrow. "That's Jase? Why doesn't he just come over here and say hello instead of making hand signals behind my back? I'm pretty sure he wants to talk to you privately, and frankly, I've been eyeing that ice cream stand over there." She jutted her chin back the way they'd come, just beyond the red-and-white 1968 Camaro whose owner had graciously let her sit in the car.

Garrett reached for her hand as though that would keep her beside him. He didn't like the idea of letting her get that far from him, though common sense told him it was only three car lengths away. Besides, he'd have a battle on his hands if he tried to tell her she couldn't go. He tried to put Cowboy's leash in her hand.

She wouldn't take it. "I don't have control over this dog the way you do. I know what you're going to say—he wouldn't let anything happen to me. That's true, but what if he perceives a threat where there isn't one? What if I can't stop him? I'd never forgive myself."

She was right, of course. There was always a possibility of an incident getting out of hand if someone didn't have complete control of an animal, especially one with the training that Cowboy had. He made a note to himself to teach her at the first opportunity. "Okay, I'll have my eye on you the whole time. You get your ice cream. I'll get Jase, and we'll meet back here. Turn your phone on just in case. Don't go anywhere else. Got it?" He was probably pushing his luck, but it had to be said.

To his surprise, she smiled. "You're kind of bossy, but I'll let you get away with it this time." She squeezed his hand before she pulled free, already digging for her cell phone.

Garrett watched the sway of her hips as she walked away, then turned toward the coffee shack his friend had indicated. As promised, he glanced over his shoulder every few seconds to track Rachel's progress.

Jase Richards had been a year ahead of Garrett in school, which made him thirty-five. He was a couple of inches shorter, but the size of his biceps and pecs kept most of the sleazeballs he encountered in his investigative work from causing problems. They'd gone through Ranger training together, going on to deployment with different units, and lost track of each other. Garrett had been promoted through the ranks, eventually making captain. Jase had finished his first hitch and opted out. When Garrett was sent stateside after the cluster that had killed most of his unit and wounded him, Jase was the first person to walk into his hospital room. They'd resumed their friendship as though only a few days had passed since they'd talked, instead of almost twelve years. Garrett still trusted him with his life.

"So...that's the beautiful lady, huh?" Jase gave a low whistle as Garrett approached. "Is it serious, or do I have a shot?"

Garrett turned to appreciate the same view Jase had. "That would be hands-off territory, Jase, and that's the only comment like that you get for free."

Jase threw his hands up. "Well, it's about damn time you got possessive about a woman. I'm happy for you."

He shoved a hot paper cup toward Garrett. "I hope you still drink a short Americano. I was worried about the caffeine keeping you up all night, but now that I've had a look at Rachel—"

Garrett slammed his fist into his friend's shoulder. "Jase. I meant what I said."

"Okay. Okay. Shit, man! That's gonna leave a bruise."

"Grab your fucking coffee and talk while we're walking. I don't like being this far away from her until we know for sure we've got her stalker under lock and key." Garrett started back toward Rachel and waited for Jase to catch up. "What are you doing here? Luke said you were flying in tomorrow."

"That was the original plan."

"And since when don't you tell me everything you know up front?" Garrett stared straight ahead, following Rachel's path.

"Keep in mind I'm just the messenger here, okay?" Jase rested a hand on Garrett's shoulder for a split second.

Rachel had purchased her ice cream in a cup and was meandering back along the line of cars they'd already looked over when the owner of the '68 Camaro approached and engaged her in conversation. The guy was harmless, so Garrett turned his attention back to Jase. "Waiting for you to spill it, Richards. What could possibly be so bad that you needed a face-to-face and a day earlier than planned?"

"Oh, I don't know. Could be I suddenly got dragged into this thing between you and your old man. As usual, he's got his own agenda, and I knew you'd be pissed as hell. So here I am if you need to take a punch at someone."

Garrett stopped and faced his friend. "What the hell are you talking about?"

Jase flung one arm up, his frustration clear. "I had a brief phone conversation this afternoon with the intruder they caught at that fucking wilderness lodge where you've apparently been hanging out. He didn't tell *me* anything either, in spite of my best interrogation techniques. Just gave me a phone number and *suggested* I call. He's one cool dude, man."

"Did you call?"

"You know I did." Jase looked toward the ground and shook his head.

"Well, who was it?" Garrett had already guessed the answer, and his patience was at an all-time low.

"Senator Harding." Jase raised his head.

Garrett smirked. Of course. He should have known. His old man certainly had the money and the clout to hire a professional like the one that currently languished back at the lodge. One of the most powerful men in the country, this wouldn't be the first time he'd used his position to his advantage. Yep. This had his father written all over it, though *why* he was interested…Garrett couldn't begin to fathom. He started walking again. "Did my father give you any useful information?"

Jase caught up in two strides. "Not really, but he's joining us via helicopter tomorrow at the Cougar Ridge Hunting Lodge." Jase groaned. "Shit! I tried, but I couldn't talk him out of it, Garrett, and he wouldn't explain why he was coming except that he had to talk to you in person."

Garrett clenched his one free fist, and for a moment, considered hurling the hot coffee somewhere into the crowd. "*That's* why you're here early—because you knew how long it would take me to get my head on straight after hearing your news. And taking quite a chance that I wouldn't lose it on the messenger, I might add." One glance at Jase's cautious expression told Garrett he was right. He looked toward Rachel in time to catch her smile in answer to something the owner of the car said, and an instant calm settled over him. In all his life, Garrett had never been able to guess what his father's reaction was going to be. That the senator was somehow involved in this, though momentarily surprising, was so very typical. Garrett couldn't wait to hear his bullshit explanation.

But—shit! Rachel was under the impression the man detained at the lodge was Jeremy, and that her life of hiding was finally over. Yet the senator couldn't be responsible for the stalker who'd killed Chance and made Rachel's life hell for the past ten years. Instinctively, Garrett knew his father wasn't involved with Jeremy. *The man detained at the lodge wasn't Rachel's stalker and probably didn't know anything about him. So who was he…and where the hell was Jeremy?*

Suddenly feeling too exposed, he searched for Rachel through a red haze of anger until he focused on her still talking to the owner of the Camaro and another man. She laughed and then shook her head, turning to go. The newcomer grabbed her left arm and didn't let go when she tried to shake him off. Cowboy growled low in his throat. Immediately, Garrett tossed his coffee cup into a nearby receptacle and jogged toward her. Jase must have noticed, too. Within a couple seconds, he was keeping pace beside Garrett and Cowboy.

Rachel dropped her ice cream and reached behind her back, flipping the edges of her jacket up. Garrett picked up his pace to cover the last ten feet and placed his hand on her back just as she would have drawn the weapon. Her sigh of relief was audible as she dropped her hand to his belt loops.

Cowboy's growl was menacing, and he stared straight at the man who had his hand on Rachel. Garrett knew just how he felt. The man released her and stumbled back, eyeing first the dog and then Garrett.

"Is everything all right, sweetheart?" Garrett slung his arm around her shoulder and smiled.

Rachel stared the man down for a second before turning to Garrett. "Uh-huh. I've been having the nicest conversation about this Camaro, but then I spilled my ice cream." She reached to scratch Cowboy's head and finally managed to drag his attention away from the man he'd been fixated on.

"Don't worry. We'll get you another one." He turned her away from the two men and headed for the ice cream stand. He knew Jase would have his back, just like always, even though they hadn't spent much time together for the past few years. Old habits died hard.

"What was that about?" Garrett leaned close and spoke in a low voice.

"I don't really know. The Camaro owner and I were talking, and then the other guy joined in and said he had a '69 Dodge Charger he thought I'd like. And then he got really insistent about taking me to see it. I tried to walk away, and you saw the rest. *Oh God!* I was so glad to see you. I thought I was really going to have to shoot someone." She hugged him around the waist as they continued walking.

"Any possibility it was Jeremy?" Garrett hated to ask, but he had to know.

She backed up a step as a small gasp escaped, and the disappointment in her eyes made her stiffen and glance around. "I hadn't considered that. I was under the assumption Jeremy was locked up at the lodge." Her brow furrowed. "He's not…is he? Is that what your friend Jase came to tell you? Oh God." Her voice dropped to a whisper as she hugged herself. "That guy…touched me. I should have shot him." She choked out a laugh, sounding close to hysteria.

He pulled her into his arms and kissed the side of her forehead. "You did just right, sweetheart. I'm proud of you. Until we know for sure who's back at the lodge, we need to operate like Jeremy's still out there somewhere. I'm sorry I wasn't there when you needed me. I won't let you get that far away from me again—not until this is over." They paused by the ice cream stand, and Garrett reached for his wallet as Jase halted beside him.

Rachel shook her head. "No. Thanks, but I couldn't eat anything now." Her smile was slightly strained, but she was clearly trying to keep it together.

"Rachel, this is Jase Richards. We've been friends since we were kids, enlisted together, and went through Ranger training side by side. You can trust him."

"Hey, beautiful lady. Garrett wasn't lying." Jase shook the hand she offered.

"I don't think we were expecting you until tomorrow. Is something wrong?" As usual, Rachel cut through the bullshit.

Jase glanced at Garrett, obviously not sure how much he should share.

Garrett wanted to put them both at ease. "You can tell Rachel anything you'd tell me." He cupped her chin and turned her face so he could study her eyes. "But maybe not tonight. I think I'll take you back to the hotel." He kissed her lips gently and looked up in time to see Jase grinning at his own feet.

"Jase." The word was a warning.

"What? I didn't say anything."

Garrett snorted a laugh. "Where are you staying?"

"Comfort Inn near the freeway."

"We'll pick you up at six, have breakfast, and hit the road."

"I'll be ready." He gave an informal salute. "It's damn good to see you, Garrett."

"You know it." Garrett shook his hand and then the two of them bumped elbows as they'd done as part of their secret handshake when they were kids. Then they both broke up in laughter. Damn. It really was good to see him. Maybe leaving the army wouldn't be the worst thing that ever happened.

"Goodnight, Jase." Rachel waved her hand as Garrett led her up the path toward the street and the Explorer.

As soon as they left the crowd behind, he unhooked the leash from Cowboy's collar and gave him the command to heel. A few minutes later, Garrett let the dog clamber over the front seat and disappear into the back before he closed Rachel inside the cab of the Explorer and strode around to the other side. He hadn't missed the fact she'd started shaking about halfway back. On the off chance she was only cold, he started the engine and turned the heater on high as soon as it warmed up. It didn't seem to help.

He was about to pull away from the curb when Rachel's phone chirped. It took her three rings to fish it from her bag. Her shaking hand, holding the device, made it clear to Garrett who was calling. He reached for the phone. "Let me take it."

Rachel shook her head. "No. Jeremy can't know you're here. I have to do this." She pressed the speaker button. "What do you want now, Jeremy?"

Garrett was proud of the strength in her voice when he knew how her insides were quaking. This answered their question. Jeremy wasn't under house arrest at the lodge tonight. He could be anywhere.

"Rachel. I'm glad to see you getting out again. It's been a long time." His voice, muffled and clearly disguised, filled the cab.

She glanced sharply at Garrett, fear in her eyes. Sitting up straighter, she pulled the phone closer to her mouth. "I couldn't care less what makes you happy. When are you going to stop hiding and face me?"

Garrett raised his hand and brought it down slowly in a gesture he hoped would warn her not to intentionally annoy him. He didn't want the jerk upset with Rachel. If Jeremy needed someone to take out his anger on, Garrett would gladly accept that role.

"Patience, my love. It won't be long before we're together. However, I'm a bit exasperated with you. Have you forgotten what I did to the last man who had the audacity to take what was mine? *Have you?*"

Rachel's face had gone white. "No, I haven't forgotten."

"Yet you flaunt your new boyfriend in front of my face?"

"He's not my boyfriend. We're just friends." Panic edged her voice.

"And you're willing to lie for him. You can see that I have no choice, right?"

Garrett reached for her hand that held the phone, pulling it toward him. "Come and get me, Jeremy. Let's finish this."

"You'll be sorry, Rachel." Jeremy was gone, the connection dead, before either of them could say more.

"Turn it off." Garrett released her hand, knowing full well she was pissed as hell at him.

"Why did you do that? I could have convinced him that there was nothing between us."

"You heard him. He already knew about us." He let his fingers trail down her arm to rest on her thigh. "I think it's safe to say he's been watching for a while now. But we've got something going for us that Chance didn't have. We know Jeremy's coming."

Rachel covered her face with her hands, slid them upward through her hair, and turned toward the window. The sun had set, and dusk's gray light settled quickly over the trees around the lake. Garrett pointed the car toward the hotel.

Rachel's silence was broken only by intermittent bouts of shaking. Shock, probably. It'd been one hell of a long day, physically and emotionally. He should have seen this coming and called a halt to anything but rest a long time ago. That's what she needed, and that's what she'd get for the remainder of the night.

On the way up in the elevator, she clung to him and trembled. As soon as the door opened, he swung her into his arms and strode down the long hallway to their door, unlocked it, and pushed it open. Cowboy followed them in and guarded the door until Garrett set her on her feet, handed her something flannel from her bag, and pointed her toward the bathroom. Then he retraced his steps to lock the door, gave Cowboy a biscuit, and scratched the dog's ears as he moved alongside him to the center of the room.

Garrett waited until he heard the water running in the bathroom sink before he stepped out onto the deck with his cell phone in his hand. Cowboy pressed against his legs as Garrett leaned into the railing and dialed Luke's number. Part of him wanted to keep the news about the senator's impending arrival to himself on the chance he'd change his mind and stay the hell away. But it wouldn't be like his father to say one thing and do another. Garrett had to warn the occupants of the lodge, because unless he missed his guess, at least one of them would be very unhappy.

"Hey, Garrett. I didn't expect to hear from *you* tonight. Everything okay?" The familiar warmth of Luke's voice made him homesick.

"Depends on your definition of *okay*." Garrett paused and raked a hand through his hair. "Jase showed up early."

"Any particular reason?" A hint of concern came through in Luke's tone.

Garrett laughed scornfully. "Came to see me personally to tell me Dad would be showing up at the lodge tomorrow."

"Oh shit. What's goin' on?" Tension flooded Luke's voice.

Garrett switched gears. "Have you spoken with Aunt Peg about Amanda?"

Luke sighed heavily. "Yeah."

"Do you believe her?"

"I don't know. I want to because she's a damn fine lady, but Dad— Yeah, he's a hard-ass and an SOB but…to cut Mom loose without trying to help her—I just don't know if I can buy that."

Garrett closed his eyes and the silence between them lengthened. He respected Luke's opinion. His honesty was exactly what Garrett needed in order to give his father a chance to be heard tomorrow before sending him packing. "I didn't want you or Aunt Peg to be surprised by the senator. He's somehow involved with the man you've got locked up. He's arriving there at noon by helicopter. If I'm not there by then, you'll have to break the news to Aunt Peg and Jonathan so no one shoots the old man before he says his piece."

"Jeez, Garrett. Do you think that's a good idea?"

"Hell no. I think it stinks, but I don't have any control over him." Garrett turned at a sound behind him. Rachel was backlit by the light from the bathroom, and Garrett's heart took on a wild rhythm of its own. Reluctantly, he turned his attention to the phone. "One more thing, Luke. This means your captive isn't Rachel's stalker, so keep your eyes open."

"Got it. I'll let Jonathan know."

"Good idea. By the way, how's Sally? I noticed you couldn't keep your eyes off her this morning." A smile curled Garrett's lips and humor vibrated in his voice.

Luke chuckled. "Isn't it time you hung up, bro?"

"Could be. See you tomorrow." Garrett ended the call, and knelt to pat the dog vigorously before motioning him inside, following him, and closing the slider behind them.

Rachel sat cross-legged in the middle of the bed. Her hair was brushed and shining, hanging in ringlets across her shoulders. The *something flannel* he'd handed her to wear wasn't the warm, practical sleepwear he'd had in mind. A teal-colored short-sleeved top hugged her breasts in stark relief and stopped about three inches short of her waistline. The cute little plaid boxers she wore with it were tight and brief, and he ached to touch her where the fabric stretched across her skin. He swallowed hard and dragged his gaze to her face.

She was apparently inspecting something below his waist, and Garrett had a pretty good idea what it was since the past thirty seconds had resulted in a raging hard-on. Continuing her perusal upward, she eventually met his gaze and a teasing smile erupted on her beautiful face.

Cowboy padded over to the bed and laid his head near her leg. She stretched forward and scratched the dog, crooning to him about what a good boy he was. Her top slid farther up her back, revealing even more skin. Garrett was sure he would bust out of his zipper, all the while wishing she was rubbing her hands over him and telling him what a *bad* boy he was.

"Are you feeling better now?" He turned away to get a grip and kicked off his shoes. Rest. That was what she needed. Isn't that what he'd told himself?

"Yes, I'm fine. Thanks for asking. I think everything got to me all at once when that guy wouldn't let go of my arm and then Jeremy called. I get a little panicky in crowds anyway. I'm better now."

"That's good." He unbuttoned his shirt, shrugged out of it, and tossed it across the back of a chair, weighing the benefits of a cold shower to his present situation.

Rachel sighed and Garrett glanced toward her to make sure she was all right. She was looking down, toying with a piece of string or something on the comforter. "Um…were you talking to Luke? Is everything okay at the lodge?"

Garrett sat on the edge of the bed and slid his hand down her satiny-smooth legs, noting an instant too late that touching her probably wasn't the best idea. "Everyone's fine." He paused, searching for the right words. "I have to tell you something, and you're not going to like it."

She didn't reply, so he glanced over his shoulder. Her eyes met his, all seriousness now. "What is it?"

Garrett gave her a quick overview of his conversation with Jase and then again with Luke. He didn't know what her reaction might be, but he wouldn't be surprised if she blew up and tried to forbid the senator from entering the lodge. Instead, she scooted closer so she could explore his biceps with her small hands. His blood heated at her touch.

He remained motionless until he couldn't withstand the torture of not touching her back. "Okay, that's enough. You're going to get some rest tonight if I have to sleep in the car." He tried to sound authoritative and convincing, but she moved closer still.

Leaning her breasts into his back, her arms encircled him, dragging the tips of her fingernails across his chest, down his abs, to where his jeans rode low on his hips. A growl rumbled from his throat as what was left of his control crumbled into fine dust.

Chapter Sixteen

"WHY ARE YOU staring at me?" Rachel stretched sleepily seconds after waking to find Garrett propped up on his elbow, leaning over her.

His disarmingly sexy smile made her heart thump as he slowly covered her lips with his in an amazingly tender kiss. Then he grinned. "I'm used to waking up with a dog in my face—literally. I'm just taking a few minutes to appreciate my change of fortune."

She laughed. "Always nice to know who the competition is, but how could a girl possibly contend with Cowboy?" She moved closer, kissing Garrett's neck just below his ear.

He moaned and enfolded her in his arms, drawing her toward him until the thick, hard ridge of his manhood pressed against her stomach. Warm lips met hers, sucking and sipping, until time seemed to stand still. "Cowboy, who?" he breathed against her lips at one point, and she giggled, the sound muffled by his tongue intertwined with hers.

Then he rolled onto his back, lifting her effortlessly until she straddled his hips. "I believe you said something about wanting the top?"

"You remembered."

"I remember everything," he said as desire darkened his eyes.

Rachel leaned forward and he lifted her again, one hand on each side of her waist, impaling her slowly and deliciously on his rigid staff. When he was fully seated and they were both breathing heavily, his grip on her backside set the rhythm. Heated friction drove her nearly mad with desire, and she closed her eyes, letting the sensations transport her to a world of unimagined delight.

THEIR EARLY MORNING antics had made them late. They'd had to get dressed and fly out the door in order to make it to Jase's motel at the appointed hour. Now, sitting beside Garrett in the front seat of the Explorer, every time his steamy gray eyes rested on her, the reason for their distraction came back in living color. Based on the grin he tried unsuccessfully to hide, he hadn't forgotten, either.

Rachel wasn't likely to ever put aside the memory of waking this morning, curled snugly in the strong arms of Garrett Harding. For the first time in many years, she'd felt as though she wasn't alone. That Garrett cared about her and was willing to prove it by standing beside her while Jeremy slammed them with the worst he had. She was falling in love with Garrett even though it was premature and irresponsible. In the end, she'd probably get hurt. Still, sometime between dinner last night, meeting Jase, and hearing the news about Senator Harding's planned visit to the lodge, she'd accepted Garrett as a man worth fighting for. Forget that he'd spent a third of his life in the army, embracing the customs of a nomad. Never mind that the only home he knew was in California. He'd be returning there in the near future…unless she could change his mind. And wasn't she always up for a challenge?

He leaned toward her as he pointed out her side window at a small herd of deer munching the tall grass of a meadow. His spicy aroma invaded her senses and intensified memories of the night before. Instantly, her breathing grew ragged, her heart drummed in her ears, and the temperature in her corner of the Explorer shot up to about a hundred degrees. All too aware of Jase sitting directly behind her, she shifted self-consciously as her barely there panties dampened.

She bore the heat for as long as she could and then hastily rolled down her window, letting the cool mountain air blow through her hair and fill the vehicle with woodsy scents. When she sneaked a peek at Garrett, feeling conspicuously like a schoolgirl, he reached to slide his fingers down her cheek, his eyes still on the road.

Within seconds, his gaze darted to her face, and he moved his hand to her arm, squeezing gently. "Damn, sweetheart, you're awfully warm. What's wrong? Are you sick?"

Rachel was sure she took on another shade of red while trying to signal him with her eyes to let it go. "I'm fine. I was just really...hot."

His quizzical expression only deepened, and his gaze swept her face for a heartbeat before a heated flicker danced in his eyes and a crooked grin settled in place. "Shit. You're killing me over here." Garrett's words were barely above a whisper.

Her lips curved involuntarily, and she shook her head slowly. "We should be bone tired and sick of each other."

"Well, you've got the bone tired part right, but we're just getting started, sweetheart." Garrett winked and desire pooled low in her stomach.

Cowboy barked, and Rachel jumped.

Jase patted the shepherd's side. "I agree, boy. They're talking all hot and nasty like we're not even here. Jeez, guys! Get a room."

Garrett's lips thinned and his eyes darkened as he glanced in the rearview mirror.

Rachel placed her hand on his thigh and shook her head discreetly when he focused on her. She laughed, maybe a bit too loudly. "Sounds like Jase is jealous."

"Damn it to hell! You've got that right!" Jase slapped the back of her seat and chortled.

Garrett's tentative smile gradually grew, and finally he joined in their laughter, but clearly, whatever had upset him still resided in the shadows around his eyes. What was it that had made him so instantly angry? He was protective of her, but did that extend to teasing remarks made by lifelong friends in fun? Or did he object to being paired with her in the minds of people he knew?

Rachel forced herself to leave that particular line of thought alone since it directly contradicted her need to convince Garrett to stay. If it turned out he couldn't, or wouldn't, then she'd know, but this was one case when she wasn't going to read between the lines.

Cowboy squeezed through the narrow opening of the seats, greeted Garrett with a lick on the chin, then leaned against Rachel, his head and neck lying in her lap. She stroked his thick fur for several minutes until he plopped down between her and Garrett, apparently settling in for a nice nap. Between the warmth of the sun in the small cab and the world flying by outside her window, she was close to dropping off herself. She was aware of the guys speaking in quiet voices, but she hadn't kept track of their conversation. Something about the letters and if they still existed. They had to be talking about the letters Amanda had written. Garrett sounded sad. Amanda had been sad much of the time as well. A family ripped apart by lies and deceit.

RACHEL'S HEAD BANGED against the door frame, and she came instantly awake.

"Welcome back, sleepyhead." Garrett smiled and winked, the same desire in his eyes that she remembered from before she'd closed hers just to rest for a few minutes.

Again, her body responded in kind, but this time she stopped short of voicing her thoughts. Instead, she glanced over her shoulder to where Jase and Cowboy lounged. "How long was I out?" Obviously, she'd been asleep for a while. They'd just turned off the highway onto Cougar Ridge Road, which led directly to the lodge. They were home.

"A couple of hours," Jase replied. "I was about to check for signs of life."

Garrett turned toward her. "Feel better? Ready to meet my father? You realize you can opt out of this, right?"

"Are you kidding? I need someone to hold all that misplaced anger I tagged you with. I wouldn't miss this." She smiled reassuringly. "Besides, your father is only a tiny blip on my screen. Don't forget I have to face Peg, too. I hurt her so badly by leaving the way I did, she may not forgive me. I may be looking for a new place to live after all."

"I wouldn't worry about that. Aunt Peg thinks you're pretty special. Even I can see that. She may be a bit upset, but she'll understand once you explain." Garrett smiled encouragingly.

They turned the last corner and the lodge appeared before them. A sleek black helicopter sat in the middle of the meadow, and three men with ear gadgets and bulges beneath their suit jackets trampled the pretty wildflowers down to nothing in a circle around the craft.

A smaller, more businesslike version of Garrett stepped out of the chopper. Senator Douglas Harding was a good-looking man for his age. He had the tan of a hardworking outdoorsman, and it contrasted nicely with his full head of silver hair, although the aviator sunglasses were a bit much.

Rachel tensed, and Garrett reached for her hand. "I'm going to let you out at the lodge. Then I'm coming back and I'm going to set a few ground rules before we get started. One thing you should know—my father invented the intimidation factor, but don't let him get to you because it's all just part of the facade."

Jonathan appeared at Garrett's window as soon as they stopped in front of the lodge. He searched Rachel's face before he focused on Garrett. "Peg's pretty upset. Said she doesn't want the senator in her home."

Garrett raked a hand through his hair, glanced at Rachel, then toward Luke, who'd just joined the group. "Well…it's her call. If she doesn't want him in there, I'm happy to tell him he wasted his time."

Jase leaned forward. "Your old man's come a long way, Garrett. Let's at least hear what he has to say. We can talk back there in the field if we have to."

Rachel touched Garrett's arm. "Jase is right. We could meet on the back patio. It wouldn't be completely private, but there are plenty of chairs, and I can ask Dory to bring out some coffee and iced tea."

Pride shone in his eyes as Garrett smiled. "Jonathan, do you think that would that be all right with Aunt Peg?"

Jonathan and Luke both nodded.

Garrett turned to Rachel again. "Will you talk to her? Explain why we have to hear him out?"

She opened her door and swung her legs out. "I'll do my best. Give me ten minutes."

Jase jumped out, and Luke hopped into the front seat. Garrett backed the Explorer out of its parking spot and retraced their path across the bridge. He stopped on the edge of the road across from where Senator Harding paced.

As soon as the car halted, Harding started forward. The two brothers stepped from the car and went to meet him. Rachel turned toward the house even though there was nothing she'd like better than to witness this reunion. Impatience had defined Harding's body language, but heaven help him if he voiced his intolerance to Garrett today. A small smile surfaced before she wiped it away and focused on the task at hand.

Quickly she made the introductions between Jonathan and Jase. "Would the two of you check the patio, please? Make sure there are enough chairs and that they've been wiped down today. Can't have the senator from California getting his ass dirty."

Jonathan snickered. "I'll take care of it, Rachel." His gaze settled on her for a moment. "It's good to have you back."

Rachel was certain his perusal had stripped her of any privacy. Surely he would guess what had transpired between her and Garrett. If he couldn't tell just by looking, no doubt the blush that heated her features and did a slow burn clear to her ears would give him the rest of the details.

"Are Sally and Jen still here?"

Jonathan nodded. "Luke talked them into staying till the end of the week, just in case."

"Good. That was thoughtful of Luke. Remind me to thank him when this is over."

"I don't think he did it for you, Rach."

Jonathan's amused grin confused her. It wasn't until he and Jase veered off to head toward the back patio that Rachel got the meaning behind his words. *Huh! Luke interested in Sally?* Evidently a lot had happened in the day she'd been gone.

Outside the lobby, Alan Taylor stood talking with another familiar guest of the lodge. Hugh Findley had made it here for every early black bear hunt Rachel could remember. It was customary for two or three of his friends to also descend on the resort, and a good time would be had by all for the better part of a week.

The way Alan and Hugh were gesturing at the helicopter and the men in the field, it was obvious what they were discussing, but they both smiled as she approached. "There you are, Rachel. We missed you at dinner last night." Alan's greeting was friendly, but she got the feeling he was waiting for her to explain where she'd been, and that wasn't happening.

She forced a cheery smile, glancing around for Mrs. Taylor, but didn't see her. "Rest assured I'll be there tonight, Alan, and Peg probably won't let me escape again until the summer season is over." She turned toward Hugh and offered her hand. "Welcome back. It's so good to see you again. I'm just going into a meeting, but we'll have time to catch up this evening. Have either of you seen Peg?"

Alan and Hugh eventually agreed that she'd been heading for the kitchen the last time they'd seen her, so Rachel excused herself and strode down the long hallway that led to the cooking and laundry facilities. Peg was alone in the kitchen, sitting at a long side table, her face buried in her hands, shoulders shaking with sobs.

"Peg?" Rachel hurried to her side. "What's wrong?"

Peg's head jerked up, and she hastily wiped her tears. She rose and wrapped Rachel in her arms. "Thank God you're home. You mustn't ever leave like that again, dear. My heart couldn't take it."

A blanket of guilt dropped over Rachel's shoulders. "I'm so sorry, Peg. I'll explain everything when we have more time. I had a good reason…or at least I thought I did, but no, I won't ever leave again without saying good-bye."

Peg's struggle to control her emotions was obvious. About halfway successful, she turned her red-rimmed eyes toward Rachel. "He's still here, isn't he?"

"If you mean Senator Harding—yes. But Garrett is here, too, and he won't let his father be disrespectful to you." Rachel wiped away a stray tear that rolled down Peg's cheek.

"I'm afraid—" She hiccupped and turned her face away.

Rachel sat in the chair next to her and pulled her into a tight embrace. "You don't have to be afraid. Jonathan, Garrett, and I are here for you, and the minute Harding says something out of line, he's out of here."

Peg smiled through her tears. "I know, dear. I'm not afraid of Douglas." She pulled a Kleenex from her pocket and wiped her nose. "Amanda told me the drugs affected her judgment—made her irresponsible. She slept a lot. She wasn't there for the boys sometimes when they needed her. I've never told anyone, but I've always had a gut feeling there was more. In all the years we had together, Amanda never told me what really happened—what convinced her to go through with the divorce and sign away custody of her boys. Did one of them fall down the stairs when she wasn't around to supervise them? Take a header off the swing set? Did she lose one at the supermarket? She never said…and I didn't ask, because I knew deep down that it would change things between us. She needed me. I was all she had."

"You're afraid Senator Harding will tell the story in an attempt to discredit her?"

"Why else would he be here, except to keep his sons from feeling anything for their mother? He'll tell them." She choked on a laugh and a bleak smile appeared for a second. "The wise woman inside of me concedes that after all the lies and secrecy, Luke and Garrett deserve answers—all of them."

"So do you, Peg. You loved Amanda all of her life. Nothing you hear today will change that. We both know what kind of a person she was. Loving, honest, and loyal. The Amanda we knew would never have hurt those boys—not in a million years. Whatever happened…it happened when she was someone else—someone who didn't know what she was doing."

Peg straightened and dried her face. "You're right. It's time I stopped being afraid. Time I accepted the truth so it can't hurt me any longer." She met Rachel's eyes, a new toughness in hers. "Let's go see what the bastard has to say."

A short laugh spilled from Rachel, and she hugged Peg again, proud of her determination. "Everyone's gathering on the back patio. Come on. We'll go out together as soon as I find Dory and order up some iced tea and coffee."

Peg whipped out her phone, dialed, and in two seconds was speaking to Dory, giving her Rachel's request. Clearly, Peg was back in control.

Three minutes later, Rachel followed Peg onto the patio. Jonathan and Jase already sat on one side of a large outdoor table. Between them lounged a man Rachel had never seen before. Dressed in black jeans and T-shirt, hair cut short, and muscles bulging on arms, shoulders, and thighs, he had to be the intruder who'd turned their lives upside down. He appeared completely comfortable in his surroundings even though Jonathan guarded him attentively.

Garrett and Luke stood off to the side with their father, although clearly there was no idle conversation between them. Garrett's hands were balled into fists, and his jaw flexed every few seconds. Cowboy sat by his leg, alert and watchful, having obviously picked up on the tension in the air. Poor Luke was straight-backed, and his gaze darted frequently toward the path that led around front, giving her the impression he was about to bolt. Obviously, Luke wasn't a fan of confrontation, especially one involving his father and his brother. He looked every bit the part of someone caught between two giant bulldozers. Luke took a seat at the table, casting his brother an I'm-so-glad-you-called-me-here-for-this glare. Garrett only nodded before turning his attention to his father.

Dory wheeled out a cart containing a thermos of coffee, a pitcher of iced tea, and cups. She studied the newcomers curiously, then hastened back the way she'd come.

As soon as Garrett spotted Peg, he pulled a chair out for her at the head of the table. She quirked an eyebrow, accompanied by the barest of smiles, and he winked. Their brief exchange put a smile on Rachel's face while he held a chair for her and then sat beside her. It touched her somewhere deep inside when he leaned back, crossed one leg over his thigh, and grabbed her hand, holding it close to his chest for the whole world to see. Jonathan, Peg, and Senator Harding homed in on the familiarity immediately. Rachel didn't know whether to blush or do cartwheels.

Jase came to her rescue. "Okay, we're all here. Just to catch you up—as you know, the intruder you captured yesterday asked to speak with me by phone. How he even knew about me, I don't know, but I'm sure Senator Harding can fill us in on that. Unless anyone has an objection, we'll give him the floor."

The senator adjusted his suit jacket and nodded toward the intruder slightly as he stepped forward. "First, I'd like to thank you all for agreeing to hear me out. Second, your intruder works for me. His name is Trent Michaels, and he's a private investigator." He ignored the looks of consternation both of his sons shot him. "Trent overheard Garrett's conversation on a tiny, experimental listening device he's currently testing for the army. That's how he knew to call you, Jase." He turned to face Garrett. "I'm not proud of it, son, but I hired Trent to keep tabs on you.

You went off half-cocked, wouldn't listen to anything I had to say. I needed to know what kind of half-truths you were being fed here."

Peg's hands slammed onto the tabletop, and everyone turned in time to see her stand.

Her face set in anger, eyes flashing fire, she pinned him where he stood. "You've got a lot of nerve, Douglas, accusing *me* of half-truths. I didn't tell Garrett his mother was a drug addict who couldn't take care of him anymore. It wasn't me who hid twenty-nine years' worth of letters from your sons—letters that would have proved she loved them and wanted to see them. How *dare* you even come here? Take your Trent Michaels and leave us in peace."

Rachel had never heard Peg's voice so cold and eerily calm. She examined the woman's face and found no trace of indecision or weakness. Pride in the matronly owner of Cougar Ridge Lodge grew until the lump that formed in Rachel's throat threatened to choke her.

Garrett released her hand and pushed to his feet. Scowling at his father, he strode toward Peg. After briefly studying her, he slid his arm around her shoulders and his unspoken message was clear—anyone who intended to cause her grief would have to go through him. Rachel practically had to sit on her hands to keep from applauding.

Garrett stared at his father. "I have to say I agree with Aunt Peg, but let's cut to the chase, Dad. I know enough about Mom now to form my own opinions. Maybe I *was* too young at five to hear all of the details, but you had a lot of opportunities to tell me…and didn't. Don't hold it against Aunt Peg for being the one person brave enough to answer my questions."

He met Rachel's gaze and the barest smile went straight to her heart. "But that's not why I came back today. When Michaels first started sniffing around, we thought he was the stalker who's been terrorizing Rachel for the last ten years. Since then, evidence has come to light proving otherwise. But I'm still going to ask—do you...or your hired man...know anything about that?"

Senator Harding's eyes shifted to her, and Rachel squirmed under his perusal, growing more annoyed with each passing second.

Suddenly Garrett was behind her chair, his hands warm and comforting on her shoulders. "Your silence speaks volumes, Senator."

A bark of laughter escaped Garrett's father. "It's not what you think. Of course I investigated the people you'd likely meet here. Rachel Maguire, Jonathan Reyes, Dory Sullivan— all of the longtime employees. I found some *gaps* in the history of a couple people. Your Rachel was one of them." His gaze swept toward Jonathan, then back to Garrett. "I figured she was running from something, so I had Trent dig a little deeper. He found the still-unsolved murder of her boyfriend in Texas. I presume she professes her innocence?"

Rachel inhaled sharply and would have jumped up to deck the SOB if Garrett's hands hadn't still been pressing her into the chair.

"Senator." This time Garrett's voice held a warning. "Apparently, Michaels isn't very good at his job if he didn't uncover the answer to that question."

Trent Michaels smirked and remained silent.

For the first time, Harding appeared deflated. "The police hit a dead end. I wanted to make sure Peg didn't have a murderer working here, so I had Trent pursue it. He had a contact that was going at it from a different angle—but I don't imagine he's been getting many e-mails since you've been holding him."

Garrett's grip tightened on her shoulders. "Will you share your information with Rachel?"

Harding laughed scornfully. "Well, I finally found something to bargain with, and from the looks of things, I'll lose either way. Just tell me, son, when are you coming home?"

Garrett's strong thumbs rubbed her shoulder blades. "I'm not exactly sure where home is at this point. I was thinking of staying here for a while. Luke will be deploying soon."

"You have two other brothers and a sister who'd like to see you."

"I'll invite them for a visit. A place like this would be a breath of fresh air to them."

Harding's derisive laugh came again. "Oh, I almost forgot—you and Luke are part owners of this place now, thanks to me. That's right. Who do you think gave your mother the money to buy this resort? How much do you think it took to get her to leave quietly? She may have agreed to leave because she was concerned about your safely, but I had to hand it to her; she knew how to get what she wanted from the bargain."

Peg's intake of air was the first thing Rachel heard, then a muted roar of indignation broke out behind her.

"Did you really come all this way to speak ill of the dead?" Garrett's hands left Rachel's shoulders, and he stepped around her. "Is your closet so clean that you can afford to do that?"

"I will do whatever it takes to—"

"That's enough, Dad." Luke's voice, vibrating with tension, made the occupants of the small patio fall silent.

Rachel couldn't get past the part where Garrett and his brother were owners...of the lodge. Amanda had undoubtedly left them her half. Of course, she would have. Rachel should have suspected, yet it had come out of left field, bounced off her glove, and hit her in the face. The worst part was that it had come from Senator Harding. Why hadn't Garrett told her? Or Peg? A burning sense of betrayal lodged in her chest.

From the corner of her eye, she saw Luke striding toward his father, his fists clenched as if he was going to do the decking she'd wanted to do. Garrett took a couple of steps forward and stood ready—for what, she didn't dare guess.

Luke stopped in front of his father. "If you're going to talk about Mom, let's hear it all. What happened? What did she do that made you pay her off and send her away?"

Behind her, Rachel heard Peg's moan and glanced over her shoulder in time to see her drop into her chair. Rachel slid from her seat and rushed to her, temporarily pushing aside the sensation of having been blindsided. Knowing how terrified Peg was of this exact revelation made Rachel tremble as she wrapped her arms around the older woman's shoulders.

Senator Harding swept his gaze from Luke to Garrett and shook his head sadly. "Since Peg seems to have all the answers, I'll let her fill you in on that as well. Now, if you'll be so kind as to release Trent, we'll be on our—"

"Wait." Rachel hated that her voice shook, but it wasn't from fear or timidity. Harding's superior attitude had finally broken through her control, and the floodgates had opened on her fury. She met his eyes with a cold stare. "I can see how you might be good at intimidating everyone around you, Senator. I suppose that goes with the job. Here, we don't give a damn who you are or what you do for a living." She could sense Garrett's eyes on her, but she didn't look away from the senator.

"This resort belonged to Peg and Amanda. Now it's Peg's. She's the top honcho. She's earned our respect, and you'd do well to remember that while you're a visitor here. I, for one, am waiting to hear the answer to Luke's question. Since Peg was never privy to that information, you're going to have to step up, for once in your life, and tell the truth."

A quick glance at Garrett sent her heart plummeting. A disappointed scowl darkened his visage for a split second before he turned and strode toward Luke. Was he really upset with her for standing up to his father? Hadn't she warned him that she'd have a few things to say? Her breath left her on a shudder. Of all the rotten ways that Jeremy had shattered her life, they were nothing compared with the disappointment on Garrett's face just now.

The senator paced angrily, darting hateful glances toward her. She tipped her chin up a notch and glared back. Garrett stopped beside Luke and placed a brotherly hand on his shoulder. He exchanged some whispered words with Luke, who then retreated a few feet, turned, and crossed his arms over his chest. Rachel could almost see the rock-solid defenses he threw up around himself. Clearly, being deserted by his mother had more of an effect on Luke than even Garrett had realized.

Silence was the order of the day, except for the angry whispers between Senator Harding and Garrett. Peg was so still, Rachel chastised herself for adding her voice to Luke's in demanding an answer. What if Peg's mind couldn't deal with the truth? Jonathan scooted his chair closer and covered one of her hands with his. Obviously, he was worried, too.

"No one's best interests will be served by dredging up the past, but if that's what all of you want, then that's what you'll get." Senator Harding looked around the patio, meeting each set of eyes, weighing each person's fortitude. When he came to Peg, his gaze lingered.

Her back stiffened. "She was my sister. I'd like to know if you wouldn't mind, Douglas." Though polite, Rachel recognized the steel that twined through her words.

Senator Harding heaved a sigh and threw his hands in the air as though to reiterate the warning he'd given. Then he pulled out a chair from another table, dropped into it, and blew out another breath. "There was a skiing accident at Vale the winter before she left. Amanda tore up her knee, and it required extensive surgery. Sometime during her recovery, she became addicted to her pain medication. I wasn't paying close enough attention. I didn't know how bad it was."

Rachel could only surmise how hard that confession had been for Harding. The question poised on her lips—why not?—went unasked.

"I was traveling. Campaign stops for Democratic candidates in the Southwest. Amanda decided to take you boys and go visit your grandmother in San Francisco. She'd called, told me her plans. It wasn't unusual—she'd made the trip many times." For a moment, the senator looked lost and uncertain, as if he was seeing something other than the rapt faces before him.

Rachel couldn't see Garrett's face. He'd turned away from everybody and stared at the back of the lodge. Tension emanated from him, and she longed to go to him, slide her arms around his waist, and lean her head against the strength of his back. Instinctively, she sensed he didn't want her comfort. The disappointment on his face earlier had changed everything.

"She'd left a note. Thank God our nosey housekeeper read it and called me. The note said she couldn't live like this anymore. I left her alone all the time. She was in pain. She was afraid for the boys." A sound like a sob choked him. "She rambled on. I couldn't understand her, but something in the things she said scared me, so I called your grandmother. She hadn't seen Amanda or you boys—didn't even know you were coming. So I had no choice. I called the state police.

"They found the car eventually, parked on a deserted logging road. She told them she was just sitting there, waiting to get up the courage to take Luke and Garrett for a walk. Just sitting there with them in the backseat and that Colt .38 on her lap."

The senator's eyes were red-rimmed as he looked toward Peg. "I called in some favors—kept her from being institutionalized. I tried to get her help, but I couldn't allow her around the boys until I knew she was all right. I was just as much to blame for not being there when she needed me. I wasn't going to make the same mistake with my sons."

Peg was crying softly.

"The worst part was she knew what she'd planned to do, and she couldn't forgive herself. It was her idea to leave. Said she couldn't trust herself and I shouldn't, either. God have mercy on me...I was afraid she was right. So I did the best I could by her. Saw she got medical care and enough money to make a life for herself."

"Bullshit!"

Rachel jumped.

Garrett's fists clenched and unclenched. The muscle in his jaw flexed in time with his steps as he stomped toward his father's chair. "Why don't I remember that?"

"You were too young." Senator Harding didn't look up as his son towered over him.

"Don't you think that at some point in my life—in Luke's—it would have been helpful to know if our mother had intended to kill us? Instead, you swept it all under the rug. For twenty-nine years. And when she got well and tried to contact us, you hid that from us, too. Is that what you call being there for us, Dad? How am I supposed to believe any of that even happened?"

Harding raised his head and met Garrett's angry gaze. "It happened, son. I'm sorry."

"Fuck!" Garrett practically roared his frustration, turned, and strode down the path that led to the front of the lodge. Halfway there he evidently remembered the dog. "Cowboy—front and center." Cowboy leaped to his feet and raced to catch up to his master. A few seconds of silence later, Garrett's Jeep started up and peeled out on the loose gravel.

Chapter Seventeen

BY THE TIME Garrett got a grip on his blinding anger, he'd been driving for over an hour, following the winding mountain roads, if you could call them that, deeper into the backcountry. As the shitload of pain in his chest began to lessen, he gradually relaxed his grip on the steering wheel. Releasing the pressure on the gas pedal, he let the Jeep coast down a short incline, noticing for the first time the breathtaking view of foothills far below the ridge he skirted.

Cowboy sat on the passenger seat, his head hanging out the open window. Every few minutes an anxious whine blew back into the cab.

Guilt got the best of Garrett, and he pulled into a wide spot beside the one-lane road. He ruffled the dog's coat and scratched under his chin when Cowboy turned his head, tongue lolling out the side of his mouth. "Sorry, boy. You don't deserve this. Just because I'm pissed off at the world doesn't mean I get to act like an ass and take it out on you. Besides, it's not going to change a damn thing."

Cowboy wagged his tail and studied him with soft brown eyes as though telling him it was about damn time he stopped feeling sorry for himself.

What in the hell was he doing, anyway? And where was he? Garrett shook his head at the overgrown trail he had followed nearly to the top of a rugged mountain thick with pine trees and fir. No damn wonder Cowboy was nervous.

He threw the Jeep in reverse and began jockeying around until he was headed back the way they'd come. He wasn't proud of the way he'd acted, but even now Garrett was unable to pinpoint one person he *wasn't* ticked off at, with the possible exception of Aunt Peg. If he believed his father, his mother had very nearly killed him and his brother. His old man had lied to him all his life, telling him his mother left because she couldn't take care of them anymore. In reality, she'd left to protect them from someone who couldn't be trusted, even if that someone was her. His father had hidden the real truth, even after the letters started coming. Apparently it was hard to dig yourself out of a hole filled with lies. How the hell could Garrett trust his father now?

As Garrett turned the situation over and over in his mind, placing himself first in his father's position and then his mother's, the truth slowly dawned on him. Each party had done what the person thought was best for him and Luke. There was enough blame to go around.

His mother had gotten hooked on prescription painkillers and let it get so far out of hand that it nearly ended in tragedy. His father's head was so far up his ass that he hadn't known she'd needed his help until it was almost too late. The bottom line was Garrett's idyllic life had been changed the instant his mother blew out her knee.

It was not so easy to excuse his father hiding the letters from them. Even though a case could be made that he'd been trying to protect them when they were younger, as adults they'd deserved an opportunity to make up their own minds. His mother had gotten well. He believed that as surely as he believed he was lucky to be alive. The possibility of ever seeing her again was gone now, and his soul ached with the loss. Garrett would bet that his father's secrecy was all to prevent an ex-wife, an addiction, and a payoff from ever coming to light. Of course, the senator would never admit to that, but Garrett had grown up showing only the best side to the public. He'd hated the subterfuge, but it was second nature to his father. It was no doubt why the senator had shipped him off to the army when he'd started to act out. Someday, when Garrett had his anger firmly in check, his father *would* answer all of his questions. For now, his lies might take more forgiveness than Garrett could muster.

What he hated more than anything was the pain Luke's question and his father's answer had inflicted on Aunt Peg and Rachel. He'd wanted to shake Rachel when she'd goaded his father into answering, until he'd seen the fear and anger in her eyes, and realized that the truth meant just as much to her and Aunt Peg as it did to him and Luke. Damn it! He slammed his hand on the steering wheel. He should have been there for her instead of getting pissed off like a pansy-assed kid and skipping out. Hadn't he given her hell for doing the same thing yesterday?

The full import of what he'd done chilled his blood. He'd left Rachel's side while Jeremy was still on the loose. Of course, she wasn't really alone at the lodge. Jonathan was there. Luke and Jase were there. Hell, his father and his entire armed brigade might still be there, but what if no one was keeping an eye on her? What if Rachel decided she needed some time alone just as he had?

Garrett yanked his cell phone from his shirt pocket and swore at the *no service* text at the top of the screen. He stepped on the gas, increasing the speed of the Jeep to well over what common sense told him was appropriate for the narrow, rocky road. He didn't care. The only thing that mattered now was getting off this mountain and making sure Rachel was all right.

Sometimes the simplest plans can be the toughest to bring to fruition. Three hours, one gorgeous sunset, several wrong turns, and a flat tire later he found his way back to the narrow, chip-sealed strip of asphalt that passed as a highway in these parts. He accelerated, reached for his phone again, and dialed Luke's number.

"Yeah." Luke answered almost immediately.

"Hey. Is everything okay?"

"Where the hell are you?" What Garrett assumed to be anger turned Luke's words hard.

"I'm sorry, Luke. I shouldn't have run out on you. I just…needed some air." Garrett blanched at his own trivial excuse. He should have been there for his brother, too. How many people had he let down today?

Luke's sigh preceded a long silence. "It's okay I guess. I mean…I get it. Are you coming back?"

"I'm on my way, about thirty minutes out. Did Dad leave?"

"He was in that chopper and out of here like a shot. No doubt he was fully aware there were a few people around here who'd like to kick his ass if given an opportunity." A carefree laugh sounded more like the brother Garrett knew.

"Are you okay, Luke?"

Another long silence hung heavily between them before Luke cleared his throat. "Did you believe him?"

"Until Jase finds something to refute his story, I don't think we have a choice. No one else is talking."

"Why didn't Aunt Peg say something before now?"

"I don't think she knew. How or why Mom kept it from her, I don't know, but I'd bet my life on it that Aunt Peg heard the story for the first time today, just like we did." Garrett glanced in the rearview mirror and noticed the only car he'd seen in the past four hours closing on him fast.

Luke laughed scornfully. "Really having a great vacation, Garrett. Glad you invited me."

Garrett smiled. Luke's sense of humor hadn't completely disappeared. "Is Rachel doing okay?"

"I think both her and Aunt Peg went to their rooms right after you left. They were pretty upset, and they didn't come down for dinner. It was just me, Jase, and

Jonathan with that guest, Alan Taylor, and a new guy—Hugh something or other. He's kind of a weird duck, but friendly enough."

Garrett checked his mirror again just as the flashing blue lights on the car behind him lit up the semidarkness. He groaned, irritation tensing his jaw. "Aw, hell. That's just great. I picked up a cop out here in the middle of fucking nowhere. I'm going to have to let you go."

"Watch your temper, Garrett. It's Dad you're mad at—not that cop. Don't get yourself thrown in jail." Luke ended the call before Garrett could answer.

Luke was getting too smart for his own good. Garrett chuckled as he dropped the phone back in his pocket and pulled over. "Chill, Cowboy." The shepherd was already in combat mode, his eyes locked on the officer approaching the side of Garrett's Jeep. He slunk into the back and lay down with a grumble.

In the side mirror, Garrett watched the officer approach with one hand on the holster at his hip and a swagger in his step. It was tempting to let Cowboy greet him first…maybe scare a little of that cockiness out of him, but Garrett respected the dog too much to turn his training into a game.

"Well, lookie who we have here. If it isn't the infamous Senator Harding's boy."

Another groan spilled from Garrett's throat. The short, stocky lawman from the backwater town of Grizzly Gulch—the one who'd momentarily considered picking up Cowboy because of Riley's bogus complaint. What were the odds that Sheriff Mike Connors would be on duty tonight and patrolling this small section of highway? The Rangers had taught Garrett to question coincidence and trust his gut, and his gut was tied in a big old knot.

"Sheriff. Didn't expect to see you out here tonight." Garrett tamped down his anger and tried for cordial.

"Why wouldn't I be here? I *own* these roads." The sheriff flicked the edge of his badge and smirked. "If you catch my meanin'."

Garrett sat up straighter. He knew only too well what Connors meant, and if Garrett wasn't careful, Luke's prophetic warning would likely come to pass. Connors was out to prove himself a big shot and what better target than the despised senator's son?

Sheriff Connors braced his arms against the Jeep's door and leaned until he was eye level with Garrett. "Last time I saw you, you were practically joined at the hip to that pretty little Rachel Maguire. Where is she now, Harding? Did she give you the boot, or did you just lose track of her?"

Something in Connors words and the threat in his eyes caught Garrett's attention. The sheriff didn't appear to have the slightest bit of respect for Rachel, and suddenly Garrett was dying to know why. He pushed Luke's warning from his mind as the thin thread that remained of his patience snapped. He pulled the handle and slammed the door of the Jeep into the officer's stomach. Connors sucked in air as he stumbled back, holding his midsection.

Garrett stepped from the vehicle, and Cowboy jumped out behind him. Sheriff Connors reached for his weapon.

"I wouldn't do that, Sheriff. You'll only have time for one shot, and there are two of us. I guarantee that whichever one of us you shoot, the other will have you by the throat before you can pull the trigger again. And, just in case you were to get lucky, don't forget that media circus I promised you. Every once in a blue moon it *does* come in handy to be a senator's son."

Connors straightened with some difficulty, his hand still hovering near his gun. "Not even a senator's son can assault a police officer and get away with it."

"What? That little bump? Sorry about that. It was an accident." Garrett smiled coldly as he stepped closer. A series of taps on his leg sent Cowboy on a diagonal path to his right. "I don't want any trouble, but I am going to ask you—do you have a problem with Rachel?"

A sneer twisted the sheriff's lips. "I don't have a problem with that stone-cold bitch, Harding. She just thinks she's a little too good for the men in these parts, that's all. And then along comes the *senator's son*...she couldn't wait to fuck you."

Garrett took a deep breath and blew it out, tempering his next words. "I see. Did Rachel tell you that? Because, if she didn't, I'm curious to know who did. Or are you just making it up as you go?"

A scornful smile spread slowly across Connors's face. "People talk around these parts. And we don't take to outsiders much. In fact, I think your welcome is wearing a little thin."

Garrett laughed derisively. "I think you're the only one who has a problem with me—you and maybe the Metcalf boys. And it all seems to revolve around Rachel. Why is that, Sheriff? Were you maybe hoping to get something going with her? Did I show up at a bad time?"

"You can think whatever you want, Harding, but watch yourself out on these back roads." Connors walked a wide circle around Garrett as he started for his cruiser.

"Sheriff?" Garrett waited until he stopped and turned so he could read his face. "That sounded like a threat, Connors, so let me be clear as well. Anyone who causes Rachel harm will have me to deal with. So if you know someone who might want to hurt her, you should probably tell me now."

Connors looked away for a moment before he smirked. "Hell, I don't know a damn thing about the woman." He continued to his car, slid into the seat, and threw gravel as he hit the gas.

Garrett had to consciously unclench his jaw as the car disappeared around a bend in the road. For a few minutes, he'd actually suspected the sheriff was Rachel's stalker, but the man seemed too preoccupied that the senator's son might get something the sheriff apparently wanted. Jeremy probably wouldn't give a damn if he was the *president's* son—he'd still just be someone to remove from Rachel's life. Garrett would still keep a close eye on Sheriff Connors. He was quickly coming around to Rachel's way of thinking. Garrett didn't trust the man.

He waited for Cowboy to hop back in the Jeep before sliding behind the wheel, starting the vehicle, and pulling back onto the pavement. His stomach was churning with dread, hoping Rachel was really in her room, and she hadn't taken advantage of his absence to disappear again.

Cowboy whined beside his shoulder, and Garrett slung his arm across the dog's back, scratching beneath his ear. "Good job, boy. Don't worry about Rachel. She'll wait for us before she takes off again." Yes, damn it, he *was* aware he was trying to convince himself.

It was the longest twenty miles in history, but he finally pulled his Jeep in beside Sally's Explorer and parked. The lodge was lit up festively, and people sat on the deck, quietly talking, enjoying the warm evening. Rachel wasn't one of them.

Luke met him halfway across the grass leading to the steps. "Sally knocked on her door a little while ago, but no one answered and it was locked."

"*Fuck!*" Garrett kept walking.

"What are you going to do?" Luke fell in beside him, opposite the dog.

"Break it down."

Aunt Peg rose from her chair and came down the steps toward him. Garrett put his hands on her shoulders. "I'm so sorry I came, Aunt Peg. This never would have happened if I'd stayed away."

"No. Don't ever say that. I would endure this and much more to have our family back together again. Your mother loved us. Whatever else happened, I believe that with all my heart." She cupped his cheek in her hand.

He hugged her gently. "You are a very smart lady. If my mother was even half the woman you are, I'd have been proud to know her." Garrett kissed her temple and stepped back. "Now, I need to apologize to Rachel, too."

"I haven't seen her since Douglas left. I was just about to go check on her."

Garrett stopped her as she pulled away and started for the porch steps. "I'll check, Aunt Peg. You wait here with Luke. Okay? I'll let you know the minute I find her." He bounded up the steps, not giving the woman time to mount an argument.

Striding past the other occupants of the porch, he nodded to Jonathan, noting his concerned expression. Jase looked more curious than anything, but didn't ask probably because he was sitting with Alan Taylor and two new guests whom Garrett hadn't met yet. He didn't have time right now, so he kept walking right through the door, into the lobby, and up the stairs until he stood in front of Rachel's silent room.

He knocked loudly enough to wake her if she was asleep. "Rachel? It's me, Garrett." His hand dropped to the doorknob and twisted. It was locked, just as Luke had said. "Please open the door, Rach. I need to see that you're all right."

No sooner were the words out of his mouth than the door whipped open. Rachel grabbed his hand and yanked him into the room. Cowboy barely made it through before the door banged closed again.

One lamp burned beside her bed, casting shadows over the rest of the room. Even in poor lighting, Garrett could see that she was a mess. A very sexy mess, but a mess nonetheless. She wore a short terry cloth robe that tied in the front and only just covered her cute little ass. He followed her long legs all the way down to bare feet. Her hair was half in and half out of a ponytail, but it was her eyes that wrenched at his heart. She'd been crying— a lot. Her eyes were red and the area around them was swollen and puffy. Apparently, her lips were going to stay pouty regardless of how angry she tried to look. And she did look angry, piercing him with a withering glare, her hands braced challengingly on her hips.

Garrett raised his hands in acceptance of whatever she had for him. "I'm sorry. The senator came here because of me. This whole thing is my fault. I'm sorry, Rachel. Would you please say something?"

She stepped into him and thumped him on the chest with the sides of both fists. When he made no move to stop her, she did it again…and again. "Where the hell did you go? I was worried about you, you big hypocrite. It's okay for you to run away, but not okay for me, huh? Well, you're done telling me what to do if you can't live by the same rules. And when the hell were you going to tell me you were my boss? I don't date fellow employees or *bosses*." She emphasized the word as if it was the worst thing she could imagine.

Slamming her fists against him again, she whirled away, but Garrett caught one wrist and jerked her around until her back was against the wall, and he held her there with one hand on each side of her.

He leaned in to kiss her but she turned her head aside. So he trailed kisses from her cheek, down the column of her throat, to the very tempting V of her robe. He was rewarded by a deep shudder, but she still wouldn't look at him.

"You're right. I got angry and had to blow off some steam. I couldn't do that here where you, Aunt Peg, and Luke were hurting as badly as I was. But that's no excuse. I shouldn't have left. I should have been here for you. As for Amanda leaving her half of this place to Luke and me—I haven't even had a chance to think about it yet, but one thing's for sure. If accepting my inheritance means you and I can't be together, I'll be selling my share before the ink is dry on the transfer papers."

A sniffle escaped her, and she finally met his gaze, her words a mere whisper. "I *really* needed you."

"I know, sweetheart, and I'm sorry I let you down. It won't happen again." He leaned forward slowly and very gently took her lips, tasting, savoring, making her his again. And she *was* his, at least as far as he was concerned. Why was he only now realizing how true, and how important, that was? More imperative, how was he going to convince her of that if he kept screwing up and making her cry?

Her small hands fisted in his shirt and tugged him closer, so he stepped up and wrapped her in his arms. He could feel her heart beat against his chest, and the cadence seemed to match his own. He breathed in the sweet, womanly smell of her as the sense of peace that had become synonymous with her proximity settled over him.

His mouth hovered near her lips as he slid his hands down her back. He cupped her bottom with both hands and drew her against his hard-on. Her short robe worked up in the process and he found himself with his hands full of bare skin.

"Oh, shit. Do you have anything on under that robe, sweetheart?" His swollen manhood jerked and twitched at the thought.

She blushed a pretty shade of pink. "No. I was just about to take a shower."

He lifted her, guided her legs around him, and pressed her into the wall. Just knowing she was open and bare before him and that he was positioned between her legs was dizzying. God, he wanted her—but he wanted all of her.

He kissed her breathless, then rested his forehead against hers and searched her eyes. "We've never talked about exclusivity, but I don't want to share you with anyone else. You're mine."

She tensed and stared at him. "That's exactly what will set Jeremy off."

Garrett shook his head. "What if Jeremy wasn't in the picture? Would you give us a shot then?

She cocked her head, as though considering her answer. Finally she nodded. "I'd like to—for as long as you're here."

"Yeah? Well, what if I decided to stay for good—be your boss? How long would you be mine then? You don't have to answer now." Garrett captured her mouth as he pressed his arousal into her. Reaching between them, he worked his thumb back and forth across the spot that made her mewl and her breath hitch.

She inhaled sharply and arched into his hand. "That's good because I can't even think right now."

He chuckled as he pressed against her again. "Wait right there," he said, setting her on her feet abruptly. He removed his wallet, found a condom, then unzipped his jeans and pushed them and his briefs down. With a grin, he handed the condom to Rachel. While she opened the package and rolled the condom on the length of him, he untied her robe and pushed it back off her shoulders, baring her beautiful breasts.

Her hand around his shaft almost brought him to his knees, so heady was the anticipation that coursed through him. And by the pleased expression on her face, she knew exactly what she was doing to him and enjoyed the power it gave her.

He rolled her nipples unhurriedly between thumb and forefinger while he devoured her mouth, raking his teeth over her bottom lip. Moving his mouth to her breasts, he lightly kissed one nipple, then licked, and immediately blew a hot breath. Rachel moaned and twisted against him. Meanwhile, her delicate hand, stroking and teasing his manhood, was pushing him past the point of no return.

Lifting her up so she could wrap her legs around him again and sink down onto his shaft, a ragged groan issued from Garrett. Rachel looped her arms around his neck and a smile curved her kiss-swollen lips. He held her tightly against him as he kissed her and let the warmth of her sheath spread contentment that he'd never known before to every part of his body. He returned her smile, briefly wondering if she shared his happiness.

He pressed her against the door, pulled out and sunk himself again, deeper than before. "You feel so good, Rach. You're the one I need, sweetheart. Only you." Again he pulled out and slammed home. The door rattled with the jolt. They both started to laugh.

"Maybe this isn't such a good idea." He glanced around and then nodded toward the center of the room. "Bed okay?"

"Wherever you're going." She held on tightly, grinning, as Garrett toed off his shoes, then obviously tried to choke back her laughter while he stepped on the hem of each pant leg and eventually pulled his legs free.

"Go ahead and laugh, sweetheart. I've got plenty of time to get even."

Once he reached the foot of the bed, he glanced at Rachel. "Any ideas how to…you know?

Her gleeful laughter filled the room for a moment. "Well, we could just start over."

"What's the challenge in that? Hold on." He winked just before he turned and dropped onto his back on the bed, holding her perfect ass in a death grip against his groin.

She squealed on the way down and her head clipped his chin, but happily, everything else was intact. He rolled her onto her back and tried to kiss the silly grin off her face. It didn't budge.

"Well, Romeo. This will be memorable." She giggled as he bit her nipple playfully.

"Shut up and hold on," he said before his mouth covered hers and his hand found the sensitive spot between her legs again. At the same time, he started moving in and out, increasing the rhythm as his climax drew closer. When Rachel convulsed and cried his name, Garrett wasn't far behind.

A few minutes passed before Garrett rolled off her. He snaked his arm around her waist and drew her close only to see sadness in her green eyes. "What's wrong? Did I do something you didn't like?"

Rachel jabbed him playfully. "You were perfect."

"And you're gloomy because?"

"Because, even if you wanted to stay, I can't keep you." She jabbed him again, presumably for daring to laugh.

"Why not? Afraid I'm not housebroken? Actually, you could be right about that." He teased her, but she wasn't buying. He cupped her chin and turned her face so she had to look at him. "What's going on in there?" He tapped her head.

Her sigh was clearly painful. "It's one thing to imagine Jeremy doesn't exist—that he can't hurt us—but that's just wishful thinking. I don't want you to stay here and get caught in his sick game. I'm serious, Garrett. I couldn't take it if he hurt you."

Garrett leaned back on the pillows, pulling her with him. "And I won't leave you to face him alone. I think he's proven that he'll find you wherever you go. It's part of the game for him. I appreciate that you're worried about me too, but I'm staying, and I'd rather have you watching my back than anyone else. We're stronger together than either of us is alone. We need each other, Rach. I need you." He kissed the tip of her nose.

She studied his eyes until he started to wonder if she'd heard him. Finally her gaze drifted downward to his lips, and she kissed him with such tenderness, he wanted to go on holding her as long as she'd let him.

"Did you mean that? You're staying?" Worry still cast a shadow over her face.

"Yes, ma'am. Is that okay?"

The most enchanting smile he'd ever seen lit up her entire face even as her eyes misted. "Yes," she whispered. "It's more than okay. It's the best gift anyone ever gave me."

She slid her arms around his neck, and he let her cry softly, safe in the knowledge they were happy tears. Having never been anyone's *best gift* before, he might have shed a couple of his own while she wasn't looking.

"I've got to see how Luke feels about this whole inheritance thing, and I'm sure there'll be some papers to sign for Aunt Peg's attorney, but first I've got some loose ends to tie up with the army. I have to report to Fort Lewis in a couple of weeks so they can evaluate my fitness for duty."

Concern furrowed her brow. "They won't send you back there, will they? To Iraq?"

"Cowboy and I were both extremely lucky." Garrett turned his head in time to see the dog's face pop up from his position curled in front of the door. He smiled as Cowboy's tail thwacked the floor at the mention of his name. "Our injuries weren't life threatening or debilitating. Miraculous really, when you consider all the strong men and women coming home with amputations or head injuries. For a long time I beat myself up wondering why I didn't die like almost everyone else in my unit. Then, when I saw some of the other wounded at the hospital, I couldn't help wondering why I'd come away with barely a scratch."

She shook her pretty head. "It still hurts you. I see you sometimes, when you don't think anyone is watching, trying to wait out the pain so you can keep on moving and pretend there's nothing wrong."

He smiled and kissed her pouty lips, sorry that she had to witness his weakness, yet proud beyond measure to have this woman in his life. "I'm a hundred times better than I was. For a few months, it looked as though I'd never walk without a cane, so I'll take what I've got now and keep trying to make it better. But the truth is: the Rangers are an elite group—the best the army has. Less than perfect, I'll be an instant washout. My fourth hitch is nearly up so they'll offer me a desk job or a medical discharge. My commanding officer already knows which one I'll choose." He smoothed the wrinkles in her forehead with his thumb. "Come with me."

"What? To Fort Lewis?"

"Yeah."

"Maybe I will."

Garrett pulled her head toward him and covered her mouth, sipping again and again until suddenly a stray thought registered in his brain. "Oh, shit! I promised Aunt Peg I'd let her know you're all right."

Rachel rolled away from him, stood, and retied the belt of her robe. "While you do that, I'm going to jump in the shower. Then maybe we could go raid the kitchen? I'm starving."

He looked her slowly up and down with a smirk. "I'm hungry, too."

She smiled secretively at his taunt, tossed her hair over her shoulder, and disappeared into the bathroom. A second later, he heard the water running.

With satisfaction warming his heart, he threw on his clothes, smoothed his hair with his hands, and opened the door. Cowboy jumped up and followed him. Garrett turned left toward the stairwell while Cowboy lingered near the door, his nose to the ground. Garrett glanced over his shoulder and tapped a signal on his leg for the dog. Cowboy's head came up, but instead of looking at his master, he focused on something at the other end of the hallway. Garrett followed the dog's gaze and saw only an empty hall, about 150 feet long, with an exit sign at the end.

"Cowboy, front and center."

Instead, the dog took off like a bullet toward the end of the hall. There'd been only one other time Cowboy had refused a command. The night his unit got hit, the dog had operated on instinct only, taking the point on the way out of the building where they'd been ambushed, leading his injured teammates to safety. He'd stalked and attacked the rebels who lay in wait to finish the job, drawing them out so Garrett could do his part. How Cowboy had been able to tell the difference between insurgents and innocents was beyond Garrett, but the dog had ignored Garrett's command to stay by his side that night, proving he didn't need a fallible human telling him what to do. Garrett hoped that was still true.

Garrett whistled loudly and charged down the hallway after the dog. A hundred feet ahead of him, Cowboy disappeared around the corner. Almost immediately, the dog yipped, a door slammed shut, and then Cowboy's fury was unleashed. He snarled and barked, scratching and gnawing at something. Had he gotten himself trapped? Garrett could already see Aunt Peg's scowl of disapproval when she witnessed the destruction this dog was capable of. But he couldn't discount the possibility that Cowboy knew what he was doing—that his odd behavior was a reaction to danger, maybe even Rachel's stalker.

Garrett slowed just before the corner and pressed himself to the wall. His hand went automatically to the waistband at his back, but he wasn't armed, having left his weapon in the Jeep. Cowboy kept up his frenzied attack on something just around the corner. He was making enough noise to rouse the dead, so this wing of the lodge must be empty. Or maybe everyone was still outside enjoying the stars. Even Rachel would be able to hear the commotion as soon as she stepped out of the shower. Garrett leaned forward, found the hallway leading to a set of stairs, and stepped around the corner.

There was a door on his left. It appeared to be a utility closet, and one twist of the knob proved it was locked. How in the hell had Cowboy gotten locked inside? Had one of the staff propped it open and forgotten? Cowboy could have knocked the prop out of the way if he'd forced his way through the crack. Anything falling could have accounted for his yip. He was definitely going to town on the door casing now. He *did not* like to be contained.

"Relax, Cowboy." He tried to get the dog's attention through the door, but the resulting silence lasted only a second or two. Garrett threw his shoulder against the door, but it didn't budge and he stepped back to consider his options. He could go to Rachel or Aunt Peg for a key, but the door frame would no doubt have to be replaced anyway, along with the door, several feet of drywall on both sides, and the carpet. He would pay for it and accept the fact that Cowboy would be banished from the lodge from here on out.

He heard something, a very small sound, like a door opening in the hallway around the corner. No doubt someone wondering what all the ruckus was. He waited a few seconds for the guest to appear, but when no one did, he strode toward the corner.

The door marked 228 was cracked open. About two-thirds of the way up, something was suspended in the opening, keeping the door from closing. It was dark in the room, but Garrett sensed someone was there, watching. A sudden stabbing pain in his arm made him glance down. He swore and yanked the feathered dart from his bicep.

"What the hell?" He took a couple of unsteady steps toward the open door. The watcher didn't move. Behind Garrett, Cowboy snarled his dissatisfaction, renewing his efforts to escape.

Garrett went down on his knees. For some reason he couldn't remember, he felt compelled to say Rachel's name, but his tongue was too heavy. His head banged against the floor as he slid the rest of the way down, but he barely felt the blow. His mind was functioning slowly, blurring the past and the present. *Who stood there in the doorway? And why was he doing this? Rachel?*

The door opened far enough for a figure to slip out. Garrett tried to get up, but he couldn't move. He blinked several times to try to clear his vision. It was a man, medium height. He circled Garrett and then leaned over him.

"No, Harding. She's *not* yours. She never will be."

That voice. Something about that voice. Why couldn't he remember?

The man bent over him again to grab his shoulders and drag him toward the open door. His face was just inches from Garrett's, and in the few seconds before the door closed behind them, recognition crystallized, and the name floated before his eyes. Eyes that would no longer stay open.

Chapter Eighteen

RACHEL WAS JUST slipping into two-inch heels that matched her blue denim skirt perfectly when someone knocked on her door with one of those upbeat, happy-to-be-alive rhythms. Her smile came unbidden. Garrett was back. She gave her image in the mirror one more inspection, smoothed her hair, and did her best not to rush to the door.

"That was fast. Peg must have—" She swung the door open, already talking, and stopped abruptly when her gaze landed on Alan Taylor. "Oh! I'm sorry, Alan. I was expecting somebody else. What can I do for you?" Rachel had never been alone with Alan before. He seemed almost creepy-nervous, his eyes darting up and down the hall. She tried to push past him so they could talk where others might see them, but he stepped in front of her.

Alan held up a cell phone. "I have a picture I'd like you to look at. Please, Rachel? It's important." He didn't wait for an answer, but brushed by her and began pacing back and forth in the center of her room.

Rachel left the door slightly ajar and turned to face him, forcing a smile. "Sure. I'm always happy to help out a guest, especially one who's been with us as long as you have."

He forced the phone into her hands and walked away as if he couldn't bear to look. Something about the way he glared at her made her shiver. She turned, prepared to insist that they take this downstairs, only to see him closing the door.

"Now isn't the best time for this, Alan. I'm expecting someone any moment. Are you sure it wouldn't be better to handle this in the lodge office? I could meet you there in a few minutes." She started to walk toward him.

"Nobody's coming, Rachel. Look at the picture." He pointed to the cell phone and his gaze drilled into her with cold deliberation.

She gave up trying to reason with him and went to plan B—placating him. Her fingers shook as she turned the phone over. "Whatever is wrong, I'm sure Peg and I will be able to come up with a solution as soon as we get to the bottom of the problem."

"The *problem* is in the picture, and it's *your* problem. No one else needs to know. Now turn the phone on and look at the picture." A sneer formed and his fists curled at his sides.

The man's belligerent attitude was completely uncharacteristic. Alan Taylor's congenial and friendly personality had vanished. Obviously, something was wrong for which he held her, and her alone, personally responsible. She should never have let him into her room, but she'd certainly had no reason to suspect he was a dangerous man. Now she wasn't so sure.

He was slightly built, but wiry. Still, if it came to it, surprise would be on her side. He wouldn't know Jonathan had instructed her in the finer points of self-defense. The worst part would be explaining to Peg why she'd broken the nose of their most long-term guest.

One more glance at him convinced her that her quickest way out of this was to do as he said. She pulled the cell phone toward her, hit the button to wake it up, and slid her finger across the bottom of the screen. The camera app opened immediately with a picture that was dark and a little out of focus. When she finally figured out what it was, her heart almost stopped beating.

Garrett!

Rachel fought back the waves of fear that threatened to smother her. The picture in front of her was replaced by images from the past that burst into her mind unbidden—Chance, spread-eagled on a bed, covered with blood. Garrett was tied to one of the king-size fourposters that graced each of the lodge's rooms, but there was no blood. He might still be alive. In the time it took for her to raise her eyes to the maniac in front of her, she pushed aside her hopes and dreams, her shame, and her fear. If there was even the remotest chance that he was alive, there was nothing she wouldn't do to keep him that way.

"Jeremy?" The name tasted rancid in her mouth.

He threw back his head and laughed. "You don't remember me, do you? All those times you walked past me while I was mowing my grandparents' yard in Plainview. You were on your way to work at that awful club, and you always looked so sad. I knew I had to rescue you from that place and those bloodsucking people you met there—like Chance."

Rachel's courage began to crumble. *Stay in the present! Concentrate on Garrett!*

"Where is he, Jeremy?" Anger burned hot within her, but she couldn't let it show.

"He's not far from here, my sweet. Did you see the pretty vest I made for him?" He pointed to the picture again.

Rachel held her breath and studied the image. After a few seconds, she raised her eyes to his. "Is that . . .?"

"A bomb? Yes." He chortled. "A suicide vest just like they use in Iraq. I made it special for him so he'd feel right at home. Except I used C-4 so there's enough explosive there to destroy this whole place."

"Why? What has Peg ever done to you? She's been nothing but kind. If you want to hurt someone, hurt me. I'm the one you're angry with." It was hard keeping her voice level and calm when what she really wanted to do was scream to the heavens.

"Oh, you're wrong. I'm not angry with you. You're just confused. I should have come to you long ago. As soon as we're away from here and the influences of these people, you'll see that we were meant to be together. You're already starting to see, aren't you?"

"I see a sick, cruel man." Hopelessness stirred within her, but she refused to give up.

"I'm not heartless, my sweet. Nobody has to die. Harding's vest is wired to blow on a signal from my cell phone. The only way I'll activate it is if you don't do exactly what I say. Do you understand?" He reached out and jerked the phone from her fingers.

She nodded dutifully. Rachel's heart felt like a cold, hard rock taking up space in her chest. She wanted to slam the heel of her hand into his nose, but if she gave in to her natural inclinations even once, Garrett would die...along with everyone in the lodge.

"If you're a good girl, I won't give the signal, and the bomb will revert to a timer set to go off in about"—he glanced at his watch—"forty-five minutes. Harding is out cold right now, but he should be awake in plenty of time. If he makes enough noise, they won't have any trouble finding him. Of course, someone will need to know how to diffuse the bomb."

Rachel gasped, and the unwanted wave of tears that had filled her eyes as he talked rolled down her cheeks.

"Enough. No more tears for that man or anyone else here. From now on it's you and me. I'll make you happy. You'll see."

"What about your wife?" She was desperate for anything that might bring him to his senses.

The grin that appeared transformed his face to nothing short of evil. "Linda was only a diversion—a poor imitation of you. I got rid of her so she wouldn't be in our way." He waved his hand in the air, as though dismissing the very thought of his wife.

Rachel forced herself to take the next breath…and the one after that. He was insane. If she left here with him, she'd be lost. Not to mention she'd be leaving Garrett when he needed her the most. She had to find him. Together, they could figure out how to disarm the bomb. If she could only get Jeremy's cell phone away from him before he could send the signal. Her gaze flicked to the heavy lamp on a nearby table, and her world went quiet as she waited for him to turn his back.

A light tapping sounded on the door, and for a moment, Rachel's hopes soared. They dropped sharply when Riley and his brother Arnold stepped into the room. The two looked just as greasy and slimy as the last time she'd seen them outside the sheriff's office. Riley's lecherous sneer nearly made her sick as her hope of escape disappeared.

"Where's the other one? I hired three of you." Jeremy rounded on Riley, suddenly furious.

"Easy now. Matt got himself in a little fight this afternoon. He's sleepin' it off at the jail. No need to get all upset. Me and Arnold took care of parkin' the getaway vehicle on the old forest service road. Delivered a few supplies to the mine too…just like you asked." Riley grinned smugly at their accomplishment, but Jeremy wasn't impressed.

"Yeah? Well, that doesn't change a thing. If I get two-thirds of what I asked for, you get two-thirds of the money we agreed on." He stared them down, daring them to argue.

Amazingly, no one did. Riley must have figured out that Jeremy was crazy, too. Rachel wasn't sure if Jeremy screwing over Riley and Arnold gave her a better chance or not. At this point, she'd take anything she could get.

Jeremy turned back to her and smiled apologetically as though he cared that she'd just witnessed him lose his temper. "It's time to go, Rachel," he said. "You're not really dressed for traipsing through the woods, but it will have to do. Riley will go down ahead of us and make sure it's all clear. Then we're going to walk right out the back door. If we should run into anybody, don't forget what's at stake." He held up his phone with the picture of Garrett plastered on the screen. "Take a good look at this and remember it if you start having any doubts. Once we're out of the lodge, we're home free. You and me." He leaned closer until his lips hovered over hers. "That is what you want, isn't it, my sweet?"

Rachel swallowed hard. *Oh my God!* How long could she pretend? The answer came instantaneously. She had no choice…as long as there was a chance to save Garrett. She nodded her head shakily.

His mouth closed over hers. She clamped her lips shut and fought to keep the contents of her stomach down. Just in time, he stepped away.

Jeremy grabbed her wrist and yanked her into the hall. She glanced around, hoping against hope that help would appear. Riley disappeared around the corner at the end of the passageway, then a moment later, reappeared and motioned to them. Jeremy dragged her down the corridor while Arnold brought up the rear, glancing at her with cold detachment.

As they approached the corner, a deafening combination of sounds broke loose. The ferocious snarling and growling had to be coming from Cowboy. Surely he'd come right through the wall of the utility closet where he was evidently trapped. That explained how Jeremy had gotten the drop on Garrett. Cowboy would have protected his master with his life if he'd been able.

Jeremy jerked her toward the stairs, and she had to concentrate to keep her feet under her as they ran down to the ground floor. There was nobody in the kitchen or the utility room. Everything was cleaned up and put away for the night. Riley stepped outside, but soon stuck his head back through the door to motion them on.

Rachel lost track of time and surroundings after that. She was aware of being led up the ridge behind the lodge, dragged along like a calf to slaughter. Once inside the tree line, out of sight of anyone who might glance their way from the buildings, Jeremy stopped, produced plastic ties from his pocket, and bound her wrists behind her back. They continued on, up and over the ridge by the light of the full moon, until they intersected an abandoned forest service road. Shortly after that, Rachel nearly ran into Riley's old yellow pickup, it was so hidden with pine boughs and a dark gray tarp.

If she'd thought walking up the side of a mountain in the dark was bad, it was nothing compared with being forced to sit on Jeremy's lap as they all shoved into the cab of the Ford pickup. Claustrophobia set in with a vengeance, and it became harder and harder to keep her mouth shut. She tried to tune out the snickers, the smell of sweat, the hands that brushed her accidentally, in favor of survival, but all the while she listened for the explosion that would signal the deaths of Garrett and everyone she loved.

It seemed an interminable length of time that they drove through the darkness, over rough one-lane trails while she perched tensely on as little of Jeremy's lap as she could manage and tried to ignore his hard-on that pressed against her hip. While he drove, Riley kept up a running monologue about his part in the night's events, about cutting Garrett Harding down to size, and about how he'd finally earned some respect in this fleabag town. Arnold sat in the middle, his legs on each side of the gearshift column, apparently oblivious to Riley's babbling and her misery.

One hand on her waist and the other stroking her arm from shoulder to elbow, Jeremy sat silently, studying the darkness beyond the passenger window. She could see his reflection. The only indication of what occupied his thoughts, his growing arousal.

Was Garrett awake yet? Had Luke or Jonathan found him? What if they got to him in time but weren't able to diffuse the bomb? The weight of despair settled on her shoulders, and cold tendrils of fear snaked toward her heart. The forty-five minutes had to have passed by now. If the bomb went off, would they have been close enough to hear? In these mountains, it was difficult to say, but for her own sanity, she had to believe Garrett was safe.

Now it was her turn. Jeremy's intentions became more obvious with each passing moment. No way in hell was he raping her. She would fight him with every fiber of her being. If he killed her in the process, so be it. There was no reason to think she would get out of this alive anyway.

Abruptly, Riley pulled off the trail, parked in a group of young saplings, and killed the engine. "Here we are."

Rachel glanced out the window and immediately recognized the deserted, partially dilapidated buildings of Addison's Mine. Her skin prickled with dread. She hated tight, underground places…even had a hard time with some basements. It was the whole idea of being buried alive that got to her.

The entrance to Addison's Mine was narrow and long, sloping off for several hundred feet before the ground opened up and swallowed anyone who wasn't paying attention. If you survived the drop, there was no way out short of scaling a sheer rock face. Why were they here?

Jeremy opened his door and dropped her, unceremoniously, on her feet outside the vehicle, then stepped out beside her. He pushed her toward the front of the truck where Riley and Arnold were waiting. Riley tossed Jeremy the keys to the pickup.

Rachel stumbled when he shoved her toward Riley.

"I know, my sweet. I want to stay with you as well, but I have some last-minute chores to attend to before we can leave. I won't be long—a few hours—and then we'll have the rest of our lives together." Jeremy started to urge her toward Riley again when Arnold reached out and grasped her elbow.

Though she scowled at him and tried to jerk free, Arnold's expression remained composed.

"Remember what I said, Riley. Keep her here. Make her comfortable. Hurt one hair on her head and you'll answer to me. Are we clear?"

"Yeah, yeah, yeah. I got it. Just don't forget the money." Riley stepped forward and jerked her away from Arnold.

Rachel cried out when the plastic ties cut into her wrists cruelly.

Jeremy was on him in a heartbeat, twisting his arm behind his back and shoving it upward toward his shoulder blade. Riley groaned and dropped to his knees.

Jeremy leaned close to his ear and whatever he whispered had Riley nodding and agreeing in short order. He jumped out of reach as soon as Jeremy turned him loose, glowering at Rachel as though it were all her fault. She probably shouldn't have rubbed it in by smiling. He turned abruptly and stomped toward the entrance to the mine.

Jeremy tossed the keys from one hand to the other as he approached the driver's door. Just before he slid onto the seat, he glanced back at her, then barely looked at Arnold. "Keep her out of sight."

As soon as the lights of the truck disappeared in the trees, Arnold latched on to her elbow again, his touch surprisingly gentle as he led her toward the mine.

"Why are you doing this, Arnold?" Rachel spoke low in case Riley was somewhere close, listening. For several seconds, it seemed he would ignore her.

The oldest, Arnold had always been the smartest of the three brothers, capable of making something of himself if his mother hadn't taken sick and passed away his junior year of high school. The boys' father was no longer on the scene so Arnold dropped out of school and got a job to help raise his brothers.

Riley and Matt ran wild, raising hell, and getting in trouble with the law. Arnold did the best he could, but the townspeople painted them all with the same brush. When a young, impressionable boy is told he's worthless over and over again, pretty soon that's what he becomes.

She jumped when Arnold suddenly pointed to the moon over the ridge to their right. "Full moon tonight. Be right pretty risin' over Amanda's cabin." He pointed again, this time down a draw that ended in darkness.

Did he mean that the cabin was that way? That she'd be able to find her way by the light of the full moon? Her hopes soared, yet at the same time, she told herself the idea was crazy. He still had hold of her arm, and she was still bound. Rachel stole a glance at him, but he looked straight ahead.

Ducking, he dragged her between the rotting timbers that served as the mine entrance. He lit a lamp just inside and led her to a stack of crates that leaned against one rock wall, covered by what appeared to be dusty sheets. Riley was nowhere to be seen, but he had to be here somewhere. She sat tentatively on one of the crates, letting her eyes adjust to the shadows, measuring the distance to the exit, and debating her chances of making it there before he caught her. Arnold moved a few feet away to another stash of crates and began digging through a metal box, obviously searching for something.

Finally, he shoved a small object in his pocket, turned, and came back to her. "This is Riley's place. He stays here sometimes when he's poachin'." He nodded toward the darkness of the tunnel. "He'll be back there lickin' his wounds…and drinkin'." He shoved his hand in his pocket and brought it out clutching a three-inch pocket knife. Before she had time to move, he reached behind her and cut the plastic ties. "He's pissed now. He blames you. I'll talk to him, but I don't think you should be here when he comes back."

Rachel glanced at the knife he pushed into her hands, and then her gaze darted to Arnold. He was watching her, a shadow of sadness apparent in his eyes.

He held something else in his other hand. "I'll only be a couple minutes, but I'm gonna leave this here." He tossed a cell phone down on a crate beside her. "No service. Need to be up higher."

Rachel couldn't believe what she was hearing. Arnold just released her from her bonds. He'd told her which way to go to reach Amanda's cabin and where she was likely to have cell phone service to call for help. Now he was going to leave her alone?

Arnold turned his back and moved deeper into the dark tunnel. A flashlight on a keychain he dug from his pocket was his only light.

"Arnold."

He stopped but didn't turn around.

"Thank you." Rachel's voice was husky with emotion.

He glanced at her and for just a heartbeat, a smile lifted one corner of his mouth, and then it was gone. "Go before he comes lookin'."

Rachel grabbed the cell phone and ran.

Chapter Nineteen

GARRETT WAS FREE-FALLING but something prevented his arms and legs from moving. The harder he tried, the angrier he became. Finally, his roar of frustration erupted—

Abruptly, his eyes flew open and…he wasn't falling at all. It was a fucking dream, although the way his heart was hammering, he might as well have been skydiving without a chute. And, *shit*, his head was pounding. He gritted his teeth and tried to sit up.

What the hell? His arms were tied to the bed-posts…and his feet. *Fuck!* Whose idea of a sick joke was this? He wrenched on his bindings as hard as he could and didn't even make the four-poster bed frame creak. His movements stopped abruptly a second later when his gaze fell on the duct-taped and wired harness of explosives that wrapped his torso.

He'd seen plenty of them…after they exploded, and it wasn't a pretty sight. Stretching his neck, he peered down to see what the wiring mechanism looked like. There was a timer attached, set at fifteen minutes, but it was inactive. Not that the information would do him any good, trussed up like a roping steer at the rodeo. He took a deep breath, and then another, and lay his head back on the bed. *Think, damn it!*

Rachel!

In a rush, the whole ugly disaster came back to him. Cowboy. Alan Taylor. That damn dart. And now this. What was it Alan had said to him? Something about Rachel being his? Was Alan Taylor Rachel's stalker? Had Jeremy been keeping tabs on her by playing a guest at the lodge all these years?

The lowlife hadn't killed him as Rachel had feared—yet anyway. That could only mean one thing: he'd gone after *her* this time. Garrett jerked his arms and legs and bellowed a string of curses in his rage. When silence prevailed again, he heard a sound, repetitive, coming from beyond the door of the room he was captive in.

Cowboy. Barking loudly and continuously. He must have heard Garrett, and he was answering. "Cowboy! Front and center!" Garrett yelled the command and the barking became even more frenzied for a few seconds, and then everything went still. Cowboy was undoubtedly scratching, digging, and chewing his way through the wall of his enclosure. Garrett smiled. Few places could hold a dog like Cowboy. The drywall inside the closet was probably already torn to shreds. All he had to do was wait until the dog was loose in the hallway…then send him downstairs for Luke. Garrett lay back.

A beep came from somewhere close by and he jerked his head up. *Holy hell!* There was a green light on the timer that hadn't been there before, and suddenly the device started counting down…too damn fast.

A quick perusal of the C-4 strapped to the harness gave him a pretty good idea of what would happen if the bomb exploded. Evidently, Jeremy didn't intend for anyone on the premises to survive. Garrett's hands flexed, itching to be around the perverted bastard's throat.

Garrett glanced at the timer again. *Twelve minutes, forty-eight seconds.* Cowboy was still quiet. Time to make some noise of his own. He yelled for Luke, Jase, and then Jonathan, filling the air in between with curses and expletives as though he were still with his unit on the streets of Iraq. Silence greeted him when he stopped.

Ten minutes, fourteen seconds.

Garrett jerked on the ropes that bound him, but all he managed was a serious case of rope burn. The bindings wouldn't give.

Nine minutes, eleven seconds. He yelled again, then whistled, long and shrill. This time he didn't go still until he heard something outside in the hallway. When he stopped, the noise came again—Cowboy! Scratching on his door.

"Good boy!" Finding Garrett was the easy part. The dog had been trained to seek out the problem. Making him leave to find the solution would be tougher. "Cowboy. Go get Luke."

The dog whined and barked, ran away a few feet, and came right back.

Garrett repeated the command twice more before Cowboy raced away down the hall, his footsteps disappearing in the distance. All Garrett could do was hope Luke would understand why the dog that he barely knew and was half-leery of was trying to drag him upstairs.

Seven minutes, twenty-five seconds. He studied the bomb. It wasn't sophisticated. Anyone could learn how to build one online. A battery, a couple of relays, a cheap timer, and about six different colors of wire. The trick was to cut the right one. Sweat began to trickle down his back as he followed each of the wires and surmised its purpose.

Suddenly he heard footsteps, heavy, and lots of them. The softer padding of Cowboy's feet reached his door first, and he barked frenziedly. Thank God…the dog had done his job.

"Cowboy, you'll have steak for dinner tonight!"

The door flew open and the first to reach him was one very happy dog who licked his face in reckless abandon. Since Cowboy had at least given him a chance, he let him get in a few licks before uttering the command to chill.

Confusion was paramount in Luke's gaze when it fell on him, taking in the bomb and Garrett's compromised position. Jonathan and Jase swarmed into the room behind him.

"What the hell?" Luke hurried to his side, studying the bomb that was presently passing the four-minute, nine-second mark.

"Cut me loose, Luke." Garrett jerked on his bonds again, the ropes scraping deeper into his skin. "Jonathan, find Rachel. I'm afraid he's got her."

Jonathan's angry expression turned stony. "*Who's* got her?"

Luke jerked open his pocketknife and sliced the ropes holding his brother's wrists, then stretched to the end of the bed and freed his feet. Garrett's arms fell to the comforter beside him, practically useless for lack of blood. He gritted his teeth as the prickling sign of the flow returning invaded his arms.

"Alan Taylor—aka Jeremy. And he's been here when the season starts every year, keeping an eye on her. Creepy bastard."

Jonathan turned abruptly and rushed from the room, his straight back and curled fists evidence of the fury that washed through his veins.

"Okay, not to rush you, bro, but we have to do something about this bomb. We're at three minutes, nineteen seconds and counting," Luke said.

"I know what to do. Give me your knife and then get everyone else out of the lodge." Garrett flexed his fingers, still trying to rid himself of the numbness, and held out his palm toward his brother.

A cynical snort proceeded from Luke. He dropped the knife on Garrett's outstretched fingers, and it promptly fell through his grasp and bounced off the bedsheets. Luke stared at Garrett and made no move to go. "Jase, get everybody out. You've got three minutes. I'm going to stay here and help my big brother."

Jase barreled for the door, already calling for Peg and Sally.

Garrett managed to land a pet on Cowboy's muzzle. "Head to the rodeo, Cowboy." The dog whined, but ran from the room after Jase. Garrett hoped to hell they'd find someone who could take care of Cowboy if this didn't go well.

A grin creased his face. "You ready?"

Luke nodded and retrieved the knife from where it had dropped. He glanced at the timer. "Two minutes, ten seconds."

Garrett propped himself up on his elbows so he could see. "Okay, from what I could determine, the battery provides the power for the timer and the blasting cap, but would they really make it that easy to diffuse? I find that hard to believe. I think there's an alternate power source where that gray wire goes behind that block of C-4."

Luke leaned closer. "So, cut the gray wire?"

Garrett shook his head slowly, then met Luke's gaze. "Cut the orange wire—then cut the gray wire."

Luke smiled of all things, and his calm acceptance of Garrett's instructions was humbling. He nodded toward the hallway. "Thirty seconds should be enough. That'll give them another minute to evacuate…just in case."

Garrett looked into his little brother's eyes. He was so proud of Luke. The navy had made a man of him the same as the army had for Garrett. The fact that Luke trusted his judgment enough to stay said it all. No one had believed in him like that since his mother left.

"ARE YOU GOING to keep your inheritance from Mom? Sign on to be part owner of this place? You know—on the off chance it survives the next few minutes?" Garrett chuckled and reached to clasp his brother's hand.

The two shook hands as they both grinned. "I don't know. I would've said no up until I met that sassy brunette and her daughter." Luke's cheeks turned a shade of pink.

"There are worse things than loving someone, Luke."

"Yeah. I suppose there are. We better do this, huh?" Luke released his hand. "Gray and then orange."

"No. Orange, then gray." Garrett chuckled as he recognized the teasing glint in Luke's eyes. His little brother had been testing him.

"Twenty-seven seconds." Without further comment, Luke clipped the orange wire. The timer flickered for a heartbeat and then continued to count down. As soon as Luke cut the gray wire, it stopped with thirteen seconds to go. They both breathed. "Damn, I used to really hate when you were right all the time, Garrett. Today—not so much."

Garrett lay back on the bed, suddenly realizing how weak he was. "Maybe you could help me out of this thing?"

"Sure. Just let me give Jonathan the all-clear." Luke apparently had him on speed dial already because from start to finish his call took about five seconds. He was just helping Garrett out of the duct-taped vest when Jonathan, Jase, and Cowboy burst through the open doorway.

Jonathan got on his cell phone right away. "Peg, it's over. Everything's okay. You can allow the guests back inside."

Garrett hoped Jonathan's *everything's okay* included Rachel. "Did you find her?"

Jonathan shook his head. "No sign of a struggle in her room. She must have gone with him willingly. I brought her sweater...for the dog." He held it out to Garrett.

"Good idea." He just happened to possess one of the best trackers Uncle Sam's K-9 Corp had ever produced. Couple that with his seeming ability to reason out a problem, and Cowboy was damn near unstoppable. He gave the dog a good whiff of the sweater. "Find Rachel, boy."

They all moved into the hallway, Garrett turning right, sure the trail would start at Rachel's door, but Cowboy didn't hesitate for a second. He turned left, raced around the corner, passed the room he'd torn apart to get out, and went down the stairs. When he was stopped by the closed back door, he twirled in a circle and barked.

"Wait. I need a weapon. Let's take five to get geared up. We don't know if we're going to be on foot or what." Garrett looked around at the other men. "Anyone want to opt out of the search, I won't hold it against you."

"Shit." The expletive exploded from Jonathan, and he strode toward the stairs. "I'll fucking hold it against you. Five minutes the man said." He continued to rant and grumble as he disappeared from sight.

The three remaining at the bottom of the stairs grinned at each other. "Yeah, what he said." Jase gave Garrett a high five as he walked away.

Five minutes later, they met again just outside the back door weighed down with weapons, jackets, water, and flashlights. Garrett held Cowboy on a leash, and the dog was antsy and ready to go. He took off at a run as soon as he was released. The men struggled to keep up over the rough terrain where the dog led them. Apparently, Jeremy had taken Rachel out of the lodge on foot and up the side of the mountain. The good news was, he probably wouldn't have carried her, which meant she was able to walk under her own power. That wasn't much consolation.

Suddenly Cowboy's desolate howl filled the night.

"He's lost the trail." Garrett didn't try to hide his disappointment as they closed in on the dog's position.

They stopped on what must have once been a road but was now nearly overgrown, with only two wheel ruts showing. Garrett called the dog so he'd stop his relentless pacing. Already he'd trampled some of the footprints that lingered in the dirt, but Garrett was almost positive there were four distinct sets of prints. Rachel's and three others.

"Over here." Jonathan motioned with his light. "There was a vehicle parked here. There are two—maybe three—sets of tracks plus Rachel, and they drove out of here."

"Fuck!" Garrett turned away from the others, afraid in his need to strangle someone he might choose one of them. God, why had he left her? Why hadn't he insisted she stay by his side? This was the end of the trail. How would he find her now?

Cowboy whined, his head pressed against Garrett's leg. "That's a good dog. You did everything you could." Garrett scratched the dog's head, floundering in his misery.

Luke stopped beside him. "Maybe we'll find a clue in the daylight."

"Right," added Jase from his other side. "Or we'll be able to follow the tire tracks."

They were trying to be supportive, optimistic, but daylight might as well be a lifetime away. What would Jeremy do to her in the dark of the night? No way in hell was Garrett giving up. He needed some quiet so he could think. His head, still throbbing from whatever was in that dart, was surely going to split wide open.

Jonathan's phone buzzed and he grabbed it from his belt. He listened for a second before he punched the speaker button, and Rachel's voice cut across the darkness.

"Jonathan?…hear me?" It was a lousy connection. Her voice was cutting out badly. "I got a…to the cabin…turned around."

"Rachel, sweetheart, it's okay now. We're coming for you. Just tell me where you are." The uncertainty in her voice tore Garrett up inside.

"Garrett? Thank God you're all right. I thought…" Her words faded intentionally this time and he could hear her harsh breaths as she fought for control.

"Where are you, Rachel?" Garrett ached to hold her close and convince her she didn't have to be afraid anymore.

"They took…mine….let me go. Got lost…fell…don't know…"

Jonathan swore under his breath. "Rach, what can you see from there?"

"Trees." She actually laughed, which Garrett took as a positive sign.

Abruptly, they lost the signal, and silence fell over the forested trail. Garrett held his breath while Jonathan redialed the last number over and over again with no luck.

A growl escaped with Garrett's breath. "I'll kill that son of a bitch when I find him."

Jonathan gave a harsh laugh. "Not by yourself."

"What now?" Jase paced back and forth between the ruts.

"We know she's in the forest, that she got turned around on the way to the cabin, and she doesn't know where she is. She can't be up too high or she'd have better cell reception. I didn't understand all of what she said, like *they took hers* and *let her go*. Did they really turn her loose out there? And took her what?" Garrett mulled over the information they'd received.

"Wait a minute. She said *they took...mine*, but the connection was really bad and there was a pause before *mine*." Luke turned toward his brother. "What if she was saying *they took me to the mine*? There are plenty of old mines around here, aren't there?"

"Damn right," Jonathan said.

"One in particular." Garrett looked to Jonathan for confirmation. "Not too far away. One that Rachel accused Riley and his brothers of planning to dump her in that day at the bar."

Jonathan nodded. "Addison's Mine. It's about six miles from here."

"What's the likelihood that Riley and one of his crew are the extra footprints we found?"

Jonathan strode toward him, his phone outstretched in his hand. When he was close enough for Garrett to shine his light on the face, he read the name *Arnold Metcalf*. Garrett furrowed a brow.

"Rachel was using Arnold's phone. Arnold is Riley's oldest brother." Jonathan took the phone back and shoved it in his pocket.

Anger burned hot within Garrett. His patience had disappeared an hour ago. He wanted to go find Rachel now, and if Jeremy or any of Riley's crew got in his way, that would be okay, too. Breathing deeply, he tried to funnel his frustration into something he could use.

"Let's get back to the lodge and get some wheels. We've got a place to start. If she's still out there, Cowboy will find her." Garrett pushed off the rutted trail back the way they'd come. He set a fast pace, pushing through the pain in his back and thigh, realizing it didn't hurt nearly as bad as the cruel emptiness where his heart used to be.

Chapter Twenty

RACHEL REDIALED JONATHAN's number a half dozen times before she finally gave up. Two bars apparently weren't enough to make the connection more than once. With her swollen and throbbing ankle, she wouldn't be climbing higher anytime soon. She turned the phone off to conserve the battery and tucked it in the pocket of her skirt.

She'd tried to tell them where she thought she was, but the connection had been spotty, and she had to face the fact that they might not have heard enough to find her. Surprisingly, she wasn't dwelling on that as she might have, because miraculously, she'd heard Garrett's voice. He was alive. She'd been so afraid that Garrett would die and that others at the lodge would be hurt. To know that they were unharmed had lifted a huge weight off her shoulders.

If only she hadn't gotten her foot stuck under one side of a huge log and toppled over, twisting her ankle before her foot finally popped free, she'd feel light enough to walk right off this mountain.

It still made her sick when she thought about sitting down at the lodge dinner table and making small talk with the man who murdered Chance. How was it that she'd not had a clue? She'd even *liked* the guy...and his wife. Poor Linda, married all those years to a perverted freak...and now, if she could believe Jeremy, Linda was probably dead, murdered as well.

A shudder washed over Rachel, and she again found herself silently thanking Arnold for letting her escape, even though she'd gotten turned around. She might as well admit now that she was completely lost. The maddening part was she'd covered all of this ground before...in the daylight with Jonathan. The darkness and her panic had not worked in her favor.

She looked out over the downhill slope before her. The mountains around her home were beautiful, and she had no fear of them. It was the omnipresence of Jeremy that scared the holy crap out of her. That's why she'd been rushing blindly through the forest to her own detriment. Finally she slumped to the ground and remained sitting at the base of a big pine to catch her breath and calm her racing heart.

It was a warm night for the month of May, and she'd have been comfortable if she'd been allowed to dress for the occasion. However, her sleeveless shirt, short skirt, and heels made less than appropriate hiking attire.

A nice breath of pine floated in on the breeze, and she inhaled it, letting it work its down-home magic on her soul. By the light of the full moon, she could see the shadowy outline of a break in the trees below her and a good distance from her position. She'd bet the river that ran by Amanda's cabin nestled in the fold. With a huge sigh, she heaved herself to her feet and leaned against the tree for a few seconds before she pushed off in the direction of the clearing.

If Jonathan and Garrett understood enough of her conversation, they'd look for her at the cabin. She bit back a cry at the sharp pain in her ankle and forced herself to put one foot in front of the other.

SHARDS OF PAIN shattered behind her eyelids every time she took a step. Rachel had long ago lost track of time and distance. The only thing that mattered was finding the cabin. Not the critters she heard scurrying through the brush now and then. Not the pain or the voice in her head telling her she'd never make it that far. Not even the one that said she was doing irreparable damage to her ankle. Garrett would look for her at the cabin, and she had to get there.

Each time she topped a rise or dragged herself to the slope of a ridge, she looked to the east to find her landmark so she could adjust her course accordingly. This time, she was close, and for the first time, optimism stole over her. She took a moment to rest and stare at the eastern sky, beginning to lighten with the first sign of dawn. The morning dew, touching her chilled skin, got her moving again.

The rush of swift water reached her ears, and she shuffled faster. As she broke over the last rise, the trees thinned and the river rolled through the clearing below. Rachel fell to her knees, breathing in the familiar scents. But where was the cabin? Slowly she turned to the right, then to the left, searching for the dock she'd sat on a hundred times, swinging her bare feet in the cool water. There was nothing, yet she had to be close. The mountains in the skyline, silhouetted by the gathering light of morning, looked just like *her* mountains. The cabin had to be only a short walk down the banks of the river.

Rachel sighed and rested her head in her hands for a moment. A short walk for her yesterday would be an excruciating trial of her determination today. Well, no sense in feeling sorry for herself. That wouldn't get her any closer to Garrett.

She used her arms to push herself off the ground, and one of her hands fell on something hard. A limb. Balancing precariously, she bent to pull one end of the limb off the ground. It was about as thick as her arm and longer than she was tall, but it was sturdy and maybe she could use it to take some of the weight off her injured ankle.

Taking a couple of hobbling steps forward, using the limb to support her right side, she marveled at the instant relief. She wouldn't kid herself, though. Bracing herself on the makeshift walking stick would take a toll on her arms and shoulders, so the fewer steps she had to take the better. Hobbling closer to the river, she studied the banks in both directions. Which way should she go?

A distant sound drifted on the breeze. She raised her head and stilled, turning this way and that, hoping she'd really heard excited barking, and that Cowboy would appear any moment...followed by Garrett. But it must have been her imagination or wishful thinking. The sound never returned.

Okay, this is nuts. Just pick a direction and find the cabin. Right. I'll go to the right first.

Rachel struggled toward the bend in the river, stopping every few feet to gauge her progress and rest. Something caught her eye in the trees ahead. *Was that a light?* The quick flicker disappeared, and she dismissed it as the white bark of a tree. She raised the corner of her shirt's hem to wipe the sweat from her eyes. *God, I'm almost there. Don't let me go crazy now.*

She hopped two more steps before the flicker was back, morphed into a circle of light that bobbed crazily in front of a dark shadow that was closing in on her.

Her heart started to beat wildly. "Garrett?" It had to be him, for the sake of her sanity if nothing else.

Why didn't he reply? He just kept walking toward her, shining that light in her direction. She lifted her hand to shade her eyes, but she still couldn't make out his handsome face or the smile she longed to see. A twinge of uneasiness sent a wave of fear that lodged in her stomach.

"Garrett? Is that you?"

The figure stopped twenty feet away. "No, my sweet. Unfortunately, your friend Garrett is dead, and good riddance I say." Jeremy's maniacal laughter drained all the blood from her extremities, and she would have fallen if not for the tree limb she braced herself with.

"Jeremy?"

"That's right, love." He strode closer. "I couldn't believe it when I learned those Metcalf boys let you walk out of the mine. Lucky for them, it didn't take too much to convince the older one to tell me where you were headed. I doubt anyone will find them down that shaft, so they're probably regretting their decision by now."

Rachel's stomach churned. "You put them down the shaft?"

"They had to be punished, as do you, Rachel." He clicked off the flashlight and took another step.

Without the light in her face, Rachel could see Jeremy's crazy eyes. He was a killer. How well she knew that. It was only a matter of time before he got around to her. There was no reason to stand still and let him take her alive. She leaned her weight on her good leg, picked up the end of the limb, and swung with all of her might. A guttural scream tore from her throat the same time the wood cracked into Jeremy's head.

He fell like a load of rocks, groaning and squirming.

Rachel stumbled with the force of her swing, resulting in a tearing pain in her ankle, and she fell to her knees. She watched in horror as he staggered to his feet. Blood trickled from a cut on his forehead, and he held his left arm immobile across his body. She scrambled to regain her feet as he strode toward her. Breathing hard, she lifted the limb, bracing it across her shoulder like a bat, and waited. He had to be close or she'd miss, and she'd have only one chance.

She let him take two more steps and then swung with everything she had. Jeremy knocked the limb from her hands effortlessly, then caught her against his body with his uninjured arm. Rachel slumped as though she were falling, and when his grip loosened, she suddenly straightened and thrust her elbow backward into his ribs. Jeremy let out a whoosh of air and grabbed for her elbow. Rachel turned her body into his, bringing her other hand up, and angled the heel of her hand toward his nose. It was a glancing blow at best, but she felt the cartilage crack, and Jeremy released her and lurched backward, sprawling in the dirt.

This time Rachel didn't wait to see if he got up. She ran, doing her best to ignore her throbbing ankle.

"You stupid bitch!" His cry of pain propelled her faster. "You'll pay for this. You can't get away."

Rachel gritted her teeth and shuffled faster. Certain she couldn't outrun him, she changed directions and took to the slope of the mountain, planning to hide herself in the thick forest above. Big mistake. Without her walking stick, she couldn't push off her bad leg, so she resorted to hands and knees to climb the slope, slippery with loose dirt and shale.

Halfway up, Jeremy grabbed her hair and jerked her head back. "You can't get away from me. I haven't kept track of you all these years to let you slip away now." His other hand delivered a punch to the side of her head that numbed the whole left half of her body.

As the numbness receded only seconds later, pain took its place, and she curled into a tight ball, breathing in short gasps because her chest ached too much to take a deep breath. Jeremy stood over her, his fist poised, and for several painful breaths, she waited for the next blow to fall. When it didn't, she rolled to the side and pushed herself up, clenching her jaw at the pain in her ankle.

THEY SWITCHED OFF the lights of Sally's Explorer as they approached Addison's Mine and coasted to a stop. The next hundred yards they'd cover on foot. Garrett was the first to reach the mine entrance, followed closely by Jonathan, Luke, and Jase. Cowboy was stuck to him like glue, anticipating a mission of epic proportions, no doubt. Hopefully, that wouldn't be the case. Quiet reigned inside the cavern until Garrett called Rachel's name. Then all hell broke loose.

"Down here! Get me the hell outta here! Hey! Whoever you are...don't leave us here!"

Riley. And he didn't sound happy.

They all followed Jonathan deeper into the mine until they stood on the edge of a hole that he outlined with his flashlight. Garrett assumed it was the mine's old shaft. It could be hundreds of feet deep. A wooden contraption that looked like a jerry-rigged elevator hung over the hole, tied off with thick ropes that looked newer than everything else the miners had left behind.

"Who's down there?" Jonathan growled.

"There you are. It's about damn time. Riley Metcalf and my brother. Some lunatic forced us into that cage at gunpoint and left us down here."

"Arnold?" Jonathan shone his light down the shaft.

"Yep. That's my brother. He's here, too." Riley was being all kinds of helpful.

Garrett stepped toward Jonathan. "Arnold, tell us what happened to Rachel."

"Get us out of here first." Riley was starting to sound belligerent.

"Shut up for once in your life." The new voice must have belonged to Arnold, and Riley did as he was told with only a small amount of grumbling.

"She slipped out of here when I went to check on my brother." Arnold's deep voice was calm and confident.

"So you don't know where she headed?" Garrett clenched his fists in frustration.

A moment of hesitation passed. "She was heading toward Amanda's cabin."

Garrett jerked his head up. "That's crazy. How would she find it in the dark?"

Several seconds of silence ticked by. "I showed her where to go."

"What?" Riley cried. "You stupid bastard. That's why Jeremy was so mad after he talked to you? You're the reason we're down here." Riley was apparently slapping his brother around for his supposed sins, but the fighting abruptly stopped when a punch landed one of them in the dirt.

Garrett presumed it was Arnold still standing since the fisticuffs had stopped. "Arnold, did you also give her your phone?"

"Yeah. Now, Riley, you just stay put. That no-good SOB that hired us is bad news. You know it as well as I do. He would have hurt Rachel as soon as look at her. Is that what you wanted? Don't you remember what she did for us? Her and Peg and Amanda? They was good to us after Mama died."

For once, Riley had nothing to say, and Garrett experienced a moment of gratitude just for that.

"Don't be thinkin' I done her no favors, though. When that son of a bitch came back and figured what I'd done, he threatened to shoot Riley, and I spilled my guts. He knows where she's goin', and he'll have plenty of time to get there ahead of her." It went quiet in the cavern below again.

Garrett glanced at the rest of the guys, and each in his turn motioned back the way they'd come and disappeared. Garrett lingered a moment longer, Cowboy moving nervously beside him. "I want to thank you for what you tried to do tonight, Arnold. We're going after her."

"What about us?" Riley was apparently into whining mode now.

"I'll call the state police and tell them where you are…and why. I'm sure they'll have a question or two for you. Arnold, when this is over, come and see me at the lodge. We'll talk." Garrett backed away, turned, and made his way to the entrance.

"Do you believe him?" Luke was waiting for him just outside.

"Yeah, I do." Garrett didn't like that she'd been turned loose in the dark, in the middle of fucking nowhere, but his gut told him Arnold, in his clumsy way, may have saved her life. He motioned for the others. "I'd like Jase and Jonathan to take the Explorer to the cabin in case she makes it that far. Keep your eyes open. Jeremy might be waiting for her, too. And give the sheriff a call to come and get these two." He nodded back toward the mine, then turned to Luke and placed a hand on his shoulder. "I'll let Cowboy track her through the woods. It could be a rough go, but I'd like you with me if you wouldn't mind."

"Shit. You don't even have to ask, bro." Luke slapped him on the back.

Garrett and Luke retrieved their gear and Rachel's sweater from the vehicle, said their good-byes, and watched as Jonathan and Jase turned the Explorer and began their descent.

Cowboy wagged his tail excitedly as he smelled the sweater Garrett held out to him. "Go find her, boy." The dog took off at a lope, and Garrett and Luke had to jog to keep up with him. Garrett clenched his jaw against pain that felt like a knife blade twisting in his lower back. With a herculean effort, he thrust it from his mind and replaced it with an image of Rachel's smiling face. Through narrow streams, over fallen logs, in and out of thickets, and across rocky ground, Cowboy traveled unerringly east, according to the GPS on Garrett's cell phone. The only spot that threw the dog for a loop was on a slope below a huge old pine tree. Cowboy circled, smelled, and dug up the ground, almost as though he expected to find her there.

Garrett stood at a distance, watching the dog's confusion, and knew exactly how he felt. Eventually, Cowboy's head came up, and he sniffed the air wafting in on an eastern breeze. He whined, fixed his big brown eyes on

Garrett, and then resumed the hunt. From then on, it was as though he knew where he was going. He didn't stop to sniff, didn't circle anything, didn't correct his course.

All Garrett and Luke could do was follow. Garrett, never having known Cowboy to lose the target he was tracking, had the utmost confidence in his abilities…but then the dog had never tracked anything so important before.

The first indication of dawn was barely showing itself when Garrett heard the river somewhere in front of them. Cowboy slowed and stopped on a rocky knoll just ahead. He cocked his head as though listening, and then he did something Garrett had never seen him do while tracking. He barked. Twice, fading to a mournful howl. His tail wagged once, and he jumped off the rocks and trotted to the bottom of the ridge.

Luke caught up to Garrett and stopped beside him, breathing hard. "This explains why you're in the best shape of your life. Even recovering from your wound, you walk circles around me. Damn, you could have warned me."

Garrett draped his arm around his brother's shoulders, feeling every inch of the tired and aching muscle surrounding the jagged scar that would end his career as a Ranger. Slowly and surely, it was healing. Tonight's mission probably wasn't doing his recovery any good, but even if he had to crawl on his hands and knees, he would keep moving until he found Rachel. "Come on. I think we're close." Garrett slipped and slid in the loose dirt following the dog to where the ground leveled off before sloping uphill again.

They walked another thirty minutes, crested a ridge, and were able to make out the banks of the river below. Garrett blew out a breath and knelt on his haunches, only too ready for a rest period. Luke joined him, dropping down on the rocky ground.

"Cowboy." Garrett tapped the side of his leg, but the dog was apparently focused on something only he could hear over the rush of the water.

"Is he always so intense?" Luke rubbed his hand over the nape of his neck.

"When he's tracking and he's close, he becomes obsessively single-minded." Garrett watched the way Cowboy stood, head lowered, weight on his front end, ears forward, and head turned slightly upriver. "I've seen him go days without food because he refused to stop long enough to eat."

"Jeez, bro. That's a little spooky." Luke regarded Cowboy with a wary respect.

The dog growled so low that Garrett barely heard him. "Not if he's on your side." He spoke quietly as he stood, motioned Luke to his feet, and put a finger in front of his lips.

The next instant, Cowboy leaped forward and hit the ground a good twenty feet down the side of the ridge. Dirt flew from under his feet as he landed and gathered himself for the next stride. At a full-tilt run and silent as the night, he raced in and out of the shadows on a straight line to the river at two o'clock.

"This is it. He's found something. Keep an eye out for Jeremy, Luke." Garrett drew his weapon, looked to see that Luke had done the same, and leaped over the side, sliding all the way to the bottom. With Luke right behind him, he shoved off the ground and sprinted after the dog.

It didn't take long for Cowboy to outdistance him, but when Garrett slipped from the trees into the clearing along the river, he spotted the dog as he lengthened his stride and bore down on the shadowy figures of a man and woman.

It was Rachel. Garrett would recognize that long hair and perfect figure anywhere.

She was just picking herself up off the ground and stumbled back clumsily, but appeared to finally get herself balanced. As the man, who could be none other than Jeremy, sidled toward her, fist raised, she delivered a right cross to his jaw that set him back a few steps. His roar of indignation echoed across the clearing as he straightened and stomped toward her. He reached out, grabbed her by the back of her neck, and flung her to the ground at his feet.

Rage exploded through Garrett and, only slightly aware of Luke beside him, he raised his weapon. *Fuck!* With Rachel so close, he didn't dare take the shot. He broke into a run, ignoring the jolt of pain with each stride, and his gaze darted to Cowboy, who was quickly closing in. The dog moved stealthier now, his body hugging the ground.

Across the sixty feet that separated them, Garrett heard Jeremy's scornful laugh, saw him pull Rachel up by her hair, drawing one fist back to strike. Cowboy lunged, clearing Rachel's kneeling figure to slam into Jeremy's chest. Man and dog flew back several feet, and there was an audible *oof* when Cowboy came down on top of him. A feral growl and the screams of a man with one seriously pissed-off shepherd two inches from his face shattered the semidarkness. Cowboy had no trouble convincing Jeremy not to move, and the bastard would never know what a good decision that had been.

Garrett and Luke approached at a jog. "Cowboy, take no prisoners." Garrett gave the dog his command to stand guard over the enemy. Cowboy immediately backed away, but never took his eyes off Jeremy. Garrett dragged the slimeball to his feet and confiscated his weapon before binding his hands behind his back. He'd never wanted to pummel anyone as badly as he did Jeremy, but Luke came up behind him, laid a reassuring hand on his shoulder, and nodded toward Rachel.

She had crumpled to the ground when Cowboy streaked by her, curling into a ball with her arms covering her head. Realizing she still lay in the same position, Garrett hurried to kneel beside her. As soon as he rolled her to her back and moved one arm carefully down to her side, her pain-filled eyes, opened and locked on him, stole his breath and his chest constricted with his need for her.

He dropped down beside her. "Are you hurt, sweetheart?" He ran his hands slowly over her arms and shoulders. God, she felt so good, yet he was almost afraid to touch her for fear she wasn't real and she might disappear again.

"Thanks…for coming, Garrett." Anguish was etched in her green eyes, and he accepted the possibility that there'd be wounds that might never heal.

He slipped his cell phone from his pocket, and while holding her gaze, he raised one brow. "Did you think I wouldn't? I'm always going to come for you."

A tear rolled down her cheek, killing him as it slowly disappeared into her hair. "I haven't been very nice to you."

It was true—they hadn't started off on the best of terms, but she couldn't resist his charm forever. "You've been as nice as I deserved."

Rachel choked on a half laugh, half sob. "Well, that's true."

There. That's what he'd been waiting for—her confidence and stubborn pride to kick in. She'd be all right...in spite of whatever injuries the EMTs found when they arrived. Needing to have her close for just a moment before he called the state police, he bent to press his lips to her cheek, but she turned her head and offered her lips.

He'd have been crazy to argue.

Chapter Twenty-One

RACHEL TIED HER naturally curly hair into a ponytail and took one more look at herself in the mirror. The past three weeks had almost completely healed the bruises on her cheekbone and jaw, although she routinely frowned at the remnants of the purplish splotches. She wouldn't be happy until they were gone.

The freedom that she'd known since Jeremy had been extradited back to Texas and charged with Chance's murder had put a smile on her face that couldn't be wiped away. Oh sure. Someday she'd have to go back and testify, but she'd be ready and willing when that day came. It had been a shock to learn that Jeremy was a grandson of the neighbors she'd been fond of in Plainview. Apparently, she'd met him one time, although she had no recollection. He'd spilled the entire story to the police once they had him in custody. After she'd left Texas, he'd hired a private investigator to find her. It'd taken him almost five years, but Jeremy was apparently nothing if not patient.

Once he'd started coming to the lodge regularly, he'd been given her cell phone number on the proverbial silver platter in case he needed anything during his stay—as were all of the guests. If he *lost* her number, all he had to do was call Peg and he'd have it again within seconds. It's true what they say—hindsight is twenty/twenty. But until the night Alan Taylor, aka Jeremy, abducted her, he'd given her no reason to suspect he was her stalker. Apparently his wife hadn't suspected him, either. They had yet to find her body.

June had come in like gangbusters, sending the temperatures into the eighties most days, although the evenings were still cool. Rachel had taken to wearing sleeveless sundresses, which seemed to make it a tiny bit more bearable to wear the big clunking boot the doctor had given her for her ankle. The X-ray and MRI she'd had showed a stress fracture in one of the small bones of her foot as well as a seriously sprained ankle. The only thing that had kept her out of a cast was her promise to wear the boot every waking hour unless she was in the shower.

Garrett had gleefully stepped in to play The Boot Nazi, and truth of the matter was she missed his bossy ways. Terribly. A week ago, he'd reported to his base for evaluation, and he still didn't have a clue what the army was going to require of him. It didn't seem to bother Garrett, but her impatience was starting to show. She wanted him home—and so did Cowboy.

She smiled at the dog where he lounged near the door. Garrett had left his beloved pet and companion in her care while he fulfilled his duty to the army. After Cowboy had saved her from Jeremy, she'd no longer had any concerns that the ex-military dog would get in trouble because of her inability to control him. His innate sense of his surroundings, as well as his intelligence, made her feel safe wherever they went, something that had been sorely missing in her life until recently. She still suffered from bouts of insecurity when she wondered if Garrett would stay in Idaho—or how long he would stay—but they were fewer and further between.

She really had no reason to doubt him. Garrett had called her every day since he'd been gone just to see how she was doing and to make sure she was wearing the boot. They'd usually talk for an hour or better about everything under the sun. He told her about his siblings and how it had been growing up in a large family. She shared stories about her alcoholic mother and what it was like to be the adult in the situation at the tender age of nine. They'd grown closer through their talks, and it was obvious that he cared for her. It was too early in their relationship to expect anything more.

Luke had left for Virginia yesterday—deploying overseas in the next week or so, promising to have a decision on what he would do with his inheritance by the time he returned. He'd become a huge help around the lodge over the past few weeks, swinging a hammer here, splitting wood there, always with a congenial smile on his face. He'd put the utility closet that Cowboy had destroyed back together in no time. The best, though, were the warm evenings he'd spent telling stories on the porch with both Peg and Sally laughing at his outrageous teasing. Rachel hadn't seen Sally enjoy herself so in years. Even Jen seemed to have taken a liking to the man.

Rachel turned from the mirror to step into the tan loafer she'd been wearing ever since the boot had become a permanent fixture in her life. She searched the closet and under the bed, and scanned the floor. Where was the darn thing?

When Peg asked her to do some actual work today, she'd been so excited and hopeful that they'd stop treating her like an invalid. She wasn't going to let a lost shoe keep her from delivering linens and food staples to the cabin in preparation for an arriving guest.

She grabbed the first shoe she could find, and as she slipped into her favorite sandal, her phone rang. The name on the caller ID screen made her smile.

"Garrett! It's earlier than you usually call. Is everything all right?"

"I had a minute and just wanted to talk to my best girl."

Those were the kinds of things he said that made her heart sing. She so wanted it to be true. "That's sweet…but I bet I know why you really called. Before you ask, yes, I am wearing the friggin' boot. And don't think for a minute that I don't know you've got Peg, Dory, and Jonathan spying for you."

"Ouch—that's harsh." He chuckled. "I guess I have been a little pushy. How about I make it up to you?" His voice dropped to a husky murmur.

"How do you propose to do that, five hundred miles away?"

"I was hoping you'd go on a date with me as soon as I get back. In fact, I'd like to cook for you. Dinner, and if I play my cards right, maybe breakfast." His smooth, deep voice literally shook her, and desire pooled low in her stomach.

Rachel glanced at her watch, slipped into a sweater, and took one last look in the mirror. She could see Cowboy's reflection, standing at the door, eyeing her impatiently as if he, too, knew they were going to be late meeting Jonathan. She limped toward the door, and the dog bounced up and down on his front legs.

"That sounds wonderful, Garrett. Can we talk about it later? I'm working for a few hours today. Peg finally decided I wasn't completely useless. But, if I'm late, she might change her mind." Rachel sidestepped Cowboy, who was prancing back and forth in front of the door, whining and going completely crazy. What was up with him? She reached for the knob and leaned her forehead against the cool wood, cherishing every minute she spent in conversation with Garrett, yet knowing each call would inevitably come to an end.

"What kind of work?" A strange edge crept into his voice.

Rachel forced a little cheerful enthusiasm into hers. "Oh, nothing serious. I'm taking a few supplies over to the cabin. We have a new guest coming in today." She straightened and jerked the door open.

Cowboy shot from the room and launched himself into the arms of the man in army fatigues who leaned against the opposite wall. Completely covered by an ecstatic dog, his face was hidden from her, but Rachel would know that tall, muscular build anywhere. Dropping her phone into her sweater pocket, she jammed her hands down on her hips and narrowed her eyes.

When Garrett finally got the dog under control, he glanced toward her and his gaze immediately filled with caution. He lifted one hand and gave her a pathetic wave. "Hi, honey. I'm home."

"What were you thinking, standing outside my door, talking on the phone, letting me believe you were still in Washington? That's the meanest thing—" She turned abruptly and stumped down the hallway.

He caught up with her in a heartbeat. "Rach, wait. I wasn't trying to be mean. I wanted to surprise you."

She turned on him, angry tears threatening to flow. "*I don't like surprises.*"

"Okay. Good to know. I won't do it again...except—"

"*Except what?*" She snapped the words and immediately regretted it when he flinched. What was wrong with her? She knew he didn't mean any harm. It was sweet really. Yet, she'd never had a good surprise. Coming home from school innumerable times to find a new man living with her mother. Discovering Chance's bludgeoned body. Learning their longtime guest was her stalker and a murderer. Rachel didn't think she could take any more surprises.

A couple of guests had stepped from their rooms and stood watching them. Garrett scowled, grabbed her arm, and pulled her toward the room she'd just vacated. He shoved the door open, nudged her across the threshold, called Cowboy, and closed them all inside.

He caught her around the waist and pulled her against him. "This isn't how I planned this at all. Can we start over?" He didn't wait for her to answer, instead covering her lips with his, kissing her so long and thoroughly that her knees nearly gave out.

She melted against him, still not quite believing he was real. Maybe it was the same for him. When he stopped kissing her, he pulled her close in a tight embrace, his face buried in the crook of her neck, and a shudder passed through him.

"God, I've missed you, Rach. You smell so damn good." He raised his head and studied her face.

Rachel smiled, recognizing his attempt to deflect her questions. "I've missed you, too, Garrett, but if there's more to this surprise you've cooked up, please tell me." She stepped back and crossed her arms.

"I've worked hard to get this particular surprise to come together. Are you sure—" He raised his hands to ward off her next suggestion. "I know, I know—you don't like surprises. Damn, I wish you'd told me before."

"You could have asked." Rachel tried hard to hide the mirth that tugged at her lips.

One of his eyebrows shot up and a crooked grin hitched one side of his mouth. It was everything she could do to keep from reaching out to slide her hands around the back of his neck—anything to have his touch on her again.

He stepped away from her to the window that looked out on the slope of Cougar Ridge. "Well, for starters, I'm the one who'll be staying in the cabin."

"You?"

He nodded. "I'm not really a guest, though. Aunt Peg sold me the place. I signed the papers this morning."

That knocked the air from her lungs, and questions swirled in her head. Before she found her voice, he started talking again.

He turned partway to look at her. "It was Amanda's favorite place. I wanted to have something of hers. I don't know why. Just one of those childhood dreams come to fruition." He took another step to face her. "I also wanted to be close to you. I plan to spend a lot of time with you...if you'll let me. Although, now that you've taken my secret weapon—surprises—off the table it's not going to be quite the same." His perusal was hopeful as it swept across her face.

Rachel placed her hand over her mouth, but couldn't stop the laughter that bubbled out.

Garrett walked toward her, his hand going to the column of her throat. "Someday, when we decide the time is right, and you agree to move in with me, I want our home to be comfortable and inviting for you."

"What? You're staying?" Rachel didn't realize how much fear the question struck in her heart until she voiced the words. At the same time, she backed away from his touch, just in case the surprise really was on her.

Garrett dropped his hand to his side. "Why would I leave? Everything I want is here. Right here in this room. I love you, Rach. Without you I'm just a guy with a dog."

Rachel laughed. "Really?" He was staying? He loved her. She would have jumped up and down if not for the stupid boot.

In the next instant, his smile turned her legs to Jell-O. "Sorry about the surprise, sweetheart, but I planned to spend the weekend with my best girl at the cabin, and—"

"No!" She stumped toward him and threw herself into his arms, placing her fingers over his lips. "Don't say any more. Surprise me."

"I thought you didn't like surprises."

"I was mistaken." She pressed a hard kiss to his lips as she laced her arms around his neck. "I love you, too, Garrett, and I love your surprise. I'm so sorry I ruined it."

"Oh, there's a lot more to come, sweetheart." He set her on her feet. "Are you ready to go?"

"If we're spending the weekend, shouldn't I pack a bag?"

"Not necessary. I asked Dory to take care of that little item. Your bag's already in my Jeep."

Rachel huffed a breath. "That's where my shoe went! You really are good at this surprise business." She leaned against his hard chest and brushed his lips with hers.

"You haven't seen anything yet, sweetheart." He grinned devilishly.

"Don't forget—two can play that game." She laughed at his wary expression as she leaned against him for one more kiss.

Give in to your Impulses . . .
Continue reading for excerpts from
our newest Avon Impulse books.
Available now wherever e-books are sold.

RIGHT WRONG GUY
A BRIGHTWATER NOVEL
By Lia Riley

DESIRE ME MORE
By Tiffany Clare

MAKE ME
A BROKE AND BEAUTIFUL NOVEL
By Tessa Bailey

An Excerpt from

RIGHT WRONG GUY
A Brightwater Novel
by Lia Riley

Bad boy wrangler Archer Kane lives fast and
loose. Words like *responsibility* and *commitment*
send him running in the opposite direction. Until
a wild Vegas weekend puts him on a collision
course with Eden Bankcroft-Kew, a New York
heiress running away from her blackmailing
fiancé . . . the morning of her wedding.

"Archer?" Eden stared in the motel bathroom mirror, her reflection a study in horror. "Please tell me this is a practical joke."

"We're in the middle of Nevada, sweetheart. There's no Madison Avenue swank in these parts." Archer didn't bother to keep amusement from his answering yell through the closed door. "The gas station only sold a few things. Trust me, those clothes were the best of the bunch."

After he got out of the shower, a very long shower which afforded her far too much time for contemplating him in a cloud of thick steam, running a bar of soap over cut v-lines, he announced that he would find her something suitable to wear. She couldn't cross state lines wearing nothing but his old t-shirt, and while the wedding dress worked in a pinch, it was still damp. Besides, her stomach lurched at the idea of sliding back into satin and lace.

She'd never be able to don a wedding dress and not think of the Reggie debacle. She couldn't even entirely blame him, her subconscious had been sending out warning flares for months. She'd once been considered a smart woman, graduated from NYU with a 4.0 in Art History. So how could she have been so dumb?

Truth be told, it wasn't even due to her mother's dying wish that led her to accepting him, although that certainly bore some influence. No, it was the idea of being alone. The notion didn't feel liberating or "I am woman, hear me roar." More terrified house mouse squeaking alone in a dark cellar.

She clenched her jaw, shooing away the mouse. What was the big deal with being alone? She might wish for more friends, or a love affair, but she'd also never minded her own company. This unexpected turn of events was an opportunity, a time for self-growth, getting to know herself, and figuring out exactly what she wanted. Yes, she'd get empowered all right, roar so loud those California mountains would tremble.

Right after they finished laughing at this outfit.

Seriously, did Archer have to select pink terrycloth booty shorts that spelled *Q & T* in rhinestones, one on each butt cheek? And the low-cut top scooped so even her small rack sported serious cleavage. *Get Lucky* emblazoned across the chest, the tank top was an XS so the letters stretched to the point of embarrassment. If she raised her hands over her head, her belly button winked out.

As soon as she arrived in Brightwater, she'd invest in proper clothes and send for her belongings back home. Until then . . . time to face the music. She stepped from the bathroom, chewing the corner of her lip. Archer didn't burst into snickers. All he did was stare. His playful gaze vanished, replaced by a startling intensity.

"Well, go on then. Get it over with and make fun of me." She gathered her hair into a messy bun, securing it with a hair elastic from her wrist she found in her purse.

"Laughing's not the first thing that jumps to mind, sweetheart."

Her stomach sank. "Horror then?"

"Stop." He rubbed the back of his neck, that wicked sensual mouth curving into a bold smile. "You're hot as hell."

Reggie had never remarked on her appearance. She sucked in a ragged breath at the memory of his text. *Bored me to fucking tears.*

"Hey, Freckles," he said softly. "You okay?"

She snapped back, unsure what her face revealed. "Tiny shorts and boob shirts do it for you?" She fought for an airy tone, waving her hand over the hot pink "QT" abomination and praying he wouldn't notice her tremble.

He gave a one-shouldered shrug. "Short shorts do it for all warm-blooded men."

"I'll keep that in mind," she said, thumbing her ear. He probably wasn't checking *her* out, just her as the closest female specimen in the immediate vicinity.

He wiggled out of his tan Carhart jacket and held it out. "You'll want this. Temperatures are going to top out in the mid-forties today. I've stuck a wool blanket in the passenger seat and will keep the heat cranking."

Strange. He might be a natural flirt, but for all his easy confidence, there was an uncertainty in how he regarded her. A hesitation that on anyone else could be described as vulnerability, the type of look that caused her to volunteer at no-kill rescue shelters and cry during cheesy life insurance commercials. A guy like this, what did he know about insecurity or self-doubt? But that expression went straight to her heart. "Archer . . ."

He startled at the sound of his real name, instead of the Cowboy moniker she'd used the last twenty-four hours.

His jacket slipped, baring her shoulders as she reached to take one of his big hands in hers. "Thank you." Impulsively, she rose on tiptoe to kiss his cheek, but he jerked with surprise and she grazed the appealing no-man's land between his dimple and lips.

This was meant to be a polite gesture, an acknowledgment he'd been a nice guy, stepped up and helped her—a stranger— out when she'd barreled in and given him no choice.

He smelled good. Too good. Felt good too. She should move—now—but his free hand, the one she wasn't clutching, skimmed her lower back. Was this a kiss?

No.

Well . . . almost.

Never had an actual kiss sent goose bumps prickling down her spine even as her stomach heated, the cold and hot reaction as confused as her thoughts. Imagine what the real thing would do.

An Excerpt from

DESIRE ME MORE

by *Tiffany Clare*

From the moment Amelia Grant accepted the position of secretary to Nicholas Riley, London's most notorious businessman, she knew her life would be changed forever. For Nick didn't want just her secretarial skills . . . he wanted her complete surrender. And she was more than willing to give it to him, spending night after night in delicious sin. As the devastatingly insatiable Nick teaches her the ways of forbidden desire, Amelia begins to dream of a future together . . .

Why hadn't she just stayed in bed? Instead, she'd set herself on an unknown path. One without Nick. Why? She hated this feeling that was ripping her apart from the inside out. It hurt so much and so deeply that the wounds couldn't be healed.

Biting her bottom lip on a half-escaped sob, she violently wiped her tears away with the back of her hand. Nick caught her as she fumbled with the lock on the study door, spinning her around and wrapping his arms tightly around her, crushing her against his solid body.

She wanted to break down. To just let the tears overtake her. But she held strong.

"I have already told you I can't let you go. Stay, Amelia." His voice was so calm, just above a whisper. "Please, I couldn't bear it if you left me. I can't let you leave. I won't."

Hearing him beg tugged at her heart painfully. Amelia's fists clenched where they were trapped between their bodies. There was only one thing she could do.

She pushed him away, hating that she was seconds away from breaking down. Hating that she knew that she had to hold it together when every second in his arms chipped away at her control.

"You are breaking my will every day. Making me lose myself in you. Don't ask this of me. Please. Nick. Let me go."

If she stayed, they would only end up back where they were. And she needed more than his physical comfort. He held her tighter against his chest, crushing her between him and the door like he would *never* let her go.

"I told you I couldn't let you go. Don't try to leave. I warned you that you were mine the night I took your virginity."

Tilting her head back, she stared at him, eyes awash with tears she was helpless to stop from flowing over her cheeks. "Why are you doing this to me?"

The gray of his eyes were stormy, as though waiting to unleash a fury she'd never seen the likes of. "Because I can't let you go. Because I love you."

His tone brooked no argument, so she said nothing to contradict him, just stared at him for another moment before pushing at his immovable body again. Nick's hand gently cradled her throat, his thumb forcing her head to lean against the door.

"I've already told you that I wouldn't let you walk away. You belong to me."

Her lips parted on a half exasperated groan at his declaration of ownership over her.

"How could I belong to you when you close yourself off to me? I will not be controlled by you, no matter what I feel—"

Before she could get out the rest of her sentence, Nick's mouth took hers in an all-consuming kiss, his tongue robbing her of breath as it pushed past the barrier of her lips and tangled with her tongue in wordless need.

Hunger rose in her, whether it was for physical desire or a need to draw as much of him into her as possible was hard to say. And she hated herself a little for not pushing him away again and again until she won this argument. Not now that she had a small piece of him all to herself. Even if it wouldn't be enough in the end.

Without a doubt in her mind, she'd never crave anything as badly as she craved Nick: his essence, his strength, *him*.

Her hands fisted around his shirtsleeves, holding him close. She didn't want to let go . . . of him or the moment.

His touch was like a branding iron as he tugged the hemline of her dress from her shoulders, pulling down the front of the dress. The pull rent the delicate satin material, leaving one breast on display for Nick to fondle. His hand squeezed her, the tips of his short nails digging into her flesh.

Their mouths didn't part once, almost as if Nick wanted to distract her from her original purpose. Keep her thinking of their kiss. The way their tongues slid knowingly against the other. The way he tasted like coffee and danger. Forbidden. Like the apple from the tree he was a temptation she could not refuse.

His distraction was working.

And his hands were everywhere.

An Excerpt from

MAKE ME
A Broke and Beautiful Novel
by Tessa Bailey

In the final Broke and Beautiful novel from
bestselling author Tessa Bailey, a blue collar
construction worker and a quiet uptown virgin
are about to discover that the friend zone
can sometimes be excellent foreplay . . .

*D*ay *one hundred and forty-two of being friend-zoned. Send rations.*

Russell Hart stifled a groan when Abby twisted on his lap to call out a drink order to the passing waiter, adding a smile that would no doubt earn her a martini on the house. Every time their six-person "super group" hung out, which was starting to become a nightly affair, Russell advanced into a newer, more vicious circle of hell. Tonight, however, he was pretty sure he'd meet the devil himself.

They were at the Longshoreman, celebrating the Fourth of July, which presented more than one precious little clusterfuck. One, the holiday meant the bar was packed full of tipsy Manhattanites, creating a shortage of chairs, hence Abby parking herself right on top of his dick. Two, it put the usually conservative Abby in ass-hugging shorts and one of those tops that tied at the back of her neck. Six months ago, he would have called it a *shirt*, but his two best friends had fallen down the relationship rabbit hole, putting him in the vicinity of excessive chick talk. So, now it was a halter top. What he wouldn't *give* to erase that knowledge.

During their first round of drinks, he'd become a believer in breathing exercises. Until he'd noticed these tiny, blond curls at Abby's nape, curls he'd never seen before. And some-fucking-how, those sun-kissed curls were what had nudged him from semierect to full-scale Washington-monument status. The hair on the rest of her head was like a . . . a warm milk-chocolate color, so where did those little curls come from? *Those* detrimental musings had led to Russell questioning what else he didn't know about Abby. What color was everything else? Did she have freckles? Where?

Russell would not be finding out—ever—and not just because he was sitting in the friend zone with his dick wedged against his stomach—*not* an easy maneuver—so she wouldn't feel it. No, there was more to it. His friends, Ben and Louis, were well aware of those reasons, which accounted for the half-sympathetic, half-needling looks they were sending him from across the table, respective girlfriends perched on their laps. The jerks.

Abby was off-limits. Not because she was taken—thank Christ—or because someone had verbally forbidden him from pursuing her. That wasn't it. Russell had taken a long time trying to find a suitable explanation for why he didn't just get the girl alone one night and make his move. Explain to her that men like him weren't suitable friends for wide-eyed debutantes and give her a demonstration of the alternative.

It went like this. Abby was like an expensive package that had been delivered to him by mistake. Someone at the post office had screwed the pooch and dropped off the shiniest, most beautiful creation on his Queens doorstep and driven away, laughing manically. Russell wasn't falling for the trick, though. Someone would claim the package, eventually. They would chuckle over the obvious mistake and take Abby away from him because, really, he had no business being the one whose lap she chose to sit on. No business whatsoever.

But while he was in possession of the package—as much as he'd *allow* himself to be in possession, anyway—he would guard her with his life. He would make sure that when someone realized the cosmic error that had occurred—the one that had made him Abby's friend and confidant—she would be sweet and undamaged, just as she'd been on arrival.

Unfortunately, the package didn't seem content to let him stand guard from a distance. She innocently beckoned him back every time he managed to put an inch of space between them. Russell had lost count of the times Abby had fallen asleep on him while the super group watched a movie, drank margaritas on the girls' building's rooftop, driven home in cabs. She was entirely too comfortable around him, considering he saluted against his fly every time they were in the same room.

"Why so quiet, Russell?" Louis asked, his grin turning to a wince as his actress girlfriend, Roxy, elbowed him in the ribs. Yeah. Everyone at the damn table knew he had a major thing for the beautiful, unassuming number whiz on his lap. Everyone but Abby. And that's how he planned to keep it.